THE TROUBLE WITH GHOULS AND SERIAL KILLERS

A CARY REDMOND NOVEL, BOOK 2

KAT SIMONS

T&D PUBLISHING

To my boys, my heroes.

1

Cary Redmond stretched, blinked her eyes open, and frowned up at the faces of her three best friends and her smallest dog Fred hovering over her. Fred woofed and licked her face.

"Ugh, Fred." She wiped her cheek. "You know you're not allowed up here."

Fred barked happily and jumped away.

"You're awake," Lucy cooed in her little girl voice.

"Finally," Marianne said, shaking her head.

"You had us worried," Angie added, her deep voice tinged with relief.

Cary sat up, looking around. "What the hell happened?"

She was in her own bedroom, lying on her own bed—she glanced down—wearing her own pajamas. Nothing seemed out of order except for her friends all being there. Her Labrador, Buck, and her basset hound, Pickles, were sitting at either side of her bedroom door, just inside the room, guarding the entrance as only a demon dog and a foo lion could. Fred plopped down next to Pickles, his tongue lolling out to one side.

She frowned at her little dog pack. They didn't usually sleep in her bedroom, even if they were guarding her.

She tunneled her fingers through her hair, encountering tangles and a loosened hair band about to fall out. She didn't precisely remember going to bed, but she felt wonderful. Fully rested. She double checked… Nope, no sore spots, aches, or pains. That was unusual. She tried thinking back to the last thing she remembered.

"You've been asleep for a little over three days," Marianne said, as if reading Cary's mind. Which was unusual since Angie was the psychic, and Marianne made magicked clothes.

"Three days!" Cary groaned. "Three days?" No wonder she felt so well rested. "What time is it?"

"Four in the afternoon," Lucy said.

"What day?" Cary asked.

"Sunday," Marianne said.

Cary gaped at her friends. "How long have you all been hovering over me?"

"Jaxer didn't tell us you were hurt until last night," Lucy said, her tone accusatory, but in her high, soft voice it just sounded like a cute little pout.

Lucy was petite, red-headed, had dark brown eyes, pale freckled skin, and was a multi-blackbelt wielding marshal artist who could fell men more than twice her size—often several of them at once. Most people mistook her voice as a sign she was a push over. They were always wrong.

Marianne sat at the edge of the bed next to Cary. Her expression soft and understanding as she patted Cary's hand. But there were creases around her dark eyes and bracketing her mouth, marring her normally smooth dark skin.

"You're okay now," Marianne said quietly. "We're here to look after you."

"Okay, someone needs to tell me what's going on," Cary said. "Marianne is being too calm and sweet."

That made the seamstress grin. "Well at least we know you're feeling more yourself," she said.

"When wasn't I?" Cary asked, rubbing her forehead. "I can't

remember coming to bed, nonetheless sleeping so long. Shouldn't I feel, I don't know, stiff or something?"

"It was a healing sleep," Angie said. The tall, lithe, super powerful witch was currently straightening up the few pieces of dirty clothes scattered across Cary's floor. "Jaxer didn't call us after that thing with the demon or we would have been here sooner to look after you," she added.

"Thing with a demon?" Cary frowned. Oh! Right. Oliver Holland. Everything came flooding back, including the fact that she'd used her powers in a way that wasn't supposed to be possible.

Being a Protector wasn't something that just came naturally to a person, and it most certainly hadn't been part of Cary's life plan. She'd been a perfectly ordinary human until six years ago. Then she'd saved a puppy from a demon and somehow ended up working for a group of North American Fae, whom she'd nicknamed the Nags because they were.

They imbued Protectors with their powers, powers that were purely defensive, and helped to keep innocents safe. Cary could now jump in between a bad guy and a good guy and the magic the Nags had given her kept the bad guys from hurting the good guys. She was like a walking, talking Kevlar vest. Which was handy when a rogue demon kept sending scary people after the kid she'd been protecting.

But Protectors couldn't *use* that power. The magic just happened, Protectors channeled it, and everything was good.

Except she'd somehow managed to do more than just channel it.

"Did Jaxer explain what happened?" she asked, sitting up a little higher in bed. Jaxer was her faery mentor, the person she'd most relied on since becoming a Protector, even if she did occasionally want to kill him.

"Not much," Marianne said. "Just that you did something impressive, and it knocked you out. Took too much out of you to handle the power the way you did."

"Damn." Cary had been awake after the face off with Holland. She remembered coming home, and… "Deacon!" He'd been with her.

Deacon Jones was a leopard shifter who had gotten it into his head that they were mates, even though it wasn't supposed to be possible and she still wasn't sure he knew what he was talking about. He was also Greek-god-gorgeous, and sexy, and occasionally scary, but mostly she kind of liked him. Which went against every self-preservation instinct she had and everything she'd learned about preternatural sex gods in the last six years.

"We were supposed to go on our first date." Cary huffed. The incident with Holland had interrupted that. "He was here when I came home. Did you meet him?" She looked up at her friends.

All three women made faces ranging from annoyed to frustrated. It would have been comic if Cary wasn't still trying to piece together the last few days.

"Jaxer was here when we got here," Lucy said. "Apparently, Deacon got called away on family business yesterday afternoon and didn't want to leave you alone, so Jaxer called in the cavalry."

"Us," Marianne said with a cheeky grin.

"Thanks," Cary said, smiling back. "So Deacon was here then? The whole time?" She could still smell him faintly in the room. The fact that they hadn't been on a date yet—or slept together—but her room smelled like him was…a lot more comforting that it should have been. She scowled at that. It was supposed to be irritating and disturbing. Damned man had wormed his way into her life and she was getting too used to him.

"Deacon and Jaxer both apparently," Angie said, coming back to the bed and sitting opposite Marianne.

Lucy jumped up on the edge of the bed, sitting on her knees like it was natural. Which for Lucy it was. "Neither of them saw fit to call us sooner, or we would have been here too," she assured.

Cary grinned. She had very good friends. With a sigh, she glanced around. "Three days." It was the longest healing sleep she'd ever had. "Well, I probably shouldn't do that with my powers again, huh? What-ever the hell I did."

"Don't remember?" Angie asked.

"Nope." Something else of the day came back to her and she groaned, dropping back against her pillow and putting her hands to her eyes. "Did Jaxer mention this seventh year business to any of you?" she asked, peaking at them from between her fingers.

The pointed silence made her drop her hands and stare at them. Maybe she didn't have such good friends after all.

Angie raised a hand. "Not before yesterday," she said, calming Cary's fears. "I would have warned you if I'd known. Especially after that wizard tried to kill you. Just before the demon did." Angie scowled. "You might have too many people trying to kill you."

"I agree," Cary said adamantly. "What did Jaxer say about the seventh year?"

"That you were gonna be on your own," Lucy said. "But you won't be. You've got us."

"And we sure as hell won't leave you out to dry like those Nags," Marianne added. "I've already started some new clothes for you, with the extra good magic in them." She grinned and wagged her eyebrows.

Cary launched up and hugged Marianne. Which started a group hug as her girlfriends surrounded her. From the door, Pickles let loose a deep, reverberating woof that Cary interpreted as happiness.

When the friends parted, Angie ducked her chin and met Cary's gaze. "Seriously, though, how do you feel?"

Cary shrugged. "Great. Better than I usually feel after a big job and almost getting killed."

Unusually for her, this particular job hadn't involved any trips to the ER, and that was always a bonus. She hated trying to explain her weird injuries to the hospital staff, because they were never what they should have been when one was, say, shot or broke their toe kicking a vampire.

"No sore muscles?" Lucy asked.

"Headaches? Tingling in strange places?" Angie asked.

Cary chuckled at that. "Nope, no tingling." Mostly because Deacon wasn't around.

"Nothing else bothering you?" Marianne asked.

"No. I'm good. Hungry." Actually now she thought about it, she was starving.

"Deacon left some bagels in the fridge," Lucy said with a grin.

"Apparently, he left donuts too," Marianne said, "but Jaxer ate them all."

"Bastard," Cary said.

"Right?" Marianne said in obvious agreement. She and Cary shared a similarly eager sweet tooth.

"That was nice of Deacon, though," Angie said, looking at Cary expectantly.

"He does that a lot actually," Cary said. "He brought me bagels and donuts every morning for most of last month."

"He's feeding you," Marianne said in approval. "Must be serious."

"We'll see." Cary wasn't sure how to feel about this thing with Deacon yet. But she did like the bagels and donuts. "We should probably go out on an actual date first, though."

"Demon hunting doesn't count," Marianne agreed.

"It could, under the right circumstances," Lucy said.

Cary laughed. Then she sighed. "I'm so glad you guys are here. I had a rough week last week." She frowned. "Actually, a rough day. And a lot of sleep." She shrugged. "But it's good to have you here."

"Come on," Angie said, patting her leg. "Let's feed you and get you cleaned up. Then we'll get you out of the house for a little fun. You've earned it."

"What do you have in mind?" Cary asked as she rolled out of bed.

"Dancing!" Lucy and Marianne said in unison.

2

———————————

arianne's girlfriend owned a small but popular nightclub in Old Town. On a Sunday night, when Cary might have expected it to be quiet and half empty, the place was packed to the rafters for 80s night. A mix of 80s pop favorites blared from the speakers and people of all ages crowded the dance floor in the middle of the club's first level. The upper area was little more than a circling gallery with tables and seats scattered around, and a great view of the people below.

Cary hadn't been to the club in ages. At least it felt like ages. She'd been working a lot. And that meant less time spent just hanging out with her friends. But if the Nags were throwing her to the wolves this year, she intended to spend more time doing fun things. Life was too short to not go dancing.

And given the fact that she wasn't entirely sure she'd be able to survive her seventh year as a Protector, *her* life might just be even shorter.

In an attempt to ignore the worry of what she faced this year, she pushed through the crowd to the long wooden bar with Lucy in tow to get the next round of beers. She was joking with Lucy about her dance moves, enjoying the energetic beat of the B52's Love Shack blasting through the club, when her cellphone buzzed in her back pocket.

Frowning, worry tightening her gut—because worry seemed to be her default state these days—she looked at the text.

Deacon: *where are you?*

Cary: *Dance club with friends. Where are you? They said you had a family emergency? Everyone OK?*

As soon as she hit send, she felt a little guilty she hadn't texted him earlier. Between him looking after her for days and then only leaving because of an emergency, she really should have thought to check on him. Oops.

Deacon: *where are you exactly? need to talk to you.*

Since he lost his mind and control when he wasn't with her for long periods of time, she assumed he just need a few minutes in her company to settle his leopard down. She texted him her location and put her phone away.

The mate thing had left him on edge and holding onto his control by a thread until—according to his *mother* (ahhh!)—they had sex. A lot of sex.

He wasn't rushing her, though, which was good because the entire thing had her more than a little freaked out. It was a weird and intimidating responsibility, knowing Deacon could lose control of his animal side just because she wasn't around. She didn't particularly like the idea. Or the responsibility for that matter. And she didn't trust the mate bond thing. Not even a little. So she was happy to take things slow with him.

At least as slow as her own hormones would allow. She was having an embarrassingly hard time resisting the man.

"Who was it?" Lucy shouted over the music.

"Deacon," Cary shouted back.

"Aw," Lucy cooed.

Cary rolled her eyes.

"What did he want?" Lucy asked.

"I think he was worried about me," Cary hedged with a shrug. "He wanted to know where we were so he could come see me."

"Is that stalker-y or sweet?" Lucy asked.

Cary laughed. "He's not stalking me. It's the mate bond thing."

"So long as you're safe?"

Cary didn't miss the question in Lucy's tone, even in the loud club. "I'm safe from him. He wouldn't hurt me," she assured.

"Good." Lucy flashed a wicked grin. "He must really like you. Not even waiting till tomorrow."

Cary made a face. "I'm still not sure, Luce."

"You don't think he's serious about you? He's been bringing you food for a month."

"Yeah, but that might just be the mate-chemistry. Wait till you see him. I'm not exactly in his league."

"If you mean," Lucy said very seriously, "that he's not good enough for you, I'll agree with you on that."

Cary grinned. "You're so loyal."

"Bet your ass."

"I love when you say 'ass' in your cute little voice."

"Well, for that crack, this round is on you."

"Deal." Cary handed over her credit card and set up a tab. Given how much support her friends were giving her, and how much she was going to need them over the next year, she figured she owed them a few rounds.

And since she wasn't entirely sure if the Nags were going to continue paying her during her seventh year, she wanted to get the payback drinks in while she could still afford them.

They were on the dance floor when a commotion near the door caught Cary's attention. She knew exactly who it was before she saw him—the mate thing apparently affected her too on some level.

She faced the direction of his approach as the crowd cleared and some of the noise around them quieted.

Deacon emerged like a mythical being, all sexy intensity and heat. The colorful strobe lights did nothing to disguise his exquisite male perfection. Dark hair, golden eyes, the body of a god inside fitted jeans and a black t-shirt. Quite a few of the women, and a number of men, gaped as he passed. One woman fanned herself. Another placed a hand over hear heart.

All eyes followed him as he strode toward Cary. Cary couldn't blame them. She couldn't seem to look away either.

And his full attention was zeroed in on her.

From behind her, she heard someone whistle, and Lucy muttered, "Holy hell."

"That's Deacon?" Angie asked.

"Holy hell," Lucy said again.

"Wow," Marianne said.

"Told you so," Cary said over her shoulder.

"You weren't exaggerating," Marianne said. "That man is exquisite."

"Hey," Lucy said, "you're not supposed to be ogling him. You're practically married."

"Gina would be ogling him too if she were here," Marianne said. "And he's not even her type."

They quieted down as Deacon approached, but why they bothered Cary couldn't guess. Given his shifter hearing, he'd have caught every word, even with the club noise picking up again.

"Hi," she said when he stopped in front of her.

"Hi," he answered, a very slight smiling lifting his lips.

"Holy hell," Lucy whispered.

"Oh my," Angie said.

"I think I just had an orgasm," Marianne said.

Their reactions broke Cary out of her deer-in-the-headlights paralysis. Though she could sympathize with Marianne. His smile had her body clenching and all her nerves dancing in anticipation of...well everything to do with him.

"What's up?" she asked so she didn't melt into a lust puddle. "Did you just need..." She trailed off, embarrassed to say "her company" in front of her friends. She wasn't sure why, it just seemed presumptuous.

"That," he said, as if reading her mind. "But I also need your help." He glanced at her friends, then met her gaze again, frowning slightly. "Your particular brand of help."

"Meaning?"

"Some of our leopard children are in trouble," he said quietly, "and I need you to protect them."

She looked back at the girls. "I have to go. Don't forget to close out my tab."

"You need backup?" Angie asked.

Cary glanced at Deacon. He shook his head.

She turned to her friends again. "Thanks, but we'll be good."

"Call if that changes," Lucy said.

"Thanks," Cary said again, squeezing Lucy's arm. "I'll touch base with you guys tomorrow."

"Stay safe," Angie said.

"Watch your back," Marianne added.

Cary nodded and followed Deacon from the club.

"I like your friends," Deacon said as he led Cary down a narrow, dark stairway. She clung to his big shoulder, careful of her footing.

"They seemed to like you too." She snorted, then had to grip him tighter as her foot slipped on a damp wooden step. "Where are we going? And why don't we have a flashlight?"

"Sorry about that," he said, glancing back. "There's one waiting below, but I don't need it yet."

She couldn't hope to read his expression, given the blackness below them, but in the very faint light from the top of the stairs, she did see him tap the area next to his temple.

She groaned. "Shifter eyesight. I'm jealous."

She had grabbed her leather jacket from the coat check on the way out of the nightclub and had moved her phone from her jeans back pocket into one of the magical pockets in the jacket to keep it safe. The phone had a flashlight app on it, but she'd have to stop to pull the phone out because she had to focus on opening the magical pocket.

Unfortunately, just the thought of stopping and doing something besides clinging to Deacon caused her to stumble again and she missed a step.

Deacon caught her, pausing while she got her footing.

She cursed under her breath. "I need my phone. Give me a sec."

"Why aren't your Protector powers helping?" he asked.

"I'm not protecting anyone yet," she said. "It'll kick in when I'm actually doing my thing." She pulled out her phone. "Speaking of which, where are we going?"

They'd gone through a hidden door at the back of a hotel at the edge of Portland's Chinatown area, not far from Gina's nightclub. The hotel's manager—a friend of Deacon's apparently—led them to the trap door in the floor of a storage closet. Next thing Cary knew they were climbing down these pitch dark, creaky stairs.

"The shanghai tunnels," Deacon answered.

Cary's eyes widened. She'd never been down into the notorious tunnels. They had never actually been for shanghaiing sailors, as was the prevalent myth. They were primarily used by the Chinese in China-town to escape raids on gambling rooms and opium dens. But they had become a popular urban legend and a great "spooky" tour for the braver tourists.

Her foot wobbled on a loose step and she nearly dropped her phone. She gripped it tighter, and tried to turn it on one handed so she wouldn't have to let go of Deacon. The light flared suddenly, so brightly she had to close her eyes against the glare. Which, given her precarious position on the rickety stairs, wasn't helpful. She squinted and angled the phone so it was pointed straight down.

When she looked up at Deacon, he was also squinting against the glare. "Too bright?" she asked.

"Can you see better?"

"Much."

"Then I'll adjust," he said, continuing down the steps.

She tried to take in her surroundings but every time she turned her head the shadows and light danced, disorienting her, and she nearly lost her footing again. So she just focused on following Deacon.

"I didn't realize there was an entrance to the tunnels here," she said.

"This isn't on the tourist route," he said. "And we're not going into an area humans go anymore."

Now he had her attention. "We're going into the Mo-Gin?"

She'd only learned about the magical addition to the tunnels a few years ago, well into her stint as a Protector. Apparently, in the mid to late nineteenth century, when the original secret passages were carved out, a handful of Chinese sorcerers created a…bubble was the word she'd seen most often used, a bubble world that was offset from reality but anchored to this realm in spots spread throughout the tunnels.

They'd called it simply the *móhuàn jìngjiè*, or magical realm.

Inside this alternate realm, they ran a whole other level of gambling, fan-tan parlors, opium dens, magical trade, and, during Portland's dry era, speakeasies. The current name came from that speakeasy era, when the locals started calling it, unironically, the More Gin. Over time, that morphed slightly to Mor-Gin, and the original name was left behind for the history books.

The realm wasn't huge, nothing like Faery, but bigger than it should have been considering where it was located. And according to the stories, the Mor-Gin had been a haven for those who understood the magical realms and wanted a place to play that didn't intersect with mundane humans—at least the mundane humans who couldn't afford the entry fee.

As far as Cary knew, a person had to be invited into the realm or they couldn't go through the barrier between it and this reality. But the thing had existed for more than a century at this stage, maybe a century and a half, well past the lifetimes of the sorcerers who'd created it. Maybe the barrier wasn't as strong as it used to be?

"Can we get in?" she asked.

"There are a few breeches in the magic," he said, "which opened the Mor-Gin up to anyone who could find it. Fortunately, most humans can't find it."

She had to agree with that. No telling what stumbling across an alternate magical realm under Portland would do to the average human's sanity.

"You haven't been down here before?" Deacon asked.

"No. Thankfully." She slipped again, and had to cling to his shoulders while trying not to drop her one source of light or blind them both by flashing it into their faces. "Are we there yet?" she grumbled.

When they finally reached the bottom, Cary took a deep breath, feeling less wobbly and likely to break her neck now that they were on solid ground.

"Better?" he asked once she released her death grip on him.

"Much." She glanced around, as he bent to retrieve a small pack from the base of the stairs. "Where to now?"

He motioned deeper into the tunnel ahead.

With only the narrow cone of light from her flashlight to illuminate their surroundings, Cary couldn't make out many details. The floor was packed dirt, the walls seemed to be dirt and wooden panels. The low, beam-supported ceiling had some piping running down its length, but no lighting system. The place smelled of damp and dirt and mold. And maybe some dead rodents but she didn't want to think about that too closely.

"Tell me more about what I'm doing here?" she asked.

"It's a long story," he said. "I'll explain the whys of this later, but some of the leopard children have been kidnapped by cougar shifters—"

"Why?" she interrupted.

"Part of the longer story." He took her hand and led her to the left.

She glanced back over her shoulder. The blackness had closed in. She couldn't see a thing. Her skin prickled. Anything could be back there. She gripped Deacon's hand a little tighter as she faced forward.

"We're here to rescue the children," he continued.

"Just us?"

"No. There are other leopards throughout the tunnels. But also cougar spies so stay sharp."

"Oh boy," she muttered.

Until she was protecting someone, her powers didn't work. She was a perfectly ordinary human woman as likely to get ripped apart by a cougar shifter as any other human. Unless that cougar was a threat to Deacon and she could protect Deacon. Then she'd be okay.

"I don't suppose these cougars will want to kill you if you appear out of nowhere?" she asked.

"Likely, yes."

He said it so matter-of-factly she scowled at his back. "Great," she said with no little sarcasm.

But she was actually a bit relieved—though she'd *never* admit that out loud. If Deacon was in danger, her powers would work. Which meant she was a *lot* less likely to get killed. Yay her.

"How much farther?" she whispered.

"We're almost to my guard," he said, his voice as quiet as hers. "He'll tell us where to go next."

She squeezed his hand tighter again before she could stop herself. With an effort, she loosened her hold, more than a little annoyed by her need for reassurance.

To be fair, she'd only just recovered from fighting a demon and his army, so that was a pretty good excuse for being shaky. Still. This was embarrassing.

As they continued through the narrow corridor, she realized this reminded her a little too much of descending into the layer of the vampire Master of Portland. There hadn't been much light there either. But at least then, surrounded by vampires and with Jaxer there for her to protect, she'd been able to see. Not being able to see beyond the range of her phone flashlight, not knowing what lurked in the blackness was…scary.

"You don't suppose there are ghosts down here?" she asked as a cool breeze brushed her cheek. She hated ghosts. She was absolutely terrified of ghosts.

"Probably," Deacon said.

She smacked his shoulder. "You're supposed to reassure me there aren't any."

"You're scared of ghosts?" he asked, a touch of amusement in his voice.

"Shut up," she said, her cheeks heating. "Where's your guard?"

"Here," a deep, quiet voice emerged from the blackness ahead.

Cary worked very hard not to jump and squeak at the sudden voice. "You knew he was there?" she accused Deacon with an irritated hiss.

"Sorry for startling you," the newcomer said.

He held up his hand to cover his eyes when she turned the flashlight on him, so she lowered the beam.

He glanced between her and Deacon, frowning a little. "Will she really be able to help if she can't see down here without that light, my…Deacon?"

My Deacon? That was an interesting slip. She filed it away behind her annoyance. Before Deacon could speak for her, she said, "Get me to the kids and nothing will get past me to them."

"Cary is very good at what she does," Deacon confirmed.

His statement, said without a hint of teasing or hesitance, mollified her annoyance and embarrassment. Somewhat.

"The breech into the Mor-Gin is this way," the newcomer said. As they moved down another narrow, pitch black corridor, he introduced himself. "My name is Lucas, by the way. And it's a pleasure to meet you, Cary Redmond."

"You too, Lucas. How the hell do you know who I am?"

"Everyone has heard about you now," he said solemnly.

"Oh good." She and Deacon had some things to talk about.

They came to a stop, and Cary's ability to see beyond the flashlight beam started to increase. She glanced around, looking for additional sources of light but couldn't spot anything.

"We're getting close," she whispered, only loud enough for the shifters next to her to hear.

"How did you…?" Lucas asked.

"I can see better now," she said. "The kids must be near."

"We just passed through the transition point," Lucas said.

Cary hadn't even noticed a change. That was either really cool or utterly terrifying.

"The others have circled the position," Lucas said to Deacon, "but there are dozens of cougars surrounding the children. Several layers thick. We can't get at the kids without risking one of them getting hurt."

"Leave that part to me," Cary said. "Point me in the right direction and I'll get the kids. Then you all can do…whatever you're planning on doing with the kidnappers."

Lucas exchanged a look with Deacon, his frown deepening. "Not to doubt you," he said hesitantly, "but…what's your plan?"

"I'll just run in and get the kids," she said. "No problem." She shrugged and flicked off her flashlight, leaving only the phone's screen to cast any light.

Yup, her ability to see in the dark had definitely improved. They'd stopped just inside the tunnel before it opened onto a larger area. As she stared, the area began to resolve into a clearer view, even after her phone screen went dark.

That was a relief. Now that she knew her powers were working, her discomfort vanished. This part she could do.

"My entrance will cause a lot of chaos too," she said, "so that should work for you guys. I'm assuming the cougars know you're here —can smell you or something?"

Lucas nodded, still frowning. "You'll just…run into the middle of all those shifters?" He exchanged a frantic look with Deacon. "That doesn't seem like a very good plan."

"It never does until I do it." She smiled. "Although, to be fair, my mentor is usually the planner. I'm more the action person." She patted Lucas on the arm, a gesture that made him blink in surprise. "Don't worry. I've got this. Which way are the kids?"

He pointed toward a narrow opening cut out of a brick wall directly opposite them, across the wide expanse of open area—a space that looked like it might have been a kind of intersection between several of the narrow tunnels she now saw crisscrossing the area. A wood plank that was probably supposed to be a door covered the opening. There were additional smaller squares cut out in the wall, which looked more like windows. Wooden slats covered those openings but not completely. She got the impression of being watched through those slats, but she couldn't see the watchers.

No light leaked out. And judging the layout beyond that wall was impossible. She could be running into another tight corridor or a giant cave for all she could tell.

Okay. Well. This should be fun.

"Got any idea what's past the door?" Cary asked. Although calling the wooden board propped up in front of the hole in the brick wall a door was being generous.

She studied the wider corridor between her tentative cover and the doorway. All that unprotected space was a little worrying. She needed to get to the kids before being attacked. They'd have to creep around the edges of the open space until she was close enough to make a run for it.

Lucas answered her question. "Our people who've been down here before said it's an open room with a high ceiling, a bar to the left of the entrance, and a loft-like wooden area above the main floor. The cougars will have people in the loft as well as on the ground. We're not sure where the kid are being held. And there's no other entrance except that one." He nodded at the panel covered doorway. "No real way to sneak in."

"Cool. Okay, let's go," she murmured. Now that she could see enough to move on her own, she released Deacon's hand and started edging around the open area.

Next to her ear, so even Lucas couldn't hear, Deacon murmured, "You're sure this will work, right?"

"Worried about your reputation?" she whispered back. "Bringing in a strange human who doesn't look like much help?" She smiled when she said it. She was pretty used to that reaction after six years.

"No," he said. "I'm worried about you."

His admission made something flutter in her stomach. She ignored it. "I've got this. I'm saving kids. This is the reason I stick with this Protector gig."

"I thought that had to do with a puppy?"

"That's what got me tricked *into* it," she said. They were nearing the door, and Cary could see the flash of glowing yellow eyes through the slat covered windows now. "They've seen us," she said.

"They've been tracking us the whole time," Deacon said. "They're waiting for us to come forward and negotiate. Or attempt the rescue ourselves."

"Quick question," Cary said. "Why haven't you tried that negotiation angle?"

"They don't really want to negotiate. They want us exterminated."

"Well, that's not good," she said, more than a little shocked by the comment. She knew some groups of shifters didn't get along but extermination seemed...extreme. "I think we have a lot to talk about later."

"Yes," he agreed with a grim sigh.

She filed that away too. Kids first, explanations later.

When they were near enough that Cary had a clear path to the door without being out in the open too long, she paused. "All your people ready?"

She looked at Lucas, who glanced at Deacon. Deacon nodded, though his gaze was on the doorway. She wondered at that. Could Deacon feel the other leopards? She'd read that tiger shifters were really good at that. But she wasn't sure about leopard shifters. Though if they could, why did Lucas look to Deacon for confirmation?

More questions for later.

"I'm gonna just walk in," she said against Deacon's ear. "I'll pretend you've sent me in to negotiate since they're pretending that's what they want. I'm a neutral human. It seems likely, right?"

He grunted but didn't respond otherwise. She took that as approval of her plan.

"I'll scream or shout or something when I've got the kids safe," she whispered. "So you'll know we're good. I can hold off the cougars, but I won't be able to chase them away. That's on you."

"We've got that part," Deacon said, his voice deep.

Now that they were within sniffing distance of the kids, she noticed Deacon's eyes glowing, his leopard near the surface. She didn't envy the cougars. But since they'd kidnapped kids and were holding them hostage, she didn't have a lot of sympathy for them either.

He glanced down at her just before she moved off, and the glow in his eyes dimmed somewhat. "Stay safe," he said. "We still have a first date to get to."

She grinned. "I'm starting to think we should count these rescue excursions as dates since it seems to be what we always end up doing."

"Not what I have in mind," he said.

The heat in his voice made her toes curl. She pressed her lips together so she couldn't give herself away and headed for the plank covered doorway ahead.

And the glowing eyes of the cougars.

Hisses and quiet growls met Cary as she stepped through the doorway into a dark, open space with a high ceiling and wooden floor that creaked under the weight of so many people. Just as Lucas had described, there was a wooden loft overhead, reached by a narrow ladder, and a dust covered bar to the left. The windows from this side of the brick wall were no easier to see through but were more obviously windows. The back of the room was solid brick—no entrance or exits that way.

And in the center of the open space, a small group of kids, maybe ten in all, huddled together. When Cary realized the youngest in that group couldn't be older than five, her heart caught and anger worked its way into her determination.

Bastards, using kids this way.

She glanced around at the cougars all staring at her, a shadowy mass of glowing eyes and dark bodies. She could really only see the faces of the ones closest to her, but at a glance, she figured there were at least forty of them in the room.

She smiled, because that tended to confuse bad guys. "Hi," she said. "I'm here to talk. For the leopards. But first, I need confirmation all the children are okay?" She glanced toward the group. "You all good?"

A girl of maybe ten or eleven, after glancing at the cougars nearest them, said, "We're fine, mostly."

"That's all of you?" Cary asked, realizing it would be easy to move a few into the loft or behind the bar to increase the cougar's bargaining position.

"That's all of them," a cougar near Cary hissed, his voice quiet and deep. "Who are you to speak for the leopards?"

"Just a friend of the family," she said, holding the girl's gaze. The girl tilted her head just a little toward the ladder leading up to the loft.

So, more kids up there. That complicated things.

"We want our lands back," the cougar said. "When the leopards leave our territory, we'll return their children."

"Huh," Cary said. "Okay. Well, let's see..." She edged through the ranks of the shifters, toward the kids.

One of the cougars stepped in front of her. "Where are you going?"

"Just making sure no one's hurt," she said. "Part of my job. You can tell I'm human, right?"

The cougar looked her over and sneered. "Yes," the woman snarled.

Cary was pretty sure that was meant as an insult. "So you know I'm not a threat here," she said. "Just doing my part to reach an equitable end to all this." She grinned at the cougar woman. The woman just stared, not moving. Cary shrugged and moved around her to get to the children.

When the cougar tried to stop her by grabbing her arm, Cary easily swung out of reach—with a grace and speed she did *not* possess when she wasn't protecting. The cougar frowned. Cary let her grin widen.

And then she dove toward the kids, setting herself between them and the cougars. The woman who'd grabbed at Cary charged forward, only to hit Cary's Protector magic and end up thrown backward onto her ass.

Silence descended over the room. Even the hissing stopped. Cary's ears rang in the quiet. She hadn't realized how pervasive the low level noise had been until that moment.

"What are you?" the man who'd first spoken said.

"Witch," someone else hissed.

"Sorceress," another snarled.

Cary glanced over her shoulder at the kids. Behind them, two more cougars where sprawled on the wooden floor several feet away, surrounded by frowning and angry looking associates.

To the kids, Cary said, "You're okay now. I just need you to stick with me. Don't run away or try to get around me. We're gonna take ourselves to a safer spot and let the grownups work this out."

Before she could move, however, the hissing and growling started up again. And a voice roared over the noise.

"Kill her!"

_C_ary and her small group were instantly surrounded by swarming shifters, all charging and bouncing off her shields. She faced the kids and opened her arms, urging them closer.

"You're safe now," she assured when the youngest started to cry as she hugged Cary's leg. Cary's heart broke and her anger at the bastards who'd done this spiked again.

Another little boy screamed when a cougar lunged right at him. He threw himself backward, closer to Cary, and she set a hand on his shoulder. She couldn't technically wrapped them all up in her arms, but they were all so stricken and scared looking, she really wanted to.

Cougar shifters—in human and now animal form—continued to launch at them and continued to get flung away by her shield, only to rise and run at them again. Though it seemed like a lot of time passed during that initial attack, Cary realized that was just because the shifters were moving so fast.

And a moment after she had that realization, the earsplitting roar of an angry Deacon pierced through the other sounds. She glanced toward the door to see the good guys pouring into the room and crashing through the slat covered windows.

"Okay," she said, "now we need a better place to be." She glanced at the older girl who'd signaled to the loft ladder. "How many more kids are up there?"

"Three," the girl said.

Cary read her lips more than heard her over the noise of the fight around them. Every so often she felt a slight bounce off her shields as a number of shifters got too near the kids and were forced away. She couldn't feel the shields at all really, even the bubbling in her blood she'd felt in the fight against Oliver Holland wasn't there. She just felt like she normally did when protecting—nothing much but the occasional back push.

The life of a Kevlar vest.

Gesturing to the children, she shouted over the noise, "Stick with me. We're going to get the others. Stay very close to me. Hold hands."

She watched them all grab the hand of another and she took the hands of the oldest and the youngest. They moved slowly and awkwardly through the fighting. Whenever one of the children gasped, Cary paused to ensure everyone was still safe. She didn't bother trying to avoid the fight, just arrowed through it, letting her powers bump and push the bodies out of the way. Worry for the missing three kids had her hurrying as fast as she could while still keeping the others protected.

When they reached the ladder, a large pale cougar leapt in front of them, snarling, its mouth open to reveal an intimidating set of very sharp teeth. Cougar shifters, like leopards, were only a little larger than their animal counterparts. If a person wasn't paying very close attention, they could easily mistake one of the cat shifters for an actual cougar. But the size and weight of even an average sized cougar was enough to make Cary's heart pound a little harder.

She frowned at the animal blocking their way, trying to decide if she'd be able to just walk through, when suddenly a black shape flew over her head, plowing into the cougar. A blur of pale brown fur and black fur writhed across the floor, and then the paler animal went flying.

Cary barely saw the move, it all happened so fast. She glanced back at the black shape, a familiar looking leopard with golden eyes. She nodded her thanks, and he grunted before charging back into the fray.

"Let's hurry," Cary said to the kids. "Mind your steps. Stay close." She led the way up the ladder, glancing back frequently to see if they were being followed. The main floor was nothing but a sea of furred and human forms, moving so fast she couldn't begin to sort them out. Once or twice, a shape diverted from the main battle and attempted to charge the trailing children. They hit off Cary's Protector magic and flew back into the middle of the fight, swallowed into the blur of motion.

"Are you a witch?" the oldest girl asked, after watching another cougar in human form get thrown halfway across the room when he tried to reach the children.

"Nope," Cary said, and left it at that.

When they reached the landing, Cary had expected to see the last three kids and at least one cougar guarding them, but the loft was empty. Damn.

"Don't suppose you know where they've gone?" she asked the older girl.

The girl pointed. "There."

Cary raised her brows. There was a narrow break in the wall, near the back of the loft, which led out of this section. She hadn't even seen it until the girl pointed it out.

She glanced at her. "Thanks. That was very helpful."

She hurried with the kids to the break. The ceiling was a lot lower here so she had to duck to get through the tight opening. A quick glance revealed a short tunnel leading to another brick wall with a very solid looking door. So much for Lucas's assertion that there was no back way in here.

Kids in close tow, she tried the door. Locked.

With a bracing inhale, she took one step back and kicked the hard wood near the frame. The wood shattered and the door swung open so fast it slammed loudly against the wall.

She had to work not to grin. Kicking open doors, something she would have broken her foot trying ordinarily, was kind of fun. She stepped into another room.

Just in time to see the remaining three children huddled in a corner as a single cougar in animal form roared and leapt toward them.

6

$\mathcal{C}$ary shouted in alarm and ran as fast as her Protector powers let her. Which, in moments like this, was really fast for a human. She got between the children and the lunging cougar just before the cougar reached them.

Because of the shifter's speed, Cary still look the full force of its attack, getting knocked backward onto her ass under the weight of the animal. With instincts she'd stopped questioning, she grabbed the big cat around its neck, tucked her legs under it, and pushed out with all her might. The shifter flew away, slamming into a wall so hard the bricks cracked and dust dropped in a choking rain from the ceiling.

Cary rolled to a crouch in front of the three kids and motioned the others still in the doorway to her. "Hurry!"

They ran—at shifter speeds, she noticed—to crowd behind her, all of them secured against the wall, with her between them and the cougar now shaking off her attack. It stared at them, its lip lifting in a teeth-revealing snarl.

"That everyone now?" Cary asked without taking her eyes off the threat stalking slowly toward them.

"Yes," the older girl said.

Cary heard their whimpers and sniffles, and every part of her just wanted them safe with their families again. "I've got you now," she said quietly. "You're safe."

"What if more come?" someone behind her said.

The cougar approaching made a strange chuffing noise that sounded suspiciously like a chuckle.

Cary made a face at the animal. "Don't worry," she said to the kids. "The whole lot of them could try and they won't get to you now."

As if to prove her point, the shifter lunged at them again. This time, since Cary was already in place, the animal flew backward without any effort on her part, so hard it hit the ceiling and slammed into the floor several feet away.

While it rose and shook off the hit, Cary said to the kids, "The other leopards are downstairs. We'll just wait here until the fighting is done."

The cougar launched and hit her magic again, this time getting tossed sideways, nearly out the door.

"While he wears himself out, why don't you tell me your names."

Three more cougars—one in human form, two in animal forms—charged in to join the one already throwing himself at Cary's shields.

"My name is Cary, by the way," she said.

"I'm Angelina," the oldest said, her voice less wobbly now.

Cary grinned back at her. "One of my best friends' names is Angela. We call her Angie."

"My family calls me Angel," the girl said. "But I like Lina better."

"Lina it is, then," Cary said. From the corner of her eyes, she watched the three animals pacing in front of her as the human stared from behind them, his eyes narrowed to slits that didn't hide the yellow glow in them.

"Who's next?" she asked the kids.

The littlest one tugged her sleeve. "I'm Sandra, Miss Cary."

Cary grinned. "You can just call me Cary."

The cougar in human form stalked closer, snarling at her. "What are you?" he hissed.

She ignored him. "So I know Sandra and Lina." She nodded to a child next to Sandra. "What's your name?"

The boy looked between Cary and the approaching cougar. "I'm Miquel," he murmured. Then squeezed his eyes closed.

Cary glanced back as the human flew backward through the room's only window—which had been solidly boarded up before it took the weight of a full grown shifter. The shifter screamed as he went through, the sound fading like he was falling some distance.

Cary winced at the thud when he landed. That had to hurt. A fall like that wouldn't kill a shifter. But it probably knocked the wind out of him. If she were very lucky, the bastard had broken a few bones too. Like most injuries, shifters healed from broken bones fast, but it would be enough to slow him down.

She'd had some experience with broken bones herself, and they weren't a fun experiences even when the bones did mend faster than normal. She figured any guy who would hurt kids deserved that pain.

She returned to getting the children's names and the remaining three shifters continued to test her shields, more carefully now, with a lot less wall-shaking blowback. As she worked at memorizing all thirteen kid names, she wondered what the hell was keeping the leopards.

Part of her started to worry about them, about Deacon, and how he was doing in the fight. She'd never actually seen him in a fight like this before, she realized. She'd only seen him in his leopard shape three times counting tonight.

He had tossed that cougar from in front of the ladder pretty easily. And she'd seen him take down a guy with a shot gun. And he'd come to her rescue once with a massive machine gun of his own—a trick his mother had taught him apparently.

But speed and anger and an ability to fire a machine gun didn't necessarily translate into skills in a fist fight. She of all people should know. Lucy had been trying to teach her hand-to-hand for more than five years now, and Cary still wouldn't have been any good in a fight if she didn't have the Protector magic to help.

If she and Deacon were going to keep ending up in these kinds of situations, she should probably ask him more about his abilities.

Two of the shifters swatted at the edges of her shields, testing, looking for a way around her. The third made another leap, this time attempting to go over her head instead of through her. He ended up thrown out through the door, breaking some of the brick frame off as he went.

She glanced up at the ceiling suspiciously as more dust dropped onto them. She hoped the tunnel could take this abuse. Had the sorcerers reinforced it against shifter fights? And even if they had, that was more than a century ago. The magic was breaking down or no one would have been able to get in here. Were there enough breeches in the magic holding this alternate realm in place to cause a tunnel collapse? And would that collapse the entire Mo-Gin?

Suddenly, being this deep underground didn't seem like a very safe idea. She should get the children out of here. Somewhere more open and less likely to fall down around them. Given she was here to keep the kids safe, they'd probably all escape uninjured, but she'd never tried that before and she wasn't in a hurry to experiment with the situation.

If she got the kids outside, maybe the leopards would follow. Then none of them would get hurt either.

She started to rise from her crouch, but stopped when the remaining two shifters swung back toward the door. A split second later, four large leopards—three spotted, one black—hurled into the room. The cougars tried to escape out the now open window, one making the leap fast enough to get out, the other too slow to react. The cougar that didn't get out of the room was taken down by two spotted leopards. The third spotted leopard went through the window after the escaping cougar.

The black leopard approached Cary and her cadre of kids. Cary smiled, recognizing Deacon on a bone deep level that she didn't really understand.

"Are you hurt?" she asked him, glancing at his muscular cat form, looking for blood in the dark fur.

She blinked and he shifted. Behind her, one of the kids gasped. For a second Cary thought it was because Deacon was naked—which he was and which was very very distracting to *her*—but then she heard a series of soft exclamations.

"Deacon?"

"You came for us?"

"Wow."

Cary frowned up at him. "There's a story here, isn't there?"

He reached out a hand, helping her stand. "I'll explain later." He glanced past her at the kids. "You all okay? Any injuries?"

A series of "no"s and "we're okay"s followed. And then Lucas came charging into the room. One of the little boys shouted, "Daddy!" and launched across the full length of the room in to his father's waiting arms.

"Aw," Cary said, her heart melting at the sight. She nudged Deacon with her shoulder. "You didn't tell me one of his kids was in here," she murmured.

"He was barely keeping it together," Deacon said. "If I'd mentioned Miguel specifically, Lucas would have lost focus and not been much help."

"Fair enough," Cary said, watching father and son hugging tight to each other. She couldn't really tell how old Miguel was, he was tall but had a baby face still which made it hard to judge, but Lucas held the boy like he was a toddler, and Miguel didn't look inclined to let go.

From over the top of Miguel's dark head, Lucas met her gaze and mouthed, "Thank you."

She smiled. Times like these, she didn't mind her job at all.

7

*D*eacon got the leopards and kids back out into the more open crossroads area. Cary was only a little surprised to see about two dozen cougars, in human and cat form, huddling in a circle, surrounded by leopards. She hadn't been sure the leopards would let any of the cougars live. Given the cougars had intended to harm kids, she was okay with a bunch of them being hurt. But she was a little relieved the leopards hadn't slaughtered them all outright for reasons that she couldn't entirely put her finger on.

Likely, something to do with being involved with one of the leopards and not wanting them to be as brutal and vicious as they'd have to have been to have killed every single cougar.

Deacon seemed unconcerned with being naked as he organized the leopards. To Cary's chagrin, he wasn't the only one who'd obviously shredded their clothing when changing to animal form. A bunch of the shifters in their human shapes, cougar and leopard alike, were naked as well. No one else, not even the kids, seemed to notice, though. So she tried to play it cool and ignore all the random nudity too.

When it came to Deacon, however, she was less successful than she wanted to admit.

Deacon ordered the cougars led out of a tunnel at the far side of the city center, an area Cary hadn't realized had an entrance to the tunnels. He also assigned a group of leopards to take the children home.

She watched in fascination. There was no question that he was in charge. Everyone there deferred to him and jumped to do as he said without hesitance. And *he* acted differently too with all the leopards around. Very controlled and emotionless given what they'd just been through. His anger had been palpable earlier. But now, he appeared almost distant from those around him. More controlled than she'd ever seen him, in fact.

And the children… The children seemed in awe of him. Wide eyes and breathless whispers. All of which Cary found very interesting.

And very suspicious.

When he joined her, he ran a finger over the scowl lines creasing her forehead. "Something wrong?" he asked.

"Just…thinking."

"Oh oh." He smiled.

"Hey," she said in mock protest. Which faded away completely when he leaned in and kissed her.

The sounds of little voices cooing and giggling made her cheeks heat. She eased away from him and rolled her eyes at his grin. He ran a hand through her hair, ruffling the remains of her ponytail, most of which was so loose now, she wasn't even sure the hairband was still there.

"I have to take care of all this." He gestured behind him to the others. "And make sure the kids get home safely. Then I'll come over."

"To talk," she said, very seriously. "We have things to talk about."

"We do." He leaned in and murmured in her ear, "But I'm not just coming over to talk."

She swallowed hard as her body tingled everywhere, a combination of anticipation, lust, and nerves. Her physical reaction to Deacon wasn't like anything she'd experienced before, and along with his insistence that she was his mate, her own inability to think straight around him scared the hell out of her.

"I thought…" She swallowed again. "What about that date we're supposed to go on?"

"You said we could count this," he said.

"I lied."

His chuckle brushed hotly against her throat and she shivered, her thighs clenching at the shot of desire that burned through her.

"We can discuss that later too," he said. He moved far enough back to see her face. "When you went to sleep and I couldn't wake you, it scared the hell out of me."

"You called in Jaxer," she guessed.

He made a half-snarling grunt of agreement.

"But you stayed with me."

"I wouldn't have left if it wasn't an emergency," he said.

"This was the emergency."

He nodded.

She cupped his cheek. "Then you did exactly the right thing, and I would have been disappointed in you if you hadn't left."

He held her gaze, heat and understanding sparking in his golden eyes. The moment was charged and intimate and when Cary remembered they had an audience, her skin flamed hot.

She made a face and looked away. "This is a conversation for private," she muttered.

"I agree," he said.

Though to her irritation he didn't look the least bit embarrassed. He took her hand, not letting go when she gave a little testing tug, and said, "How's your eyesight now that you're not protecting the kids?"

"It's a lot darker than it was earlier, but not as bad as when we first came down here. I guess my eyes have adjusted." There were two storm lamps set up near the captured cougars, which provided enough light for shifters to see. But it wasn't nearly enough for an ordinary human.

"Stay with me on the way out anyway," he said. "Just in case. I don't want you lost down here. Especially while we're still inside the Mor-Gin."

She shuddered. She didn't much like that idea either.

The leopards guarding the cougars went one direction while Deacon led the group with the kids another. Cary glanced over her shoulder at the group with the cougars, wondering what would happen to them. She looked up at Deacon but he didn't meet her gaze. Which likely meant she didn't want to know what would happen to the cougars.

They followed a series of underground streets before reaching another brick wall—a wall they all ended up walking right through. Not through a door or climbing through a window. No. They moved into the bricks and passed through them as if they weren't there.

She stared back at the breech once she'd moved to the other side, amazed. There was no sign of an entrance into another realm, no hint that there was even anything beyond that brick wall. She hadn't even notice a change in temperature with the transition. The sorcerers who'd set this up had done one hell of a job.

When she faced forward again, she realized they were at the base of a staircase leading up. Out into the open. Where normal people would see them.

She gave Deacon a sideways glance. "Are you going outside naked?"

She'd been making a concerted effort not to look below his chest area, because her mind might explode, but he wasn't the only one without clothes.

In answer to her question, one of the leopards at the rear of the group tossed a backpack forward and Deacon caught it effortlessly. She recognized it as the pack he'd picked up when they'd first entered the tunnels.

"We came prepared," he said.

"Oh good." She released his hand so he could dress before they went above ground, turning away so she didn't have to watch—the temptation to look at more than his chest would be too strong. The male perfection of his upper body was more than enough, thank you very much.

But as she stared at the bricks, she realized she could see details she hadn't been able to see a few minutes earlier, the area seeming lighter than it had been. She glanced up but no light was leaking from the top of the steps. She couldn't even see the top of the steps. There weren't any flashlights on, just the single storm lamp Lucas carried. No additional sources of light to explain her clearer vision.

And then she felt the warning tingle along her spine, the nudge that let her know her particular brand of help was needed.

She turned to face the brick wall and the breech leading back into the Mor-Gin, zeroing in on a direction perpendicular to the way they'd come. A sense of urgency hit her the minute she faced that direction.

She squeezed Deacon's arm. "I have to go. I'll meet you later." She started back toward the magical section of the tunnels, but stopped when he grabbed her hand.

"Where are you going?" he asked.

"To do my job," she said, with a sigh. "Again."

8

*C*ary spotted the man huddled amidst a pile of what looked like rags and bones, his eyes wide but glazed, and at his waist a solid black stain on his light colored t-shirt. She didn't have to wonder if the stain was really blood or not. The smell mingled with the scents of rotted wood and cloth, mold and dust, too obvious for even her human nose to miss. So strong, she worried his side wasn't the only place he was injured. She needed to get him to a hospital and quick.

But first, she had to get between him and the shadows slowly lurching toward him.

Despite her heightened eyesight, she didn't realize what those shadows were until she was standing between the man and the forms.

Then she gaged. "Ew," she said. "Ghouls. Ghouls?"

When one reached toward her, she squealed through her teeth, hoping the gray bony hand wouldn't be able to touch her, and sighed when her Protector magic worked. Gray and black skin sloughed off the creatures skeletal bodies, dropping in occasional thick globs onto the dirt floor. They were dressed in ragged clothes, like they'd risen from the grave. Their eyes were white and seemingly sightless. A few sprouts and tufts of white hair sprang from their heads. She couldn't have said if they were male or female, and she was too grossed out to remember her basic ghoul biology. Did ghouls have distinctive genders or were the just…ghouls?

They started to moan and scratch at the air, attempting to get past her to the bleeding man she was guarding.

"Yuck," she said when one's finger fell off. "What are you all doing?" She pointed at the nearest creature. "You have one job. And it's in the graveyards eating decaying things. What the hell are you doing *here*?"

She glanced down at the man behind her. He didn't seem to realize she was there. He was staring at the ghouls, breathing heavily, his arm resting across his stomach as he pressed his hand against his wound. His dark hair was mussed, his skin ashy, his brown eyes still glazed, like he wasn't entirely present.

But the one overwhelmingly obvious fact was that he was still very much alive.

Grossed out or not, she knew with absolute certainty that ghouls ate dead things. They did not go after the living.

"Hey," she said to the man, trying to get his attention.

A ghoul standing only a foot away moaned louder and the hair on Cary's arms stood up. She glanced at it, watched a cockroach crawl across its face before the ghoul snatched the bug and ate it with a sickeningly loud crunch.

So much for not eating living things.

"I'm gonna throw up," she said. She nudged the man behind her gently with her foot, trying to get his attention. "Mister, we need to get out of here. Now."

If she had to, she could carry him, especially if the ghouls followed and she had to continue protecting the man from them. But he wasn't exactly a small guy, a fact that was obvious even with him crumbled and injured on the ground. This would be a lot faster and easier if he could manage to stand and walk. He didn't look up, though, and she wondered if he *could* stand.

"Sir," she tried again. "How badly are you hurt? Can you move?"

He didn't take his gaze off the ghouls. "They'll attack if we move."

He spoke so quietly she barely heard him. His voice was scratchy and harsh, the words choked out. His lips were cracked and dry, a small line of blood welling in one of the cracks. He didn't move to lick the dripping blood away.

"You're okay now," Cary said, her gaze jumping between the man and the ghouls. "They won't get to you. We can move." She winced. "That is, if you can move. Do you need me to carry you?"

For the first time, his gaze jumped away from the ghouls to look at her. "I'm too big for you to carry."

She shrugged. "I'm stronger than I look."

He blinked, the first time she'd seen him blink so she took that as a good sign.

"Who are you?" he asked. "What are you?"

"Just a concerned bystander," she said, reaching a hand toward him. "Can you stand?"

He gripped her offered hand and lurched upward. Cary stumbled to take his weight, reaching out to grab him when he listed to the side and looked like he might collapse again.

"I got you," she said.

One of the ghouls let out a moan so loud it sounded close to a scream. The others joined in, the noise making Cary wince. The creatures flung themselves toward her and the man, scrambling to get closer, their mouths opened wide. For the first time, Cary noticed their rows of sharp yellow teeth, like a series of serrated razors in their mouths.

Those looked like they would hurt. A lot.

As she adjusted her balance, her foot slipping once on something, but she didn't want to look down to see what it was. Her brain had only slowly processed that the bones the man had been laying on were likely human, the rags the remains of clothes. She really couldn't think about that more until she was someplace else, but she filed it away. Something not good had happened here. She was going to have to tell...well, someone about it.

Despite their look of decay, the ghouls didn't smell like rotten flesh themselves. They smelled of damp soil, the slightly sweet scent of detritus, and the misty coolness of night. But their breath… When they got close enough for her to get a whiff of their breath, she gaged again. Their breath smelled like death and rotten meat and things much much worse.

Given their usual diet, that really shouldn't have surprised her. Still. Ew.

"How're you doing?" she asked as she helped the injured man take slow steps toward what she hoped was an exit.

The only one she was sure she could get to was the one she'd gone with Deacon to just before sensing that her help was needed, so she headed that direction. She hadn't the first clue how to get out of the Mor-Gin otherwise. And the last thing she wanted was to get lost down here in these decrepit tunnels, in a magical realm offset from her reality, with no idea how to get out, and with ghouls following them.

She'd lost track of time but she was pretty sure they still had another half hour until sunrise. If she remembered right, ghouls stopped functioning at sunrise. Although, according to her readings, they also didn't leave graveyards, so she wasn't taking anything for granted.

When the man didn't say anything, she glanced at him. He was as pale as stone now, his lips pressed together in a hard line.

"You gonna pass out?" she asked, adjusting her hold to take more of his weight.

He shook his head, barely, but enough that she knew he was still in there somewhere. The glazed, glassy look in his eyes was not reassuring.

Without having to look over her shoulder, she heard the ghouls following at a steady pace, their moans rising and falling like a wave. They didn't run to keep up or get ahead of her—unlike zombies, ghouls could move fast when they wanted to—but they didn't drop back far either. They stayed just beyond the effects of her shield, relentlessly pursuing.

Sweat trickled down her temples, a few drops falling into her eyes and blurring her vision. "Can you tell me your name?" she asked the man she was mostly carrying now.

"Justin," he muttered, so quietly she barely heard. The sound came out like a breath more than a word.

"Justin, it's nice to meet you. Sorry it was under such shitty circumstances." She risked a glance over her shoulder. Yup, still there.

It felt like ages passed as they shuffled inch by inch through the passageways. Cary was starting to think it might be easier to just carry Justin, which would be interesting and awkward but at least they'd be able to move a little faster. A sound from ahead of them stopped her in her tracks. The ghouls behind them stopped, too.

She sighed. What now? If it was more ghouls she was going to be very unhappy. If it was the cougars, she'd be pissed. If it was Deacon, she was going to thump him later for not taking care of the kids.

The woman who lurched out from behind a curve in the tunnel was a bit of a surprise.

She was tallish and thin, almost skeletally thin. Her cheeks were hollow, her dark hair hung in a long braid that had seen better days, and her clothing was dusty and sported a rip here and there. Cary couldn't quite tell if she was human or not, but something about her looked vaguely familiar.

"Get away from him," she said in a deep voice the echoed off the low ceiling.

The power in her voice made the hairs on Cary's arms stand up. She blinked and shook her head. "I think I'll stay right here," she said.

Justin pulled in a deep breath and on its release said, "She's not talking…to you."

Cary frowned at him, then looked at the woman again. Her expression was intent and focused. And not on Cary and Justin. Cary glanced behind her.

The ghouls were holding their heads, their moans turned to grunts and a strange scrambling noise that sounded a bit like rocks rolling around. One tried to lurch forward only to drop to its knees while the others started to fall back. The one who'd dropped to the ground—to Cary's astonishment—began to fall apart, bits and pieces of its body hitting the dust like they hadn't actually been attached. The thing opened its mouth to make a sound and nothing came out. Its jaw dropped next, followed by its head very gently tilting to one side and popping off its neck. The head rolled a few feet, stopping with the face pointing toward Cary. Its white eyes stared at her, and the tongue in its mouth flopped around.

She gaged. Again. And looked way.

The rest of the ghouls had vanished into the shadowed darkness, so completely Cary couldn't hear them anymore. But since she was still able to hold Justin upright and see decently in the blackness, she assumed he wasn't out of danger yet. Her powers stopped working once the threat was gone.

The skeletal woman jogged toward them, moving easier than Cary would have guessed.

"Justin." She took the man's face in her hands. "I thought I wouldn't get here in time. How badly hurt are you?"

"Bad," Cary answered for him. "We need to get out of here. The ghouls haven't left entirely."

The woman looked at her, blinking as if she couldn't quite fit the pieces of their situation together. "Yes. There's an exit this way." She took up the place on Justin's opposite side, gently putting his arm over her shoulders to take some of his weight.

Together they covered the short distance to another staircase. This time, Cary felt the transition between realms like a ruffle of static electricity across her skin. There was no wall to walk through or obvious signs of the transition point, just that sense of something soft rubbing against her skin and creating static. She wondered if that meant there was more magic here and that this breech in the barrier was more recent than the ones she'd crossed through with the leopards. She'd have to ask about that. Who she'd ask she wasn't sure, but that was also a problem for later.

The staircase the woman had led them to was a metal spiral that looked as rickety and unstable as the wooden stairs Deacon had used to bring her down here. It was also too narrow for the three of them to walk side by side. Cary took the lead, still supporting as much of Justin's weight as she could manage, while the other woman took up the rear, her hand braced against Justin's back.

The wooden trap door at the top of the stairs creaked and groaned as Cary shoved it a few times, but it didn't budge. Locked? Damn. She shoved a bit harder, putting her shoulders into it and leveraging with her legs. Something made of metal screeched, the pressure on the door abruptly ended, and she was able pushed it upward. The heavy wood fell all the way open, making a loud thud on the floor above. Dust rained down on them. She coughed, waving a hand in front of her face to clear the air.

"Did you come this way?" she asked the woman. If so, someone had locked the door behind her.

"No," the woman said, her tone quiet and emotionless.

"Oh good. So we don't know what we're walking into," Cary muttered. That was always fun.

To her relief, the trapdoor was part of an old wine cellar that looked like it hadn't been used for a while. Wooden racks set in pretty diamond shapes lined the walls but they were empty and a patina of pale dust covered every surface. She climbed out of the trapdoor, sitting on the floor to brace herself so she could help Justin out. The woman hurried up behind them, closing the trap door when everyone was clear.

Cary glanced around. The windowless space was smaller than she'd thought at first. It was dark, too, but Cary was accustomed to a lack of lighting now and was able to make out most of their surroundings. Her Protector vision was starting to fade, though, which she took as a good sign that they were no longer in trouble from the ghouls. It was going to make it harder to get out of this basement, though.

Before her vision returned to normal, she spotted a stone staircase that looked like it led up into the building above. With effort, she and the woman got Justin onto his feet. One hand bracing Justin, Cary took her cellphone out of her jacket pocket and turned on the flashlight app. If she couldn't see anymore, she was pretty sure her charges wouldn't be able to see either, and the last thing Justin needed was to fall down stairs.

Although the woman hadn't had a flashlight with her and had still managed to find Justin underground. Cary wondered how she'd been able to see. A question for after they got Justin to the hospital.

They emerged into the kitchen of a restaurant that looked like it hadn't been a working restaurant for some time. The relief of not having to explain themselves to strangers left Cary a little dizzy. Or maybe that was the exertion of the night after she'd only just recovered from the standoff with Holland. She blinked back her weariness. Time for that later. Justin need an ER and quick. His wound was dripping blood down his side again, leaving a trail of smeared red behind them.

They had to unlock the kitchen door to get out, which meant they had to leave it unlocked. Cary felt a twinge of guilt for that, but maybe she could come back later and make sure everything was sealed up again. Or maybe just call the landlord.

They came out into a back alley area that stank of garbage. The ground was damp from a recent rain shower. The air was cold and biting after the humid coolness below. She glanced at Justin, who wasn't wearing a coat, and shivered for him.

When they moved out from behind the building, Cary took in their surroundings, gauging their location as only a few blocks from Chinatown, not far from where she'd entered the underground with Deacon. That surprised her as it had felt like she'd gone a lot farther. The Mor-Gin was definitely bigger inside than the actual area of Portland it covered.

Letting the woman take most of Justin's weight, she turned off her phone's flashlight. The sun was starting to come up, turning the sky a lighter gray even as the streetlights dimmed. Away from the garbage behind the restaurant, the air smelled of more rain and a nearby coffee shop. Cary nearly groaned aloud at the thought of coffee.

"We need to call an ambulance," she said as she thumbed through her saved numbers for the nearest hospital. Yes, she had all the local ER numbers in her phone. She spent way too much time at hospitals.

At least this time, it wouldn't be for one of her own weird-and-hard-to-explain-to-normal-people injuries.

"No!" The woman lurched forward and knocked Cary's phone from her hand, sending it crashing to the hard ground.

"Hey!" Cary snatched it up. "You want to break it?"

The magic pockets Marianne had put into Cary's leather jacket ensured her phone didn't get crushed while she was saving people, but her phone was not indestructible outside the pockets—despite the heavy duty case she'd put it in. She really didn't want the hassle of having to replace it now. Especially when she still wasn't sure if she'd be making money over the next year.

She flicked on the screen, surprised and relieved when it still worked. Letting out a breath, she glared at the woman. "He needs help. He's close to bleeding out."

"We can't go to the hospital."

"He's gonna die if you don't," Cary said bluntly. "Why bother saving him from ghouls only to let him die now?"

"I'll take care of him."

"Who are you?"

"His sister. And we'll be fine. Thanks for your help." The woman turned and started to stumble away.

"Wait," Cary called. But the woman didn't acknowledge her.

Now what? Did she call the ambulance anyway? Or the police? She'd hate to bring the police into this since she didn't like to be on the cops' radar. It complicated her job. But she could hardly let the man she'd just saved die because his sister didn't want help.

She thought back to what the woman had done to the ghouls. Cary couldn't say for sure what kind of power that had been, but she had a suspicion. And if her suspicions were right, she could understand why the woman didn't want to involve other people in this. Necromancers were notoriously private.

But Cary couldn't just let Justin bleed out. When the pair turned down a side street, she cursed under breath and hurried after them. By the time she reached the street, however, they were gone.

Shit. She put her hands on her hips and hung her head. Had she just saved someone, only to let him die? Her Protector senses weren't going off to indicate he was in mortal danger. In fact, she realized, they hadn't triggered when the woman walked away with him. Maybe his sister would be able to help him, and he wasn't about to die from blood loss.

Boy, Cary hoped so. She'd feel like crap if the poor man died now. Some Protector she was.

9

ary pushed into her house and was met by a pile of doggie welcomes. She sighed and sank to her knees in the entryway to hug them all. "Hi guys. You need out?"

The sun was high enough that her neighbors were starting to wake up and head out to work. Cary had hurried from the taxi and ducked inside, hoping anyone who'd spotted her just thought she'd been out dancing all night. Seeing Cary roll in at all hours wasn't an unusual sight for her neighbors. She sometimes wondered what they thought she did for a living. But she was pretty sure she preferred not knowing.

With a groan, she got up from the floor and headed through the kitchen to the back door, three happy dogs in tow. She was wrecked and exhausted, but mostly because she was still worried that Justin might have died from his injuries before his sister got him help.

Fred yapped, bounced off her thigh with the kind of enthusiasm only a dog with terrier blood could swing, and pushed past her to get into the cold morning air the instant she opened the door. Her basset hound Pickles followed at a more leisurely but still happy trot, taking a moment on the top of the raised porch to survey the landscape below before dropping down the three steps to the grassy yard. Buck, the golden Labrador, put his big, warm head in Cary's hand for a scratch before following the rest of the pack.

She grinned at them as they went about exploring their yard, then turned back to get their breakfast ready. Pickles would be expecting food soon.

Cary had just finished doggy food prep and making herself a pot of coffee when her front doorbell rang.

She didn't get random visitors. She had to allow people to find her home or they couldn't thanks to a glamour spell her bosses put on the house. All Protectors were given one safe place, a location that was disguised and impossible to pinpoint even if the Protector was followed. Cary had to consciously give permission for someone to find her house. This morning in the taxi, she'd had to mentally give the driver permission to see her address just to get her here. And the minute she was inside, she'd taken that permission away.

She had no idea how it worked, only that it had for more than six years now. As she reached the door, the realization that it might not work for much longer hit her hard and she paused, her hand halfway to the doorknob.

What if her house wasn't a safe place where she could hide from the bad guys anymore?

A second knock on the door made her jump, but then through the wood, a familiar voice.

"Cary? Why aren't you opening the door?"

Deacon. With his wicked shifter senses of smell and hearing.

She sighed and let him in. The instant the door was out of the way, he was inside, pulling her into a tight hug. The suddenness of his entrance made her gasp. The heat and strength of his body pressed against hers left her breathless. His mouth covered hers before she fully regained her senses and then she was kissing him back because it felt too natural not to. The edge of desperation, the hunger and need, the way he was somehow both gentle and aggressive in tasting and teasing her, left her knees wobbly.

She might not be sure where this relationship was going, but she did enjoy the kissing part.

He ran his hands over her back, a slow glide that made her thighs clench as he stroked down her spine. He moved from kissing her mouth to nibbling and tasting his way across her jaw and over her neck. She dropped her head to one side and shivered. He knew exactly how to make her head spin. That should probably scare her a lot more than it did at the moment.

"I've missed you," he murmured against her throat.

She chuckled. "You just saw me four hours ago."

"Too long. Plus the day and a half when I had to deal with other things and couldn't look after you. You scared the hell out of me, passing out like that."

"Yeah, that hadn't really been part of the plan," she said. Then groaned when he nipped at the skin between her neck and shoulder.

"You're okay?"

"You can stop asking me that now," she said. "I just had to sleep. All better now."

"No, I meant after you left us last night. You're not hurt?"

"I'm fine. Are you? How are the kids? Did you get hurt during the fight? Where are the cougars you took? Why are you trembling?"

He chuckled under his breath. "Slow down, I'm missing every other question."

"Tell me why you're trembling then? Are the kids okay?"

"Fine. Being reunited with their parents as we speak." He leaned back a little and cupped her cheek. "You've officially earned the loyalty of a lot of leopard shifters by helping to rescue their kids."

"Any time," she said. And meant. She never hesitated to protect kids. Or animals. Or women in danger. Or old people.

She did occasionally argue about having to protect fully grown men who should be able to take care of themselves. She had her biases.

Thoughts of Justin and what bad shape he'd been in reminded her quite sharply that sometimes grown men needed her help, too. She still got grumpy about it, though. At least in front of the Nags. Couldn't let them think she accepted all this happily.

"I'm trembling because I needed to hold you," Deacon added.

He buried his face against the skin on her throat as he pulled in a deep breath she felt as his chest expanded against hers.

Suddenly, he leaned away, frowning. "What's that smell?" He pushed her to arm's length, holding her by the shoulders, and his scowl turned fierce. "You're hurt!"

She looked down. "Oh. Oops."

Her shirt was dark and stiff with dried blood. She hadn't even noticed, though given how much Justin had been bleeding she shouldn't have been surprised. No wonder the taxi driver had been given her such funny looks all the way home. Her sense of smell was apparently pretty messed up from being underground and surrounded by ghouls because she couldn't smell it either. Not that she had a Deacon-level sense of smell or anything. But she usually knew when her clothes got covered in body fluids.

She'd taken her jacket off when she'd come in, but hadn't really thought about her shirt or the state of it. And the dogs hadn't reacted to the blood. Which was odd. Buck would normally have at least snuffled at it to make sure she wasn't hurt. The fact that she'd been wandering around the kitchen with someone else's blood on her shirt and hadn't noticed was gross, too. She really needed to go change.

"What happened?" Deacon brought her attention back to him. "Why haven't you gone to the hospital?" He started tugging her out the door.

She pulled back. "It's not mine. Relax. Deacon." She waited until he looked her in the eyes. "It's not mine. The man I went off to rescue was wounded. It's his blood."

The tension in Deacon's shoulders eased, but his scowl remained. "What happened?"

"I'll tell you over coffee." She closed the door and gestured him toward the kitchen. "Go say hi to the dogs. I'll go shower and change."

Something shifted in his expression, his eyes darkening, his gaze taking on that lazy, speculative expression. The look sent a series of sharp tingles and awareness through her, making her very conscious of her body. And what he could do with her body if they were naked right now.

Damn, how did he do that with a look? How could she read that look so well after only knowing him a little over a month?

She pointed a finger at him. "No. You can't help. I'm too tired and... We still need to go on a date... And stop looking at me like that."

His smile rose. "I warned you I wouldn't stop trying to seduce you. You can't blame a man for trying."

She sniffed in mock offense and waved her hands at him. "Go wait in there. I'll be out in a minute."

"If you're sure." He sauntered away, giving her an excellent view of the most perfect, denim clad backside in all of Portland.

Everything in her fluttered as she watched him, his muscles moving beneath his jeans and t-shirt—because of course even though it was cold out, he hadn't bothered with a coat thanks to his shifter metabolism. He was impossible not to watch, despite her exhaustion, and a part of her she kept trying to control wanted to call him back and take him to bed. She'd been having trouble resisting that impulse since meeting him.

He did that to her on purpose, she was sure, but she couldn't figure out how.

He'd say it was the mate thing, that he was her mate and they were supposed to feel this way about each other. She suspected, given her friends' reactions to him, that maybe it was just Deacon.

Since that brought up more worries she was too tired to think about, she hurried to her bedroom to grab clean clothes and then to the bathroom for a quick shower.

The smell of coffee drew her to the kitchen more insistently than knowing Deacon was there somewhere. Having him in her house now, when there was no one else around to function as chaperone, made her a little edgy. Some of that good and excited edgy.

Some of it...not good.

She knew he never wanted to crowd her. He was conscious of that. And she would have been surprised if he hadn't shown up sometime this morning given they'd been apart for a few days—he had to be around her or his waning grasp on his self-control got worse, making him very dangerous. But she'd had her house to herself for years now, just her and her menagerie of pets. Having people in her home for long periods of time was…intrusive. And all of November, she'd had visitors here.

She reached the kitchen expecting to see him standing near the coffee machine. Instead, she found him out in the yard, throwing a ball to the ever-energetic Fred while Pickles slept on the porch beside him.

Her little pack had welcomed Deacon into the family already. She wasn't sure if that was good or bad.

Buck nudged her aside to go into the house, not even stopping for a head scratch or any other acknowledgment of her—which surprised her. The dogs usually hung out together. They even slept in the same area of the living room at night. She frowned after Buck, wondering if he'd left some food behind or if something else was wrong. He'd felt a little warmer than usual this morning when she'd hugged him. But she'd assumed he felt warm because she was chilled from being outside.

Deacon pulled her into his arms from behind, wrapping her in heat and his delicious scent. He'd obviously taken the time to shower before coming over because he smelled faintly of soap. She hadn't noticed earlier. Her own shower must have cleaned out her nostrils.

"What's wrong?" he asked, his mouth against her neck.

Well, that was distracting. She leaned into him, breathing in deeply and enjoying the feel of his breath against her skin even as she fretted. "I'm hoping Buck isn't getting sick. He seems a little off this morning."

"We have an excellent vet who visits the shelters here in the city. You want me to call her and see if she can see Buck today?"

Cary smiled. Deacon and his family ran animal sanctuaries around the country. It was one of the things that she really adored about him.

"Thanks," she said. "Let me watch him for another few hours first, though. The house has been pretty busy for the last month. He might just need some quiet."

Cary wasn't sure about taking Buck to an ordinary vet at any rate. She never had—he wasn't a normal dog and she was a little afraid of how he'd react to being poked and prodded by a doctor. Since he was a puppy, Buck had kept to his "ordinary dog" form, never showing any signs outwardly of the demon dog he was. He was protective of her, and he guarded the house with Pickles, but he didn't let on he was anything but a typical dog. After all these years, she'd gotten used to him just being a dog. She never forgot he was a demon dog, but she hadn't considered the implications of that either. Maybe she should have paid more attention to his heritage and his medical needs.

Damn, she wasn't a very good dog mommy. She'd better do some research on vets specializing in "unique" animals.

The other two dogs pushed past them, then, crowding back into the house. Which meant playtime was over, and it was time for a nap. She smiled and followed them in. She'd never understood why people said "a dog's life" like it was something negative. As far as she could tell, dogs had great lives. At least, hers did.

Inside, still *aware* of Deacon with every nerve in her body, she opened the fridge to see what they could scrounge up for breakfast. Only to have that irritating tingle go down her spine. The one that warned her the Nags were coming.

"Shit," she muttered and closed the fridge. Good thing she'd slept for three days because it looked like she wasn't getting her own nap any time soon.

"What?" Deacon asked, setting aside the glass of milk he'd poured himself.

She waved to the living room and headed out.

I O

*L*iruk and Wisat stood in the middle of Cary's living room, opposite the couch, in front of her small fireplace. They were…well, a pretty impressive sight.

Wisat was all black and red—red skin, black hair and clothes, the twin, interwoven halos crowning his scalp covered in red velvet-like fuzz. Liruck was gold and white. Her skin a flawless golden brown, her hair a white blonde veil, the two little horns appearing through her hair a deeper, metallic gold. They both had shockingly green eyes, like the richest forest Cary could imagine. Nothing like a shade of green a human might have.

They were from a North American faery species, known to the original inhabitants of this continent by many names. Her favorite was the name given to them by the Passanaquoddy: Nagumwasuck. Mostly because she could shorten it to call them Nags. Because they were, and it annoyed Liruk when she did.

She crossed her arms and met their gazes. "So. This seven year thing," she stated without preamble. "Care to explain why you blind-sided me with this?"

Wisat blinked. Liruk showed no outward reaction.

"Protector, you're needed," Liruk said.

Cary shook her head. "Seventh year explanations first. Unless it's a kid about to die. Then I expect an explanation immediately after I save them."

Wisat glanced at Liruk, then back at Cary. "Jaxer didn't explain?"

"We got interrupted. Oliver Holland." She waved that away. "I'm sure Jaxer told you all about it given…"

She trailed off. Given she'd done something she wasn't supposed to be able to do—used the Protector magic offensively. Her powers were strictly defensive. She shouldn't have been able to level an army of supernatural bad guys with them. And yet she had.

At least, that's what she thought she might have done. She really didn't know for sure. And she couldn't remember the night clearly enough to pinpoint *how* she'd managed to use magic she shouldn't have been able to control. Jaxer hadn't understood what had happened either.

She wanted to ask the Nags about that, how it had been possible, what had happened exactly, and was it likely to happen again. But she needed to understand the seventh year trial first. Because her trust in her "bosses" was at an all time low just then, and she wasn't sure she could believe any explanation they might give her for what she'd done.

"Back to the point," she said. "What happens now with the seventh year? Do you still pay me? Do I still have to jump into chaos whenever you show up? Do you still show up with jobs or do I just protect whoever I come across? And my house…?"

She didn't finish because she was very aware of Deacon just behind her, listening to this conversation. She still hadn't told him about the glamour on her home. She hadn't known him long enough yet. In fact, she wasn't sure she would ever tell him. Only Jaxer knew about the spell. And the Nags, of course, since they'd set it. But she hadn't even told her best friends. She was a little worried it would stop working if she let too many people know about it. And of all the shit the Nags had put her through, the protections on her home were one of the few things she'd really really appreciated.

"Your house will continue," Wisat said, staying as vague as Cary had. "You will have to continue doing your job."

"If I don't?" she asked. "If I want to quit now?"

That was always a question with her anyway. She'd been tricked into this Protector gig. She'd grudgingly accepted it—mostly because she *did* like being able to help people who needed her. But she'd never felt fully up to the task. She'd never been confident she was capable of doing the job long term, despite six years of managing to save people and not die. She was so ordinary for a Protector, so…human. She was always worried about failing.

And that fear had been confirmed during her fight with the demon a week ago. She'd failed to save one life. The failure weighed on her. Would likely weigh on her every time her insecurities raised their heads. Maybe she just wasn't good enough to be a Protector.

In which case, she was fucked this year.

"You can't quit," Liruk said. Liruk was always the hardass, the one most critical of Cary's performance as a Protector. "You are required to complete this year."

"But what if I don't?" she said. "What if I just hide here in the house and don't do anything?"

"You will no longer be paid," Wisat said, almost apologetically.

"And your house will no longer be…safe," Liruk added.

"But the dangerous beings you've already faced in the city will still be aware of you," Wisat finished.

Cary narrowed her eyes at them as her temper rose. It was a threat, though subtly spoken because of Deacon. And the fact that they were threatening her very life, after six years of working for them, pissed her off more than anything else they could have said.

She'd confronted a lot of bad guys in this city, and she'd built up a little circle of people who wouldn't object to killing her. Just the most recent list included some vampires that wouldn't mind getting her out of the way, anyone from Holland's army who'd survived, and a trio of witches Cary was pretty sure would come after her given the chance.

Then there was Sheldon the wizard, who should be dead but might not be, in which case he would definitely be angry enough to want to kill her.

She'd rescued Deacon from Sheldon, that was how they'd met, and everyone had thought Sheldon was dead. But his body had disappeared. And then she'd sworn she'd seen him amongst Oliver Holland's army. Plus a wizard had tried to kill her outside Angie's place not long ago. Even if the wizard wasn't Sheldon, there was still someone pretty damned powerful out there gunning for her.

Without the spell on her house, any of those people would be able to find her, track her down, and kill her quite easily. They wouldn't even have to try hard because she had no magic or special skills to ward off a personal attack. The few martial arts skills she'd managed to pick up training with Lucy wouldn't do her any good against wizards and witches and vampires.

She was vulnerable. More vulnerable than most Protectors. And the Nags knew it.

Bastards.

Snarling, she ran her fingers into her still damp hair, tugging a little to alleviate the pressure building in her scalp. "You're blackmailing me, then," she said through her teeth. "Do this dangerous thing, risk my life, or else I'll be left out to the wolves."

"It is this way with all Protectors, Cary," Wisat said gently. "You must be tested. You must survive that test."

"What happens after?" she asked. "Jaxer said I come into my full powers. I thought I had those already. What does that mean?"

"It means nothing until you survive the year," Liruk said. "You won't understand before then."

Cary cursed out loud and started to pace the room. A quick glance at Deacon confirmed he wasn't any happier about this than she was. His body was tensed, his muscles flexed. His nostrils flared, and his eyes were narrowed, the faintest glow of yellow showing his leopard was near the surface. The fact that he was holding his tongue and not attacking the Nags showed some pretty impressive restraint given his control wasn't the best at the moment.

On one pass, she caught Wisat's glance at Deacon. While she couldn't read Wisat's expression, she fancied he was nervous about the angry shapeshifter in the room. And she took an inner, mean sort of pleasure in that. She liked Wisat most of the time. Of the two, he was her favorite boss to deal with. But at the moment, she might just hate him enough not to care if Deacon attacked.

No one would get hurt. Wisat would just vanish in that way they appeared and disappeared in a blink. But it would be satisfying to watch him and Liruk have to run away.

Feeling petty for the thought, she stopped pacing, put her hands on her hips and hung her head. With her eyes closed, she clarified, "So you will keep paying me, keep sending me out on jobs, and leave my house as is for the next year. But I won't have Jaxer's help. And you won't be able to give me any clues, hints, or advice. Right so far?"

"Correct," Liruk said.

"And I have to do all the jobs you send me on," Cary continued, "or the payday and house stuff stops?"

"Yes," Wisat said.

"Any other details I should know about?" She opened her eyes and looked up at them, meeting their shockingly green-eyed gazes. "Any other complications I should be aware of?"

The two exchanged a look she couldn't read.

Cary dropped her hands to her side and faced them fully. "What? What?"

"It is nothing," Liruk said after a beat that clearly let Cary know there was something else. They just weren't going to tell her.

"I really hate you guys right now," Cary muttered.

"You are a fine Protector," Wisat said. "You will do well."

"Right," she said, with no little sarcasm. "Like the way I kept Nira alive you mean?"

The snake shifter had been manipulated and then killed by Holland. And Cary hadn't been able to stop that murder. She'd almost gotten Jonathon, the kid under her protection, killed too.

Fine Protector my ass, she thought sourly.

"Nira was not a failure," Liruk said, unaccountably gently for her. "Nira was what happens sometimes. You are one woman, Cary. You can only do so much. It is…one of the lessons you will confront this year."

"Well, that's not good," she said, her voice rising. "You're telling me I'll lose people? People will die, and I won't be able to stop it, and I'm somehow supposed to be okay with this?"

"Yes," Liruk said.

Cary let loose a strangled cry of anger mixed with no little bit of anguish. She couldn't do that again. She couldn't face letting someone die because she was not good enough at her job.

"It is the way it is," Wisat said. "It is important, this year."

"And now you know everything you need to know," Liruk said. "You have a job to do."

Cary shook her head. She wanted to cry. "I just recovered from the fight with Holland. I've spent the night rescuing shifter children and a man being attacked by ghouls—"

"Ghouls?" Deacon said, the first time he'd spoken. His voice was harsh and loud.

She winced. Oops. She'd forgotten they hadn't gotten around to talking about that yet. "Yeah," she said, "that blood, the man I saved... He was being attacked by ghouls."

Deacon's scowl deepened.

"I was gonna tell you," she said.

His jaw muscles flexed and he briefly closed his eyes. "Jesus, Cary."

She shrugged.

"Justin Klein and his sister Beatrix are the reason we're here," Wisat said.

Cary blinked and faced the Nags again. "Wait, what?"

"We need you to protect the necromancer and her brother," Liruk said. "Or she could end the world."

Oh boy.

ary studied the house from beside her car, parked on the dirt road outside the place. It was a shabby little building, located well east of Portland, past Gresham, in an area surrounded mostly by farms. The house stood alone on a small plot of land bracketed by evergreens, the nearest neighbors a quarter mile away.

Winter brown grass and dirt covered the front yard, a few muddy puddles attesting to the last hour of rain. There was no fence circling the property, and no sheds or outbuildings that Cary could see from her vantage. A single beat up Jeep was parked out front. The small wooden porch leading up to the front door looked like it had seen better days and was empty but for an unused terracotta pot pushed against the far railing.

Everything was eerily quiet. Even the birds were silent.

She pulled in a deep breath, catching the scent of foliage and something danker, a kind of sweet, spoiled scent that made her gag. She wasn't sure she wanted to know what that was.

"Rotting meat," Deacon murmured at her back.

She lifted her lip in disgust at the news. Yeah, she hadn't needed to know that.

Despite her giving quite logical reasons why he shouldn't come with her, Deacon had insisted on joining this little excursion. And since she'd never had to deal with a necromancer before, at least on this side of the Protection racket, Cary had given in to having his company. She'd pretended to be irritated, but inside she was grateful. She was still reeling from this being-on-her-own seventh year business. Having Deacon here—having someone she'd have to protect if things went wrong—meant she wouldn't die yet.

That was a relief.

She glanced back at him, then at the front door. "Do I want to know what kind of meat is rotting or will it gross me out more?" she asked.

"It'll gross you out, but you should probably know. It's human meat."

"Ew." She swallowed hard. "Long dead or…recently?"

"Relatively recent," Deacon said, a faint hissing growl in his voice.

She thought of Justin's wounds and wondered if it was him. It had taken her more than an hour to get here from Portland, with traffic. Long enough for Justin to have bled out from his wounds if his sister didn't stop at a hospital to get him help.

Although it was really too soon, and too cold, for him to be rotting yet, even if he had died. The very thought left her throat clogged with guilt. She sure hoped he hadn't died.

It occurred to her that since his sister Beatrix was a necromancer, she could probably just resurrect him, but that was equally icky to consider so Cary pushed the thought aside.

Necromancy was a kind of magic, ancient and uncommon, and most people considered it bad. Throughout history, non-wielders of magic claimed to be necromancers that could divine the future by reading a dead body or animal innards—sometimes they called themselves other things, but necromancer got thrown in to the mix.

Real necromancy, though, required magic. And real necromancers were a lot scarier and more dangerous than the snake oil augurs. They could call spirts—against the spirit's will—from the grave and make them talk. The really powerful necromancers could raise the dead, forcing them to impart information or even using the dead like weapons to kill.

Typically, human communities didn't suffer real necromancers for long, especially not the ones who could actually raise the dead. Mostly because no one wanted to be raised after they died. Some of the earliest "witch" burnings were in fact local necromancers that were caught showing off their skills.

A lot of laypeople equated necromancy with dark or black magic, but it was, as far as Cary had read, a completely different skill set. Not everyone who dabbled in so-called black magic could raise the dead, or even talk to them. Necromancy was unique.

And, fortunately for most dead people, it was also a very rare trait.

Cary studied the quiet front door of Justin and Beatrix's house. Anyone inside would have seen her and Deacon by now. They weren't exactly sneaking up on the place. And given she'd saved Justin's life, Cary was *pretty* sure his sister wouldn't try to kill her. But dealing with someone who could call the dead wasn't something Cary did every day. In fact, she found her heartbeat thumping almost as hard as when she'd gone into the catacombs to meet Ariel—the former Master vampire of Portland. Only the knowledge that vampires should *not* drink from kittens and her outrage over having come across one that did had kept Cary going then.

This time, she was here to *protect* the person she was nervous about. Which had a way of complicating her feelings on the matter.

"You okay?" Deacon asked quietly.

"No. Yes." She sighed. "Let's go. If she wanted to kill us with a dead person, she probably would have sicced them on us by now."

"You're here to keep her safe from…whatever is threatening her and her brother. Why would she want to kill you?"

"Because she obviously didn't want me to come find her or she would have left contact information. She would have taken her brother to the hospital. And she can control ghouls. That was some serious magic." Cary glanced at Deacon and winced. "She deals with…ghosts and spirits. I don't like ghosts." Her cheeks heated. "Fine, ghosts scare me a lot, okay."

"From the woman who not a week ago faced off against an entire army of supernatural beings who all wanted to kill her?"

"Don't laugh," she warned without looking at him. "That was different."

"If you say so."

"Shut up." She snarled but still refused to look at him because she was embarrassed at being scared.

Some big bad Protector she was. But seriously, ghosts did freak her out on a very primitive level. She was a lot less nervous around demons and shapeshifters. Though, to be fair, she'd dealt with a lot more demons at this stage. And shapeshifters. And vampires.

Okay, she'd hidden from anything hinting of ghosts before now. This particular job was playing right into her irrational fears. That did not help.

"You must be scared of *something*," she said, giving Deacon a look from the corner of her eye. "Spiders?" The thought of a big bad shapeshifter being afraid of spiders amused her a lot. "Lightning? Swimming pools? What scares you?"

"Losing you," he said.

Her eyes widened and her heartbeat tripped over itself. "Well. That took an unexpected turn."

"Not sure how to react, are you?"

"Not even a little bit." So for the moment, she was going to ignore it.

She dipped her head toward her shoulder on one side, then other, until she heard two very satisfying pops. Then she let out a long breath and straightened her shoulders.

"Let's do this," she said and headed toward the door.

She knocked as loud as she dared in the quiet. For some reason it seemed weird to make too much noise when even the insects and animals were silent. The door was rough, the paint—she thought it might have been blue at one stage—was pealing. The brass knocker looked like it hadn't moved in years. There was a mat at the foot of the door. It had once had something written into the straw-colored face of it, but now it was just this damp and squelchy blob. Cary avoided stepping on it.

As she waited for the person she knew was standing just the other side of the door to decide if they'd open up or not, she crossed her hands in front of her to avoid fidgeting. Deacon was a welcome, reassuringly warm presence at her back.

Her nerves were stretched to the near breaking point, and she was about to shout something—a reassurance or her name or something—when the door suddenly swung open.

She had to swallow a startled screech. She couldn't control her instinctive step backward, though.

Frustrated with her reaction, she covered it with a smile. "Hi. Remember me? From a few hours ago? And the ghouls?"

Justin's sister stood in the dark doorway blinking at her. "How did you find us?"

"Long story," Cary said. "But I wanted to check on you and your brother. You know, make sure he didn't bleed to death."

"He's fine," she said. "Thank you. Goodbye."

She swung the door closed, but Cary caught it with a hand on the flaky wood. "Can we... Can we talk? I might be able to help you."

The woman's gaze narrowed. "Who says I need help?"

"The ghouls attacking your brother and the serious injuries he was sporting." Cary stepped closer, ignoring the squelchy mat now. "The fact that you were afraid you might not find him in time, that you apologized. I know there was a lot happening in that moment, but those were pretty clear signs to me that a lot more was going on. You need help. I can help."

"How?"

Cary glanced past her, not seeing much inside the dark corridor beyond the door. "Can we talk? It's hard to explain what I can do until I know better what kind of trouble you're in."

"No, thank you," Beatrix said and started to close the door again.

Cary kept her hand in place and was a little surprised she was strong enough to keep the woman from closing the door. Her Protector powers must be working because she wasn't that strong normally. Or else the woman was so drained, her physical strength was minimal just then. Either way, Cary knew now without doubt she needed to be here, that this woman needed her help. She had every intention of keeping Beatrix and her brother safe.

"What's your name?" she asked, realizing they hadn't formally introduced themselves. She felt bad just thinking about her as "the necromancer" but since Beatrix hadn't introduced herself, Cary felt equally weird about already knowing her name. "I'm Cary," she added belatedly.

"Why are you here?" Beatrix asked.

Cary let out a breath and decided to resort to truth. At least as much of it as she was able. "I know you're a necromancer," she said. "I know you're in trouble. And I'm here to keep you safe."

Beatrix scowled at Cary, shoving at the door again in an attempt to close it. "How do you know what I am? How do you know what necromancers are?"

"The way you dealt with the ghouls gave you away," Cary said, still holding the door without having to exert much effort.

"How do you know about necromancers?" Beatrix hissed.

Cary had to swallow an urge to step away from the woman in that moment. She looked angry and scary and like maybe she might want to send dead people to kill Cary.

"I study," Cary said evasively. "Look, I'm not here to hurt you or your brother, Beatrix." As soon as the name left her mouth, Cary pressed her lips together.

The woman's eyes widened. "You know my name?"

"Justin must have said it," she hedged, trying not to wince visibly at the lie. "I swear, I'm not here to hurt you. I'm here to keep you and Justin safe from whatever is after you."

At the mention of a separate threat, Beatrix's anger morphed to fear. "Did he send you? What do you want? I told him I wouldn't say anything."

"Whoa, whoa," Cary said. "'He' who?"

Beatrix frowned. "You said… I don't… Who the hell are you? Who sent you?"

"No one sent me," Cary lied without hesitance that time. "My name is Cary Redmond and I have this…habit of helping people who are in trouble. It's what I do," she finished, defensively.

Beatrix glanced behind her. "And him?"

Cary shrugged. "My friend."

"Her boyfriend," Deacon said at the same time.

Cary scowled at him over her shoulder, even as her cheeks heated. He kept introducing himself that way even though it wasn't true. You had to date before you got to the boyfriend/girlfriend stage. Did you?

Beatrix's expression relaxed a little as she glanced between Cary and Deacon. "Does she know she's your girlfriend?" she asked Deacon.

"It's complicated," Cary put in before he could answer. "And not why we're here."

"Why are you here?" Beatrix said, wariness coming back into her voice.

"To help. I'm not sure how many more ways I can say that."

"I don't need help. We're fine."

"Yeah, I wouldn't be here if you were fine. Call it an instinct."

"If you have an instinct for helping people, where were you two weeks ago when I needed you?" Beatrix's bottom lip trembled briefly before she covered the reaction with a snarl.

Cary raised her hands in helpless gesture. "Sorry about that. I was…busy."

"Doing what?" Beatrix snapped.

"Keeping a demon and his army from invading a Naga city," Cary said.

Beatrix stilled for a long moment, not even blinking as she stared at Cary. Then she dipped her head to one side in a shrug. "Fair enough. Come on it. Ignore the smell if you can."

Cary stared after the woman's retreating back, not sure what had just happened. "That was…easy?" she murmured to Deacon.

He grunted a non-committal sound and followed her inside.

1 2

The inside of the house wasn't in much better shape than the outside. To the right was a living room type area but it was crowded with boxes and the table in the center was covered with metals and what looked to Cary's untrained eye like smelting equipment, maybe for making jewelry. She didn't get a chance to look too closely at the various bits and pieces scattered across the table, but they could have been medallions of some sort, and she glimpsed a few colorful looking crystals.

To the left of the entrance was another room with the door closed. Cary got a stronger whiff of the rotting meat smell from that room and had to swallow back her bile. Since she was here to protect Beatrix, she was pretty sure she was happier not knowing what was inside that room.

A long hall led to the back of the house, the creaking wood floor in need of a polish and no carpets to warm the area. The walls were a green color, but faded and like everything else looked like they could use a fresh coat of paint. There were no pictures or other real decorations except for a strip of black and white wallpaper circling the top of the wall, just at the ceiling. Cary couldn't identify the pattern in the dimness, but wondered if Deacon with his super shifter senses could see it. She'd have to ask him later.

They passed two more closed doors, which from the size of the space could have been closets or bathrooms. Maybe bedrooms but they'd be very small bedrooms. Then they emerged into an open and shockingly bright kitchen. The back wall was almost all windows, with clean white curtains framing them. The appliances were shiny chrome, the cabinets a light colored wood, the counter tops pale colored granite. The floor was stained a darker color here, making a nice contrast to the light colors. And the wall was a clean, bright yellow. Against one window, a cozy table in a nook surrounded by mismatched chairs gave the place a very homey feel.

The brightness and cheerfulness of the space contrasted sharply with everything else about the house. And if it weren't for the smell of rotting meat still coming from the front room, Cary might have thought she'd stepped through another magical portal into a completely different home.

"Beautiful kitchen," she commented, trying to cover her surprise.

Beatrix snorted. "You mean compared to the rest of the place."

Well, she hadn't wanted to say that out loud, but…

"You want some tea?" Beatrix asked, going into the open kitchen and setting a kettle onto the stove.

"No, thank you," Cary said. The space around her might have appeared friendly, but the stench was still pervasive. Her stomach rebelled at even the thought of drinking or eating anything. "Where's Justin?" she asked.

"Sleeping."

"His injuries?"

"I stitched him up."

Cary raised her brows. "You can do that?"

"Our mother was an army medic. She taught us a lot of first aid." Beatrix turned away from the stove and settled her backside against the counter, folding her arms across her chest. "I don't know why you think you can help us, so there's really no point in you being here."

"Maybe, you could explain who 'he' is and why you worried he'd sent me?" Cary looked around, wondering if it would be rude to sit.

Beatrix lifted her mouth in a half smile, half smirk and gestured at the table. "Sit. Both of you. He's too tall to keep looking up at."

Cary chuckled at that. Deacon was pretty tall, though not like basketball star sized or anything.

She only realized how relatively small Beatrix was in that moment, though. While she carried herself with substantial presence and had appeared much taller in the tunnels, she was actually maybe five-foot-three, five-foot-four at the most. She still looked a lot thinner than seemed healthy, though. Her cheeks were hollow, her skin in the bright light looked ashen and dry, her dark eyes were rimmed by puffy purple smudges. She had her brown hair pulled back in a low bun now, the style accenting her sharp, hungry features. In the daylight, Cary noticed stripes of white hair tucked under the brown, something she hadn't seen before.

"Been a tough few weeks?" Cary asked before she could filter the comment. Beatrix looked worn down to her bones, with few reserves left.

"How can you help me?" Beatrix asked, ignoring Cary's comment.

"Depends on who 'he' is," Cary said.

"He won't be a problem soon. I'm taking care of it. I always do."

That was what Cary was worried about. "If you're intending to send dead people after him, that might not be…a great idea."

"You don't know him. What he's done. He deserves no less."

"Was he the one who hurt your brother?"

"A threat. A warning."

"Looked more like he wanted Justin dead," Cary said.

"If he'd wanted him dead, he would have killed him and dumped his body on my doorstep." Beatrix's muscles flexed in her forearms and she glanced out the window, not meeting Cary's gaze. "He was playing with us," she murmured. "He likes to play games."

"And *he* is?" Cary prompted.

Beatrix met her gaze again, but the woman looking at Cary now was hollow, dead inside. Numb to what was happening to her. Cary blinked in surprise. It was like looking at someone completely different from just moments ago. How had she done that? Why had she done it?

Cary tried not to squirm in her seat. If Beatrix was raising power, calling on dead people or whatever, Cary would be able to sense it. Probably. Because Deacon was here and would be in danger.

But the deadness in Beatrix's expression now was haunting.

"He," Beatrix said, her voice sounding deeper and just as emotionless as her face, "is our boss."

Not another boss, Cary thought. Everyone had called Oliver Holland the Boss. Did she have yet another demon to face? Beatrix couldn't be talking about Holland, but…

"Boss. As in your employer?" Cary asked carefully.

"He's a serial killer," Beatrix said. "And he uses us to help dispose of the bodies."

For a very long moment, Cary could only stare at the woman as what she'd said sank in. Every word of that had sounded…wrong somehow. And also scarily plausible.

She swallowed, opened her mouth to comment, had to swallow again. "Your boss is a serial killer?"

Beatrix nodded.

"And you found this out when? After you went to work for him?"

"No. We knew when he found us what he was and what he wanted. He didn't hide anything."

Cary felt sick. Beatrix and her brother had willingly helped a serial killer dispose of bodies. And she was supposed to protect them? It sounded like they were the bad guys. What the hell had the Nags gotten her into? She didn't protect bad guys. At least, not if she could help it.

Okay. Sometimes she couldn't help it and did end up protecting bad guys but still…

What the hell?

Deacon put a hand on Cary's arm. "We should leave," he whispered, quietly enough that Cary wasn't sure Beatrix would have heard him all the way across the kitchen.

Cary wanted to agree, but the Nags had sent her here for a reason.

She wasn't sure she could walk away from this job without risking… Well, she wasn't entirely sure. But she had the feeling keeping Beatrix and Justin safe from the serial killer was necessary to preventing Beatrix from destroying the world. Or something…

Shaking her head, Cary said, "You, uh, you helped a serial killer. How exactly?"

"You aren't asking why first?" Beatrix asked. "Most people would wonder why?"

"We can get to that part eventually. I do need to know the hows of it first, though."

Beatrix shrugged and turned to the now whistling kettle. With her back to Cary and Deacon, she said, "I'm unique even among necromancers. For a long time, I didn't even know what this…gift of mine was. I could bring our dead pets and animals back to life, sort of. Though they were never really the same after." She glanced over her shoulder, not quite looking at them. "That book, you know with the cemetery for pets that brought the pets back to life? It was like that. But it was me, not the sacred ground that did the resurrecting." She returned to making her tea. "They didn't have to be buried even. Just dead. And then they were mine to control."

"That must have been scary to realize," Cary said quietly. She would have been majorly freaked out by that ability.

Beatrix shrugged. "It was natural. I didn't know I was supposed to be bothered by it, not for a long time."

"Justin obviously knows?"

"Of course. He's my twin. We know everything about each other."

"Your parents?"

"Dad died in Afghanistan when we were little. I don't really remember him. Soldier like mom. She retired to take care of us, but… She was what some would call eccentric." Beatrix faced them then, a slight smile giving life back to her previously dead expression. "Although I suppose you have to be rich to be eccentric. Without the money, it's just crazy, right?"

Cary didn't respond to that. Instead, she asked, "Is your mom still alive?"

"She died when we were sixteen. Self-inflicted gun wound." Beatrix made the words sound sour. "Suicide, though no one wanted to say that to us. Justin found her out back." She glanced out the windows again. "Poor mom. They'd call it PTSD, I suppose. If they'd bothered to explain much about it to us. No one wanted to."

"You been on your own since?" Cary asked.

Beatrix faced her, cradling her mug as steam wound up from the tea. She didn't sip any, just held the cup. "We had to fight for that," she said. "They wanted to send us to foster parents. But Justin and I had been taking care of ourselves for a few years at that stage. We didn't want some stranger trying to tell us what to do."

"How did you support yourselves?" Cary asked.

Beatrix's mouth lifted in a faint smile that didn't look entirely pleasant. "Used what we had. There were military benefits from mom and dad but they didn't cover everything. The house was paid off, so we at least had a place to live."

"How long ago was all this?" For all the dark circles, ashen skin, and white streaks in her hair, Cary couldn't really gauge Beatrix's age. She could be anywhere from eighteen to forty. Most people had the same issue with Cary's age, but Cary had an excuse for that. Protectors aged slowly. One of the few benefits Cary saw in the job.

"Mom killed herself four years ago," Beatrix said.

"And you've been managing ever since."

"We have skills to sell. We got by."

Skills? "You sold your…ability to question the dead?" Cary knew that was how sham necromancers made a living. Like false mediums, it was a lucrative business for those gullible or desperate enough to turn to anyone that offered comfort. In this case, Beatrix could actually speak to the dead, so maybe it wasn't such a bad way to make a living?

"At first," Beatrix said.

Cary waited her out. She had a lot of questions but at this stage, she needed to know what Beatrix was prepared to tell her and what she wasn't. The woman was being surprisingly open so far. Cary wasn't sure if that was good or bad, but it was useful.

"My brother's talented, too," Beatrix added, raising her chin in a proud and defensive gesture. "Makes jewelry. Beautiful stuff. Very valuable."

"Nice," Cary said. "That's his workroom in the front of the house."

Beatrix nodded. "Not just ordinary jewelry either. Special stuff. With magic."

She threw those words out like she expected Cary to scoff or argue with the assertion. Obviously the twins had made the mistake of revealing Justin's gift to people who didn't believe in magic before this. It appeared to be a knee-jerk reaction for Beatrix.

Cary just said, "Handy talent, I'd guess."

Beatrix pursed her lips. "You don't startle easily."

"You telling me you went to work voluntarily for a serial killer was startling. If that helps at all."

Beatrix looked away. "It wasn't really like that," she said softly. "We aren't evil like people say."

"Necromancers get a bad rap," Cary agreed. "People get squicky about things like zombies and ghosts and dead things rising."

"Justin's not a necromancer," Beatrix said. "He's a good man."

Cary noticed Beatrix didn't apply that defense to herself, or necromancers in general. "So did you go to work for the serial killer because you needed the money?"

She didn't glance back toward the front of the house, but her implication was obvious. Their home wasn't in the best of shape. And they'd been on their own since they were barely of legal working age. Money was an obvious motivation. One Cary sympathized with.

"Sort of," Beatrix hedged. "He offered us… Freedom."

Cary narrowed her eyes. "From what?"

Before Beatrix could answer, a hesitant voice from the doorway drew all their attention. "Bea, what's going on?"

Justin leaned heavily against the doorframe, looking from Cary and Deacon to his sister. He was shirtless so the thick bandages wrapping his waist were obvious. His sweatpants hung loose on his frame so Cary couldn't tell if he'd had any more injuries. Since there wasn't blood dripping anywhere and the bandage around his waist looked clean, she assumed any and all of his wounds had been dealt with.

Beatrix hurried to his side. "You shouldn't be standing yet. You'll tear the stitches."

"What's going on?" he said, his tone firmer now.

Cary stood to face them. "I don't know if you remember since you were pretty out of it, but I'm Cary Redmond. We met earlier today?"

"You saved me from the ghouls," he said, nodding. "I remember. What are you doing here?"

"I came to help."

He glanced down at Beatrix. Even leaning on the doorframe, he was still several inches taller than his twin. He likely had half a foot or more on her standing at his full height.

"What's she talking about?" he asked.

"Actually, I don't know yet," Beatrix said, frowning at Cary. "But she says she can help us with Greenson."

Justin met Cary's gaze, his own flicking between her and Deacon. "The only way to help with Kenneth Greenson is to kill him."

13

ary let out a breath. "That's not exactly the help I'm offering."
Although, sometimes when people attacked her, her powers ricocheted their attack back on them and killed them. But Cary didn't typically kill people. She frowned a little. Except for the army of bad guys who'd tried to get into the Naga city. She'd killed a bunch of them. Kind of on accident.

It was a sobering thought. She killed more people than she'd considered, even if she didn't do it on purpose. She made a face. That didn't feel...good. Granted, they were always the bad guys and brought it on themselves—usually getting killed by their own magic or whatever. Still...

If she hadn't just been thrown to the wolves by her bosses, this was exactly the kind of thing she'd talk to Jaxer about. Except she hadn't seen Jaxer since the attack on the Naga city. And now it was too late for him to help her.

She shook off the thoughts. She could brood about her own circumstances later.

"I'm here to keep you and your sister alive," she said to Justin. "Not to kill anyone."

"He won't stop until he's dead," Justin said. His voice was deep but rusty sounding, like his throat was dry. And he was even paler than he'd looked that morning.

"You should sit down," Cary said.

Beatrix draped one of his arms over her shoulders. "She's right. Sit. Before you fall down and ruin all my hard work."

Deacon stood and gave Justin his seat since it was the easiest to reach. The younger man eased down with obvious pain, his face set in a grimace as he settled.

"Better?" Cary asked.

Justin let out a breath that was probably supposed to be a chuckle. "Sure. Better." He met her gaze. "Thank you for saving me."

"You're welcome."

"How did you do that?"

"I have a particular set of skills that come in handy in those kinds of situations," she said.

"You a witch?" he asked.

"No," she said with a slight smile. "Not a witch." That was everyone's first guess.

"But you're not here to kill Greenson?" he asked.

"No. I didn't even know about him until just a few minutes ago. I just knew you and your sister were still in trouble. And I came to do what I can to keep you alive."

Justin exchanged a look with Beatrix. "We're fine. We can take care of ourselves."

"Obviously," Cary said without sarcasm, gesturing to his clean bandage. "Beatrix said you've been taking care of yourselves for a long time now. But I wouldn't be here if this was a situation you could handle without me."

Justin frowned. "Meaning?"

"Meaning, I show up when I'm needed." Before Beatrix could remind her, she added, "When I'm not helping elsewhere. It's complicated. But I'm here to do what I do to make sure this killer former boss of yours doesn't murder you. Fair enough?"

"Who says he's our former boss?" Beatrix asked.

Cary faced her. "You can't be serious. He tried to murder your brother. You said yourself he was playing with you. You still intend to work for him?"

"That was the point," Justin said.

Cary frowned, processing that. "You tried to quit already," she guessed. "And nearly murdering you was a warning to keep up the job or else?"

Justin tapped his finger to his nose. "Bullseye."

"Huh. Well, my job is coming more into focus now," Cary murmured. She glanced at Deacon who was frowning at her. "Can't let a serial killer keep using them, now can I?" she said.

He didn't look convinced, but since it wasn't his job or his decision she ignored him and concentrated on the twins.

"What magic do you have that he's exploiting?" Cary asked Justin. "Is it to do with your jewelry?"

He glanced at his sister.

Beatrix shrugged. "It came up."

"She was bragging on you," Cary said.

His mouth lifted at one side in a faint smile and he shook his head. "Not something you should be proud of me for," he said to Beatrix.

"Why not? You're amazing and the world should know."

"The world would lock me up in a lab and try to study me like a rat if they knew," he said.

Cary didn't comment since she agreed with him. The mundane world didn't have a lot of consideration for those that weren't strictly typical. And obviously Justin's skill was something that could be used for evil or he wouldn't have ended up working for a serial killer.

Unless the killer was using Justin to control Beatrix. She asked that out loud.

"No," Beatrix said. "He wanted Justin's talent as much as mine. Though he came for me first."

"What *exactly* do you help him with?" Cary asked.

"I dispose of the bodies," Beatrix said bluntly. "I make sure they can't be found."

Cary sat in her previously abandoned chair, realization sinking in. "You call the ghouls and have them eat the remains."

"Nothing left but a few bones afterward," Beatrix said. Her expression had gone blank again, that emotionless mask that was as scary as her admission.

"And I use the bones," Justin said. "I tie them into my jewelry."

"To what end?" Cary asked.

"Depends. But for Greenson, I've been working them into an amulet. A power amulet."

Cary had a feeling she already knew, but she asked anyway, just to be sure. "What kind of power?"

"To control the ghouls," he said.

"Yeah, that didn't work out so well, did it?" she said.

Justin exchanged a look with his sister. "Greenson offered us a lot of money. Enough that we could fix up this place, or even move if we wanted to. The amulet was supposed to be our out. Beatrix takes care of the bodies until I get the amulet done. Once it's ready and he's tested it, we can go our own way."

"Instead, he tested it on Justin," Beatrix said. "And it worked."

"But…" Cary rubbed a hand across her forehead, forcing herself to recall what she'd studied about ghouls in the past. "As far as I knew, ghouls only eat *dead* things. That's their job, just clean up rotting meat, keep the whole ecosystem rolling over, so to speak, in areas where the dead are most dense. Like cemeteries."

Another thing the mundane world didn't know about or believe in, but ghouls were just part of the natural order of things. They helped the bugs and other organisms that digest and redistribute nutrients from dead things. They looked horrible and scary, and the way they went about things—coming out from the ground, digging up bodies, and eating them—was a bit, well, ghoulish. But they weren't normally a threat to living people.

"They don't kill," she finished out loud. "Ghouls don't even approach living things. They certainly don't attack them."

Another look between Justin and Beatrix.

"That was—" Justin started, but a knock on the door stopped him.

Everyone in the kitchen fell silent, looking toward the front of the house.

"Expecting company?" Cary asked. Tingles of awareness crawled up her spine. Danger waited outside that door. And her Kevlar vest type of magic was needed. She was standing, heading toward the kitchen doorway before Beatrix answered her question.

"No, we aren't," Beatrix said.

Another knock, this one louder. And a voice filtered through the rough wood. "Come out come out my helpers. I know you're in there."

"That doesn't sound creepy at all," Cary said quietly, but heavy on the sarcasm. "I assume that's our serial killer?"

Justin and Beatrix both nodded but didn't look away from the door.

"Okay," Cary said, "I'm gonna go stand in front of you guys while you talk to him." She waited for them both to face her. "That's how *my* magic works. I'll just stand there making sure he can't get at you or hurt you. You tell him to fuck off or whatever works for you. Got it?"

"That won't work," Justin said. "He won't go away. Not now."

"Yeah, you're going to have to explain that later," Cary said as another pounding knock sounded. "Right now, let's just get him to go away. We'll work on getting him to stay away after that."

She started down the hallway, stopping when Deacon called her name. She glanced at him.

"I'll stay in the shadows and guard your backs," he said. "Be careful."

"Thanks. You too."

She faced the door, wincing as the man outside pounded on the worn wood hard enough it sounded like it might crack. She pulled in a deep breath—which was a huge mistake as it coated her mouth and throat with the rotting meat stench—held it, let it out slowly. Then she headed for the door, Beatrix and Justin a step behind her.

To face a serial killer.

Fun.

14

He was exactly what Cary would have expected from a human serial killer.

Kenneth Greenson was average height, with ordinary brown hair and eyes, ordinary Caucasian features that were neither too handsome nor too ugly, wearing jeans, a t-shirt, and a baseball cap. His coat was a padded rain coat, nothing fancy. And if you didn't look closely, he looked like an ordinary, average man you might pass on the street in any given city in the country.

Only two things really stood out. One was the thick, solid silver chain and amulet around his neck. The amulet was an intricate folding and weave of decorated silver and carved bones with a clear quartz crystal in the center of the complex design. The fact that he had his "ghoul control" necklace on was a pretty good sign he wasn't here for a friendly visit.

The other thing about him that ran contrary to his ordinariness was something in his eyes. They were sharper and deader than a normal man's, but there was also the very faintest hint of red in the depths of the brown, so faint she could almost convince herself she was imagining it.

Cary blinked when she saw that. That only happened with demon hunters.

"Shit," she said aloud. "Not more demons."

The man tilted his dead to one side. "Who are you?"

"Hi," she said, to recover from her shock. "No one in particular. Friend of the twins. Just…you know, hanging out."

Even as she stood her ground between him and Beatrix and Justin, her mind spun. He couldn't be a demon hunter. Could he? Weren't they supposed to be the good guys? Maybe there was another reason for the hint of red in his eyes. Maybe it was just the light. She'd have to look this up when she got home. There had to be another explanation.

Greenson narrowed his eyes at her, then glanced past her to Beatrix and Justin. "We need to talk. Tell your friend to give us some privacy."

"Nope," Cary said. "I stand here. You talk around me."

When he scowled at her, she grinned. It really irritated bad guys when she grinned at them, but it also kept them off their game. A serial killer who didn't know quite what to do about her was probably a good thing. Hopefully.

"This is none of your business," the man said.

She shrugged. "Tough. I stand here. You talk around me."

His eyes narrowed to little slits and the faint red seemed to flare brighter. "You will move out of the way, return to your car, and leave now."

His voice had dropped an octave, and Cary could actually feel the force of his will rolling over her. She pressed her lips together so she wouldn't laugh at her own unintended joke—"feel the force" as he was trying to use a Jedi mind trick. Her amusement must have shown because the man's expression turned downright deadly. Oops.

"Are you laughing?" he asked.

"Nope," she said, then pressed her lips together again so she wouldn't. Not really the time to be amused by her own accidental puns. The fact that he was using a tone and force of will in the way a demon hunter might should concern her more, so she focused on that.

He tried to make her leave again by the sheer force of his will, this time the roll of his power making her skin crawl. This was interesting.

She'd never been on this side of a demon hunter's willpower before. Both impressive and terrifying if she wasn't protecting someone.

After a moment, the man straightened and glared at her. "What are you?"

"Concerned friend," she said. "You're here to talk? Talk. Then you can leave."

"How do you resist?" he asked, more quietly this time.

"Talent," she murmured.

He smiled, just a little, a really terrifying lifting of lips that revealed very white teeth. "You'll have to explain that to me sometime."

"Nope," she said again. "Get on with it. My tea is getting cold." Well, it was Beatrix's tea, but he didn't need to know that.

He held her gaze a moment longer, the red in his eyes fading but still there. And obviously not a trick of the light or her imagination. Damn it.

He finally turned away to address the twins. "We're not through. My message was clear?"

"Crystal," Justin said, touching his bandaged waist. "But you hired us for the amulet. You have it. Our work is done."

"What else do you want?" Beatrix asked the million dollar question.

"The charm is flawed," he said.

Justin laughed, the sound bitter in the quiet afternoon. "It worked or I wouldn't have nearly been eaten."

The man smiled faintly, his gaze turning inward. Cary had a real gross suspicion he was imagining the "eating" part. She controlled her expression so she didn't lift her lip in a disgusted snarl.

"But your sister overrode the amulet," Greenson said. "You have given me half of what I wanted. You haven't finished your job."

"We didn't promise you something that was stronger than my magic," Beatrix said. "We can't do that. Not—" She cut herself off, but not quick enough.

"Not what?" Greenson asked. His voice held that same creepy, softness that he'd used when calling through the closed door for them.

Beatrix didn't answer for a long moment.

"Not what, Beatrix," he said again, still soft but with that edge of will rolling through his tone.

Cary held up a hand to get his attention. "That trick won't work." When he looked at her, she said, "Just to let you know. That trick you're trying right now, with your voice and willpower? That's not working."

He glared. She shrugged. He looked past her to the twins again.

"I want a fully functioning amulet, children," he said. "I've paid well for it. And I'll be back for it." He glanced at Cary. "When we have some privacy to…talk."

Well, that didn't sound pleasant.

Before Cary, or anyone else could comment, Greenson turned and walked away. Cary watched as the dead grass under his feet charred in his wake. She frowned at that. It was hard to hide that and come across as ordinary. That didn't quite jibe with what she'd assumed about him.

Even as she mulled over the incongruity, the grass charring stopped and he continued to walk without anything out of the ordinary happening to his surroundings.

She continued to stand in the doorway, protecting the twins, until Greenson was well out of sight down the road—still walking. The faintest hint of sulfur remained in the air, filtering through the stench of dead things.

She frowned. Demon *hunters* didn't exude sulfur. Freed demons like Oliver Holland didn't either, not if they were powerful enough to hide what they were. Freed demons who did stink of sulfur were usually not powerful enough to hide from the demon hunters for long or had only just gotten free into this realm.

Greenson was walking around with eyes like a hunter, but the stench of a newly freed demon. So what the hell was he?

Once she was sure the man was gone, she turned around to face the twins. Deacon stood behind them now, staring out the door.

He met her gaze.

"Demon or demon hunter?" she asked him. With his sense of smell, he could usually figure these things out. He'd known Holland was a demon on first sniff.

Deacon's mouth turned down in a slight frown. "I don't know. I couldn't tell."

Well, that couldn't be good.

Shit.

ary waited until Beatrix had boiled the kettle again and set fresh tea in front of Justin and herself before she started asking questions. Both twins looked nervous, their gazes darting about, not making eye contact with either Cary or Deacon. They were hiding something. From Greenson, yes. But also from Cary. Which made her job more difficult.

She didn't like when the people she was supposed to be helping made her job *more* difficult.

"Talk," she said when everyone had settled at the cozy little table in the brightly colored kitchen that felt worlds away from demon hunters, serial killers, and ghouls.

Beatrix lifted her shoulders in a shrug that conveyed an awful lot of defensiveness. "About what? That was our boss. As you can see, he isn't ready to let us quit yet."

"Your boss is more than an ordinary human serial killer. You could have overcome a normal human." Cary glanced at Justin. "Your jewelry, you fix magic into it. Can you add any kind of magic, any sort of power, or just specific stuff?"

Could he imbue his jewelry with "willpower" on par with what demon hunters had access to?

Justin looked away, not meeting her gaze when he said, "So far, everything I've tried has worked."

"You gave him limited powers over the dead on purpose then?" Cary said.

"No, actually," Justin said. "I gave him what I could as soon as I could. But… I didn't limit it on purpose. Necessarily."

"Meaning?" Cary prodded.

"He needed more…" Beatrix started, but trailed off when Justin glared at her.

"Come clean," Cary said. "Hiding this stuff from me isn't going to help you."

"You did what you came here to do," Justin said. "You made him go away. Aren't you done helping now?"

"He's coming back," Cary said. "You're still in danger. And he knows as well as I do that you're hiding something." She narrowed her eyes. "Are you responsible for his will or did he have that when he found you?"

"What do you mean?" Beatrix asked.

Cary studied the young necromancer. "You know anything about demon hunters?"

Beatrix frowned and shook her head.

"How about you?" Cary asked Justin.

He shrugged. "Didn't know there was such a thing until you mentioned it. Not exactly part of our skill set." The last was said with only a hint of sarcasm.

Cary leaned back in her chair, considering whether to explain this or not. It wasn't exactly common knowledge she supposed, outside the demon and demon hunting circles. If Justin didn't know such a thing existed, he wasn't likely to figure out how to make jewelry that could carry a demon hunter's main source of power. Given he'd gone to work willingly for a murderer, that was probably a good thing.

So she changed the subject a bit. "What exactly did you give him?" she asked.

"An amulet to control ghouls," Justin said. "Just like he asked."

"Did he ask for that?" Cary said. "Or did he ask for powers like Beatrix's?"

The twins exchanged a look and Cary knew she'd hit the point. "So," she said, "when Beatrix could override the ghouls he'd commanded to eat Justin, Greenson had confirmation that you hadn't given him *her* powers at all."

"I can't give him *her* powers," Justin said. "They're hers. They're a part of her."

"If he killed more people and gave us their bones, Justin could make a stronger amulet," Beatrix said.

Justin hissed at her. "Enough. She knows enough already."

"But it still wouldn't be my powers," Beatrix finished, ignoring her brother's warning.

"Could Greenson do necromancy?" Cary asked. "With what you have or could give him?"

"A bit," Beatrix said. "Controlling ghouls is a very specific part of my skill set, a higher level of it really. Giving him that much took a lot of death and Justin's magic already, though."

"More death would make that part of his new skills stronger?" Cary asked.

Beatrix nodded. "But still not stronger than my ability to counter what he does."

"What would be strong enough?" Cary's suspicions were growing. She wasn't a psychic witch like Angie, but she'd been studying and knew just enough about magic to have an inkling of what it might take to give Greenson Beatrix's exact powers.

Beatrix held Cary's gaze, very obviously not looking at her brother when she said, "The only way he gets powers like mine, as strong and as complete as anything I do is with—"

"Beatrix, enough," Justin hissed.

She still didn't look at him. "He'd need me dead," she said, her tone even and calm. "He'd need my bones."

16

---

ary hadn't wanted to leave the twins after Beatrix's admission, but she needed more information about Greenson. If he had the skills, the willpower, of a demon hunter, he would eventually get the truth out of Beatrix about needing her death and bones. He'd figure out a way to control Justin long enough to have him make the amulet. And then he'd probably kill Justin too.

The only way to stop all this was to take down the killer. But that wasn't in Cary's job description. She needed help. And since she wasn't going to get it from Jaxer or the Nags, she needed to find someone else who could.

Which meant research and a few phone calls.

She had insisted the twins go somewhere Greenson couldn't find them. She'd almost volunteered her own home, so she could protect them at the same time as she did her research. But frankly, she didn't want them in her home, or even knowing where it was. If something went wrong and she lost the glamour that kept her house hidden from uninvited guests, she didn't want a necromancer knowing where she lived.

After much hemming and hawing, Beatrix and Justin had decided on a tiny cemetery that they hadn't been too since they were kids, a place with a little one room cottage where a grounds keeper had lived before the cemetery was abandoned. No one new had been buried there in a long time. The place was down a remote dirt road, miles outside of Portland, and mostly forgotten. It wasn't a place Greenson would think to look, probably didn't even know it existed. The twins claimed it wasn't even on most maps anymore. All of which made it a good hiding spot. If you didn't mind cemeteries.

Cary got the directions so she could find the twins when she was ready, and she gave them her cell number so they could call if they needed her.

She'd felt that hint of guilt at leaving them, that without her around they might be in danger. But now that she knew Justin hadn't died of his injuries, and that they'd be someplace really difficult to find, the guilt wasn't loud enough to make her forgo the security of her own home.

She parked in the garage, and Deacon followed her inside without a word. He'd been silent on the drive back. Since Cary had needed to think, she didn't try to force conversation. His silence was worrying, though. So once she'd let the dogs out into the backyard and put on the coffee pot, she faced him with her arms crossed over her chest.

"Spill," she said. "What are you thinking so hard about?"

He smiled a little as he closed the space between them and pulled her close. She dropped her defensive pose and settled her hands on his waist before she realized what she was doing. Her unthinking comfort with him, the way they flowed together physically with such ease, as if they'd known each other for years instead of weeks, really annoyed her.

They *still* hadn't been on a date.

Deacon must have sensed her irritation because his smile grew. "You're worried about liking my touch again, aren't you?"

"Stop that. You know it bugs me even more when you read my mind."

"Stop being so easy to read," he countered.

"What were you thinking about in the car?"

"When was the last time you slept?"

"I woke up from a three *day* sleep yesterday afternoon."

"So you've been awake for twenty-four hours now?"

She glanced at the clock on the microwave. "Bit over. Why?"

"You should sleep."

She ducked her chin and gave him a look. "I slept for *three days*. I'm good for a few more hours. Besides, it's like jet lag. I need to get back on a regular sleep routine and go to bed at a normal going-to-bed time." Not like she had a normal sleep routine with her job, but he didn't need to know that. "And you haven't been thinking so hard about my sleep schedule," she said. "Come on, what are you worrying about?"

"You mostly," he said, seriously. "I seem to worry about you all the time. Even when I should be thinking about other things."

"Then stop worrying about me so much. I'm a grown up. I can take care of myself."

"You're my mate. I will always worry about you."

"Deacon…"

He set his lips to hers, a gentle touch that stopped her in mid-protest. Caught off guard, she responded automatically, returning the gentle touch with a searching pressure, rising on her toes to deepen the contact.

His kiss pulled her under as he tightened his hold around her waist and followed her lead deeper. Sweeping his tongue into her mouth, a hint of urgency answering her soft moan. She was over-whelmed so fast, so completely by the sensation, she forgot she'd had questions. She forgot she had things to do. She forgot the world existed outside his arms. She pressed against him savoring the feel of his solid, hard body, and let herself go in the sweet bliss of his scent and heat.

He backed her up against the counter, his hands stroking up her spine in a delicious movement that had her arching against him. Her pulse pounded hard, her breathing sped, and without thinking, she started to tug at his shirt. The feel of his hot skin under her palms as she moved her hands up under his shirt made her sigh. She scrapped her short nails over his back, loving the way he shivered in response.

He ground against her, his cock hard and solid between them. And it was an act of will not to reach down and rub that thick ridge.

She had never wanted a man this much, never gotten swept up in need and lust so quickly with anyone else she'd ever met. A touch, a look, a smile, and she was lost.

The whole thing scared the hell out of her. Almost as much as ghosts.

When she felt herself falling too far, knowing she wouldn't stop if she didn't put some distance between them now, she ended the kiss and eased him back from her. The air felt colder when she wasn't enveloped in his heat.

"How does that happen so fast?" she asked, her voice sounding embarrassingly husky.

"You know how and you know why," he said.

"Yeah, yeah. I'm just still having trouble dealing with it."

"Which is why I'm going to stand a few feet away now," he said with that sexy smile that made her knees weak.

She shook her head at the smile. He knew exactly what he was doing with that, even as he gave her the space she'd just asked for. Bastard.

"You distracted me," she said, though she didn't sound as accusing as she'd intended. "You weren't just worrying about me on the drive home. Tell me what you're thinking."

She turned to the cabinets for a coffee mug and a glass so she didn't have to stare at him. It was always easier to keep her hormones in check if she didn't look at him constantly.

"Greenson," he said. "He's human, but not…fully?"

"You don't sound sure."

"I'm not. He smelled strange."

"I caught the sulfur."

"It was more than that, though. He smelled human, but not like a demon hunter."

She glanced at him as she took the milk from the fridge. "What exactly do demon hunters smell like?" She wasn't sure if he could explain but she was curious anyway.

"Actually, they don't smell like much at all unless they want to," he said. "They tend to be almost scentless. It can be disconcerting for a shifter."

She chuckled. "I bet. That's some trick. Do they do it on purpose?"

"I've never asked, but I suspect so." He shrugged. "They don't do a lot that's not on purpose."

That she could believe.

Demon hunters mostly faced demons who'd been brought through a crack between realms by some hapless person looking for power or wishes or whatever. A demon hunter showed up when the person's ability to contain the demon had run out and the demon was about to break free into this realm. The hunter's job was to ensure that didn't happen, and the fights to prevent a demon from getting free were reputed to be…impressive.

Hunter's fights tended to involve a lot of show, a big production—using religious paraphernalia, or scientific gadgets, or pagan rituals from different cultures, sometimes entering into challenges the demons offered up. All depending on how the demon was called and what was used to manifest it and bind it in this realm, sometimes combined with the type of demon called.

But all of that was just outer trappings. For show. Maybe to help the hunter focus. None of it was necessary. All a hunter really needed was a will stronger than a demon's. If the hunter's will was stronger, they overcame the demon's attempt to escape and sent them back to whatever realm they'd come from. A hunter who failed, whose will wasn't strong enough, died. Simple as that. The ones that survived were the strong ones, the ones that could and did do things that shouldn't be possible. All through the sheer force of their wills.

"This guy had a scent, though," Deacon continued. "He smelled like a human, mostly. There were hints of Justin's magic and the death magic Beatrix wields. The sulfur only came out when he walked away and scorched the grass, like he'd done that on purpose."

"And he had that faint red in his eyes that demon hunters get," she added. "He could have done all of that on purpose, as a show for us and the twins."

"True," Deacon said. "But there was something… I don't know if I can pinpoint it and that's what's been bothering me. He isn't precisely reading as demon hunter."

"And he's definitely not a demon?" she asked, hopefully. She'd had enough of demons in the last few weeks.

"He's not a demon," Deacon said. "They can't hide their scent signatures the way a hunter can. Most demons wouldn't even try."

She supposed that was true enough. If anyone had been strong enough to hide his nature it would have been Oliver Holland. He'd been old. And a freed demon for centuries according to Deacon's sense of smell. Yet he hadn't bothered, even knowing Deacon would scent his nature. Holland had been content with them knowing exactly what he was.

Given Greenson's arrogance, Cary doubted he'd have tried to hide his nature from them if he was a demon. Especially since Deacon hadn't shown himself, so Greenson wouldn't have had any reason to believe any of them had the sense of smell to figure it out.

"Do you suppose he's trying to make the twins believe he's a demon?" she asked as she poured Deacon his milk and herself a cup of coffee. "I mean, Beatrix and Justin don't have your sense of smell. But Greenson did throw out hints—like the sulfur and the grass charring. Really deliberate stuff."

"Maybe." Deacon frowned. "Why hint, though, and not just tell them he was a demon?"

She shrugged. "What if they called him on it? Or got in touch with a demon hunter?"

"They didn't know hunters existed, remember."

"Right. Right." She handed him his milk, as ever bemused by the big cat who drank milk. "I don't know. If they don't know much about demons, it seems silly to even pretend at it. And why would a demon want Beatrix's powers? They called him a serial killer. Beatrix disposed of bodies for him, but…" She cursed under her breath. "I never asked more about how he killed, who he killed, how often… Damn it. That was a mistake. I need that information, don't I?"

"We got distracted," Deacon said.

"No. I made a mistake. Fuck. I've only been on my own, what, less than day, and I'm already making mistakes. How the hell am I going to survive this year?"

"Your job is to protect people and you kept Greenson from the twins. How is that a mistake? Your job isn't to stop a serial killer."

"How do you know? The Nags said Beatrix could destroy the world. We still don't know how, because I forgot to ask. And maybe the only way to protect them is to stop him. Plus, you know, protecting his other victims falls into my job description." She ran a hand through her hair, loosening her ponytail. "I got distracted by the demon/demon hunter thing and forgot to get all the information I needed from the twins."

"You want me to go talk to them again?" he offered, setting the glass down gently on the counter. "I wanted to make sure you got home safely, but I can go back out and grill them more."

She stared at him a moment, startled to realize… "You can help me and that doesn't go against the seventh year rules."

"Exactly."

"But…" She nibbled on her bottom lip. "But does it break the rules? I'm supposed to survive on my own."

"Using everything you have at your disposal." He spread his arms wide. "And I'm at your disposal."

Her heart thumped hard at that, the truth of it. Plus he looked incredibly sexy standing there and for just a split second, "at her disposal" carried a completely different, much more erotic, implication for her.

She shook that off and refocused. "Thank you. It would be really helpful. I need to know what Greenson does. Who he kills, how, when, how often… I need to know more about the 'serial killer' part of all this. While you're gone, I'll make some calls about the demon hunter problem. If he is a former demon hunter, he could be using that will of his to send the twins mixed signals about his nature, just to keep them from understanding what he really is."

"If he's a former hunter, that would explain why he didn't hide his scent, or give off the other signs of being a hunter. Maybe he wasn't good enough."

"That's what you've been thinking about, isn't it?"

He nodded. "He definitely isn't a demon, but he's not giving the full signs of being a hunter either. If he wasn't quite strong enough to remain a hunter, he might have quit before being killed. He'd still have enough tricks to pursue…whatever it is he's doing now. It might even be how he gets victims."

"Yeah, I definitely need to know if that's what's happening," Cary said. She set her mug down and crossed to him, taking his face in her hands, she said, "Thank you again." And kissed him hard and quick.

When she leaned back, he smiled. "If that's how you thank me, I'm going to be helping you a lot."

She chuckled as he left, working hard not to notice the way her tummy danced in happy little jitters. She really didn't have time for the new-relationship-giddiness right now. She had some research to do.

eacon pulled his SUV to the side of the dirt road, wet and muddy from the rain that had pelted the traffic all the way here, and cut his engine as he took in his surroundings.

Though there was a break in the clouds now, the sun was behind the horizon, submerging the area in shadows. Trees bracketed the road, leaving only a narrow shoulder of rocky dirt and scraggly grass. He stepped out into the damp evening air, breathing in the scents as he oriented. Wet soil, pine and maple trees, the faint scent of local animal life, though distant as if they weren't in the immediate area anymore. His hearing confirmed his sense of smell. There weren't any animals nearby. Even the insects seemed quiet and distant.

Ten yards up the road, the rickety wooden gate for the cemetery hung on its hinges. The cleared space that held rows of non-descript tombstones was open to the surrounding woods, no fence or border circling the area to separate the graves from the rest of the land. Grass grew around the graves in rough patches, with several large maple trees scattered in the otherwise open space to give shade in the summer months. Now their branches were bare, naked arms stretching over the dark lines of stones.

Underneath the natural scents, Deacon picked up a hint of rot, mostly wood rot but also just a little of the muskiness of dead animals —or humans as the case may be. The graves inside the yard were all dated from the previous century or earlier. As he walked along one of the narrow paths through the yard, the most recent date he spotted was in the 1950s. Some of the stones were tilted sideways or laid out flat in the muddy grass. Others had defied the elements to remain straight and solid markers to the people buried beneath.

A faint scrapping noise set Deacon to full alert as he made his way slowly toward the small wooden cabin at the back of the yard. He'd never dealt directly with a necromancer, or anyone who could raise the dead for that matter. He wasn't any more comfortable with Beatrix than Cary was, but for Cary he was willing to quiet his agitated leopard and speak with the woman.

Her scent made his nose itch, though. She smelled of death and decay, under a layer of desperation like a too-sweet perfume. The combination was nauseating to someone with his heightened senses. Justin didn't smell much better. Whatever magic he'd been working had tainted his naturally earthier, clean scent with a bitterness that reminded Deacon of mold mixed with blood. It wasn't at all pleasant, and it made his leopard edgy and eager to escape.

There was something very unnatural about the twins—which coming from a shapeshifter might have seemed strange. But shifters were part of nature, their existence not in any way working against the order of the natural world. Whatever magic the twins wielded, felt completely contradictory to the order of things, and it triggered Deacon's instincts. He wanted to rid the world of that taint. The part of him that would one day be responsible for all of his people wanted to protect them and clear the area of anything this…wrong.

But that wasn't why he was here. He was here to help Cary protect the twins, to keep them alive. For his mate, he'd do just about anything —even quiet his own instincts to protect. At least as much as he could.

There was still a faint gravely note to his voice as he called out to the twins. He knew they were aware of him. He hadn't shifted or tried to sneak closer. The hairs on the back of his neck prickled under their gazes, even though he couldn't see them. The cabin's wooden front door was closed, the windows boarded up. The peaked roof appeared solid enough. The wood that made up the shed-sized building's walls was turning green with mold in places, though, and worn thin in others. Frankly, he was surprised the place was still standing. It looked like no one had entered it in years.

He imagined it was the kind of place two kids drawn to dead things might find appealing. As a kid, he and his twin brother and sister would probably have loved the place, too. Their own private playhouse where their parents or younger siblings weren't likely to find them.

"Why are you here?" Beatrix called from inside as Deacon neared. "Where's Cary?"

"Figuring out if Greenson is a demon hunter," Deacon said, keeping his tone even, hoping she couldn't hear his faint growl through the windows. He sensed more than saw the movement just inside the front of the cabin and waited a few feet from the door for them to decide if they were willing to let him in.

"Is anything wrong?" Justin called.

"No," Deacon said. "I just have more questions. About Greenson. Things Cary needs to know."

"Why isn't she here herself?" Beatrix asked.

"She's doing her part," Deacon said. "I'm doing mine to help her."

He couldn't read their scents from this distance, not with all the other less pleasant things coating the area. But their distrust of him was obvious even if he hadn't had shifter senses. He couldn't blame them. Given what they could do, he imagined they didn't trust most people.

"What do you want to know?" Beatrix asked.

"Are we having this entire conversation like this?" Deacon said. He glanced at the surrounding gloom. "It's going to be pitch dark soon."

"Does the dark bother you?" Justin asked.

Deacon smiled without humor, showing teeth. "No. Does it bother you?"

There was a snort from inside that might have been a laugh or a derisive gesture. He couldn't really tell. Since he was here to help keep them safe, having to go through hoops just to have a conversation with them was more than a little irritating.

He pulled in a deep breath, let it out slowly. For Cary, he thought. This is for Cary. The image of his mate, frustrated and in need of help, bolstered his determination and helped tamp down on his leopard's need to fight.

"The ghouls come out soon," Beatrix called.

"I'm not dead yet," Deacon answered. "And I'm as strong as a ghoul." The twins didn't know he was a shifter, and he wasn't going to tell them. Let them think whatever they liked about him. The less they knew for sure, the more prepared for anything he felt.

Silence followed that, for so long Deacon's ears rang with it. Not just from inside the cabin. The pervasive silence of the entire area was oppressive. He was in the middle of the woods, surrounding by nature and there should be noise, the sound of night birds waking up, the faint sound of scurrying animals heading into burrows, the chirping and buzz of bugs. Nothing moved here. Even the air was still and heavy, cold and sharp and dead.

If fog rolled in, he'd be convinced the twins were somehow doing this on purpose in a bid to scare him.

He didn't like the silence, but he wasn't scared. Just leery. And itching for a fight. With his control still sketchy at best, and his mate in need, a fight sounded like a wonderful option.

Finally, the cabin door cracked open. "Come in, then," Beatrix said, a shadow in the darkness of the cabin. "But I'm not sure what we can tell you that we haven't already."

"I need to know what and how Greenson kills. How many people that you know of? Who? I need you to tell me everything you know about him."

He stepped inside. The cabin was just a single, open room with no furniture. Dirt covered the wooden floor. A storm lamp in the center of the space cast the only light and left the corners growing darker as the night rolled in. The twins had brought two sleeping bags, which were stretched out on the floor around the storm lamp, and backpacks with some supplies were tossed against one wall. Other than that, the room was empty.

Beatrix remained by the door after closing it. Justin stood against the opposite wall, his gaze steady on Deacon.

"You don't like us," Justin said. "You don't want your girlfriend helping us."

Deacon hissed a silent curse. He hadn't realized he'd been so obvious about it. He was usually better at hiding his feelings. Especially from humans who couldn't smell his emotions. The fact that they'd read him was more than a little irritating.

Since meeting Cary, his control—the one thing he'd depended on most of his life, that he'd needed to maintain to keep from hurting people—had almost entirely abandoned him, and he held onto his human logic by a very thin thread. His leopard remained at the surface most of the time, just one strong emotion away from emerging. Whenever he wasn't with Cary, he felt like he was losing his mind. Becoming more animal than human.

He was dangerous right now. He was even more dangerous when he wasn't around his mate. The fact that he couldn't hide that from strangers was enraging. And terrifying.

"It's not about whether I like you or not," Deacon said. He moved to a spot in the middle of the room where both Beatrix and Justin could see him, then he sat on the floor, trying to look as non-threatening as he could manage. "Cary needs to help you. I need to help her. It's as simple as that."

The twins exchanged a look but they didn't move to sit down. Smart kids, Deacon thought—a little sourly since he should have better control than that.

"Your eyes are glowing," Beatrix said. "Faint but they are. Greenson's eyes do that."

Deacon's jaw tightened. Damn it. "I'm not like Greenson. You don't have to worry about that."

"You're a killer, though," Justin said. "You've killed before."

"Not for fun," Deacon said. "Not because it gives me a thrill like it does your boss."

Justin winced at that, which gave Deacon a mean sense of satisfaction. The fact that they'd been willingly helping a serial killer dispose of bodies didn't leave them a lot of moral ground to judge him and what he'd had to do over the years.

"What are you?" Beatrix asked. "Your eyes are…yellow. They glow like a night animal."

"I'm here to talk about Greenson," Deacon said. "Not me. I won't hurt you so you can relax."

Neither made a move to sit, but they weren't running away either so he supposed that was something.

"Fine," Deacon snapped after another prolonged silence which stretched his limited patience too far. "We'll talk like this. You start. What kind of victims does your boss take? And what does he do to them?"

"You sure you want to hear this," Beatrix said.

"It's not pleasant," Justin added.

"Tell me," Deacon said, and braced himself for whatever came next.

1 8

---

*C*ary pushed back from her computer and rubbed her hands over her eyes. Her head spun with all the information on necromancy she'd been reading. To catch up and remember things she hadn't needed to know for a while.

She slouched in the large comfy chair behind her huge executive desk, staring at her surroundings as she mulled over her research.

She loved her secret attic where she kept all her research books, her big desk, and her special computer which was linked into search sites not normally accessible to ordinary humans. This was where she did the learning part of her job. Thanks to her tech guru, Chris, she had computer access to all the dark corners of the internet without having to worry about hacking or being traced by a tech savvy enemy. And when she couldn't find what she needed online, she took to the library of print books stacked neatly around the open, airy space.

She kept her work-related library and research up here so that casual visitors—like her parents—wouldn't accidentally stumble across it. Her parents thought she did research for a former professor who wrote popular science books on animals. They wouldn't understand why she kept volumes on demon phylogeny, the current thinking on spellcasting techniques, and histories of preternatural creatures down through the centuries.

She'd gone so far as to ensure the ceiling door was hidden from casual view, so no one would even realize she had a finished attic. Only Jaxer, Chris, the Nags, and her dogs knew about her secret lair. She liked it that way. It was like being a superhero with a secret bat cave. Except there were no bats in it. And she'd painted it a lovely shade of creamy yellow to keep it bright and cozy.

She glanced at the stack of books on her desk. She hadn't had much luck identifying Greenson as a type of demon, so she was pretty sure he was a demon hunter, or at least had their skills. Or he knew about them and could put on a pretty decent imitation of a hunter. She couldn't imagine why he'd do that for the twins since they didn't even know what demon hunters were, but it was a possibility. Maybe just a way to appear even scarier?

Like enjoying killing people didn't make him scary enough.

Cary had called Angie, and through her, gotten in touch with a demon hunter currently in Portland. They'd set up a meeting for later that night, so Cary could ask her a few questions.

In the meantime, Cary decided she'd better read up on necromancy. And if possible, see what she could learn about Justin's skills. His magic had actually been more difficult to identify than Beatrix's. But Cary had been able to learn that people like him could bind certain types of magics through ritual and spellcasting. Some bound that magic to metal or stones—what Justin seemed to do. Others used plants or leather. What kind of magic they could bind, how they did it, what sort of materials they used was all unique and specific to the person doing the binding.

Which meant anyone familiar with the magic could actually trace it back to the spellcaster.

That had been an interesting bit of information. It meant someone could, in theory, trace Greenson's amulet back to Justin. She wondered if he knew that.

Her research into necromancy was more straightforward and she hadn't uncovered anything new. The refresher had been good, though, because she'd forgotten that necromancers often used fresh kills to call the dead—a sacrifice, usually animals, which spilled blood as a trigger for the magic a necromancer used. The blood-letting could be minor, even just a few drops, if all the necromancer wanted was to wake a spirit for a conversation. Pulling the physical body of a dead person from a grave took more blood. Calling forth more than one dead corpse with their spirits in tow took a lot of blood.

The most horrifying part, though—something Cary had blocked from her memory—was that a necromancer, with enough blood and sacrifice and magic, could raise an army of corpses to do their bidding. Literally an army of walking dead complete with their trapped spirits sent to do the will of a necromancer without being able to refuse.

It was worse than zombies, as far as Cary was concerned, because the spirits of the people who'd once occupied those bodies were forced back into existence, into a rotting, decaying corpse, and without any control over their actions. Yet still…themselves.

Zombies didn't have minds and spirits. They were bodies directed by instinct and hunger. What necromancers raised were…more. Worse.

No wonder human societies rarely tolerated them.

The ghoul controlling part of Beatrix's skills was just as gruesome, though, if the information Cary found online was true.

Poor ghouls. Just trying to do their job and then getting caught up in some human magic like that, being made to do things that went against their natures.

Ghouls weren't pleasant beings, by any means. They were inordinately strong, had those damned sharp teeth, a taste for flesh, and were able to burrow through sacred ground to move between graves. They rose at night to clear away any dead things at the surface, or dig up anything that needed to be eaten, then sank back into the soil as the sun rose.

Research done by one particularly eager scientist with chip trackers placed on a few ghouls showed that they were active during the day as well, just underground away from the sun. They had a sensitivity to light which was why you never saw a ghoul after sunup. And though they had eyes, they could navigate by taste and sound underground. From what the eager scientist had discovered, the things never really slept. Just continually moved around eating and cleaning up decay.

There was a lot of debate in the literature on how a ghoul came into being. Some specialists said they just grew, for lack of a better word, in cemeteries where the body count was substantial and typical human decay took time. Others claimed they were former humans who had been bad people in life and were "cursed"—by either a god or a witch or an angel depending on which book you consulted—to serve as ghouls. The fact that ghouls tended to have scraps of clothes on, and didn't show up in every single cemetery, argued strongly for the second option. But advocates of the "ghouls grow in cemeteries" theory claimed the ghouls simply picked up clothes from the dead they ate and didn't grow in cemeteries with low body counts.

The one thing everyone agreed on, though, was that ghouls served a very clear purpose. Because if buried bodies were eaten, they couldn't be raised. No vampires. No zombies. No necromancer led armies.

Ghouls kept the numbers of dead-returning-to-life to a bare minimum. And all the experts agreed that it was a lucky cemetery to be blessed with ghouls.

Taking them out of their natural habitats and making them do things they weren't meant to do seemed cruel to Cary. Like torturing animals for sport. The fact that Beatrix did that, and that she and Justin had passed that power on to a serial killer, left a bad taste in Cary's mouth.

She pushed away from the desk and headed back down to the main part of the house to get ready for her meeting with the demon hunter. She should probably be more worried about the serial killer and what he might do to the twins—or make them do for him. But after all her reading, Cary was most concerned with what they'd been doing to the poor ghouls.

Her dogs were waiting at the foot of the ladder, patiently napping—or in Fred's case not so patiently—until she'd finished. She pushed the latter and door back up into the ceiling, making sure her secret attic lair was properly hidden. Then turned to give the dogs some attention.

Buck nudged against her hand, taking a little scratch behind the ears, then he walked away to the back of the house. She frowned after him. He really wasn't acting like himself. She'd better find a vet for him tomorrow. Despite her job, and the fact that Buck didn't like vets, the health of her dogs came first. They were part of her family, and they always took precedence.

Fred barked and pounced off her leg to get her attention. She rolled him over and scratched his stomach even as she mulled over Buck's strange mood.

"Do you know what's wrong?" she asked Pickles who was content to sit nearby watching Fred get scratches.

The basset hound that was actually a foo lion raised her head a little and let out a deep woof, then rested her head on the floor again, her long ears flopping out beside her wrinkled face.

"Yeah," Cary said. "I'm worried about him, too."

She glanced at the time on her cellphone. Damn, it was getting late. Buck was a worry she'd have to push to the back of her head for a bit longer. She had a demon hunter to meet.

She frowned when she realized she hadn't heard back from Deacon yet. Not even a text.

Her stomach tightened a little. She tried to shake off her unease. He was probably just busy grilling the twins. He was a grown man—a leopard shifter was super strength and senses. He was perfectly capable of taking care of himself. Two magic wielding young people and a serial killer weren't likely to catch someone like Deacon Jones off guard. The serial killer didn't even know Deacon existed. And while the twins could do some scary impressive things, all of what they did took time and concentration.

And blood.

Glancing up at the ceiling, remembering the drawings and images of corpses called by necromancers, she bit her lip.

What would the sacrifice of a powerful shapeshifter's blood call?

She shook her head and snatched her car keys and jacket from the hall on her way to the garage. She and Deacon were trying to *help* the twins. They'd hardly try to hurt him. And he'd sense the danger and get out if they were a threat. No need to worry. Deacon would be just fine.

But, boy, she couldn't wait to be done with this particular job.

19

As soon as she pushed into the roadside diner north of town, Cary was hit by the smells of fry oil and cooking burgers. Her stomach growled, reminding her that she hadn't eaten much since last night. The girls had made sure she was well fed before they all went to the club, but since then, she hadn't had much time for anything more than a few protein bars and coffee.

She'd considered getting a sandwich at one stage while she'd been researching, but the images of corpses and blood sacrifices had dampened her appetite significantly.

Until she got a whiff of freshly cooked French fries.

She glanced around the tidy, narrow, brightly lit restaurant, and mentally thanked Angie's demon hunter friend for picking a meeting place that had food.

She actually had to scan the diner twice before she spotted a woman sitting by herself at a booth in the very back of the restaurant, near the kitchen door. Cary frowned. She'd sworn that booth was empty just a moment ago.

As she headed toward the woman who fit Angie's description of the hunter, Cary studied her. She was very…ordinary looking. Not stunningly beautiful, but not unattractive either. She had a very common shade of brown hair, pulled back into a braid that hung over her shoulder. She wore an unadorned t-shirt, no jewelry, no obvious makeup, but she wasn't obviously without makeup either. Everything about her screamed "nothing to look twice at," and Cary was more than a little startled to realize she could look away from the woman and not feel any need to *see* her again.

She slid into the booth across from her. "Aidan?" she asked.

"Cary?" the woman returned. Her tone was pleasant but again nothing particularly stood out about her voice. Nothing about her seemed unique or interesting.

Cary leaned her arms on the table. "How do you do that?" she asked.

Aidan smiled suddenly, and some of the ordinariness finally left her expression. "Willpower is a handy thing."

"Yeah, it is," Cary said, leaning back again. "That's very impressive. Just by willpower, really?"

"Really. That's how it works."

"Is that why I didn't see you at first when I came in?"

Aidan tilted her head to one side in what might have been a nod, though Cary couldn't be certain.

"Why don't you tell me what I can help you with," the hunter said.

Cary pulled in a deep breath. "I need to know if someone I've come across lately could be a…" She glanced around. No one was looking their way or paying any attention to them. Probably more of Aidan's will at work. "A failed demon hunter," she finished. "Someone who left and went…rogue."

"Doesn't happen most of the time," Aidan said. "A failed demon hunter is a dead demon hunter."

"So no one retires or quits?"

"Why do you think you've come across a hunter?" Aidan asked rather than answer the question.

Cary gestured to Aidan's eyes. This close, if Cary looked closely, she could see the faint glow of red in the woman's ordinary brown eyes. "This man had that red thing. And he wasn't a freed demon."

"You're certain?"

"My…friend—" she stumbled over the word, not sure what to call Deacon, "—he's a shapeshifter and could smell the difference. But he wasn't certain this man was a hunter either."

"What's the man's name, do you know?"

"Kenneth Greenson."

"What is he to you?" Aidan asked. "Why do you need to know if he's a hunter or not?"

"Because according to two of his employees, he's a serial killer and he's a threat to their lives."

Aidan nodded, but didn't show any other sign of emotion, and Cary couldn't tell if the news upset her or concerned her at all.

After a quiet few minutes, Aidan asked, "What are you? Since Angie gave you my number, I'm assuming witch?"

"No. Just a concerned citizen."

"With a shapeshifter *friend* and a powerful witch best friend?"

Cary shrugged. "A girl's got to have friends."

Aidan smiled a little at that. "Fair enough. Kenneth Greenson isn't *technically* a demon hunter. The eye thing—" she gestured to her own eyes, "—can happen in other ways."

"You're sure he's not a hunter? How do you know?"

"There are only so many of us. Living anyway. We all know each other. We keep a history of past hunters as well."

"Cool." That was a new bit of knowledge for Cary. "So how else can you get the demon hunter red glowy eye thing?"

Before Aidan could answer, Cary's stomach growled loudly. Cary made a face and put her hand over her stomach. "Sorry about that. I need food."

Aidan raised her hand and a waitress appeared, notebook at the ready.

Well that was impressive. Cary ordered a burger and friends. "You having anything?" she asked Aidan.

"Just a soda, please. *Not* diet."

The waitress grinned at that and left to get their orders.

"I have to work later," Aidan said. "Don't like to have food in my stomach during a fight. Never know what smells might come up and throwing up disrupts the battle."

Cary nodded. "That makes sense. But…am I keeping you? I mean, if you have a demon to fight, shouldn't you be…getting to it?"

"We have time. The dumb ass calling this demon won't get started until three a.m. He's got it in his head that's the necessary time." She shrugged. "Anyway, I'm good for another couple of hours."

"Great. So, how do you get the glowy eye thing?"

Aidan glanced out the window, her brow furrowed. "This man is definitely human?" she asked.

"According to my shifter friend." Cary was pleased when she got the "friend" part out without stumbling.

"Then there's only a couple of way this can happen. The reason it happens to hunters is because we spend so much time with demons. Not necessarily moving into a demon realm, although that happens occasionally, but so close to them that we…take on a bit of them. With every fight, we…absorb some of that energy."

"Is that good or bad?"

"Depends on the hunter. The strong ones survive it. The weakest ones are killed. The ones in between…" She sighed and faced Cary again. "They get consumed."

"Eaten?" Cary asked. Ew.

Aidan chuckled. "Not that kind of consumed. They absorb so much demon essence without being able to channel or control it that they essentially…become a demon. That's the best way I can describe it. They are human. They don't change into a real demon. That's not possible. But they manifest demon qualities and traits."

"Ah," Cary said on a long breath. "That explains a lot." At Aidan's questioning look, she said, "The grass at his feet charred, but only for a few steps. Then everything was normal. I thought he might be faking that, or using an illusion."

"He still could have been. Illusion demons are tricky bastards."

"But…" Cary frowned. "You said this guy *wasn't* a demon hunter. What you're describing happens to demon hunters who are strong enough not to get killed but too weak to take the exchange of demon energy. If he wasn't ever a hunter…?"

"There are humans who tamper with demonology and calling demons without ever becoming hunters. Ordinarily, they're either killed or a hunter shows up to fend off the demon or demons they've been summoning. If they're killed before a hunter arrives, the demon can get free. Those we go after."

"I fought a centuries-old freed demon last month," Cary said. "What about him?"

"Did you? Who?"

"Oliver Holland."

"Ah. Yeah, he's a…unique case."

"He shouldn't have been," Cary said bluntly.

Aidan shrugged. "He wasn't my decision."

Cary narrowed her eyes. "One day, we'll talk more about that. But right now, I need to focus on my serial killer."

Aidan nodded. "It's possible he's strong enough to have been a hunter which is why he hasn't been killed yet. We usually find those types of humans and train them or dissuade them from summoning demons anymore."

"Dissuade?" Cary raised her brows in question.

"Some do slip by undetected, though," Aidan said as if Cary hadn't spoken. "Because they want to and they have the will to ensure no one notices them. The problem is, without training and help, without knowing how to channel all the energy they're picking up every time they call a demon, what's happening to your serial killer can happen to them."

"Seems to me, someone who calls demons regularly enough to have this happen, and is able to hide from demon hunters through their own will, might want to absorb that demon energy."

"Oh likely," Aidan said with a disconcerting matter-of-factness. "That's almost always why humans call demons and try to control them. Power, wealth, the usual suspects. Sometimes revenge. Every once in a while, more noble reasons."

"There are noble reasons for summoning demons?" That was a new one for Cary.

"I've had to fend off demons called by desperate parents trying to find a cure for dying children. Sometimes there's more to it than greed."

Cary's heart hurt at the thought. She could only imagine a parent desperate enough to do something like that, and it made her chest ache in sympathy. "Poor people," she murmured.

The food arrived then, and they fell silent for a few minutes, but Cary was very aware of Aidan studying her as the waitress laid out their food and drinks.

Cary took a few bites of her burger, sighing in satisfaction, before continuing the conversation. "So Greenson is likely someone who called or is calling demons and survived," Cary said, "and has done it often enough to get the glowy eye thing. You said there were other ways, though."

"He could be half-demon. Some of the freed ones have reproduced. That doesn't usually produce a human-looking child, but it can happen."

"Wouldn't someone like that smell like a demon to a shapeshifter, though?" Cary had read about but never met a half-demon before.

"Depends on how good they are at disguising themselves," Aidan said before taking a sip of her soda.

"He wasn't disguising his scent. At least my friend said he wasn't. My friend compared it to the way hunters can smell like nothing if they want and that this guy wasn't doing that—which is why he didn't think Greenson was one of yours."

Aidan shrugged. "It's just one of the options. A rare one."

"I'm working with a lot of rare at the moment," Cary muttered, "so I won't write it off. What are the other possibilities?"

"The only other option I can think of for someone who's human is that he's an illusionist, creating these impressions for intimidation reasons. He might not even know they're signs of demons and demon hunters. He just wants to give the impression of being strange and powerful."

"We considered that," Cary said, mulling as she finished her burger. The last bite came as a surprise. Wow, she'd been hungry. She moved on to the fries. "So my options for Greenson are could-have-been-a-demon-hunter human, half-demon who looks human, or an illusionist. That's it?"

Aidan nodded.

"Well, how the hell do I keep my people safe from him, then? I'm not exactly a demon hunter myself."

"How did you deal with Oliver Holland?" Aidan asked.

"He wasn't human."

"Right. He would have been more difficult than any human to fight. How did you and survive?"

Cary made a face and glanced away. "I kind of flattened his army." At Aidan's raised brows, she said, "It was an accident. I'm not sure how I did it."

"Hm. Someday we'll talk more about *that*."

Cary dipped her head and stuffed a few more fries in her mouth. It was embarrassing that she didn't know how she'd flattened Holland's army. Especially when talking to a demon hunter. Something occurred to her, though.

"Angie got Holland's phone number from a demon hunter friend. That was you?"

"Not me," Aidan said. "But Angie knows a few hunters from back in the day."

"Back in the day? What the hell does that mean?"

Aidan's expression went carefully neutral. "You'll have to ask her about that."

What the hell? Angie was supposed to be her best friend and she hadn't told her about "back in the day" with more than one demon hunter? Oh, they were definitely going to talk about that soon.

She opened her mouth to ask more about fighting a could-have-been-a-demon-hunter human when Aidan suddenly straightened.

"I...have to go. Seems my fight might happen sooner than I thought."

"Oh!" Cary waved the waitress over and paid the bill, leaving a generous tip and shoving a handful of the remaining fries in her mouth before following Aidan outside.

The hunter paused on the sidewalk outside the diner door, slipping into her nondescript coat. Her gaze unfocused, turning inward. "Yeah, the dumb bastard will need help soon." She faced Cary. "Good luck. Let me know if you need more information."

"Thanks," Cary said. "I—"

A ball of glowing blue energy flashing through the dark, heading right toward her, cutting her off mid-sentence. Cary screeched, a deer in the headlights, unable to move in her shock. Useful skill in a Protector. Not so useful when a deadly mage bolt was heading right for her.

The energy ball slowed to a crawl, inching forward in horrifying clarity. And then she found herself on the ground with Aidan covering her as the bolt exploded in a blinding flare of light and deadly power.

"Shh," Aidan said against her ear.

Cary lay still, looking at the scorch mark in the parking lot tarmac less than six inches from where she'd just been standing. She couldn't have spoken just then if she'd wanted to.

From the opposite side of the lot, she heard a murmured, "Where is she?"

Then a man Cary had never seen before eased closer. He was tall and thin, his features sharp, his hair thinning and gray, his blue eyes too bright, his pale skin wrinkled and spotted. He looked quite old, but his movements were that of a much younger man. He was dressed in black pants and a black turtleneck under a black peacoat.

Cary racked her brain but nothing about him seemed familiar.

He reached the scorch mark from the mage bolt and frowned at it. Cary held her breath because she and Aidan weren't exactly hidden from him now. But as he looked around the lot, his gaze passing right over them as if they weren't there.

"Bitch," he muttered, snarling, and spun away, stalking back across the lot and out of sight.

Cary remained motionless for a long time. The tingles along her spine that warned of danger when she had to protect someone weren't there, but the hairs on her arms were raised in fear. That man, whoever he was, had been after *her*. He hadn't been any sort of threat to Aidan or Cary's powers would have kicked in.

After a few moments, Aidan glanced down at her. "You okay?"

Cary grunted an affirmative, and they stood. She glanced at the scorch mark. "The bolt slowed down. And he didn't see us. That you?"

Aidan nodded.

Wow. Real demon hunter willpower was…impressive up close. "Thanks."

Aidan glanced toward where the man had disappeared, then she faced Cary. "Looks like someone wants to kill you."

"Yeah." Cary sighed. "That happens a lot."

———————

Cary was edgy and nervous on the drive home, waiting for another bolt to careen toward her car. This was the second time in less than a months that someone had tried to kill her with an energy bolt. Oh, people tried to kill her all the time, but usually because she was standing between them and some poor innocent they wanted to get at, and they wanted Cary out of the way.

Having someone deliberately come after her, someone she'd never even seen before, was disconcerting. Not the least because she didn't know who he was. What the hell had she done to him to make him that angry with her?

She wasn't surprised she'd angered someone enough that they wanted to kill her. That happened all the time, too. She was just surprised she couldn't remember this particular guy.

She let out a long, relieved breath when she parked in her garage and cut the engine. At least she was safe here. For the moment. Pulling out her cellphone, she checked for messages. Still nothing from Deacon.

Well, now she had something more to worry about. She rang his number, and almost as soon as she'd pressed the button she wondered if he was even in human form. His leopard would hardly be able to answer.

The phone rang out and went to voicemail. Her gut clenched tight. Not good, not good. She left a message she hoped didn't sound too frantic but she heard the shaking in her voice. Partly from the earlier attack, partly fear for Deacon.

She frowned at her steering wheel for a painful few minutes, debating going out to the cemetery to find him. What if he was in trouble and needed her?

What if the man who'd just tried to kill her followed her?

"Fuck it." She started the car again, pressed the remote to raise the garage door, and started backing out.

Her phone rang before she'd left her driveway. Throwing the car into park, she fumbled to answer the call.

"Hello. Hello."

"Cary?"

She let out a relieved breath when she heard Deacon's voice, sounding strong and sure.

"Are you okay?" he asked. "Your voicemail sounded worried."

"I was worried, you ass. Why haven't you been in touch? Where are the twins? What did they say? Where are you now? Do you need my help?"

"I'm fine," he said.

In a soft, satisfied tone that made her scowl. He sounded much too pleased with her worry.

"I'm on my way back to your place now," he said. "I had to pull over to answer the phone. Forgot to connect the Bluetooth to the car system."

"Fine. I'll be here when you get here. Did they tell you anything?"

"A lot. I'll tell you everything when I get there. It'll probably take me another hour. Lots of traffic."

"I'll wait up."

She pulled back into the garage and went inside, her body shaking with the adrenaline of the last hour and a tiredness she'd been ignoring. She greeted the dogs, let them out for one last pee break, then went to change her clothes. There was a faint scent of burnt ozone clinging to her shirt and she didn't want Deacon to pick that up and ask what had happened. He'd get distracted worrying about her and not tell her what she needed to know fast enough.

After changing, she let the dogs back in. Buck seemed his normal self, bumping her for a scratch and hanging with the other dogs like nothing was wrong. She watched him for a bit, but he showed no signs of distress or being sick now. Maybe she'd been worried for no reason. Or whatever was wrong had passed?

She hoped so. Worrying about her dog at the same time as having to protect a necromancer from a possibly could-have-been-a-demon-hunter serial killer was one anxiety too many.

Glancing at her coffee machine, she gave serious consideration to making a pot. She'd need to sleep soon. She'd officially gone well past twenty-four hours of being awake and the three days of sleep she'd had before that were no longer making up for the constant wakefulness now. If she drank coffee, that would keep her up a bit longer. But maybe also interfere with her getting any sleep.

Hemming and hawing, she startled when her doorbell rang. She glanced at the microwave clock. Deacon had made good time.

But it wasn't Deacon at the door.

"Jaxer!"

Her erstwhile faery mentor stood in all his gorgeous glory on her doorstep, smiling at her as if nothing had changed in the last two weeks. Blond hair, green-blue eyes, sharp stunning features, pale skin, and a perfect body, he was almost too handsome to look at.

Which he did on purpose.

His most powerful magic was glamour, and he used it ruthlessly. Sometimes to look more handsome just to irritate her. Sometimes to look more human so people weren't scared off by him. Cary had a suspicion, though, that if he dropped the glamour altogether, he'd be too beautiful to behold.

He pulled her into a hug that made her grunt and scowl.

"I'm glad you're feeling better," he said into her hair.

"Stop that." She pushed him away. "What are you doing here? I got the impression I wouldn't be seeing you again. The Nags said…"

"You're on another assignment already?" he asked.

She stepped back to stare at him. He was genuinely surprised. "Why wouldn't I be?" she asked, wondering—again—what she didn't know. "My seventh year has officially started and the Nags said I still have to do these jobs."

He walked into her living room without an invitation and flopped down in a graceful slouch onto her couch. "You do have to keep doing the jobs they give you. I'm just surprised they gave you one the day after you recovered from the Holland fight."

"Protections wait for no one," she said sourly, closing the door. "What are you doing here?"

"I came to check on you. Last time I was here you were unconscious."

"Thank you for getting the girls to come look after me," she said, sincerely.

"I'm sorry I couldn't be there when you woke."

She frowned at his tone—all soft and sincere and earnest. "Jaxer, one of these days you're going to explain to me why you've started acting so weird. Is it just the seventh year stuff?"

"No. But we'll get to that. Did the Nags answer all of your questions? We didn't have time to finish talking before."

He'd been in the middle of explaining the seventh year trial to her when she'd been called to the fight with Holland. And she hadn't seen him since.

"They told me I'll still get paid and have the protections on my house, so long as I keep working." She crossed her arms as she considered him.

He patted the couch. "Sit. You're making my neck hurt."

She snorted. "Right." But she sat because she was tired.

He frowned a little, brushing his fingers across her cheekbones. "Have you slept?"

"You mean since walking up from a three day nap?"

His mouth lifted in a faint smile. "Since then."

"No. I will soon. But Deacon's on his way with information about this latest job I'm on."

"Is he?" Jaxer's expression turned bland.

Supposedly, Jaxer and Deacon were friends. But every time she'd seen them in the same room together, they'd been at odds. Testosterone poisoning run amok. She got the feeling "friends" wasn't exactly the right word for them.

"Tell me about the job," he said.

"I thought you weren't supposed to help anymore. Is this breaking the rules? And if it is, will that cost me my house protections?"

"Is that what they threatened you with?" Jaxer asked.

"Yes, the bastards. I can't afford to lose that glamour. Especially now."

"Why especially now?"

She sighed. She wasn't sure whether to tell him or not. She hadn't decided if she'd tell Deacon yet either. Deacon would get all protective and not want to let her out of his sight—he barely did that as it was—and Jaxer… Well, she didn't know what he'd do, and she was a little afraid to find out.

A part of her suspected he'd just brush off the threat to her life. And that reaction from her former mentor would hurt more than she cared to admit.

"Cary," he said on a sigh. "You can still talk to me. That doesn't break any rules."

"Fine." She told him about the two attacks—the first at Angie's, the second tonight. She told him Angie had said the attacking wizard was powerful and tonight Cary had finally got a look at him. "I have no idea who he is, though. Not even remotely familiar. You'd think I'd remember someone I pissed off that much."

Jaxer frowned, his expression fierce and angry. "What did he look like?"

Cary described the older man. "Sound familiar?"

Jaxer looked away. "Fecking hell," he muttered.

"You know who it is?" she asked. When Jaxer didn't reply, she pushed his shoulder to get his attention. "Who is he?"

"I don't know either," he said.

He met her gaze and she narrowed her eyes at him. He raised his hands defensively.

"I mean it," Jaxer said. "I'm not lying. I don't know who he is. That's the problem."

"Well, hell. So some stranger wants to kill me. Great. Suppose someone hired him?"

Jaxer shrugged, the gesture so elegant and sophisticated she wanted to roll her eyes, but he hadn't done it on purpose. Just his natural grace.

"It's possible," he said. "You have made a number of enemies over the years."

"Which is why I can't afford to lose the glamour on my house."

"I won't let the Nags take that way," he said.

"You can't promise that and you know it. I'm on my own now, and you can't intervene anymore."

"Not officially. But I'm not going anywhere."

He cupped her cheek in one hand, his thumb caressing her cheekbone, a gesture that felt entirely too intimate. He was a touchy-feely kind of guy, but lately he'd been ratcheting up the touching and the feeling. Even to the point of kissing her on the mouth once or twice. She couldn't understand the shift and it irritated her as much as it confused her. She wanted her old friend and mentor back. She didn't need any more things to worry about.

"Tell me about your current job," he said. "I might not be able to help or advise, but at least you can walk through it out loud."

He had a point there. She'd intended to mull this stuff over with Deacon, but Jaxer would work as well.

She explained everything that had happened in the last thirty odd hours, pausing in her story when he grilled her about helping the leopards.

"What the hell was Deacon thinking, getting you involved in that?" he snapped.

"That I'd want to help protect innocent children," she pointed out.

"That was leopard business. He had no right to use you that way, for something that wasn't part of your job."

"Who are you to talk? You were always sending me off to do your person dirty work. That's how I met Deacon, remember."

"Yeah," he said, his lip lifting in a faint snarl. "I still regret that."

"You sure you two were ever friends?" she asked.

"I'm reevaluating that now," he said. "Finish your story."

She rolled her eyes but continued until she'd caught him up on her dinner with Aidan.

"So my serial killer could either be a could-have-been-a-demon-hunter human, a hybrid demon—which sounds ridiculously scary—or an illusionist who wants the twins to think he's something to do with demons even though they don't know much about demons."

"I'd lay money on could-have-been-a-demon-hunter," Jaxer said.

"That's helping. Stop before the Nags find out."

"Not helping," he said, putting a hand to his chest in protest of his innocence. "Just telling you were I'd place my bet."

"Sounds suspiciously like trying to help," she said aloud, then mouthed, *Thanks*. Because it did help but she didn't want to risk saying so.

She wasn't even sure the Nags would hear or know. They'd never been particularly forthcoming with how they did things and what they knew. According to them and Jaxer, they used premonitions, research, and sometimes intuition to figure out who needed protecting and when —a system that wasn't perfect but did do some good so she couldn't argue with them about that. But they'd refused to clarify how they knew where she was at any given point in time, or if they could hear and see her even when they weren't around. The idea that they could sometimes freaked her out so she tried not to think about it too closely.

"If I'm dealing with someone with the kind of willpower Aidan demonstrated tonight, I'm in a lot of trouble," she said.

"Aidan is a legend, though. There aren't many demon hunters like her."

Cary raised her brows in surprise. "Really? Cool. I didn't realize. Guess that's why Angie gave me her number. Though I'm surprised she had time to see me."

"If it turns out this serial killer is a half-demon, you might consider calling her again. Expert help wouldn't go amiss."

"That feels like you're advising me," she said, her eyes narrowed.

"Just a suggestion. Friends can suggest things to friends."

"Right." She wondered how long he'd be able to keep this up before the Nags intervened.

"Like, I can suggest you go take a nap," Jaxer said. "I'll wait up for Deacon. He can tell me what you need to know, and I'll pass it on."

She lowered her chin to stare at him. "You're intending to just hang out while I sleep?"

"Of course. You'll feel safer if there's someone here looking out for you."

"I will, huh?" She shook her head. "Jaxer, you have never once offered to babysit me while I slept. What—and I can't emphasize this enough—the hell?"

"We have more to talk about. But I don't want to talk while you're so tired."

"Then go away and come back."

"Will Deacon be staying?"

The growl in his voice made her lean back. "Again I say, what the hell? First, none of your business. Second, really really none of your business. Third, why do you even care?"

"I don't like him claiming you as a mate," Jaxer said bluntly.

So bluntly it surprised her. She blinked at him. "Why not?"

He ran a hand through his hair, looking as honestly at a loss for words as she'd ever seen him.

"It came out of nowhere," he finally said, his tone harsh. "I don't like it. He's cornering you in, making you responsible for something you don't need to be responsible for. And all of it happening when you're going to be under a lot of stress. If he cared at all, he'd go away and give the mate thing time to break."

She was so busy being stunned at his outburst she almost missed the last sentence. Then it sank in. "Wait." She held up a hand. "The mate bond thing can be broken?"

"You're human. With you it can."

"But he loses his mind when he stays away from me for too long. I've seen some of it. He had to go back to his family home and spend most of Thanksgiving week as a leopard because he's so affected by this mate stuff. And you're telling me that if he just did that for a little while longer, he could break the bond and be…okay?"

"You're more worried about him being okay than you being trapped?"

"That's not what I said. I don't feel trapped." Not in a way she'd admit out loud to Jaxer anyway. "I asked if he's sacrificing his control…his sanity, to keep the bond between us."

"Seems to be, yes," Jaxer said.

"Well shit."

The doorbell dinged and Cary and Jaxer both looked at the door.

Cary went to answer, not entirely sure what she wanted to do or say about this latest bit of news. Because despite her worry over the bond, her fear that it was happening too fast…she didn't want Deacon out of her life.

She might even be in love with him, though that seemed really ridiculous when they hadn't been on a date yet.

When she opened the door, Deacon smiled down at her, leaning in to brush a gentle kiss across her lips. His scent filled her head with lusty thoughts and his warmth seeped into her skin despite the cold night air. Her stomach tightened, dancing in delight at his mere presence. Her body obviously wanted to keep him.

But could her conscious allow it?

2 1

"Jaxer," Deacon said, his tone belying the greeting. "What are you doing here?"

"Visiting my friend and making sure she's doing okay?" Jaxer said. He leaned back in the couch, his arms spread across the back like he owned the place.

Cary sighed. More testosterone poisoning. They always did this when she was too tired to deal with it.

"Okay, I can't take you two posturing at each other right now," she said.

"Posturing?" they both said at the same time, sounding equally offended by the description.

That made her smile. "Jaxer, thanks for stopping by and everything else. Since we still have things to talk about, come over tomorrow. Or maybe the day after. I have to deal with the could-have-been-a-demon-hunter first."

"The what?" Deacon asked.

She waved away his question. "Later. I need you—" she pointed at Deacon, "—to tell me everything the twins said. Then you can go home, too. We both need some sleep." She frowned at him. "You've been awake as long as I have. When did you last sleep?"

"I'm fine," he said. "I can go longer than you without sleep."

"I wouldn't bet on that," she said.

"I look forward to finding out," he murmured.

Her ears heated with a blush she was as embarrassed by as her reaction to Deacon's sexy innuendo.

Jaxer cleared his throat. "I'll hear what Deacon has to say. Maybe there's something I can contribute."

"If you get me into trouble with the Nags, I swear to god, Jaxer…" She glared at him, her hands on her hips.

"I won't." He raised his hands, palms facing her. "I promise."

"Fine." She closed the front door and waited for Deacon to sit—on the couch so she had to sit in a chair. She wasn't sure if he'd done that on purpose so she wouldn't be sitting next to Jaxer or not, but it did save her the trouble of refereeing between them.

"Spill," she said. "What did Beatrix and Justin say about Greenson."

"Nothing pretty," Deacon said. "He kills a lot. He doesn't seem to pick a particular type of person—though as far as Beatrix knew they were all human."

"She could tell from the bodies?" Cary asked.

Deacon nodded.

"Gross," Cary said. "What else?"

"He…sacrifices them apparently. A lot of pain and blood-letting involved. The more pain the better. The twins said he worships a god of some kind that requires regular sacrifice. And everything he does is in service to this god."

Cary exchanged a look with Jaxer. "Demon?" she asked.

"Possible." Jaxer shrugged.

"The bodies are pretty obvious sacrifices—what's left of them," Deacon continued. "I'm not sure you need as much detail as Beatrix gave me. Some of it, he does himself, but some of it is the god…feeding. There's no real hiding the connection between the murders. And that's apparently why he went looking for them. His god told him to make sure the remains were eliminated."

"Makes sense," Cary said. When Deacon and Jaxer frowned at her, she said, "Obviously if all the dead shared similar wounds, and the cops found a lot of bodies killed the same way, they'd know they had a serial killer on the loose and they'd be hunting him. This guy seems to have been working under the radar." To Deacon, "How long has he been killing?"

"The twins didn't know for sure," Deacon said. "Just that he was well practiced by the time he found them. He'd dumped some of the bodies in the Mor-Gin, but the god apparently warned him that wasn't enough. The evidence had to be more thoroughly eliminated."

Cary remembered the bones and rags where she'd found Justin and shivered.

"Greenson went looking specifically for a necromancer who could raise ghouls," Deacon continued. "Someone somewhere knew enough about Beatrix to point Greenson in her direction."

"Why not just…burn the bodies or something," Cary wondered aloud. "Or bury them in a cemetery where the ghouls would get to them naturally? Or bury them inside the Mor-Gin where no mundane human would find them? Why bother with a necromancer at all?"

Deacon pressed his lips together in a tight line before answer. His hesitance made Cary's pulse pound a little harder in dread.

"Beatrix said Greenson watches the ghouls devour the bodies and… He gets off on it. Sexually."

"Ew." She shook her hands as if shaking off the image. "Ew ew ew. That's extra super gross." She suddenly felt sorry for Beatrix who was no doubt around while Greenson was…enjoying the show. "Yuck. Anything else?"

"Apparently, he needs to feed the god regularly, so he kills every few days. A lot of homeless people, so they're not missed, but he's opportunistic. He just needs bodies and he doesn't care where they come from. He's also claimed the god has some grand plan and all the death is part of it, but the twins don't know what the plan is. They're not even sure if there's really a god or if Greenson is just sadistic and delusional."

"Doesn't really matter," she said. "Either way he's crazy dangerous."

Deacon nodded.

She leaned back in the chair and considered everything. "Okay, so… He's sacrificing humans—either to a demon or something like that, or to his imaginary god. He went looking for Beatrix to help dispose of the bodies not the least because he likes to watch ghouls eat the remains." She lifted her lip in a disgusted snarl. "And when he realized Justin could make him an amulet imbued with Beatrix's powers, or something like them, he decided he wanted that. If there is a 'god' Greenson's sacrificing to, then it's either a demon because Greenson is showing signs of prolonged contact with a demon realm, or the god-thing is giving Greenson powers of illusion or something like that." She frowned. "Although, he could have had those already."

She glanced at Jaxer who shrugged.

Deacon frowned. "What did you learn?" he asked.

She gave him a quick rundown on her research and her meeting with Aidan.

"You should have called me before that meeting," he said. "I would have gone with you."

"I can meet with sources on my own, thank you very much." She made no effort to hide her annoyance. She knew he was protective—she was getting to be protective of him too—but she was a grown woman and this was her job.

She did, however, leave out the part about the wizard attack. That wouldn't help her argument. She very carefully didn't look at Jaxer when she glossed over that part of her night.

"So what do I do about this guy?" she said aloud, not looking at either man, mostly talking to herself as she considered her options. "I need to make sure he leaves the twins alone. That's my job. But… how? I doubt I can use the same trick that I used with Holland." She winced. "And that didn't work out very well in the end anyway. But beyond that, I'm pretty sure I shouldn't just leave a serial killer running around Portland sacrificing innocent people. Right? I mean, stopping him isn't the job the Nags gave me, but it would solve all the problems. It would protect the twins. And a lot of other innocent people. Except, I don't know how to stop a serial killer who may or may not have the skills of a demon hunter, and who might have the help of something he thinks is a god. Ugh."

She rubbed her fingers in circles over her temples. She wasn't really the strategist here. Jaxer used to do that for her. For six years, she'd mostly just ran in and got between good guys and bad guys. She was pretty good at that part. But planning beyond the action…not so much.

Unfortunately, she'd proven her lack of strategic skills against Holland. And it had nearly cost her the life of her charge. It did get someone else killed.

What did the Nags expect her to do here? And why had the last two jobs involved her having to do things she didn't normally do? It was like a conspiracy to ensure she failed. Her gut tightened in a wave of anxiety that felt a little too much like fear.

Sighing, she faced the two men on her couch. They were both frowning at her. Jaxer looked very uncomfortable for reasons she couldn't figure. Deacon looked…suspicious and he kept glancing at Jaxer. She was very tempted to ask what that was about.

But she had a feeling she needed some sleep before she'd be able to deal with whatever was going on between them. "Are the twins safe right now?" she asked Deacon.

He nodded. "I doubt Greenson will be able to find them where they're hiding. It's as isolated and forgotten as they said it was."

"That's something." She let out a long breath, ran her fingers through her hair, and made a plan. Sleep first so she could do her job. Then another conversation with the twins. The rest…,

Would have to wait. Her job was to protect the twins so they didn't somehow unleash hell. It was someone else's job to take care of Greenson. Maybe Aidan would be able to help if Cary could prove the guy was calling demons. Sounded like a job for a demon hunter.

And that plan, at least, seemed like it might work. Which was good.

"Okay, I have to sleep now," she said, putting her hands on her knees. "Thanks for all your help today, Deacon. Jaxer, I'll talk to you soon."

Both men looked startled as she stood and walked toward the door.

"Would you like me to stay?" Jaxer asked.

"Are you sure you want me to leave?" Deacon said at the same time.

She looked over her shoulder to see them both growling at each other. "Stop or you'll freak the dogs out," she warned. "Both of you have to go so I can sleep. Goodnight."

She opened the door and waited on them. She was grumpy and out of sorts and not entirely sure where to aim her irritation. Between the information about Greenson, the near death by an angry wizard, and Jaxer's revelation about the mate bond—a little fact Deacon hadn't bothered to tell her—she wasn't sure she trusted herself to be in either of their company right now. Better to be alone so she could figure it out. Otherwise, she was likely to say something she might regret.

She did that enough already.

At the door, Deacon hovered as Jaxer stepped out into the cold night. He glanced at Jaxer who stood on her stoop staring back, his brows arched expectantly.

"Give us some privacy," Deacon said.

"No," Jaxer said with a wide grin.

Cary rolled her eyes. "You two need to work out whatever this thing is between you because I don't have time for it." She pulled Deacon's head down to her and gave him a solid kiss—not deep or long, because of their audience, but enough to wish him a goodnight. "I'll see you tomorrow?" she asked mostly because she couldn't imagine him staying away but it felt presumptuous to assume.

"Do you want breakfast?" he asked, his voice husky and sleepy sounding.

And way too sexy for company. "No donuts," she warned. "I have to save my donut calories for the holidays."

He smiled, that deadly lifting of the lips that made her shiver, dropped a brief kiss on her lips and joined Jaxer. Jaxer gave them both a little scowl Cary chose to ignore. If he hadn't wanted to see them kiss goodnight, he shouldn't have hovered and refused to give them privacy.

"We still have things to talk about," Jaxer said, holding her gaze.

He looked so intent and serious, she started to worry again without really knowing why. "Sure," she said. "You know where to find me."

Jaxer brushed the back of his knuckles over her cheekbone, then turned and walked away.

Deacon growled at his back. "Stop touching her," he said, following Jaxer.

"No," Jaxer said, his smug-tinged voice fading into the darkness.

"Both of you stop talking about me like I'm not here," Cary called after them, then slammed the door shut.

One day soon, when she wasn't in the middle of a job and a career crisis, she had to sit the two of them down and hash this out. She couldn't have them at each other's throats right now.

She had way too many more deadly things to fight.

2 2

---

ary shivered on her way toward the small, dilapidated cabin set at the back of the graveyard. It was cold enough that her breath misted in the air, but that wasn't the reason for her reaction.

She couldn't believe the twins had spent the night out here. Even in the bright sunshine of mid-morning there was a cloying dampness and eerie green lighting around the area. Not like the lovely sun-dappled light you got in the woods, but more… She wasn't sure. Moldy. Dank.

Anyway, it was weird and creepy. And she felt a little guilty that she'd left them out here last night instead of having them safely in her house. Especially given Justin's injuries. But she'd slept great and felt a lot better this morning, so she stomped down the guilt as she picked her way past gravestones.

The sense of being watched sent a rush of tingles across her shoulders, awareness and wariness making her muscles feel stiff and awkward. She was pretty sure the twins were the ones watching her and Deacon. But given the wizard attack last night, she still found herself glancing around the surrounding woods, wondering if he'd somehow managed to find her.

The thought that maybe a ghost was watching her didn't help her feel less nervous.

She shook off the ghost idea and knocked on the cabin door. Justin answered.

He looked tired, with dark circles under his eyes, his hair rumpled, his clothes from yesterday wrinkled.

"Did you sleep?" she asked. "You need rest after that wound. Is it too cold out here?" More guilt. "We should find another safe place for you."

"I slept a little. We took turns." He opened the door wide to let her and Deacon inside.

Beatrix was huddled on a sleeping bag, a steaming cup of something held between her bare hands. Her braid was coming undone around the edges, parts of her hair sticking up in places, and her heavy coat seemed to swallow her like a blanket. She nodded in greeting, but didn't say anything.

"Give her a few minutes to wake up," Justin said, amusement in his tone. "She's not a morning person."

Beatrix huffed something under her breath and took a sip from her steaming cup.

"You want some tea?" Justin asked.

"No thanks," Cary said. "How are your injuries?" She glanced at the hard floor and the second sleeping bag that had obviously been Justin's.

"Fine. They'll heal. I'm taking the good drugs today."

She raised her brows at him.

"Aspirin," he said.

"Those are helpful," she agreed. She knew all too well from her myriad injuries over the years that a good dose of old school painkillers went a long way in the healing process.

She sat on the wood floor, between the two sleeping bags, while Deacon hovered at the wall opposite the door, leaning against the rough wood with his arms crossed over his chest. He looked intense and not a little intimidating.

The twins pretended to ignore him, but Cary noticed Justin's occasional wary glance.

She'd have made Deacon sit and relax but there was something too reassuring about his looming presence so she let it go.

Why the twins set off her nerves instead of her protective instincts, she couldn't say. They were usually the kinds of people she had no problems protecting. Maybe it was just that Beatrix's particular brand of magic gave Cary the willies. Or maybe it was because they'd worked voluntarily for Greenson.

"Tell me more about this god Greenson sacrifices to," she launched in without any more preamble. She really wanted this particular job done soon. "Cause if he's calling a demon, I know people who can help." At least, she did now. *Thanks, Angie!*

"Why do you think it's a demon?" Justin asked.

"Because of Greenson's red eyes and that ground crisping thing he did. If this isn't about demons in some way, then he's an illusionist, or delusional, or some combination of the two. Either way, I need to know what we're dealing with so I can sic the right people on him. Once he's out of your lives, you'll be safe to go back to…whatever it is you want to do." She tried not to think too hard about what their next moves might be.

Justin glanced at Deacon. "We told you everything we know yesterday." Back to Cary. "I have no idea if he really summons a god or what it is. We haven't been around for the sacrifices. He calls Beatrix in once it's done. And I go with her to watch her back."

"Damn." She'd woken assuming that if she could just confirm demon—somehow—she'd be able to pass Greenson off to Aidan, or some other available demon hunter. They'd stop him and all would be well.

"He's due to sacrifice again tonight," Beatrix said.

Her voice sounded scratchy and unused, a little deeper even than yesterday. She didn't have the same circles under her eyes as Justin, but her lids were heavy, as if she might drift back to sleep again.

"How do you know that?" Cary asked, her pulse jumping.

"He has to sacrifice someone every three days," Beatrix said, then yawned. "Sorry. I really don't do mornings if I can avoid them."

"Do you know why he sacrifices every three days?" Cary leaned in a little closer, ignoring the faint scent of death that clung to Beatrix.

Every three days? She finally understood why Greenson would need a way to dispose of the bodies and couldn't just bury or burn them, or dump them in the Mor-Gin—beyond the fact that he enjoyed watching the ghouls eat the remains. She swallowed hard at the thought. He was building up a lot of dead bodies if he'd been killing someone every three days for who knew how long. Even trying to bury or burn them in that amount would draw attention. Shifters would eventually sniff out the evidence if he dumped all the bodies in the Mor-Gin. At the rate Greenson was killing, someone would find him out, sooner rather than later.

It did occurred to her to wonder why the Nags hadn't detected him, though. They, at least, should have…sensed the danger and sent her in to protect the victims before this. Unless Greenson's god was somehow masking the murders? Something to ask her bosses next time she saw them.

Beatrix shrugged. "Says the 'god' requires it. I just figured he liked killing."

The fact that the young woman wasn't more bothered by the killing was disturbing. Cary held her feelings in check and said, "Do you know where he does this, or does he bring the bodies to you from wherever he…works?"

"He started by bringing the bodies to an agreed cemetery," Justin said.

"Now, he just kills there and calls us when he's ready for the ghouls," Beatrix finished.

"How do you know?" Cary asked.

"There's left over stuff," Justin said. "Candles and salt and a chalk pentagram and stuff. He usually has the pentagram brushed into the ground and grass so it's hidden by the time we arrive, but we got there fast once and I saw what it was."

Sounded like the right kind of paraphernalia for demon summoning —potentially. Most of the stuff used to call demons was just for show, so this could still be something else. But Cary got the impression Greenson liked the show.

She leaned back and glanced at Deacon. If she got to the place before the sacrifice began, she could save whoever Greenson had targeted next. Stop him "feeding" his god. Maybe even stop him permanently if she had some specialized help.

Would Aidan come if she wasn't positive it was a demon?

Cary could at least call and ask. If Aidan or another demon hunter couldn't or wouldn't show, maybe Angie could help. Since apparently there had been a "back in the day" with demon hunters.

The Nags said Cary couldn't turn to Jaxer for help anymore, but that didn't mean she couldn't take advantage of the skills of her other friends.

She *was* starting to wonder why she seemed to be up to her ears in demons lately, but maybe it was that time of year or something.

"I could call in some backup," Deacon said, as if reading her thoughts. "There are a few of my people that would happily help you now."

She smiled. "That could be very helpful." Her smile dropped away. "But I don't want to risk too many lives. We'll keep them in reserve, if that's okay?"

He nodded. "Just tell me what you need."

Her tummy did a little happy dance. They might not have had that date yet, but she really did like that he seemed to have her back.

And if they ended this job tonight, she and Deacon could finally get to their first official date.

"Will Greenson expect you to come help him tonight?" Cary faced Beatrix again. "After what happened with Justin, given he's got his own ghoul-control necklace now, will he still call you?"

Beatrix shrugged and looked at Justin. "He still wants a stronger amulet from Justin. You heard him yesterday. He still expects us to work for him."

"Or else," Justin said sourly, touching his waist.

"Yeah, it's the 'or else' that worries me," Cary said. "I'd rather you weren't there at all." Two less people she'd have to protect. "If you can handle one last night here, I'll go catch him before he sacrifices some poor person, hopefully stop him—" somehow, "—and then you should be safe going forward. Sound good?"

The twins exchanged a longer look this time. Long enough Cary briefly wondered about that idea that twins could communicate without talking. She was close to her younger sister, but she'd always been glad they couldn't read each other's minds.

"We should be there with you," Beatrix finally said. "If he calls ghouls, I can put them down again."

"I can protect everyone from the ghouls," Cary said. "They'll settle again at sunrise, and everything will be finished by then." One way or the other.

"He doesn't have enough control of them," Beatrix said. "They could hurt someone after you've left."

"But unless he sics them on someone, they won't attack the living." She looked between brother and sister as they both refused to meet her gaze. "Right?" she said, her voice hardening.

"The amulet…" Justin started, stopped, then shrugged. "The amulet kind of…distorts what Beatrix does."

"Justin thought it would make things better," Beatrix said, "That Greenson wouldn't have as much control of them, so he wouldn't be able to cause as much trouble."

"I fucked up," Justin said. "Badly. I used a stone that had flaws. It robs the spell of purity."

"You didn't do this on purpose," Beatrix said.

"I should have known," he snapped. "I knew I was giving him a flawed piece. I should have known…" Justin swallowed hard and turned his back on them. "I should have known."

"What, exactly, do these flaws make the amulet do?" Cary asked warily.

After a silence that stretched Cary's nerves to near breaking, Beatrix finally answered. "The ghouls Greenson calls with it become hungry for flesh period," she said quietly. "Not just decaying stuff. Living flesh will do."

"What?" Cary stood in her agitation. "Are you telling me we

left flesh eating ghouls in the underground the other night? When people—tourists!—go down there? Especially at night for ghost tours?" True, mundane tourists didn't go into the Mor-Gin, but the weakening magic meant a tourist *might* stumble into those areas. Or the damned ghouls might stumble out, lured by the smell of human flesh. "Why the hell didn't you tell me that?" she finished.

"We didn't know enough about you," Justin said without looking at her.

"We had no reason to trust you," Beatrix added. "It was our problem to take care of."

"Can you?" Cary asked. "You turned them away. Can you…get them back to just wanting decaying stuff?"

"I think so," Beatrix said.

"You think so." Cary put her hands on her hips and hung her head. "Fuck me," she muttered. "Okay. Two things then." She faced Deacon. "Before tonight, I need to make sure the ghouls aren't running amok. Can you check with your cop friend and maybe hint that they should close off the underground tours for the night? For the next few nights. The less people underground, the less likely the ghouls will be lured out of the Mor-Gin."

"The tourists went underground last night," Deacon pointed out.

Unnecessarily. Cary was already in a panic about that. "I know and I'm just hoping no one disappeared. The Nags didn't come get me so I'm assuming the ghouls weren't a threat last night. They're part of this. The Nags would have sent me in to protect people if they were going after tourists." At least, she thought her bosses would. They didn't expect her to have known about the danger ahead of time, did they?

Shit.

Panic crawled over her skin. "We need to ensure no one goes down into the underground for a few days, until we can track to loose ghouls and, *hopefully*—" she glared at Beatrix, "—fix them before anyone gets hurt. Tonight, I'm going to get between Greenson and his sacrifice, end his 'god feeding' routine, and get his amulet away from him so he doesn't fuck up anymore poor ghouls. Is everyone good with this?"

She narrowed her eyes and looked between the twins. "You two, you will stay here tonight, out of the way. I will not have you getting killed because you think you can take care of Greenson yourself. Once he's been neutralized, you can try to fix the ghouls. But you are not to get involved until I say it's safe. Got it?"

Beatrix lifted her chin as if she might argue but when Cary stared her down, the young woman dropped her gaze to the wooden floor and nodded in agreement. Justin finally faced her and with a deep breath agreed to Cary's terms without any sign of argument.

Guilt will do that to you, Cary thought sourly.

"Where the hell is this cemetery," she said, still so angry she wanted to spit.

Once the twins had laid out where and when everything usually happened, Cary reiterated that they should stay put. If they tried to stop Greenson on their own, Cary promised she would *not* react well to that.

She had no idea how she'd carry through on her implied threat, but so long as they were worried about what she might do, everyone would be fine.

She hoped.

2 3

ary drove back into Portland while Deacon made phone calls to his cop friend as well as some of the local leopard community.

"They'll go down and look for the ghouls," he told her when she frowned a question at him.

"Wait, don't send them in there without me to protect them?" she objected immediately. "It's too dangerous." From the corner of her eye, she caught Deacon's stare. "What?"

"You're worried that leopard shifters won't be able to handle themselves against ghouls," he said.

"Well. Yeah. Living-flesh eating ghouls who've been screwed up by flawed magic."

"You've seen them fight now. You know how fast and strong we are."

"Still…" She glared at him when she caught sight of his smile. "Stop that. I'm serious. I don't want any of them getting hurt. Why are you smiling at me like that? It's freaking me out."

He chuckled. "I guess I like that you're protective of my people."

She made a face even as her cheeks heated. "It is kind of my job. Protector and all." Why was she embarrassed? She had a feeling there was more going on in this conversation than she realized and that didn't help her mood.

"They'll be fine," Deacon said softly. "They'll just go in to locate, not engage. I'll warn them these ghouls are different, just in case they have to…intervene."

"If they have to *intervene*, it means someone needs my brand of help. I should go with them."

"They'll be faster without—"

He cut himself off but she got the implication. "Faster without a poor human in tow?" she asked.

"That's not exactly what I meant. But even your Protector powers can't help you keep up with running shifters."

"If I'm going to help someone, I can move almost as fast as a shifter."

Which wasn't precisely true. She could get between an innocent and a shifter moving at top speed, if needs be and if she was close enough to start with. She could do the same with fast moving vampires or anything else that moved at inhuman speeds if necessary. But unless she was protecting *from* a shifter, her powers wouldn't give her the speed she'd need to keep up with shifters.

For all she could fend off an entire army of bad guys under the right circumstances, her powers definitely had their limitations.

As Deacon made his calls, she mulled over those limitations. Is that what the Nags meant when they said she'd come into the full use of her "magic" after this year? She'd be able to do things like keep up with shifters if it meant she would reach someone that needed protecting faster?

If so, that gave a whole new perspective on the seventh year trial.

She was deep in thought when Deacon disconnected his call. She blinked away her distraction and said, "So, will Trevor close the tunnels to tours?" Officer Trevor McKinsey was Deacon's friend and contact in the local police force. While Cary tried to stay under police radar, having a cop friend did have its benefits.

"He's going to try. He's got to convince his bosses the danger to tourists is significant enough to warrant it. And since he needs to do that without telling them there are flesh-eating ghouls on the loose—"

"Which would get him locked up for sounding crazy," she added.

"Exactly, he has to find a way to talk them into it with a story they'll believe."

"Serial killer on the loose? There is one."

"I think he's going to go for something like gas leak. A little less 'fill the streets with cops' kind of excuse."

She nodded. "Yeah, that's a better plan. Did you tell him about our serial killer?"

"You weren't listening?"

She winced. "I was thinking. Did you?"

"No. I don't want the cops going after this guy on their own. They won't know what they're getting into and some of them might get hurt."

She grinned at him. "That's what I would have done."

"We make a good team," he said.

Huh. Maybe they did.

THEY MET DEACON'S SHIFTER FRIEND LUCAS IN THE SAME LOWER-level hotel storage room where Deacon had first taken Cary into the tunnels.

"How's Miguel doing?" Cary asked.

"Recovering a lot faster than I would have expected," Lucas said with a faint smile. "Now that it's all over, it was a great adventure, and as far as he's concerned you are the best things since Spiderman."

"Really?" She grinned. "Hey, that's cool."

Lucas chuckled. Then grew serious as he said, "I can't ever thank you enough."

"You don't have to," she said, in all seriousness. "I'm very glad I could help."

"Still, we owe you."

She nodded to the open trapdoor just behind him. "You're paying me back now. What's the word?"

"We've located about twenty ghouls in an isolated section of the tunnels, still well inside the Mor-Gin. Not close to any of the places where the magic is weak and they could slip out. And so far, no telltale recent human remains anywhere."

Cary closed her eyes and breathe out a sigh of relief.

"A lot of rodent bones, though," Lucas finished.

"You haven't gotten close enough to attract their attention, right?" Cary asked, her chin tucked.

"Who's attention, the rats or the ghouls?" Lucas said.

She scowled. "You know what I mean. The ghouls. They're really dangerous right now."

"Deacon warned us. We're keeping our distance. Their sense of smell is pretty impressive, and their sense of movement even better— they pickup vibrations in the ground like a worm. But we've found a distance they can't sense us and are keeping watch. We've set a few of our people to guard the breeches in the magic barrier, too. At least the breeches we know about. That should help keep them contained."

She glanced at Deacon.

"Good enough for now?" he asked.

"So long as the ghouls don't start roving around." To Lucas, "Are there enough of you to help if a human gets too close to danger?"

Lucas nodded. "Don't worry, we'll turn humans away before they get anywhere near potential trouble. None of the entrances into the Mor-Gin are on the tourist routes anyway. But that's why we set up guards at the breeches we know about, just in case. One of our people owns a construction company." He looked at Deacon. "Sherri got us some gear so we'd look official. We'll tell people there's tunnel damage and the area is closed off."

"Great work. Tell Sherri thanks for me," Deacon said.

"She feels like she owes Cary, too," Lucas said. To Cary, "Her daughter was one of the children you saved."

"She doesn't owe me anything," Cary insisted. "But I'm really really glad I could help her daughter."

As they left Lucas to return to the tunnels, Cary felt her heart swelling, just a little, with gratitude. Knowing she helped people, knowing she could save kids like Lucas's son and Sherri's daughter... These were the moments she could forget about all the irritations and stress that came from dealing with the Nags—and sometimes Jaxer—and appreciate the job she'd been tricked into. Sometimes, she was even glad to be a Protector.

But she had no intention of admitting that out loud.

In the car, on the way back to Cary's house, Deacon said, "My people do owe you, you know."

"Nope," she said. "No one owes me anything. I protect kids because it's one of the few redeeming features of my job."

"Still... My mother is grateful for what you did."

She glanced at him from the corner of her eye. "Your mother?"

He nodded. "She's really looking forward to meeting you."

"Why do those words terrify me?"

He chuckled. "She can be scary."

"That's not helping."

"But she won't be with you. You're my mate."

"Uh huh."

Except she was human. And apparently, they could end this mate business if they wanted too. She pursed her lips. They had bigger things to worry about at the moment. They still hadn't even been on a date. It wasn't important for them to discuss this yet.

And if she was being completely honest with herself, even though his claim they were mates scared the crap out of her, she didn't want the bond to end. Not yet.

But the longer they were together, the more likely it was to become permanent. According to him, they had to have sex first—and lots of it—before that started to happen. If she was going to end things with him, she'd have to decide sooner rather than later. For both their sakes.

She glanced at him before focusing on the road. He was unbelievably sexy, unreally handsome, but that wasn't what made her so hesitant to let him go. It had more to do with what he'd said earlier, something that struck her as…well, important when considering your future mate.

They made a good team. He had her back. And for a lot of reasons she was afraid were purely selfish, she didn't want to give that up.

2 4

---

ary rang Aidan's number twice without getting an answer. She left a voicemail after the second call, then rang Angie.

"You okay?" Angie said before Cary got a word out.

"Yeah, fine," Cary said. "Why do you sound so worried?"

"I heard about the attack last night. That's the second one."

Cary glanced toward the kitchen, where Deacon was talking with the dogs and getting himself a drink. She hadn't told him any of this yet. And this seemed a bad way for him to find out. She went to the bedroom and lowered her voice. His hearing was good, but hopefully this would give her some privacy.

"You talked to Aidan?" Cary asked.

"She texted. We need to do something about these attacks. This guy will just keep trying until he does kill you."

Cary closed her eyes. "I don't even know who he is," she said. "I have no idea why he wants me dead. I told Jaxer, but Jaxer didn't recognize my description either."

"When the attack happened here, you thought it had something to do with that kid wizard who tried to kill Deacon. Do you still think it does?"

"Since the wizard that came after me last night wasn't Sheldon, I don't know anymore. I thought I saw Sheldon in Holland's army, but…" She snorted. "I was under a lot of stress just then. I could have imagined it."

"What did your attacker last night look like?" Angie asked.

Cary described him. "Familiar to you at all?"

"Nope. But I'll ask around. Someone with that kind of magic won't be a stranger to the local witchy crowd."

"Thanks," Cary said on a sigh. "Maybe if we can find out *why* he wants to kill me, we can figure out how to make him stop trying."

"That's the plan. Did Aidan help last night? Besides saving your life."

"Yes. Thanks for putting me in touch with her. That's kind of why I called, though." Cary explained all the new information they'd gathered. "I could use a demon hunter tonight, in case whatever this thing is that Greenson is calling is a demon. But I can't prove that's what's happening. Will Aidan think it's a waste of time? Will she even show up?"

"Did you tell her what you needed in the message you left?" Angie asked.

"No, just asked for her to call me back."

"Text her the name of the cemetery," Angie said. "With a 'may or may not involve a demon summoning' message. If it is a demon, she'll show."

"She'll know the difference ahead of time?" Cary frowned at her bedroom window. "How?"

"That's how it works. She'll get a…vibe. The way you do when you sense someone needs protecting? She gets a sense of demon summonings."

"Then why hasn't she felt these before? Greenson's been doing this for at least a month, probably longer." The same question she had for the Nags. Why had no one stopped this guy sooner?

"If her guess was right that he could have been a demon hunter, his own will would probably mask the summonings, and up to now, he's been able to keep the demon from escaping. Most hunters only show up once the demon is on the verge of breaking free. But once Aidan is clued in, she'll be able to sense if this is to do with demons or not."

"She mentioned something about you knowing a lot of demon hunters 'back in the day,'" Cary said. "Is that how you know all this?"

"Said that did she?"

"You have a past I don't know about," Cary said, her tone just shy of accusing.

"It's complicated," Angie hedged. "But if you want to hear the sordid details one night over a bottle of wine, I can tell you some of it."

"Only some? I thought we were best friends."

"Some of it I'm not allowed to talk about, Cary."

Cary wanted to argue with that, but she kept so many secrets herself. Some stuff even Angie didn't know. She really wasn't one to talk here.

"Fine," she said, "I won't push. But I do want the details you can share."

"Deal. It will require wine, though. And maybe some Tequila."

Cary groaned. The last time they'd had wine and Tequila in one night, she'd ended up with a killer hangover. It'd be worth it for this story, though.

"If Aidan doesn't show," she said, "does that mean I'm not dealing with a demon for sure? Or could she just be busy?"

"If she's busy," Angie said, "someone else will show up."

"Where were all these hunters when Holland was going after the Naga city?" Cary asked with no little annoyance.

"They aren't allowed near Holland," Angie said.

As if that answered anything. "Why?"

"They won't say. But he's not an issue anymore is he? You beat him."

"He was still alive, though."

"The Naga's have him. He's not a threat."

Cary wanted desperately to believe Angie on that. She really did. And since she had another kind of demon to deal with tonight, she decided to go with that feeling. "If you hear anything I need to know, call," she said. "And definitely a night of storytelling with wine soon."

"Deal. Good luck. Call if you need backup."

"Thanks." She disconnected, grateful for her friends. Even with their secrets.

*U*nlike the cemetery where the twins were hiding, this one was huge and well kept. Rolling hills of gravestones interspersed with trees and the occasional crypt spread out from a wrought iron gated entrance. The roads through the cemetery were clean and smoothly paved, with only a few puddles from a short afternoon shower. Though the cemetery was surrounded by city, the size of it meant very little traffic noise reached her once she and Deacon had moved into the middle of the place.

According to the twins, Greenson called them to an older section of the cemetery where few people went even during the day. Though the gates had been securely locked against car traffic, most of the cemetery wasn't enclosed behind any fences. Anyone could walk through the gravestones at any time. Which could bring innocent bystanders into the mix. But the area Greenson used for his "sacrifices" was far away from any potential thrill seekers sneaking into the cemetery at night.

At least, Cary hoped so. That's what the twins had told her. Since she'd already have her hands full with a serial killer, a potential demon, and whoever Greenson had lured here to murder, she really hoped she could trust their information. The fact that she didn't entirely left her uneasy.

She did wonder how Greenson got his sacrifices and all the demon summoning paraphernalia into the cemetery without being able to drive in. Did he carry all the gear plus a person? That would make him scary strong, but also wouldn't *someone* have spotted him hauling a person into the cemetery before now? Or maybe he drugged his sacrifices so they came willingly? For all she knew, he had a wheelbarrow or cart and people mistook him for someone who worked in the cemetery.

As she and Deacon picked their way through the headstones, she decided she really didn't want to know. The less she knew about how a serial killer worked, the better she'd sleep.

The moon was halfway to full, which helped, but it was still pitch dark inside the grounds. Cary inched around the darker shapes of the gravestones, careful of her steps, wishing she had Deacon's eyesight. And his ability to move without making any noise. That'd be really handy about now.

As they crept closer to the section they were aiming for, Cary kept her sense open, waiting for her Protector magic to kick in. Her first hint that something was wrong was the quiet. The cemetery was already a quiet place despite the surrounding roads, but the silence that fell over them was almost deafening.

She exchanged a look with Deacon. He was frowning, and the yellow glow in his eyes was stronger now. She swallowed hard. He'd left a backpack with spare clothes in her car, in case he had to shift, which for some reason wasn't particularly reassuring.

The quiet hum of noise, when it came was almost shockingly loud in the stillness. A chant with words Cary couldn't hear well enough to identify. But any noise at all felt like a knife in the darkness. Faintly now, she could see lights ahead, flickering and shadowy. As they crept closer, the sounds of the chant got a little louder, the lights a little brighter…

But she still couldn't see very well in the darkness.

She stopped in her tracks, her senses open as she evaluated how she felt. Deacon paused beside her, frowning a question at her. She shook her head for him to give her a minute. Something was wrong and she couldn't place it. Something felt…off.

It took her several erratic heartbeats before she recognized what was so strange. She wasn't feeling that tingling along her spine she got when someone needed protecting. She wasn't feeling any sense of someone *else* being in danger. Her eyesight and other senses were all perfectly normal—no heightened night vision, no heightened sense of smell or hearing to help her protect someone.

She widened her eyes and stared up at Deacon. Her powers weren't working. Nothing was triggering them. Which meant whatever was happening ahead of them, no one was in danger.

Either Greenson had already murdered his sacrifice, or something had gone very wrong.

She pulled Deacon's head close to her and whispered her realization in his ear. He scowled down at her as if to ask if she was serious. She shrugged.

And in a blink, the black leopard that was Deacon's other form stood in front of her.

She sucked in a gasp. Damn he could do that fast. She'd never met another shifter who could change shapes that fast. He'd shredded his clothes—as usual—but in this form, he was almost impossible to see in the darkness. So black he was little more than a shadow with glowing yellow eyes.

He nudged her back behind a tree, and she got the hint. She was supposed to hide while he went to check on things.

She would normally have argued. He was putting himself in danger. And if he was in danger, her powers would work to protect him. But something felt so off, she actually agreed to stay where she was and let him handle this part.

She'd probably never hear the end of this when he shifted back to his human form.

He vanished in the night, moving fast and silent. She pressed her palms against the tree, trying to slow her racing heart. She got nervous when going in to protect others, sometimes even scared, but she rarely felt truly vulnerable. She was always more worried about screwing up and getting someone else killed.

But her already shaky confidence going into this seven year trial felt completely absent tonight. She felt vulnerable and in danger and she couldn't tell *why*. Was the wizard who wanted her dead somewhere nearby? That might explain it. Though this feeling wasn't quite like that sense of being watched she got when the wizard was around.

She kept thinking about the twins sending her here, telling her their boss would be sacrificing someone tonight, and the fact that he was still, technically, their boss. Would they have set her up? But why? It didn't make sense when she was just trying to keep them alive.

And was she seeing betrayal and feeling so suspicious just because she didn't like their particular brand of powers—or their moral compass for that matter? Was she worried about their motives because she didn't particularly like them?

She nibbled her lip, stretching her hearing as far as it would go even though she knew she'd never hear Deacon coming, and tried not to fidget as she waited. She wasn't great at waiting.

The feel of something nudging her thigh made her jump and she had to slap a hand over her mouth to keep from screeching aloud. Deacon stood there still in his animal form for another half moment then he was in his human form. He stepped close to whisper in her ear, which was good because she was too startled to truly appreciate him naked just then.

"Greenson is there with what looks like an alter set up," he said. "A blanket on the ground in the middle of a chalked outline of a pentagram. Candles set at the points. A salt circle surrounding the pentagram. I could only get so close without risking him noticing me. But from my vantage, It didn't look like he had a sacrifice there."

"No body or anything?" she whispered back.

"Nothing. Not even…blood that I could smell. There are tools. A wicked looking knife and some bowls. But I can't see or smell what he might be using for a sacrifice. Not even any animal smells."

"Well, that's not good," she mouthed, almost silently. What the hell was going on? "Can he call a demon without a sacrifice?" she asked, not expecting Deacon to have the answer but needing to ask the question.

According to the twins, Greenson had to sacrifice every three days to this particular god of his, but they hadn't said—and likely didn't even know—if he could call the whatever-it-was without spilling blood. Not all demons *required* sacrifice just to be summoned.

"I don't like this," Deacon said. "We should leave."

"I don't like it either. But this may be our only chance to stop him."

"There's no one here for you to protect. How do you plan on stopping him when you don't have your magic?"

Like she needed the reminder.

She glanced around the tree in the direction of Greenson's circle. "We should at least see if he's calling a demon or not." She hadn't heard back from Aidan, but if the hunter showed up, she'd probably appreciate knowing if this was really a job for her or not.

"I don't want you anywhere near that man while you're vulnerable," Deacon hissed against her ear.

She shivered at the heat and protective anger. And a part of her really really wanted to listen to him. She didn't have the skills for this. No magic. No shields. No shifter senses. No nothing that might help. This wasn't part of her usual job.

Her only hope would be if something went wrong and Greenson went after Deacon. Given the glow in his eyes, Deacon would probably dive into a fight, which meant Greenson would probably try to kill him, which meant she'd be okay because she could protect Deacon.

But there were a lot of *ifs* and *probablys* in that sequence of events.

She pulled in a deep, silent breath and held it. She couldn't just leave. She had to take the chance and find out what Greenson was doing. Maybe he was delusional and all this show didn't actually *do* anything. That would be important to know. He might just be killing people here and pretending to call his god. He might think he's doing magic when he's not actually accomplishing anything with the deaths.

And if she left now, she wouldn't have any idea which possibility was the truth.

"I have to have a look," she finally said against Deacon's ear. "We have to know what he's doing, if he can do anything... I just have to know."

His scowl darkened. She could see he wanted to argue with her and she braced for it.

Instead, he said, "I'll carry you into the tree I used in my leopard form. You will stick with me, and if anything goes wrong, I'm getting you out of here as fast as I can move. Agreed."

"Absolutely," she said without hesitance. She'd gotten herself so freaked out at this stage, she would happily let him run away with her if chaos erupted.

She tried not to smile at the thought of him "running away with her" since it wasn't the time for humor. She did whisper, "No more dates like this, okay? Next time we should just do dinner and a movie."

His soft snort was his only reply before he lifted her into his arms.

Moving at shifter speeds was a stomach-churning experience when you weren't a shifter. She closed her eyes, opened them a moment later, and they were in a tree. She'd felt the leap, but not the run to this spot. She wanted to comment on his speed, but now that she could see Greenson, she didn't dare speak even in a whisper. In fact, she was having a lot of trouble just breathing.

The large oak was winter bare so they weren't hidden among leaves, but it was far enough away from Greenson's set up Cary hoped he wouldn't even glance this way.

From this vantage, she saw the full set up Deacon had described. Greenson was inside the salt circle, at the bottom edge of the chalked pentagram, chanting rhythmically. And though she couldn't see as well as Deacon, it was obvious Greenson didn't have a sacrifice with him. No bodies, no nothing.

It occurred to her he might be practicing calling the ghouls. But without a body to feed them, why would he bother?

Cary listened closely to his chant, trying to pinpoint his intent. The language sounded like Latin. She wasn't great at languages, but she'd learned just enough Latin to recognize a few words here and there.

She thought he might be saying something about "great one" and maybe "my soul". She snarled in frustration, wishing she was better with this kind of thing. She could read Latin well enough to fumble through some of the old texts she had to study, but hearing it spoken, especially in Greenson's rhythmic chanting, complicated things. Was that "darkness binding" or something else? *Sanguis*. That was definitely blood. She recognized that one.

Vocationem ore exíbit gládius acútus.

She squinted as she tried to translate. The *acútus* part sounded familiar. It was a phrase she'd seen before, she was sure of it. It just sounded so different when spoken.

She wondered if Rosetta Stone had a program for Latin. Might do her some good to get that if they did.

Greenson raised the knife Deacon had seen earlier over his head, holding it up in both hands like he was about to use it, and for a heart stopping moment, Cary wondered if he was planning on using it on himself. Could she stop that? Would her powers work to prevent it?

Did she want to prevent it?

Deacon's arms tightened, holding her solidly in place. And they both watched as Greenson cut a deep slice along his palm. He said something too quietly for her to hear, then with the blood dripping down his arm, flattened his palm into the soil in front of him.

A deep reverberation hummed over her bones, like the gong of a temple bell. Every hair on her body stood up, her nerves jumping in reaction to the energy buzzing in the air now. So strong she could feel it even with her ordinary human senses. She felt Deacon's muscles tightened, and caught the faint sound of his hissing gasp. They held still, as still as the rest of the night, as that reverberation of energy grew and deepened and expanded, filling in the air until Cary could barely breathe around the thickness of the magic.

She had to blink several times before she spotted the darkness in the center of the pentagram, collecting in a thick shadow over the blanket she'd assumed was there for a sacrificial body. At first, she just thought the candles behind the deepening murk were flickering and dying. But there was no air movement, nothing to make the candles flicker. And the closer ones barely danced on the wicks, as if there were no air currents at all.

Then the shadow deepened, coalescing into something solid, a fog of indistinct shape.

Cary hadn't attended any demon summonings. She thought back over her interactions with demons in the past. Nope. No actual moments of summoning. They were usually just...there when she arrived. So watching this whatever-it-was materialize into this realm was both fascinating and horrifying.

The scales tipped to horrifying when the vague shape solidified and from the thick darkness an actual *thing* emerged. Huge, and muscled, with red eyes and skin that looked like black lava rock moving on the top of glowing red lava. Horns sprouted from its head, glowing white hot in the darkness. Over the top of its rock skin, chinks of silver like metal moved into view then folded back and melted into its skin, almost as if it wore chainmail, but the chainmail kept melting and reforming continually in the being's immense heat. Its features were thick and carried just enough of the look of a human to be recognizable, but those same features kept blurring, making it impossible to really *see* its face.

Except for the eyes. The red red eyes with black pupils slit like a cat's were the most solid thing about the creature.

Exactly what she might have expected a demon god to look like.

What she hadn't expect was for the demon to turn its head, look directly at her...

And smile.

"Cary Redmond," it said. "At last."

2 6

eacon moved so fast Cary didn't even register the change in position until they were already on the opposite side of the cemetery. Her stomach rolled as the urge to throw up from motion sickness swept through her.

She barely noticed the need because she was still in shock.

"How the hell did that thing know my name?" she said, her voice hollow and high.

Blackness seemed to be crawling into her vision. Shock, she thought, and wondered if she might actually pass out. That wouldn't be a good idea when there was a demon nearby *who knew who she was*!

"I don't care how it knew you," Deacon said. "It knew you. We're getting out of here."

She couldn't get around her shock long enough to argue, and wasn't sure she wanted to argue anyway.

This was so not good.

"Was that the demon you saved the puppy from?" Deacon asked as he carried her to the side of the cemetery where they'd left her car parked on the side of the road.

"No." She shook her head. "That one looked more like Holland. At first anyway. Just an ordinary guy, until I got between him and the puppy. Then his eyes glowed, and he sprouted scales and horns, and his fingers started dripping acid, and I thought I was dead so I wrapped myself around the puppy and closed my eyes."

The memory of those moments had never really faded. She just tried not to think about it too closely or too often. She and Buck were just fine now. No one had been melted by demon acid. But she'd never forgotten that particular demon's face. She'd know him again anywhere.

"Holland was hiding in his human guise," Deacon said. "That demon you faced when you became a Protector was hiding in a human guise, too."

"Yeah, I know. Well, sort of. But he let me see his real self right before he tried to kill me," she said. "That…that thing we just saw was not the puppy-kicking demon." The puppy-kicking demon wasn't even close to as scary as the thing Greenson had called.

Which only scared her more.

Deacon leapt the chainlink fence that lined this section of the cemetery, landing on the sidewalk beyond so easily it was as if he'd just jumped over a small puddle. She'd be impressed when she thought about that later.

"Where the hell is Aidan?" she asked no one in particular.

"This does seem like a job for a demon hunter," Deacon said. He glanced over his shoulder at the cemetery, his features set in a scowl.

"What?" she asked.

"Listening. I don't hear them."

"You think they could have followed? I thought the demon was contained in the circle unless Greenson releases it. That's how these summonings usually work."

At least, that's how they were supposed to work. A demon knowing who she was had knocked her confidence in her own knowledge a bit.

Later, she'd use that as an excuse for why she'd almost missed a very very important bit of information.

Greenson had been *inside* the salt circle. Outside the pentagram in which the demon materialized, but he'd been inside the circle with the demon.

That wasn't good. She just wasn't sure what it meant yet.

"It's not breaking free," a familiar voice said from the shadows under a tree. Aidan stepped into view, her brown eyes ever so slightly redder. "Not yet anyway," the hunter added, her gaze unfocused as if she were concentrating on some internal vision. "Your serial killer has a strong enough will to contain what he's called. But not for much longer."

"I take it this is your demon hunter," Deacon murmured.

Cary raised her brows at his faint growl. She pushed at his shoulders and he reluctantly let her down. But he kept his arm around her waist.

"Deacon, Aidan, Aidan, Deacon," Cary made a quick introduction.

Aidan nodded at Deacon, smiling just a little before facing Cary. "Sorry I'm late. I had another call tonight." She glanced toward the cemetery, her eyes narrowed. "A distraction I think. What's been called in there… It's more than usually moves into this world."

"You going in?" Cary asked.

"Not tonight."

Cary raised her brows in question.

"It's not getting out tonight," Aidan said. "I'd waste energy."

"I assume you're sticking around to fight it when it does start to get out, though. Right?" Cary asked, both hopeful and a little desperate. This was definitely outside her usual job description.

Aidan nodded. "I'm sticking around. Want to tell me why you're so freaked out?"

"That obvious, huh?" Cary snorted. "The thing knew my name. It had no reason to know who I am. Greenson doesn't know my name. The twins wouldn't have had time to tell him… At least…" She glanced at Deacon, frowning. "I don't think so."

"I think the twins have some questions to answer," he said, snarling faintly.

Cary didn't envy Justin and Beatrix just then. To Aidan, she said, "We came here tonight thinking Greenson would be sacrificing someone to that thing. He didn't have a sacrifice, though. He called it with his own blood."

"So," Aidan said. "He's bound himself to it. That explains why his eyes glow and he occasionally chars grass. He's not likely doing that on purpose. He may not even realize it's happening."

"Is the fact that he's bound himself to the demon why he was inside the circle when he summoned the thing, instead of safely outside it?"

Deacon hissed a curse under his breath, and she realized he'd missed that detail, too. Which was something of a relief. It hadn't just been her.

"Yeah," Aidan answered with a sigh. "I don't know if he realizes this or not, but he's going to die soon."

"What?"

She shrugged. "The demon is…inhabiting him. Blood binding can allow demons of a certain power level to control a human body, a way into this world that doesn't sacrifice as much power since they're still linked with their own realm."

"Huh?" Cary said.

"Yeah, we'd better talk more about what that demon is, and soon," Aidan said. "Unfortunately, I have to go now." She made a face. "Another distraction, but a dangerous one if I don't do something about it. I'll call you tomorrow." She turned to walk away, paused, and turned back. "By the way…" She nodded at Deacon while smiling at Cary. "Mazel tov."

Cary raised her brows at the hunter's back, then glanced at Deacon. Standing there in all his naked glory.

Ah.

"You need clothes," she said. And hurried back to her car.

BACK IN THE SAFETY OF HER HOME, CARY LET OUT A SIGH OF RELIEF and gladly fell into the happy greetings from her dogs. Buck nosed at her, nudging her a few times until she looked directly at him. He let out a low rumbling bark, and nudged her again.

"You smell the demon?" she asked.

He barked again.

"I'm okay," she assured him. "Nothing to worry about."

He bumped against her again, and to Cary's surprise, he felt really hot. She held him at arm's length, looking him over. "Do you have a fever or something?" She felt his nose, checked to make sure his lips and tongue weren't too dry. Heat pumped from under his fur, but otherwise, he didn't show signs of a fever.

Maybe she was just freaking out after the night she'd had.

Deacon gave Buck a pat, frowning at the Labrador. "He does feel warm. You want to take him to our vet?"

Buck knocked Deacon's hand away with a sharp jerk of his head and walked away back to the bedrooms. Cary stood and stared after him. "That is not typical Buck behavior."

"He knew you'd been around a demon tonight," Deacon said. "How?"

She glanced at Deacon and realized she'd never actually told him this. So much had been happening since they'd met. They still had so much to learn about each other. And that realization felt weird tonight, because she was starting to feel like she'd known Deacon for a lot longer than a month and a half.

"Buck is the puppy I saved from the demon," she said. "He's a demon dog—his preferred term. Call him a hellhound and he'll growl at you. He knows demons when he smells them."

"He didn't react so strongly to Holland," Deacon commented.

"He did, just more subtly. Somethings wrong with him right now. I'm just not sure what." She ran her hands through her hair, pulling her ponytail completely out, then scratched her scalp. "Lot of unanswered questions," she muttered. "I hate that."

He cupped her face between his palms and set his forehead against hers. "Would you mind if I slept in the guest room tonight?"

She pulled back enough to give him a look.

He smiled a little. "I'm not rushing you, I promise. I'll keep my hands to myself."

"It's not your hands I'm worried about."

His smile widened. "I just want to keep watch over you, if you don't mind. Confronting a demon that was happy to see you has me a little…edgy."

She snorted. "Me too. You sure you can stick to the guest room?"

There was still a very faint yellow glow in his eyes. His leopard had calmed a lot on the ride home, but it was still pretty close to the surface. When he was like this, the call to be with his mate seemed to ramp up. And if they started making out now, she was pretty sure they wouldn't stop at just a few kisses. They didn't have a chaperone. And she was just edgy enough herself that she liked the idea of burning off all this residual adrenaline by losing herself in Deacon's arms.

But sex with Deacon wasn't just sex. It would tighten the mate bond. Settle it into something more permanent.

And she wasn't ready for that step yet. For reasons she was still working out.

"I can stick to the other room," he said quietly. "I'd rather take you to bed with me. But not before you're ready."

"What happens if I'm never ready?"

"I will spend a lot of time in cold showers."

He said it so seriously and solemnly she started to laugh. The laughter felt good after the scare she'd had tonight. And the worries she still had.

"Thank you." She kissed him, gently.

"As soon as this job is over," he said. "Dinner. A movie. The whole thing. A date that doesn't involve danger and potential world-ending consequences. Deal?"

"Yes, please," she said. "I'd like to talk about some things, too."

He tilted his head to better meet her eyes. "Like what? We can talk now."

"I'm still working out what I want to ask and say," she admitted. She hadn't had time to digest what she'd learned from Jaxer yet, and she was afraid of rushing the conversation before she knew how she felt or even what she thought.

"Should I be worried?" he asked.

"Depends on what you want," she said. Then shook her head. "Sorry. I'm talking nonsense because I'm still a little shaky. We'll have plenty of time for the personal stuff after Beatrix and Justin and Greenson and this demon god are no longer a thing."

"If you're sure." He didn't look convinced.

She kissed him again, a little more lingering this time, because she needed to. Because his heat and warmth, the taste of him on her tongue, the feel of him holding her tight felt solid and real. Because her world felt like it was spinning out of control. Because she was worried about her dog. Because she was worried about her future.

Because at the moment, she wasn't sure about anything.

When Deacon went out the next morning to get them some food for breakfast, Cary snuck into her attic and brought down some of her books on demonology. She definitely needed to know more about what she was facing, and while she'd studied this subject frequently over the years, she always felt like she was forgetting more than she learned.

The fact that she'd gone from necromancers and ghouls back to demons was just…irritating.

By the time Deacon walked through the back door with a bag of bagels, she was deep in her reading.

"Okay, I think I know what Aidan was talking about now," she said without looking up from the huge tome in her lap. The brown leather binding was soft and supple under her fingers, but the yellow pages crackled with age.

Deacon plunked down next to her on the couch and she swatted at him. "Careful of the book," she said. "I made them give me this version instead of the one made of skin, because gross, and the paper is delicate."

"Sorry," he said, half smiling, half grimacing. "What have you found?"

The smell of bagels from the bag he set on her coffee table made her stomach growl. She gave the bag a hungry look but wanted to finish what she was doing first.

"So, according to this, the reason there aren't more freed demons like Holland is because there's a loss of power when a demon moves from demonic realms into this one. They have to give up some of their strength and power. The mid-level demons don't care. Getting here from there with whatever power they have is fine by them, and that's why they work so hard to get those that call them to screw up so they can get out. The really really strong demons, the high-level ones, most of them have to give up *a lot* to get into this realm. The more power a demon has, the more it sacrifices to move into this world unfettered. And most of them aren't willing to do that because, according to the scholars, the loss is permanent. There's one researcher here who claims they can get some power back if they're rebound by a containment circle linking them back to their realm, but all the other authorities claim they can't ever get the power back."

"Which means Holland must have been pretty fucking powerful to still be so strong in this realm," Deacon said.

"Exactly! But also, he must have been pretty eager to be in this realm instead of his own to have given up whatever power he gave up. I got the impression from a few things he said that he didn't want to go back either. A lot of that night is blurry now, but I swear he said something about not wanting to go back, and something about his father, and that's why he needed Naga power. Or something. Anyway, it was pretty clear he wanted to stay in this realm."

"What does this have to do with our current demon threat?"

"Not sure exactly, except that I think this demon god of Greenson's may really be as powerful as a god—or close to it. So powerful, it isn't going to just drop all that power to step into this realm. But, but!" She sat up and carefully turned a few pages so she could point at the relevant passage. "There's a way for a demon to remain in their realm and still access ours freely."

"They occupy a human body," Deacon guessed. "Is that what Holland did?"

"I doubt it or he wouldn't be worried about being dragged back. Because when they occupy a human body, they're still *in* their own realms technically. It's kind of like their…essences are split in half. Part of them is still in their own realm while another part is in this realm—the way they'd be in both realms inside a containment circle when called, except free to move beyond the confinement of whatever is used to bind them."

"Does this happen…often?" Deacon asked.

"Ha! No, because most human hosts can't handle it and die. And the demon can't keep moving the body around for long afterward."

"Definitely not what Holland did, then."

"The process also requires a *lot* of blood sacrifice and blood offered up freely from the human potential host, and enough visitations, and a host strong enough to take the demon in without dying—and the more powerful the demon, the ones who might actually try this process, the more likely they are to kill the host. Plus, if the host finds out, unless they're like fanatical or good with being martyred, they aren't likely to go through with it since they'll end up dead."

"The demon could lie and say the host would have all their power," Deacon suggested.

She shrugged. "Actually, that's likely, isn't it? But still… The whole process is so damned difficult. And in the end, very few human hosts survive for any length of time."

Deacon frowned, absently running his finger over her shoulder and along the exposed skin of her neck as his brow creased in thought. She tried to ignore the gesture, but the simple touch made her nerves dance with anticipation and excitement. And it was hard to think past wanting his hand to move to more interesting places.

"If Beatrix could keep the human body animated, through her necromancy magic," Deacon said, slowly, "then would that extend the time the demon could use the body for its own ends?"

Cary's eyebrows shot up. She hadn't thought of that. Whoa. "That means when the demon sent Greenson for a necromancer…"

"He wasn't just thinking of body disposal," Deacon finished.

"Oh no." She closed her eyes and dropped her head back against the couch.

"What?" Deacon asked.

"I might have to protect the serial killer to keep the demon from getting into this realm. Shit." She snarled. "And yuck. I don't want to protect Greenson. He's evil and gross."

"Then don't," Deacon said matter-of-factly. "Let him get killed by the demon he's called. We just have to prevent Beatrix from keeping his body animated."

"If we can." Cary wasn't sure about that yet. "But what if Greenson can take the demon god into him and manage to survive even for a short time? The havoc a freed demon like that could cause is…too scary to think about."

"You suppose this is what the Nags meant when they said if you didn't protect Beatrix, she could end the world?" he asked.

"Maybe. Sounds like a pretty dire consequence even if it wasn't what they meant."

No sooner had she said "dire consequence" than her stomach rumbled loudly. She squirmed under Deacon's chuckle.

"Stop laughing and give me a bagel," she said. "Thank you for going out to get them."

"You're welcome." His voice deepened as he leaned in to kiss her neck.

Her stomach danced from something other than hunger by the time he leaned away and reached for the bag. She focused on setting the delicate book to one side, carefully closing it and setting it on the floor so it wouldn't fall off the couch. Buck, who was laying under the living room window with Pickles and Fred, raised his head and look at the book for a pointed second. His lip lifted in a slight, soundless snarl. Then he laid down again, his chin on his forepaws.

Cary had never wished she could read her dogs' minds more than she did in that moment.

Deacon called her attention away from Buck with food. When he handed her a raisin cinnamon bagel already smeared with cream cheese, she sighed. He knew her shockingly well for such a short period of time.

Deacon studied her face. "You said no donuts," he pointed out.

She smiled. "I'm not sighing unhappily," she said. "This is perfect." She took a big bite to prove her point.

Deacon's expression changed, from worry to contemplative in a breath. She watched the heat filling his golden eyes, the way his nostrils flared. She knew he wasn't focused on the smell of the bagel. She swallowed, but she couldn't look away. And when he leaned in, she forgot about the bagel in her hand.

"I thought you were going to keep your hands to yourself," she said, her voice husky.

"That was last night. This is today." His lips lifted as he stopped close enough to kiss her without actually touching her. "And I am keeping my hands to myself."

"Oh?"

"I'm not touching you, am I?"

"Yet."

"Is that an invitation?"

She gulped again. Because she was a little afraid it had been.

He brushed his lips against hers in a teasing, soft caress that didn't last nearly long enough for her. She kept still, waiting to see what he would do, but part of her wanted to lean in and kiss him like there was no tomorrow.

"Technically," he said, "I bought you a meal. And we're alone. We could…if you wanted to…think of this as a date."

"Not sure discussing demonology counts as romantic."

But her pulse was pounding in anticipation and it was very tempting to agree that this could count as a date. It wasn't out of the house. But it also wasn't fighting off bad guys. They were alone. Except for the dogs. And for a little while anyway, no one was expecting either of them anywhere.

"I could talk about how delicious you smell," he murmured. "Would that help?"

She gasped when he started nibbling the skin along her throat, down to her shoulder. He nudged her t-shirt out of the way so he could kiss more of her skin.

"I could talk about the fantasies that kept me awake most of the night. Would that help?"

"No," she groaned and dug her fingers into his hair to keep him close.

"Knowing you were so close, so warm and soft," he murmured, moving his mouth to the other side of her throat. "Imagining you in my arms, naked and gasping my name."

She did exactly that when he scrapped his teeth over her collarbone.

"Imagining how I'd touch you," he murmured, and cupped her breast in the heat of his palm. "Imagining how I'd taste you."

A desperate sound escaped her, and she wasn't even sure what it meant. She was afraid it meant "do that" instead of "maybe we should stop now."

The sound of her cellphone suddenly ringing shocked her back to her surroundings. If that was her mother calling, she was going to be mortified.

She fumbled for her phone on the coffee table. Realizing as she did that outside of cupping her breast, Deacon hadn't been touching her with any other part of him but his mouth. All that erotic seduction with just his mouth. She very nearly rolled her eyes as lust made her body pulse. What would he do once he got his hands really involved?

She swallowed hard and answered the call before checking the caller id. She blinked in surprise at hearing Aidan's voice.

"Did I wake you?" the demon hunter asked.

"No, no. Just…eating." She pressed her lips together when Deacon chuckled, and she was very glad Aidan wasn't there to see her heated blush. "What's up?"

"I confirmed a suspicion last night in my final fight," Aidan said.

"How many did you have?" Cary sat up straighter.

"Three after I left you. Nothing too serious. They were all low-level demons, and the people who'd called them weren't even completely sure why they had. But I was able to get some reluctant answers from one of the demons."

"Greenson's demon god is trying to get into this world by using Greenson as a host body?" Cary guessed.

"Been doing some reading, huh?" Aidan said with a touch of humor in her tone. "Your serial killer has enough will he can probably survive the process long enough for this demon to cause some serious damage to this realm."

"We might have figured out what the demon intends even if Greenson doesn't survive the process," Cary said. She explained about Beatrix and her brother and wasn't surprised by the silence on the phone following her explanation.

"That complicates things," Aidan finally said.

"Uh huh. Although, none of this explains why that demon knew who I was."

"You're going to need help with this," Aidan said.

"Yes. Please and thank you."

Aidan chuckled. "Meet me at the diner tonight."

She disconnected before Cary could ask or say more. Help from Aidan seemed like a very good idea just then, but Cary did not want to go back to that diner. The wizard who'd tried to kill her had found her there. He could find her there again. She couldn't afford to get killed by a vengeful wizard yet.

She had to save the world first.

2 8

"We need to go talk to the twins," Cary said into the silence following Aidan's call. "And then meet Aidan tonight." She looked up at Deacon and realized… "Wait, it's a weekday. Why aren't you working?"

"Caitlin still won't let me anywhere near the business right now," he admitted with a shrug.

His younger sister, who ran the Portland wing of their animal shelters with him, had made him leave last month when he'd almost shifted in front of some of their employees, answering the challenge of a mundane tiger his shelter was trying to relocate to a suitable sanctuary. His control on his leopard was so tenuous at the moment, working around other predators was out of the question.

That reminded her that they still had to discuss the fact that he could break the mate bond if he wanted to. That she knew it was possible, and maybe, just maybe, they should consider that option.

Six weeks after meeting, they still couldn't cobble together enough time for a simple date. And despite her temptation earlier, bagels on her couch surrounded by books on demonology really didn't count.

She wasn't sure guilt was the right word for what she was feeling.

175

Maybe frustration. And worry. But she wasn't sure anymore if she was worried about their relationship continuing, or ending.

"You're thinking things I don't want you to, aren't you?" he asked, his golden eyes narrowed.

"Probably," she said. "Also, stop doing that mind reading thing."

But there was no heat in her scolding. She shook off the personal worries. Like the vengeful wizard, her personal life would have to continue waiting until she saved the world from another demon, a serial killer, and potentially the necromancer who enabled them.

"Let's go talk to Beatrix," she said and stood. "I'm a little worried leaving them alone this long anyway. We should bring them some food or something."

"I'll drive," Deacon said. "We can pick up some stuff on the way."

On the drive, Cary debated how to broach the subject of demon gods and Beatrix's ability to animate Greenson's corpse. Whether she even wanted to tell them about that possibility. If Beatrix didn't know, she wouldn't try to do it.

Then again, she could be tricked into it. Or bribed. The twins needed money, and they didn't have a lot of scruples about how they got it. With enough power and money on offer, Beatrix might be willing to help the demon without even realizing what she was doing.

After talking through the options out loud to Deacon, she finally decided on just telling them the truth. If they helped a demon to hurt other people, Cary would intervene and stop them. If they didn't want anything to do with letting a real life scary ass demon loose into their world, then all the better and Cary would keep them safe so they didn't have to.

Still, her nerves jumped as she pushed into their cabin with a couple bags full of food. Uncertainty seemed to be her best friend these days.

"Thanks," Justin said, taking the bags from her. "We were starting to run low." He looked inside one of the sacks.

"Did you stop Greenson? Can we go home now?" Beatrix asked.

"No," Cary answered both questions with that single word.

Beatrix's shoulders hunched.

"I thought you liked it here," Deacon commented in a neutral tone.

She shrugged without looking at him. "It's great for a few days. It's claustrophobic when we can't go anywhere else."

"Yeah, sorry," Cary said, feeling genuinely bad. She still didn't feel bad enough to bring them into her home, but she could sympathize with them feeling stuck out here and isolated. They probably had enough isolation in their lives already. "We've discovered a few things I think you should know. And we need to talk over what all this means for your safety."

Over a lunch of sandwiches and chips, Cary told them about the demon Greenson summoned, and that he could call it with his own blood. She left out the part about the demon knowing her name. She wanted to judge the level of surprise from the twins. If they'd given her away to Greenson or the demon, she figured she'd be able to see it in their expressions, in the way they reacted to her news.

Justin's eyes widened throughout the telling until he was up and pacing the cabin. "I knew he was evil," he said without looking at anyone. "I knew he was dangerous. I didn't actually believe he was calling a god. I thought it was all in his head to feed his taste for death and…" He paused and looked at Cary with a faintly guilty expression. "And murder," he admitted. "All of it, I thought it was all really just him."

"We didn't know there was a demon involved," Beatrix said quietly. She was sitting on her sleeping bag, her knees up to her chest and her arms wrapped around them. She rocked a little as she spoke, her gaze on the wooden floor. "I thought Greenson was the ultimate evil in all this."

Cary watched them closely. She'd ask Deacon later if he picked up any deception with his super sense of smell, but with her ordinary human sense and instincts, she believed the twins were telling the truth. They hadn't really ever believed the "god" story. They'd just thought Greenson was a murderer and used the story as part of his sick obsession with killing.

"There's more," Cary said. She went on to tell them what she'd just learned that morning about how a high-level demon might gain access to this realm without sacrificing its powers. "The host dies pretty quickly most of the time," she finished. "Humans just can't take that much power."

Beatrix was staring at Cary now, her eyes wide. Cary held her gaze for a quiet moment as the information sank in, before finally asking, "Could you animate a demon possessed corpse? Could you keep the body moving and function with your magic?"

Beatrix trembled and hugged her knees tighter. "I don't know for sure," she said, her voice small. "But I'm afraid I could."

For the first time, Cary really saw how young the woman was, how vulnerable. It triggered her protective instincts in a way she hadn't been feeling before. Suddenly, protecting Beatrix didn't seem so complicated.

"Would it trap Greenson's soul in his body, even though the demon had control of it?" Cary asked quietly.

Beatrix nodded, the movement jerky and fast. She pressed her lips together and looked up at Justin.

He knelt beside her and pulled her into a hug, then met Cary's eyes. "What do we do?" he asked.

"We keep Beatrix away from Greenson," Cary said. "And maybe don't raise his corpse once he's dead, even if you're sure the demon isn't inside him anymore."

"The amulet I gave him," Justin said, "it's pretty specific to raising ghouls even if it is corrupting them. But... That's part of Beatrix's power. What if the demon uses it to animate Greenson's corpse? What if it sends Greenson to kill Beatrix and force me to make an amulet with her full powers in it?"

Cary had only just considered that possibility on the drive here. "Again, we keep you both away from Greenson until he's stopped. Or properly dead. The demon won't be able to stay here with its full powers if it doesn't have a human host."

"But it knows about us now," Beatrix said. "Greenson will have told it. It can just look for new hosts, more people, until it gets to us..." A tear dropped down her cheek when she said, "How can we know it will leave us alone? Ever."

Justin held her closer, but he looked just as worried.

Cary didn't have answers for them. She didn't know if this particular demon would keep coming for them or not. If it would even be able to. She had a feeling the only way to find out would be to ask the demon itself.

Which was her least favorite plan of the day.

AIDAN WAS SITTING AT THE BACK BOOTH JUST AS SHE'D BEEN THE LAST time Cary had met her.

"Déjà vu," Cary said as she sat down. "If I believed in the Matrix, this would be a little scary right about now."

Aidan grinned. "I love that movie. Sorry for the repeat location." She shrugged. "They have good food."

"So, you do eat?" Cary asked.

"When I get time." She glanced at Deacon. "Nice to see you again."

Deacon nodded in greeting, but kept silent.

The waitress arrived then, as if called, even though no one had looked her direction. Aidan ordered food, which Cary assumed meant she wasn't planning on fighting demons tonight. That was either good for them, as there were not going to be any scary demon summonings in Portland, or bad because she wasn't actually going to help them fight off this demon of Greenson's.

Cary ordered a burger and fries, hoping for the first option.

When the waitress left, Aidan said, "The demon I got to talk last night gave me some really interesting information."

"That's the kind of interesting that's going to complicate my life, isn't it?" Cary said.

"You're a very smart woman. Seems the demon being summoned by Greenson is actually what most demons would consider a god. Not just super powerful and scary. Not just a higher-level demon. One of the highest level. One from a realm hard for the average demon to even access. In fact, the hunters thought this particular demon was just a myth, told to scare other demons. The god is called Ho'Lud, but the hunters usually referred to it as just Lud since invoking a demon's full name can be…potentially dangerous."

"So, all this talk of demon gods wasn't just hyperbole?" Cary's gut tightened. "That's definitely not a good kind of interesting."

"I'm not sure how your serial killer was able to call this entity," Aidan said. "Demons like this don't come on command. That's why almost everyone considers Lud a myth. And fortunately for us, demon gods don't bother trying to get into this realm. They don't need to."

"Why would any demon need to?" Cary asked, genuinely curious.

Aidan frowned a little. "I've never really asked individual demons why they want out of their own realms. Mostly, I'm too busy sending them back. But, the consensus among hunters and demonology experts is that most demons want into this realm either to wreak havoc, because it feeds them, or to escape…something. Many are evil and like pain and suffering. They want to inflict that here. Those are the ones we go after."

"You don't go after all of them?" Cary asked, a little amazed by that news.

Aidan shrugged. "Of those that get free, the ones that aren't evil and just looking to escape, we don't waste our energy on them."

"Holland was evil, why was he still free?" Deacon asked.

"There are demons who aren't evil?" Cary asked at the same time. Then, "Wait, answer his question first."

"Holland killed two hunters before finally calling a meeting and making a deal." Aidan's gaze turned inward a moment in thought. "He was one of the ones escaping something. He wasn't exactly…not evil. But he wasn't here for pain and power. He was here to get away from something, and he was willing to keep to himself and just become obscenely wealthy in exchange for…sanctuary I guess you'd call it."

"He tried to take over a Naga city," Cary said. "He raised an army of supernatural beings to do it. And he killed. That's not really just hanging out not getting into trouble."

"And if the hunters had known what he was doing," Aidan said, "one of us would have shown up to help stop him."

"Why didn't the hunters know?" Cary asked. "I got his phone number from a hunter."

"That's the other part of what my demon last night revealed. The hunters were all very busy during that period of time. Lot of summonings and near escapes. A lot more than is usual. I had to fight off a near escape almost every night for a couple of months. Sometimes more than one. Like last night, some of the people didn't even remember why they'd called a demon and were surprised they had. It was a very strange period of time."

"Has it stopped since the Nagas took Holland?" Deacon asked.

"Slowed. Not stopped. And it seems like the pace is kicking up again."

"Not tonight?" Cary asked, nodding vaguely toward the kitchen. "You ordered food."

"I won't know till I'm called. That's the way it's been. So, despite my preferences, I need to eat while I can. If I have to throw up, I throw up." She shrugged.

"Something big is happening," Cary guessed. "Something like...a real, not exaggerated, demon god trying to get into this realm. Not just a powerful ass demon, but an actual god type thing that is pushing other demons to distract anyone who might stop it."

Aidan pointed a finger at Cary then tapped her own nose. "Got it in one. According to the talkative demon last night, that's what has been causing all the havoc over the last few months."

"Well hell." Cary glanced at Deacon.

"That would be a world ending disaster," he said.

"So...literally hell," she said. Then winced.

Oh boy.

2 9

$\mathcal{C}$ary climbed into Deacon's SUV after dinner without the first clue what to do now.

There was a demon god trying to enter this realm. She had charges to protect so they couldn't be used to help the demon god stay in this realm. A serial killer on the loose who had to feed said demon god soon since he hadn't last night. The little complication of said demon god actually knowing who *she* was. And…

Well, that seemed like it should be more than enough all on its own. But then there was the serial killer's amulet that controlled poor ghouls, and the wizard running around wanting her dead, and the fact that she couldn't call Jaxer to ask for help.

She rubbed her hands over her face. And she'd thought facing down an army of supernatural bad guys had been challenging.

"What do you want to do now?" Deacon asked the million dollar question.

"I want to stop Greenson. If we stop him, we stop the demon getting here. Since the whole process of a demon this powerful being able to occupy a human body is time consuming, if we stop Greenson now, we stop the demon." She winced. "At least for a while. But now that the hunters know what's going on and why they're being distracted

182

with lower level demons, they can get onto the job of stopping the big demon. Beatrix and Justin will be safe. The ghouls will be safe. And my job will be done."

"Good plan," Deacon said. "How do we stop Greenson?"

"Yeah, there's the part I haven't worked out yet." She huffed out a laugh that had no humor to it. "I really should have been working on tactics more over the last six years. Seems like I need that kind of skill a lot more than I have in the past. Jaxer always took care of that, and I need to ask him what to do, and I can't anymore. That sucks a lot."

"Jaxer didn't do a good job of training you then," Deacon said with a growl in his tone. "He claimed he'd trained you well enough to survive this year."

"Did he? When did he tell you that?"

"Last month. When he told me about the seventh year."

"Did he say how many times he'd done this before?"

"He said he'd only ever lost one Protector during their seventh year and that was the Protector's doing, not a lack of training."

"Then why do you sound so angry, and why are your eyes glowing?" she asked.

She leaned away from him not because she was scared but to get a better look at him. His face was held in very hard lines, his jaw so tight he could probably break rocks. He gripped the steering wheel tight enough that his knuckles were white. And the muscles in his arms were bulging against his long-sleeved t-shirt.

"You look like you're about to shift," she added. "Maybe you shouldn't be driving."

"You're upset," he said between clenched teeth. "It's harder to keep my leopard in check when you're hurting." He pressed his lips together and looked away from her before saying, "And when you turn to Jaxer for help instead of me."

She sighed. "He's my mentor. I've always turned to him for work related help. That doesn't change just because we met."

"Logically, I understand that," Deacon said. "My leopard doesn't and he's more in charge than usual."

"Tell him to calm down, then," she said. "Because I can't go to

Jaxer for help anyway. And frankly, while I do like having the backup, I'd send you away now too if I could."

He faced her, his frown fierce. "Why?"

"Because there's a demon god with my name in his mouth about to break into this world. I want you somewhere far away and safe. I don't want even the risk of you getting killed just because you feel the need to help me." She swallowed hard. "This isn't right, you risking your life because of my job."

"It's not about right," he said, his voice finally softening. "It's about want. I want to be here with you. I want to help you. And you couldn't send me away now, with you still in danger, even if you wanted to. I'd follow and guard your back no matter what. So stop worrying about me."

"Right. Just like you'll stop worrying about me?" she asked, though her guilt over sucking him into her life lessened.

"Fine. Worry. But I'm still going to be beside you."

She pulled in a deep breath, held it for a beat, then released it on a loud sigh. "Fair enough. Just…don't get killed okay?"

"You either." He reached across and took her hand in his hands, squeezing gently.

She squeezed back. "Thanks for having my back."

"You're welcome. Where to now?"

She closed her eyes tightly, forcing down her fear, before she answered, "The cemetery."

THE DARKNESS AND GLOOM WERE NO LESS OPPRESSIVE TONIGHT THAN they'd been last night. But Cary noticed a change the instant they hit the dirt inside the grounds. She could see ever-so-slightly better. Her night vision hadn't magically improved overnight. Which meant someone nearby needed her protection.

While she didn't particularly like that there was a person in danger, she was embarrassingly relieved to know her own magic would work now.

"You're not as nervous tonight," Deacon whispered against her ear.

"I can sort of see," she said in answer.

The fact that he didn't have to ask what that meant made her smile.

They reached the place they'd watched Greenson call the demon last night but no one was there. Cary frowned, searching the area. Her senses were hopping and that tingle along her spine, her Protector instinct nudging her toward danger, was at full force now. But despite those signals, she couldn't spot the trouble.

"You smell them?" she whispered.

Deacon shook his head, then stilled. Cary had felt the faint breeze shift, blowing into their faces, almost at the same instant. Deacon turned slowly, his face lifted. Then pointed toward another part of the grounds.

As soon as Cary was facing the same direction, her every instinct hit high alert. Without waiting to see if he followed, she took off at a looping run. She wasn't a runner by choice and she didn't move fast or gracefully over uneven ground normally, but someone needed her fast, which gave her the speed and agility she needed.

She reached Greenson just as he raised that same wicked-looking knife from the night before. She had a half second to spot the person on the ground beneath him and then she crossed his circle and threw herself on top of the prone victim. The sounds of screams from more than one voice echoed in the otherwise quiet night.

Cary glanced down at the person she'd just saved, ignoring the feel of the knife bouncing harmlessly off her back as she chalked up another bruise. The woman was probably in her forties or fifties, based on the laugh lines around her dark brown eyes and the strands of grey in her black hair. She looked soft and friendly, a bit like someone's mother.

She also looked stoned out of her mind. Whatever Greenson had given her left the poor woman completely oblivious to what was happening around her. With a wide smile, the woman reached up and tugged at Cary's ponytail where it hung over her shoulder.

"Hi," the woman said. "You have soft hair."

Cary grinned back. "Thanks. I like your hair, too." She looked over her shoulder to see a black leopard sitting on top of Greenson with Greenson's throat in his mouth. There was no blood and Greenson's eyes were open and alert so apparently Deacon hadn't killed him. Yet. But by the vibrating muscles running along the big cat's legs and body, Cary had a feeling it would only take a wrong breath for Deacon to rip Greenson's throat out.

She eased away from the woman still lying flat in the grass. The woman giggled and batted at something imaginary in the sky above her. Cary remained between the woman and Greenson and hunted the grounds for the knife he'd had. He still gripped it in one hand, which nearly made Cary's heart stop. That knife would make quick work of Deacon if Greenson saw an opening.

She scrambled to her feet and stomped down on Greenson's wrist, to keep him from using the knife. "Fancy seeing you here again," she said. "You'll want to loosen your grip and drop this knife or I'm going to press down hard enough to crush your bones. Or maybe I'll just tell my friend here to go ahead and rip your throat out."

Greenson turned his ever-so-slightly red eyes toward her. He didn't look worried about having his throat torn out. Cary narrowed her eyes. To Deacon she said, "Loosen your hold enough to let him speak, please."

The leopard widened his jaws fractionally.

Greenson smiled. "Kill me, and he comes."

"But he can't inhabit a dead body," Cary pointed out.

Greenson's smile dimmed a little, and Cary realized she'd surprised him with that comment.

"You don't know what you're doing, do you?" she asked. "He didn't tell you how this all ends?"

"Death and blood and delicious pain," Greenson said. "All the pain and blood I can drink."

"Ew," Cary said.

She stepped down harder on his wrist until he grunted and his hand opened. She very carefully picked up the knife and looked at it. She wasn't entirely sure what to do with it but leaving it lying around for someone to pick up seemed a bad idea. It was probably tied into all this mess with all the blood it had spilled. She'd have to take it to Angie and see how best to dispose of it. Carefully, she put it into her jacket pocket and pressed the pocket edges together, sealing the magic so the knife wouldn't fall out but also wouldn't actually slice through the battered leather and cut her.

Marianne had made her one hell of a handy jacket.

When she was sure the knife was no longer a danger, she glanced back at the woman who was still swatting at the air. "What the hell did you give her?"

"She'll only feel the pain when it happens," Greenson said. "It's better this way."

"Oh my god, I'm going to have the leopard rip your throat out just for being so gross," she said with a snarl. When she heard a choking noise, she faced them again and raised her hand. "Wait! Don't kill him yet. We need more information."

Deacon's jaws eased, but blood dripped down Greenson's throat now. Cary frowned at that.

And the fact that they were still inside his demon summoning circle.

And even though they'd broken the barrier getting in here, it was entirely possible the demon could still show up if blood hit the ground.

"Fuck," she muttered and hurriedly put her hands under the blood before it could drop. "Gross." She wasn't particularly keen on someone else's blood dripping into her hands. To Deacon, she said, "We need him beyond the circle. I don't know if this will call the demon or not, but it comes for blood."

Greenson giggled. "He'll kill you. He'll eat you. He'll leave bloody bones for the ghouls."

"You need to shut up now," Cary said. "Really, just don't say anything until I ask, okay. You're icking me out."

"He knows you," Greenson continued as if she hadn't spoken. "He *wants* you."

"I'll need to hear more about that in just a sec," she said. She looked around for some of Deacon's torn clothes and for once was glad he'd shredded everything to shift. Scraps of jean material and cotton t-shirt were close enough for her to reach without moving too far. She snatched up what she could, carefully so she wouldn't drip blood, then had to hurry to press her impromptu bandage to Greenson's throat before more blood dripped.

"We really need him out of here," she said. The blood seemed to be falling fast for the small nicks Deacon's teeth had left, soaking into the clothe instantly.

She'd seen the wounds. Deacon hadn't cut that deep. But blood was starting to flow as if Greenson's artery had been pierced.

She cursed and pushed at him to get him outside the circle before the flow overwhelmed her attempt at staunching it. "What the hell?"

Deacon took hold of Greenson's belt and pulled hard with his shifter strength while Cary lifted Greenson's head and carried the upper half of him out of the circle.

Greenson laughed, choked on blood, then chuckled again. "Too late," he murmured.

The air started to hum with energy, running along her skin like electricity, sending waves of shock through her and stealing her breath. She dropped Greenson outside the circle and spun back, intent on getting the drugged woman out.

Deacon hissed at her, but she ignored him as she hurriedly gathered the woman in her arms and lifted. She was small but not insubstantial. Cary grunted as the woman flopped over her arms, dead weight that didn't help with the carrying part of this. The ground rumbled beneath her feet, sending her stumbling sideways before she could right herself. Greenson giggled again, his voice surprisingly loud against the grinding sound of earth moving. Cary stumbled a few more steps even as she felt a flash of heat scald her back.

And then like a brick wall she hit the circle's edge and couldn't step out.

She looked wide-eyed at Deacon. The leopard howled and threw himself at the circle barrier, but crashed into it, unable to get through.

A deep, reverberating chuckle sounded behind Cary, so deep and resonant she felt the sound more than heard it. Sweat dripped down her temples, and her heartbeat jumped to triple time. Slowly, still holding her charge in her arms, she turned.

"At last," the demon god said. "I've been waiting for you."

3 0

ary trembled so hard she almost couldn't stand. The woman in her arms glanced at the black mass that was the demon, then up at Cary. "He's very dark, isn't he?" she said.

That was such an understatement Cary very nearly laughed. Lud was like looking into the depths of death itself, so black with only those hints of silver and melting lava beneath the skin, a shadow against the shadows.

Its glowing red eyes, with the cat-slit pupils stood out solid inside that darkness.

"Do you think you can stand?" she asked the woman.

"Nope," the woman said without a care in the world.

"Okay." Cary widened her stance and adjusted her hold on the woman so she could manage her weight easier. Behind her, Deacon snarled and howled loud enough to make the hair on her arms stand up.

Lud chuckled. "Your mate is upset. Poor kitty."

"He'll be okay as soon as I get out of here," Cary said.

"What makes you think you will?" Lud asked, its tone genuinely curious rather than smug and demanding.

She shrugged. "Just a hunch."

Holland had known what Protectors were. He'd killed at least one

—or so he'd claimed. But Holland had lived in this world for centuries. According to Aidan, Lud's realm was difficult to access and demon gods didn't really care about this world. There was every chance Lud —even though it was a god—didn't actually know what she was. If it didn't know what she was, it probably wouldn't know how to get around her powers.

She hoped.

It reached toward her and the woman and Cary's breath stopped as she waited to see if it would be able to touch her. Its hand stopped within inches of her face. The woman's eyes grew along with the heat of having the demon so near. She must have finally realized the danger because Cary felt her start to shake.

The demon turned its head to one side as it contemplated them.

From outside the circle, Greenson said, "Kill them, eat them, leave me their bones, please, my master."

Cary winced. Yuck. On many levels that was just...yuck. She didn't dare look away from the demon, but she was pretty sure Deacon wouldn't be able to listen to Greenson without killing him for that.

The demon looked past her toward its servant, then looked at her again with its red hot cat's eyes. "Your bones would be powerful," the demon said. "Shall I give them to him?"

"I'm still using them, so I'd rather you didn't," she said, trying for casual and failing completely. Her voice most definitely trembled.

The demon reached for her face again, and she braced for its burning touch but again its hand stopped a few inches from her face. The scent of sulfur was strong, but not as strong as she'd expected. Not so strong it made her gag. The heat, however, had sweat dripping down her back and chest, under her clothes.

Lud glanced down at the woman in her arms and reached for her. Cary turned the woman slightly, blocking her with her own body even as the woman started babbling a panicky stream of denials. Cary took a brief moment to check the woman's expression. She looked a lot less stoned now, which meant she was way too aware of what was happening.

Would have been easier on her if she didn't know what was going on.

"It'll be okay," Cary said to her. "I've got you. You're safe."

"He'll eat her!" crowed Greenson.

Cary scowled and said, "How are you still talking? Haven't you bled out yet?"

Greenson laughed. "I'm becoming a god. I can't be killed."

"Don't tempt the leopard," she said. And to Deacon, "But don't kill him yet! I don't know what that might do here."

She faced the demon again, as much as she could while still keeping the woman half turned away from it. The woman had wrapped her arms around Cary's neck now, which made holding her a little easier and gave Cary more stability.

Lud was still studying her, seemingly undisturbed by anything happening.

"What are you?" it asked.

"Concerned citizen," she gave her usual answer. "And really I can't let you into my realm. So best if you just head back to your own realm. I'm sure there are demon minions eager to have their god back and all that." She swallowed to wet her dry throat.

And the demon reached for her again. "I can't touch you. But you have my slave's blood on you. You should be mine."

She winced. She'd forgotten the blood on her hands. "I'll be sure to wash up soon, then."

"Our meeting is overdue."

"Oh, I don't know," Cary said. "I could have gone on forever without meeting you."

Another of those deep chuckles that made her teeth hurt. "My son hates and adores you. I see why."

"Your...son?" What the hell?

"He calls himself Holland here. It's time for him to come home."

Cary's head spun and she nearly dropped her charge. If not for the fact the woman was clinging to her now, she might have.

"You're..." She almost couldn't say it aloud. "You're Holland's...father?"

Oh this was so so not good! Her heartbeat raced. Horror welled up so fast, spots danced in her vision.

"He doesn't like you very much," she said while the shock of all this numbed her nerves. She couldn't even feel the woman in her arms anymore. And only willpower and maybe her Protector magic kept her upright.

She'd barely survived Holland. She hadn't been able to stop Holland from killing someone. And this…thing was his father.

The demon's laughter shook through her, rubbing rough against her nerves. "He will be returning home soon."

"Okay," she said. "Wouldn't want to interfere in a family squabble. Don't really like Holland myself. But I can't let you kill any more people to get at him. And I can't let you into this realm."

"Why not?"

"Which why not?" she asked mostly to stall because her brain was spinning so fast she was having trouble concentrating enough to speak.

"Why can't *you* let me kill more people?"

"Oh, that. That's just what I do."

"My son covets you. I understand why."

"Hate me, yes," she said with a slight shrug. "Covet, no I doubt that very much."

"He does, though. He wants you for his own."

"His own what?" she asked before she could stop herself. She really really didn't want to know what Holland might want from her now.

"His slave of course," the demon said. "He wants you to worship him as I am worshipped. I think you will worship me instead."

She almost laughed. A strangled sound that could have been a laugh actual burst out of her. "Uhm. No."

"No to which?" the demon said, his tone echoing hers from a moment ago.

She glared at that, getting the distinct impression she was being mocked. "No to slavery and worshipping demons just in general," she said. "Now, if you'll just go back to where you came from, I'll be on my way."

The demon lunged toward her suddenly and without warning. Cary screeched through her teeth as much from surprise as fear. It was like having a cockroach fly at her face, the suddenness of it as shocking as the ick factor.

The demon hit her Protector shield and slammed to a stop like it had hit a steel wall, but the reverberation from his attack knocked her backward into the solid barrier of the protective circle. The circle's power stung her nerves like an electrical burn. She hissed and jumped awkwardly away from it but was afraid she had another injury to heal. Damn.

The demon snarled, its first signs of frustration. "What are you?"

"Ready to leave. Not going to help you. Definitely not going to worship you. Take your pick." She hefted the woman into a better position and the woman buried her face in Cary's shoulder as the demon lunged at them again. This time she was ready for the attack and only forced back two steps instead of all the way into the circle's edge.

She narrowed her eyes at the demon. "Go away," she said. "Now."

Its head jerked upward. "You are not one of these…hunters."

It said more than asked that, so she chose not to respond. Let it think whatever it wanted.

It lunged again. She stood her ground. It snarled when it still couldn't reach her, and she snarled back.

"Go away," she repeated, lowering her voice to a deeper register. "Go back to where you came from. Now."

"You heard her," said a newcomer from outside the circle. "Time to leave."

Cary recognized Aidan's voice but didn't turn to face her.

The demon looked past Cary. "You are a hunter. You have been fending off my attacks."

"Among other things," Aidan said.

Lud looked at Cary again. And smiled.

She blinked and instead of the demon, a stunningly gorgeous human man stood in front of her.

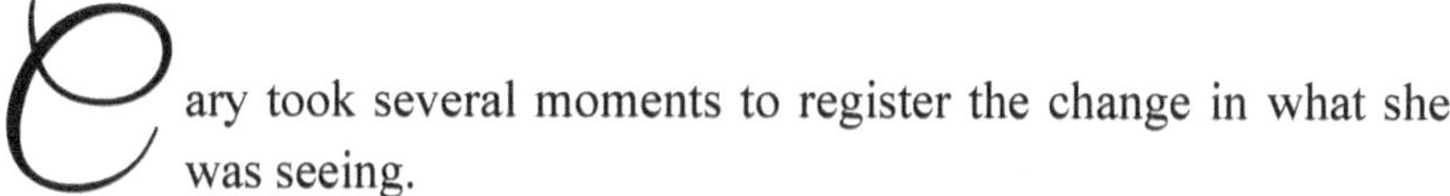

ary took several moments to register the change in what she was seeing.

The man that was the demon was so overwhelmingly handsome it was just ridiculous. Broad and muscled, black hair, blue eyes, a face that reminded Cary of the pictures of Greek gods.

Well, that made sense seeing as how this thing was a god.

He was dressed in a black suit that fit perfectly, a black shirt, and a blood red tie. The outfit might have seemed clichéd but for the fact that the demon wore it so damned well.

The man smiled at her, his blue eyes heavy-lidded and sparking with seduction. The woman in Cary's arms gasped and leaned away from Cary toward Lud. Cary tightened her hold, scowling down at her.

"She's so perfect," the woman said on a sigh.

"He's so deadly," Cary muttered, pointing out the obvious.

Though from the woman's comment, Cary realized the man she was seeing wasn't what the woman in her arms was seeing. The demon had obviously taken the form of whatever an individual viewer found sexually attractive, which meant all of them were seeing something different just then.

Was this affecting Deacon? Was he seeing a seductive, perfect woman? She didn't dare look over her shoulder to check on him, but the idea bothered her a lot.

A faint scent of musk and something like extra fine cologne wafted toward her, distracting her from her faintly jealous thoughts. The scent circled her in masculine yumminess that made her blink in surprise. The smell was almost as delicious as Deacon's natural scent, and gave her a very similar tingling through her body that urged her to lean in close and breathe in deeper.

"She'd never hurt me," the woman said and tried to struggle out of Cary's hold, lunging toward the demon with surprising strength.

"Whoa whoa whoa. Stop that." Cary held the woman tighter and was grateful her magic gave her the strength to resist the woman's frantic bid to get away.

She looked up at the demon again. His smile deepened, and Cary felt that look this time, felt the eroticism of it sneaking under her skin and straight to her core. She gasped. She'd learned how to deal with preternaturally handsome men a long time ago, thanks to Jaxer. And until Deacon, she'd developed a healthy distrust of men that perfect looking. Several of them had tried to kill her in the past, so it had been an important lesson to learn. She hadn't even trusted her attraction to Deacon because he was so unbelievably gorgeous.

But this was...different. Almost like her response wasn't entirely within her control. Not like the way she felt swept away by her feelings for Deacon. This was truly intrusive and manipulative. Like her body was lusting for something her mind rejected outright.

The feeling was so weirdly wrong, she wasn't sure what to make of it. Her body was growing hungry for the man in front of her even as her mind winced and reeled away from him.

"This affecting you?" she asked Aidan without looking back at her.

"Bit," Aidan said, matter-of-factly.

"Damn," Cary muttered. The woman in her arms struggled to get away from her again, stronger this time, and Cary had to concentrate on keeping her close. Again, she wondered if this was affecting Deacon, but in his leopard form, he couldn't exactly tell her. Was he seeing a woman or was he seeing the demon in male form trying to seduce Cary?

Lud laughed, the sound now like a caress over her spine. Her body tightened and she took a single step toward him before she caught herself. The shock of that had her eyes widening. Her Protector powers should be insulating her from this game. Yet her body was still not entirely under her control just then.

She shook her shoulders trying to dislodge the feeling. "Okay, just stop that now," she said. "I'm spoken for. And besides, you're not my type."

"I'm everyone's type," the man-demon said. His voice was deep and sexy now. Not the same as when it was in demon form.

Her thighs clenched. "Stop that," she said more firmly. "Enough with the weird sex bit. I'm not interested. And I'm not letting you seduce this poor woman out of my protection. And you need to leave. Now."

Behind her, Deacon roared, sounding like a wounded animal. She still didn't dare turn to face him. But his roar was definitely more enraged than lusty. Which meant the damned demon was torturing Deacon in a very different way than he was torturing Cary. Instead of showing Deacon a sexy woman and inciting lust in him, the demon was letting Deacon see Cary lusting after a different man. Just to piss Deacon off and make him feel powerless.

That was just rude. Especially since she wasn't really mentally lusting after the demon's male form anyway.

Her anger on Deacon's behalf lessened the heat of lust crawling over her skin, putting distance between the demon's attempts at seduction and her actual physical reaction.

She met the demon's deep blue-eyed gaze. "Enough," she said more firmly this time. "You're pissing off my boyfriend. I can't have that. You're done here."

"She's right," Aidan said. "You're done here."

Cary could almost feel a layer of strength being added to her own words from Aidan. It was another odd sensation but a much more welcome one than the demon's attempt at physical seduction. So welcomed, she embraced it.

"Go," she said. "Enough. You have to leave. Now."

Aidan said almost the same words at the same time. And Cary felt the power in their combined words in a way that was both foreign and yet seemed wholly part of her. Like her words alone carried a kind of magic.

She heard Aidan murmur, "Willpower." And realized she was using the demon hunter trick. Cary wasn't trained in it, and doubted her willpower alone was enough to fend off a demon—she could barely resist a donut nonetheless a demon—but she was in full Protector mode. And Protector magic gave her what she needed.

Right then, she needed the will to send a demon god back to its own hell.

She pulled in that knowledge, wrapped herself up in it, fitting the willpower around her like another shield. And when Aidan repeated the words, "Go, now," Cary spoke simultaneously, same words, same strength and power in them.

The man snarled at them, his blue eyes turning back to the demon's red-hot cat's eyes again. The seductive façade ripped away to reveal Lud in its natural form.

It turned the full force of its gaze on Cary. "Your will alone cannot command me, woman," it said.

"Then why are you leaving?" she asked. And as soon as she said it, she knew it was true. She willed it, with all the strength she could put into that truth, pulling on whatever the Protector magics would give her.

"Another day, Cary Redmond," the demon said, chuckling now. "It's obvious why he wants you. I will make you mine."

In a flash of smoke and light that Cary cynically thought a bit over-done, the demon vanished. The smell of rotting eggs mixed with burnt grease hung in the air in the wake of the vanishing act.

"Ew," she said, narrowing her nostrils in an attempt to not breathe in the stench too deeply. Her stomach did roll and bile threatened. Now she got why Aidan didn't eat before a fight. Bleh.

She turned to face the circle barrier and this time she was able to step over the line as if it was no more than chalk in grass. She blinked a few times to get the world back into focus. Deacon nudged her leg, still in leopard form, his lips lifted in a teeth-revealing snarl she wasn't sure he could control.

"I'm okay," she assured him. "You?"

He chuffed, a noise she took to mean he was fine. At least, she hoped so. He didn't seem to be injured anywhere except for a few singed spots in his fur on one side. He must have thrown himself at the barrier enough to get hurt. Damn it.

She gently set the woman in her arms on her feet. The woman blinked at her, glanced at Deacon, then very gently collapsed into a heap on the grass. Cary sighed. Looked like she'd be carrying her again.

Cary faced Aidan and only then realized that Greenson was nowhere to be seen. She groaned and closed her eyes. "He got away."

"The demon?" Aidan asked.

"The serial killer who called the demon," Cary said, opening her eyes. "He wasn't here when you arrived?"

"Just your leopard throwing himself against the circle," Aidan said, almost apologetically. "Sorry I was late. Had another demon to send back first. This one fought a little harder than the last few."

"Guess our god there wanted more time with me." She shivered at that thought. "Lud is Oliver Holland's father. Don't know if you heard that part."

"Missed it. But that's…interesting news," Aidan said and asked at the same time.

"Yeah. Right. Interesting. Good word for it. Apparently, he's trying to get Holland back for whatever reason—I really don't want to know."

"That probably wouldn't be good for any realm," Aidan said.

"Not that I'm keen on helping either one of them," Cary said, "but why bad for this realm? Wouldn't we kill two birds so to speak? Get them both out of this realm to have their family fight somewhere less dangerous for humans?"

"Anything Lud wants badly enough to go to the trouble of getting into this realm won't be good for anyone anywhere anytime."

Cary sighed. Yeah, she was afraid it wouldn't be as easy as just handing Holland over to his dad to end this.

She narrowed her eyes. "What were you seeing?" she asked Aidan. "When the demon was trying that seduction trick?"

Aidan sighed and settled her hands on her hips, her gaze turned inward. "Someone I never thought I'd see again actually. Someone I haven't seen in fifty years."

"Fifty years?" Cary asked.

Aidan smiled a little, her gaze still distant. "The one who got away, you might say."

"A romantic someone. From *fifty* years ago?"

Aidan shrugged. "I'm a little older than I look."

"Yeah, you are," Cary said. And she thought her job made her look younger. Since becoming a Protector, her aging had slowed, but she was still aging. She might look like she was in her early twenties, but she definitely looked older now than she had six years ago when this all started. Given that Aidan appeared maybe mid-thirties at the oldest, Cary could only imagine how old the hunter really was.

One day, she'd love to learn more about what the hunters did with their willpower from an actual hunter. It was apparently more than just fending off demons.

Though, that reminded her… "Did we really *will* that god away?" Now that it was all over, it seemed entirely too easily done, even though in that moment it hadn't felt easy.

"Sort of," Aidan said. "But it was a bandaide. Mostly, he chose to leave and regroup. He's not at full strength inside our realm. Yet. But he'll be back. And he learned what he needed to know about hunters in that standoff."

"Meaning?"

"He's been testing us with the other demons," Aidan said. "Learning how we work, what the best of us can do. What you and I just did, we didn't bother with the trappings. Just sheer willpower. I have a feeling that was a test to see if we needed the rituals."

"A test? Did we pass or fail?"

"Depends on your point of view," Aidan said. "But I doubt willpower alone will send him away again. Which means demon hunters alone won't be able to stop him."

Well hell.

---

*D*eacon shifted back to human form and dressed at the cemetery, but he remained mostly quiet while they delivered the woman to a nearby hospital—with the cover story that they'd found her outside unconscious and didn't know what was wrong with her but thought it might be drugs. Cary wanted them to check for whatever Greenson had given her.

After leaving the hospital, Deacon didn't speak at all. And the silence between them left Cary very leery. She wanted to question it, wanted an explanation, but she was afraid of the answer she might get.

Her gut was tight with anxiety by the time they walked into her house, though.

When she knelt to greet the dogs, Buck actually reared back from her, his dark doggie eyes widened in a way that looked exactly like human surprise. She reached toward him and he back up a few steps.

"Buck? What's wrong?" A bubble of panic rose into her throat. Buck had never balked away from her touch.

He let loose a low bark, a deep sound that echoed in a way his regular barks didn't. His nostrils flared and he sat back on his haunches, whining slightly.

Cary closed her eyes, as she realized… "The demon god smell is bothering you?"

At the cemetery, while Deacon dressed, she'd washed her hands and gotten all the blood off, thanks to a very large bottle of water Aidan had given her. But her clothes no doubt still stank of her night's adventures.

Buck let loose another deep bark. Pickles nudged him in the shoulder, then sat next to him. A gesture Cary couldn't interpret. Fred bounced back and forth between her and Buck in seeming oblivion to the tension.

"I'm sorry, boy," Cary said to Buck. "I promise that demon isn't in this world." Yet, she thought but didn't want to admit out loud. "I'll go change and get its scent off me, okay?"

Buck actually nodded.

She reached for him again, but he held back and Cary's heart broke a little. This was the very first time, in the entire six years she and Buck had been together, that her dog didn't want her to touch him. And this wasn't the first time she'd encountered demons or fought them off. Something about Lud, though, must really rub Buck the wrong way.

One more reason for her to hate this demon god.

She rose with a sigh and turned toward the hall, only then realizing Deacon was standing in her living room, arms crossed over his chest, watching silently, scowling at the scene.

"What?" she asked, feeling irritable and upset about Buck. Deacon didn't deserve her ire, but so much had happened and she was so off kilter, she just couldn't take anymore.

"What did you see earlier?" Deacon asked, his voice low. "With the demon. You weren't seeing me."

"No. Just some random handsome man. Why?"

"You were attracted to him. I could smell it."

"Not because I wanted to be. It was some weird demon trick. Pretty irritating, actually. And intrusive and invasive, and all the other 'i' words for gross."

"Aidan saw a former love."

"Yeah. So?"

"You didn't see me."

She glared at him. "What did you see?"

"You falling for someone else."

"A demon trick, you knucklehead. He was torturing you. Torturing me. I'm *never* attracted to men that are preternaturally gorgeous anymore." She made a face. "Except you. He tortured Aidan with the sight of a lost love. The woman we saved was probably seeing either a past love or someone she could fall for."

"You weren't seeing *me*," Deacon said, his voice coming out a growl.

"Because I knew you were right there behind me. Why on earth would the demon show me you? I would know it wasn't you and the trick wouldn't work."

"Maybe he didn't show you me because I'm not—" He cut himself off and looked away.

"What?" she asked. "You're not what?"

"Not the man you want," he said, facing her. "You've been resistant to our mate bond from the beginning. Maybe the demon was showing you what you really want."

She sighed. "No on so many levels, Deacon. What he showed me was a generic handsome man. Not even really my type. I was serious about that." She almost hated to admit this, but, "You're not technically my type either."

"Is Jaxer?"

"Don't with the Jaxer thing again. This isn't about him and whatever is between you two. But for the record, Jaxer isn't my type either."

"Who is?"

"I usually go for more ordinary looking men," she admitted. "Nice men that wouldn't necessary make you stop in the street to stare after them."

"I'm not a nice man?"

"Stop," she snapped. "I never said that and don't put words into my mouth. You know I think you're nice. You know very well how attracted I am to you. You know with that damned way you can read my scent that I'm more than just attracted to you. That I care about you a lot more than I should at this stage. But you're pissing me off right now when I have other things to worry about. No, you're not the usual kind of man I date because I don't usually get hit on be men who look like you unless they want something from me. Or want to kill me."

She shook her head. "The fact is, I'm not your type either." She raised a hand when he opened his mouth. "Don't try to deny it. I'm cute but ordinary. You are not ordinary in any possible way." She paused, not sure if this was a bad time for this or not, but since they were down the rabbit hole. "Jaxer told me you could end the mate bond. Enough distance, enough time between us, and you wouldn't have to be bonded to me anymore."

"Is that what you want?"

"I'm asking if it's what you want," she said bluntly. "You're the one who can't even go to work because of the chemistry of this bond. You're the one who is forced into proximity to me because of pheromones. You didn't choose me because you wanted *me*. You got stuck with me."

"You're stuck with me, too."

She lowered her chin. "Only because I want to be. I might be scared out of my mind by what's between us, but if I didn't want you around, you wouldn't be around. But my chaotic life isn't exactly helping things. And this is it, this is my life for the next year."

"We've had this conversation before," he said, still growling, his arms still crossed. "I made my choice clear."

"You failed to mention then that you had an out. You made it seem like this was a done thing for you and it was up to me to figure out how to adjust to it."

"I don't want you to just put up with me because you feel like you have to." He glanced away. More quietly, he said, "We needed time. I don't want to end our bond. That's why I haven't brought it up. You've been so hesitant about our relationship, I was afraid if you knew, you wouldn't give us a chance."

"Stop hiding things from me," she said. "I'll make my decisions like a grownup. And you'll live with them."

He pressed his lips together and nodded. When he faced her again, his expression was carefully blank. "What is your decision? What do you want?"

She shook her head and cross to him. "You really are a knucklehead." She took his face between her hands and forced him to meet her gaze. "I want you, Deacon. I don't *want* to end things between us before they even get started. But I don't want you forced into a relationship with me against your will any more than I liked being forced to feel lust for that demon tonight. It's… It's awful and wrong and if that's what's happening with you, then that's not the basis for a long term relationship."

"I'm not being forced into something I don't want," he said. "Why the hell do you think I've been fighting so hard to keep you? If I truly didn't want this relationship, I would have told you from the beginning about the option to end the bond."

"You're sure? Because there will come a time when we can't just walk away easily."

"That time for me was the night we met," he said quietly. "I would have come looking for you even if you weren't my mate."

She snorted. "I seriously doubt that."

"Then you haven't been paying attention." He brushed his lips softly against hers, gentle and testing. "I don't want anyone else but you, Cary." He buried his fingers in her hair, doing in the remains of her ponytail. The band dropped to the ground and her hair fell around her shoulders. "If you leave me," he said, "you'll be my one-who-got-away, and fifty years from now, if some demon tries to torture me, they'll be showing me an image of you."

She smiled a little. "That was more romantic that it should have been."

He chuckled, but turned serious again. "Can you forgive me for keeping the truth from you, about being able to end the bond?"

"Probably." She leaned into him. "Honestly? It makes me feel better about our relationship."

"Why?"

"It means you are with me because you want to be. You could have broken the bond last month, at any time you could have just put distance between us and toughed out the effects until the bond broke. You didn't."

"I didn't want to. I don't want to."

For the first time since meeting him, the weight of uncertainty about his presence in her life lifted. Maybe there was hope for them after all.

"I have to shower so I'm not freaking Buck out anymore," she said.

He nodded, a soft smile taking the tension and worry from his expression. "Should I go make you some coffee?"

Her heart hammered a little harder as she looked up at him, this man she'd grown so attached to in such a short period of time. She had other things to worry about and there was every possibility she wouldn't survive the next year. A less selfish person would let him go.

Turns out she was a lot more selfish than she realized.

"It's too late for coffee," she said. "Why don't you join me in the shower instead."

He held very still for a very long moment, and Cary started to wonder if he'd refuse.

"We haven't been on that date yet?" he said, his voice hoarse and choked.

"At the rate we're going, an ordinary date seems unlikely to happen any time soon."

He swallowed visibly, his gaze traveling over her face. "I'm trying not to rush you."

"If you're not ready…"

He laughed harshly and jerked her hips close to his. "Does this feel 'not ready'?"

His cock was a hard, solid line against her lower stomach. Yes, he definitely felt ready. Her entire body pulsed in anticipation and heat and need.

"You're upset and worried about your current job," he said, though he didn't sound like he was trying to talk her out of anything anymore.

"I'm sure the shower will help," she said. "I'm sure getting you naked will help even more."

His low groan made her smile. She'd never wanted a man like this before, so much she trembled with the need. And she didn't want to deny the feelings anymore. Not when so much could go wrong. Not when she might get killed before the year was up.

She pressed tighter against him, rising on her toes to put her mouth nearer his. The movement rubbed her body against his and he sucked in a breath as his hands clenched her jeans.

"You feel good," she murmured.

He grunted something she assumed was supposed to be a response.

"You smell delicious," she said, burying her face against his neck and breathing in deeply.

He trembled and she thought she heard material rip.

She returned to his mouth, letting her lips linger tantalizingly close to his. "I don't feel like letting you sleep in the guest room anymore," she said. "But if you want to wait longer, we can."

"I don't," he said, his voice so deep it rumbled. "I don't want to hurt you either." He nodded down and she followed his gaze.

He'd actually ripped the waist of her jeans, the tattered indigo material bunched in his fists. She raised her brows at that. Wow, he was strong.

"I'm not completely in control of myself," he said. "And you're not a shifter."

"You won't hurt me." She held his gaze. "And I heal fast."

"Your clothes aren't going to survive," he said even as the material over her hips loosened and the sound of tearing denim was loud in the otherwise quiet room.

"I need to dump this stuff anyway," she said, thinking Buck wouldn't mind if Deacon tore her clothing to shreds.

"I still feel guilty destroying your clothes," he said, not sounding the least bit guilty.

"You can buy me more."

"I'm running out of excuses," he said.

She grinned. "Good."

She kissed him, hard and sure and oh so happy to give in to all the lust and need that had been building in her for weeks. All pretense of resistance vanished. He wrapped his arms around her and dove hard into the kiss, tasting her like he'd never get enough. The sound of her t-shirt ripping along the spine made her laugh and shiver in delight. She probably should have more concern for her clothes, but Deacon's intensity was too sexy, too irresistible.

His mouth still on hers, he edged her back enough to remove her shirt, then pulled her close again, his shirt and her bra the only thing between their bare skin. Even like this, he felt hot and perfect and solid. She rubbed her breasts against his chest, loving the contrast of her softness and his hardness. His arms flexed around her, flattening her against him and she savored that too. But she wanted more bare skin involved.

She tugged his shirt from his jeans, pushing it up until he had to ease away to toss the shirt aside. She hummed in the back of her throat, finally able to savor his chest without feeling a little guilty for looking her fill. He was all cut muscle and perfect symmetry, dark hair covering his chest and arrowing down his abdomen to the waist of his jeans. She rubbed her hands over his skin, relishing the scorching heat of him. Needing a taste, she leaned forward and flicked her tongue against his nipple, a quick gesture that made him suck in a sharp gasp. She loved hearing him react, so she did it again, then she ran her lips over his collarbone, tasting the salty flavor of him.

Another snap and she realized he'd torn apart her bra strap. She laughed. "That would have been easier to just open," she said.

"I don't have that much dexterity right now," he said.

His voice was so deep and harsh it was like another kind of caress, thrilling her every feminine nerve. She let the remains of her bra drop between them and then his hands were on her breasts. He pinched her nipples, kneaded her fullness, until she was near boneless and panting. He kissed a hot wet line down her throat, nipping at her skin where her shoulder and neck met. She gasped, so on fire with need her skin felt feverish.

She reached between them to rub her palm along his cock, still encased in his jeans, shaping and feeling him. "You feel so good," she murmured. "So hard and hot."

"Stop," he groaned against her shoulder. "Or I won't last long enough to get out of my jeans."

"You'd better get out of your jeans, then," she said without moving her hand away from him.

He removed the rest of his clothing so fast it was a blur. The speed made her laugh. Then he was naked and she could enjoy that lovely view finally without guilt or feeling like she should look away. Taking in Deacon in all his nakedness was a glorious thing and she delighted in the sight until he pulled her back into his arms. She wrapped her fingers around his cock again, without the material between him and her palm, and stroked the hard length of him. He was thick and perfect, so silky and hard. She ran her thumb over the tip of his cock, spreading the moisture there, thrilling in his harsh groan.

He took her hands, gently but firmly and eased both of them behind her back, holding her hands there by her wrists. The position pushed her breasts against his chest, his hair a rough delicious texture against her peaked nipples.

"You can explore all you want soon," he promised. "But this time…"

His mouth traveled from her jaw, down her throat to her shoulder.

"This time?" She gasped.

He kissed lower, until he took her nipple into his mouth, sucking her hard. She jerked, a line of heat spreading from her nipple to her core in such a strong pulse she felt close to coming.

"This time?" She forced the words out her tight throat as he moved to her other nipple.

With a last swipe of his tongue, he stood and pressed her hard against his chest again, her arms still pinned behind her back. "This time," he said, "ladies first."

Her eyes might have rolled back in her head, but she was too busy kissing him to notice. Lust overwhelmed her, so strong she was barely aware of her surroundings. She only realized her jeans were hanging off her, both sides ripped well past her hips when she felt him pushing the material down. She wiggled and with his help got the remaining material down to her ankles.

Only to realize her boots were still in the way.

She laughed, but when she tried to move back to remove her shoes,

Deacon stopped her. He dropped to his knees in front of her and took her foot in one hand. She braced against his shoulders as he removed first one, then the other boot, and pulled the remains of her jeans off. She expected him to stand again, but he stayed on his knees, his gaze traveling over her, taking her in the way she'd enjoyed looking at him.

She'd never felt so damned sexy in her life. When he leaned forward to place a soft kiss on her stomach she gasped, her muscles flexing. He looked up long enough to meet her gaze, and his wicked smile made her knees tremble. Then his mouth was on her again, licking and kissing a trail of heat across her stomach and over her hip. Her underwear didn't fare any better than her jeans or t-shirt, but she was so lost in the feel of his mouth, she barely noticed him ripping away the cotton. The heat of his breath against her curls made her head spin.

When he kissed the place where her thigh met her hip, she almost lost her balance. When he licked a long hot stroke across her feminine folds, her knees did buckle. He held her in place with one arm around her hips. He was so strong, she practically sat on his arm and he didn't even notice her weight. Which was pretty impressive given she wasn't a small woman.

His licked into her, finding the little bud of bundled tension and nerves. He sucked and nibbled and kissed and licked her until she couldn't think beyond the building tightness, the urgent desperation sweeping through her, coiling where his mouth devoured her. Panting, her fingers buried in his thick hair, she held back as long as she could, until the desperate pressure burst through her in a body shaking jolt of release.

She jerked and trembled against him, forcing his mouth away from her because she was so sensitive now, she needed a little space. "Ladies first," she said, her breathing harsh and shaky. "I like it."

He chuckled. "I like it, too."

"I'm glad you're strong because I don't think I could stand on my own now if I wanted to."

"You don't have to." He stood and swept her up into his arms before she could worry about falling down. "Bed or shower?" he asked.

She hummed at the delicious possibilities. "Bed first. Then shower."

"Anything you want. Everything you want."

She kissed his throat as he carried her to bed. "We aren't getting any sleep tonight, are we?"

"Not even a little bit," he agreed. "Do you mind?"

She grinned. "Not even a little bit."

3 4

In her room, Deacon took his time setting her on the bed, kissing her, caressing her, a languid exploration that, at first, delighted her. She'd assumed his control was so tentative that he wouldn't have the patience for more foreplay. And so, she returned the seductive teasing, savoring the taste of his skin and the delicious pressure of his kisses. Enjoying the way his body reacted to her touch, hunting for the spots that made him moan.

But after a while, she realized he was holding back. She could feel the tension in his hands and body, the hard length of his erection against her hip. She was certainly tangled up and ready for more again. He had her body humming with need, her skin trembling with his every caress.

And yet, he seemed almost distant. Like he was detached from the feelings and sensation sweeping her away.

That wasn't good.

They were on their sides, so she leaned back and took his face in her hands, meeting his gaze. His eyes were glowing yellow, and she could see his desire in the way his jaw muscles jumped, the way his nostrils flared. She didn't think he was resisting because he didn't want her.

"Is something wrong?" she asked.

His eyes widened a bit. "No. Why?"

"Well, not to be too pushy, but why aren't you inside me yet?"

He closed his eyes and his jaw tightened. "You have no idea what you do to me."

"I'd have a better idea if you'd stopped holding back," she said.

"That's the problem."

"You're going to have to explain that a little better."

"If I don't hold back," he said through his teeth, "I might hurt you."

He opened his eyes, and the glow was brighter. Under her hands his muscles were so hard it was like touching warm steel.

"We've been through this already," she said. "I heal fast."

"I don't want to lose control and scare you," he said, his voice a low growl. "I want you so much I can feel the edges of my control fraying."

"Then stop trying to control yourself," she said with a huff. "Do I look even remotely scared to you right now?"

"I've been going slow."

"Too slow when neither one of us wants slow. Fuck me. Now."

His groaning growl was fierce as he covered her mouth with his. "You drive me insane," he muttered and kissed her harder.

With a gesture that made her gasp, he flipped her onto her back and pulled her knees up to his hips. He paused long enough for her to catch a breath, and then he was inside her. Finally, finally, finally. The full length of him filling and stretching her. Nothing had every felt so good and so so right.

He didn't even attempt gentle now. His hands on her thighs and butt were rough and bruising, his teeth scraped almost painfully along her throat, and the pace he set pushed her to her limits. She loved every minute of it. She urged him faster and harder, taking every pounding beat as the tension coiled tight in her core again, until she could barely breathe, until she was lost in the rhythm and heat of him. She dug her short nails into his back and met his thrusts, desperate to give as much pleasure as he gave her. Her body exploded in a trembling burst of release that wiped away thoughts. Everything but the sound of him saying her name, his voice harsh and not entirely human anymore, as he found his own finish. She wrapped around him in a full body hug, absorbing his pleasure as her own.

And when he collapsed against her, she smiled at the weight.

"See," she murmured when she could speak. "That was much better, wasn't it?"

He laughed against her throat and hugged her tight, but to her amusement, very gently. "You have bruises now."

He wasn't asking and she wondered how he knew that already. She was still floating on pleasure and could barely feel anything beyond that thrill yet.

"They'll heal before we're done in the shower," she said. "Stop worrying about me."

"We both know that's not going to happen. Not with your job."

She chuckled. "Fair enough. Stop worrying about me in bed. I can take you."

"I've never been so grateful for anything in my entire life."

He lifted up, rolling to one side but keeping her tight against him. "You haven't mentioned birth control," he said quietly.

"I have an IUD," she said, snuggling close to his heat.

"Probably good. I hadn't planned on seducing you tonight since we haven't had that date yet. I wasn't exactly prepared."

"We can double up on birth control going forward," she said, "but there's no reason to worry tonight."

"I wouldn't exactly be worried about it," he said quietly.

Well that was terrifying. "What do you mean?" she asked.

"You're human," he said, shrugging slightly. "Even though you're my mate, we may not be able to even have kids."

"Does that bother you?" she asked.

It hadn't even crossed her mind. Though the thought of the whole family and kids thing did kind of freaked her out. She was a happy auntie.

And her world wasn't exactly safe, so while she loved children, she didn't think she could have them while she was still working as a

Protector. It hadn't occurred to her to even consider the subject in general, nonetheless specifically with Deacon yet.

"Not as much as I would have expected," he answered her question. "And it's too soon to worry about that anyway." He caressed her shoulder. "I'd like to have you all to myself for a while yet."

She smiled a little at that.

"This between us," he said slowly, staring up at her ceiling. "I need you to know… I do want this." He finally looked at her. "I'm grateful to Jaxer, even though he pisses me off and I'm jealous of his relationship with you. Because if it weren't for him, I might not have met you. And I can't imagine my life without you now."

She kissed him because she didn't have the words. Yet. She suspected the words were those three little scary ones, and she wasn't ready to say them aloud yet. But she couldn't imagine her life without Deacon anymore either. A terrifying admission after less than two months.

She only hoped they both survived long enough to see where this thing between them went.

3 5

———————

She hadn't been asleep very long when Deacon woke her with his mouth moving over her body, across her shoulder, down to her breast. She smiled but didn't open her eyes, wanting to prolong the delicious process of waking up to Deacon's attentions. The faint glow behind her lids confirmed it was likely morning, sun coming in past her half open curtains. She was almost sorry about that. Night gave them some insulation from the real world. Soon she'd have to face the knowledge that she had no idea how to defeat a demon god.

But for a little bit longer, she decided not to care.

She buried her fingers in his hair, holding him close, wallowing in the heat of his mouth on her. When her cellphone rang, she groaned.

Deacon kept up his erotic ministrations as she scrambled on the bedside table for the annoying phone.

"Hello," she murmured.

"Cary. Are you okay? Aidan said this demon thing is a real god."

"Angie?" Cary pushed her hair out of her eyes and tried to focus. But Deacon, after pausing for a brief moment, went back to sucking her nipple and it was extremely distracting.

"You're okay, right?" Angie asked.

218

"Yup," she said, her breathing speeding up. "Fine. Just fine. Just… Little busy. Can't talk now."

There was a pointed pause. Then, "Is Deacon there?"

"Yup."

"Really," Angie said, a slightly smug tone wiping away her worry.

Cary wanted to say something smart and snarky, but she was too busy trying not to pant as Deacon's hand moved across her hip to stroke slowly up her inner thigh.

"Are you having sex?" Angie asked.

"No!" Cary bit down on a groan. Not yet anyway, she thought.

"Why not?" Angie asked.

Deacon moved up from her breast to her ear opposite the phone and whispered, "That's a good question."

"Uh, Ang, he heard you," Cary said.

"Wow, good hearing." Another pause, then, "Does he agree with me that you should be otherwise occupied now?"

"Yes," Deacon whispered.

"Yup," Cary squeaked.

"Then I'll let you go," Angie said, with a chuckle. "Call when you're free."

"Yeah, yeah. Will do." Cary disconnected and tossed her phone aside because Deacon was kissing his way down her waist, across her stomach, moving lower, and she couldn't have thought about anything just then if she'd wanted to.

ANOTHER SHOWER, MORE SEX, AND A HALF A POT OF COFFEE LATER, Cary felt like a new woman. She couldn't remember the last time she'd felt like this—sated, exhausted, and content all at once. Despite everything else going on, she couldn't seem to muster enough energy to worry yet.

Even Buck seemed his usual self that morning, watching on as Fred begged for food from Deacon while they sat in the kitchen at her tiny two-person table for breakfast, letting Cary scratch him as she filled his bowl, ambling outside with the other dogs to enjoy the cold morning air. Seeing Buck act like himself was a huge relief. She would have to find a demon dog expert vet soon, but at least her beloved friend seemed to be feeling like his old self. For now anyway.

As she came back inside for another cup of coffee and a soft kiss from Deacon, her little world felt lovely and whole, distanced from the danger and death of her job. A sensation she wanted to hold onto for as long as possible. A bubble of peace to offset the chaos.

Her phone rang at the same time as her front doorbell buzzed, bursting the bubble. She sighed and answered her cell as she went to get the front door.

Beatrix was on the phone. Jaxer was at her door.

She frowned at Jaxer but focused on Beatrix. "Are you okay? You're still safe?" she asked.

"No one has found us here," Beatrix said, "but I was talking to, uh, to some of the dead here in this cemetery last night."

Cary tried not to wince. "Okay." She motioned Jaxer inside without really looking at him.

"There's something happening," Beatrix said. "The ghouls still in the tunnels, something is going on with them. The local dead can sense it even though the ghouls are still in the Mor-Gin."

Cary glanced toward the kitchen. Deacon stood in the doorway, his arms crossed over his chest, his expression impossible to read. She was pretty sure he could hear the phone conversation with his super hearing, but she couldn't tell from his expression.

"We have people keeping an eye on the ghouls," Cary said.

"The dead here couldn't tell me what was happening," Beatrix said. "They're too distanced from it and that magic barrier blocks a lot from getting out. But the vibration is moving through the ground outside the Mor-Gin. Like an echo in all the cemeteries around the area."

"Is this affecting all the ghouls?" Cary asked. "Or just the one's Justin's charm called." She almost said damaged, but that sounded accusatory.

"They couldn't say and I can't tell," Beatrix said. "I spoke to the dead last night, though, because I can feel something's wrong. I can't explain it. It's rubbing against my skin like sparks. What happened after you left here yesterday?"

"Talked to the demon god," Cary said, matter-of-factly even though the incident hadn't felt so casual at the time. "It's not going away any time soon."

"I was afraid of that." Beatrix's voice trembled a bit before she firmed it up. "Greenson was there."

"Yeah." Cary did wince this time. "And he got away. He still has Justin's amulet."

"You're going to need my help," Beatrix said, her tone almost emotionless now. "No one else can control the ghouls."

"You're still in danger," Cary said. "We discussed this. You can't be near Greenson when he calls the demon. We can't risk it."

"We can take care of the ghouls today," Beatrix said. "I can settle them permanently so they're at rest."

"You can do that?" Cary asked.

She paused a beat before saying, "I can."

"Does that kill them?"

Cary hadn't read anything anywhere that said you could kill a ghoul. If the whole they-were-cursed-former-humans theory of ghoul birth was true, they were technically already dead. But since you could kill a vampire and they were *technically* dead too, maybe there was a way to permanently put a ghoul to rest.

"I've never done it before," Beatrix said. "They serve a purpose and it seemed unnecessary."

Cary sat on the edge of her couch, staring at nothing as she asked, "Do you know how they come to be?" If anyone knew it would be a necromancer who could call them. They'd had so much else to talk about Cary hadn't thought to ask Beatrix before this.

"All the ones I've called have been cursed," Beatrix said.

"So, that theory is true then. They don't just spontaneously form in cemeteries." Cary bet there were a whole bunch of scientists who'd love that bit of information. Well, at least the handful that actually studied this stuff. Okay, that one guy with the ghoul tracking chips would probably be interested.

"We need to quiet the ghouls in the Mor-Gin permanently," Beatrix said. "I shouldn't have left them that way, but…"

"But you had a serial killer after you who was calling a demon god," Cary finished for her. "And I made you stay in hiding." She glanced over her shoulder to Deacon who hadn't moved from the kitchen doorway. "Deacon and I will come get you. Does Justin need to be there or will it be safer for him to stay put?"

"He wants to come with me," Beatrix said. "He'll guard my back while I work."

Cary wanted to point out that *she'd* be there to guard Beatrix's back, but that seemed redundant. If Justin wanted to look after his twin, Cary wouldn't be able to keep him away. She was surprised he'd want to see those tunnels again, though.

"We'll be there in an hour," Cary said.

She disconnected and finally faced Jaxer. He was leaning against her small fireplace, looking casually elegant in tailored slacks and a silk shirt. He had his arms crossed as well and Cary realized he'd positioned himself opposite to Deacon, with her in the middle. She scowled at that bit of maneuvering.

"What's wrong?" she asked him.

"Just checking on you, sweetie," he said. "Angie told me about the god. Holland's father? You're going to need some extra help."

"She has help," Deacon said.

Cary sighed at the growl in his voice. After last night, the question of jealousy shouldn't really be on the table. "You can't help," Cary pointed out to Jaxer. "Unless the Nags are willing to make an exception?" She was embarrassed by the hint of hope in her tone. She needed all the help she could get, even if it meant Deacon and Jaxer had to deal with each other.

"No," Jaxer said with a sigh. "Not even for world-ending events."

"That seems unreasonably harsh," Cary said. "What if I fail and the world ends?"

"You won't," Jaxer said.

He sounded a lot more confident than she felt. The peace of a few minutes ago was thoroughly gone now, as if it had never been, and Cary's gut was once again tight with worry.

She stood. "We have to get Beatrix," she said. "At the least, we can settled the ghouls in the tunnels so they're no longer a threat. As for the demon god…" She shrugged. "What kind of help were you offering, Jaxer?"

"I can't help with Lud," he said. "But I can help with the wizard trying to kill you."

She narrowed her eyes. Damn him, she hadn't had a chance to tell Deacon about that yet—or decide if she was going to or not. While she didn't turn to look at Deacon, she could feel the tension in the air ratchet up a few degrees.

"How?" Cary asked shortly.

"I'll track him down for you so you can concentrate," Jaxer said. He looked smug, like he was pleased with having dropped that bomb into the room.

Cary snarled at him, her back still to Deacon so he couldn't see. "You came all the way over this morning to tell me that?"

He glanced past her toward Deacon, before saying, "I came to talk about some other things but my timing isn't good."

"No, it's not," Deacon said.

The sound of his harsh tone made Cary flinch. Great. They were about to have a very badly timed fight. Not exactly what she needed this morning.

"Fine, whatever." Cary stalked to her front door and opened it for Jaxer. She narrowed her eyes at him as he sauntered up to her. "We'll talk more later," she said through clenched teeth.

He held her gaze, something in his blue-green eyes she couldn't read.

"Made your decision, then," he murmured.

"What?" Which decision?

He gently tugged at her ponytail where it hung over her shoulder. "Stay safe, love," he said. "We'll talk soon." He cupped her cheek in one hand, a brief gesture that left her frowning after him as he left.

"That faery is so strange sometimes," she muttered.

She closed the door and turned to find Deacon standing at the couch now, staring at her.

"What?" she demanded.

"There's a wizard trying to kill you?" he asked, his tone as carefully neutral as his expression.

She wasn't fooled for a moment. "Yes. And yes, I didn't tell you about it on purpose. I probably would have eventually. But you worry enough about me as is. And frankly, it's not the first time someone has wanted to kill me. In fact, you've met a few of them." She was thinking of the still-alive Oliver Holland and anyone in his army who'd survived.

"You told Jaxer?"

"It came up. I'm used to telling him things."

Deacon's jaw muscles flexed. She could almost hear him grinding his teeth together.

She sighed. "Are you upset that someone is trying to kill me, or that I told Jaxer about it?"

"Both. Why didn't you tell me?"

"I just told you why. Are you going to make this a big deal thing?"

"It is a big deal thing, Cary. You're my mate. After last night—"

"Last night just happened last night," she pointed out. "The after is only just the last half hour. I didn't have time to tell you anything yet this morning and to be honest I wasn't even thinking about any of this. I was thinking about you naked and how much I enjoyed having your mouth on me. Would you rather I was thinking about Jaxer and the wizard?"

Deacon scowled, but she saw the tension easing from his shoulders. She almost smiled because he looked more confused now than angry.

"Deacon, I didn't want you to worry more than you already do," she said. "And we have a demon god to stop and ghouls to take care of, and... Do we have to fight about this now?"

He let out a harsh breath and stared at the carpet for a few moments, long enough that Cary was afraid they were going to have to fight about this now.

Finally, he looked up. "Please don't keep things like this from me in the future," he said quietly. "You're my mate. You can turn to me."

"Fine. Since you said please." She crossed to him and wrapped her arms around his neck. "Thank you for understanding."

"I don't," he said, his hands on her hips, keeping her close. "But I'll try to deal with it."

She studied his expression, the slight yellow glow in his eyes. "Your control is still wobbly, isn't it?"

"Yes," he admitted. "And it will be for a while."

Until he felt more secure in the mate bond. "So…more sex is necessary then?" she asked as casual as she could manage, though she had to work hard not to purr at the prospect.

"'Fraid so," he said, that wicked smile of his lifting his lips.

She sighed with feigned resignation. "Fine. I guess if we have to."

His chuckled, and kissed her.

And for a brief moment, she let her worries go.

"This isn't going as well as I'd hoped," Cary muttered as they eased through the tunnels under the city center, well inside the Mor-Gin.

The cops had convinced the tour companies to steer clear of the tunnels for the last two nights. And the blockade set up by the leopards had held. No humans had gotten past, and everyone had assumed the ghouls were still safely inside the magic realm. Lucas had assured Cary that they'd heard them just last night, but no one had gotten near enough to check on them. Because Cary had warned them not to.

The only problem was, now, the damned things were nowhere to be found.

She and her group had wandered through huge sections of the magic realm—the place really was a lot larger than it should have been—and still no signs of the ghouls. No bones from recent food. No scent the shifters could follow. No telltale bits of dropped material from their tattered clothing. Nothing.

Which was *not* good.

"You're sure there are no other ways out of this area?" she asked Lucas. Again.

They'd come to a stop at a deadend tunnel, the path blocked by a brick wall. Inside the Mor-Gin, that wall could have been an illusion, a solid real wall, or a section of the magic barrier between realms still too intact to move through. To Cary, the wall looked like it bricked over another tunnel, but nothing was that straightforward in the Mor-Gin. And without the original sorcerers to ask, there was no way to know for sure what they were facing.

The one thing she could be sure of was that *they* couldn't get past the wall.

She put her hands and her hips and turned in a slow circle. The low ceiling and dirt floor underfoot gave a very cave like feel to the area, and the air was cold and damp. The strong musty scent reminded her of the river. Her Protector magic was working—she could see here without the help of the flashlights the group had brought with them. She could *feel* danger in the air coming from somewhere, but she couldn't pinpoint it. Not directionally. The threat seemed to be coming from all around, as if the walls of the tunnels themselves contained some sort of danger.

Thoughts of ghosts made her shiver.

"What's wrong?" Deacon asked near her ear.

"Beyond the fact that the ghouls are missing?" she asked. She didn't want to mention ghosts out loud in case that somehow summoned them. Especially with a necromancer around.

"We've had them blocked in," Lucas insisted. "There was no way for them to get past us. We had guards at every breech in the magic barrier we know of."

"The Mor-Gin is big and purposefully convoluted," Deacon said quietly. "It's possible a new breech has opened and the ghouls slipped through."

Cary glanced at the brick wall. "You suppose that's blocking a tunnel? The ghouls burrow underground. They could have just dug their way to a blocked off section."

The ghouls couldn't have burrowed under the Mor-Gin's barrier because that's not how magic worked. This was called a bubble realm on purpose—all directions were enclosed inside. But if there were sections of the Mor-Gin that had been physically bricked off, or even magically, while still remaining technically inside the realm, it was possible for the ghouls to sneak into those sections.

"They're around here," Beatrix said. "It's like a vibration I can feel. They're…" She trailed off and frowned, turning in a circle with her flashlight. "I can't pinpoint them." She faced Cary. "The ground in this area is pretty rocky for them to burrow through. They need the softer, moister soils of dug up cemeteries. Unless something pushed them to try, I'm not sure they'd voluntarily try to dig out of here. Especially since there hasn't been any threats to them directly."

"Greenson?" Cary said. "He's still got Justin's amulet. If he came after them, to control them, they might try to get away."

"Except no one has gotten past our blockade," Lucas pointed out. "We'd have smelled your serial killer, nonetheless seen him, if he'd tried to sneak past into the Mor-Gin."

Deacon said, "It's hard to fool a shifter, and Greenson stinks of blood."

Cary frowned and made an attempt to stuff her hands into her coat pocket, only to remember she'd sealed one. The sacrificial knife she'd taken from Greenson was still in her pocket.

"I can see," she told Deacon quietly, knowing he'd understand. "But I can't pinpoint the problem."

"What time is it?" Beatrix asked.

"Four twenty-five p.m.," Lucas answered after glancing at his watch. "At least outside the Mor-Gin that's the time. Inside…" He shrugged.

Time, like size, wasn't the same inside the magic realm as it was outside. "We've been underground a while," Cary said to no one in particular. She hadn't realized they'd been here so long. No wonder her stomach felt empty.

"The sun is setting," Beatrix said.

Her tone had suddenly taken on the hollow deepness that made the hair on Cary's arms stand up.

"The ghouls are waking," Beatrix said.

She closed her eyes and knelt on the ground, setting her hand against the bare dirt. From a pocket in the side of her canvas pants, she pulled out a small wrapped bundle. When she unwrapped it, Cary's lip lifted involuntarily. It was a dead gray squirrel. Without opening her eyes, Beatrix pulled the poor dead animals head off and let its blood spill over the ground in front of her. She started to chant, a low rhythmic sound that rubbed wrong against Cary's nerves.

"Did you know she had that on her?" Cary asked Deacon close to his ear so only he would hear.

"Beatrix always smells like death," Deacon whispered back. "Today, like fresh death. But I didn't realize she was carrying an animal carcass with her."

Justin glanced at them. While he couldn't have heard them, he spoke as if he knew what they'd been discussing. "She needs the sacrifice blood to control ghouls."

Cary nodded, keeping her expression as neutral as possible and her thoughts to herself. She had a real soft spot for animals. The fact that Beatrix had randomly killed a squirrel did not go over well with her, and it took a great deal of effort not to show her disgust and anger.

Deacon subtly rubbed a hand down her arm, as if he knew how she felt. Given his sense of smell, he probably did.

They watched Beatrix work for a few moments, then Cary felt that sharp charge of danger across her shoulders, the sign that her powers were needed. She took up a defensive position between the small group and the open section of the tunnel.

Over her shoulder, to Deacon, she said, "Make sure everyone stays behind me. No heroics."

He eyes were glowing yellow now, but he nodded Lucas and Justin closer to Beatrix, ensuring everyone was in a small space. The small clustering of the group made her job easier. Less likely someone would dodge around her and put themselves in danger by abandoning her protection.

They had to *let* her protect them. If they tried to get around her, to run into danger, there wasn't a lot she could do—short of jumping between them and the danger and taking whatever hit was meant for her erstwhile protectee. Unfortunately, when she had to guard a group, that kind of thing could leave the rest of the group vulnerable.

She faced the open tunnel again, stretching out her senses as best she could. She heard echoes, sounds she hadn't heard before, but she couldn't tell if she was hearing anything new or just things her human ears hadn't picked up before.

Behind her, Beatrix continued to chant. The scent of decay rose in a choking miasma, and Cary didn't envy the shifters just then. She heard something like scrambling, and her nerves jumped. She'd expected the ghouls to come from the ground beneath them if they were here at all.

Instead, they dropped from the ceiling.

Cary started to lunge back to the group, to cover ducked heads and keep the ghouls from falling on anymore. But just then, a sound farther up the tunnel reached her.

"They're mine, Beatrix," Greenson said, his voice a harsh directionless echo. "You might have called them, but these are mine to control."

Cary backed up closer to the rest of the group and took a quick glance at the ghouls surrounding them. They were standing in a half circle behind them, staring at Beatrix. Beatrix faced the ghouls instead of Greenson, while Justin stood at her shoulder watching the approaching serial killer. Cary turned toward Greenson as well. Beatrix would have to handle the ghouls. But since Cary was in full Protector mode, she was pretty sure if the ghouls turned against them because of Greenson's amulet, Cary would still be able to keep everyone safe.

She hoped so anyway.

She wasn't sure if Beatrix having called down the danger, quite literally, would change anything. Beatrix continued speaking under her breath, but Cary couldn't focus on what she was saying. She was trusting the necromancer a lot, and the skin on her neck tingled with unease.

That strange feeling like bugs crawling over her skin, which happened after she'd been protecting someone from a magical attack, hit her hard, making her shiver. The danger wasn't passed. She was still in Protector mode. So why was she feeling that sensation already?

Weird.

Greenson shuffled closer, distracting her from the strange sensation, demanding her full attention. Her heartbeat hammered as she watched him emerge from the darkness. His eyes shown red in the illumination from their flashlights, dispelling any idea that he might be harmless despite his very ordinary appearance. He narrowed his eyes at the increase in light, but otherwise didn't show any discomfort from the sudden flashlights in his face. He seemed to approach without weapons, but the amulet hanging around his neck was obvious against his plane black t-shirt. The dark color of his clothing made his face stand out against the blackness behind him, eerily looking detached from his body.

Cary waited for him to say something even as Beatrix continued to speak in a low tone behind her. The ghouls' steady moaning echoed strangely through the tunnels, making it seem as if ghouls were surrounding them.

The sensation of bugs crawling over her in increasingly frantic movements intensified for a moment before fading away. She frowned. When she was in full Protector mode, those kinds of sensations made her nervous. She normally didn't feel much of anything at all, at least not until the protecting was over. Or unless she got hurt in the process. Or when she was facing someone very very powerful like a Master vampire.

But Greenson was just a relatively ordinary man with a serious will and an amulet that called ghouls. Outside of that, she was certain he didn't have additional magical skills. She shouldn't feel his efforts to get through her shields at all.

Was her magic failing? Was she failing? Again.

Or was being inside the Mor-Gin somehow affecting her powers? It hadn't while she'd been protecting the leopard children, but where magic was concerned, anything was possible.

"What are you trying to do?" she asked Greenson.

He smiled, stopping about ten feet away. He glanced around as if searching for something. "You're very good with shields, witch," he said.

She smiled back. "Not a witch. But thanks."

"My will is stronger than your shields," he said.

"Nope," she replied.

At least she was pretty sure it wouldn't be. Just in case, though, she used some of what she'd learned last night with Aidan and poured her own will into the shields, willing them to be stronger than ever. Just in case.

After another few moments of skin crawling standoff, Greenson scowled. "How?" he asked.

"Talent," she replied, with a casualness she didn't entirely feel.

The echoes of ghoul moans seemed to be increasing. She was afraid to look behind her, to see what Beatrix was doing. With Greenson so close, she didn't even dare ask Beatrix anything out loud. But it was starting to sound like there were a lot more ghouls around them than there had been just a few minutes ago.

"You didn't save the woman from *him*," Greenson said. "He let you go."

"Yeah, we figured that," she said, only half paying attention to him. She could hear the ghouls in the tunnels behind him now. No longer just behind her. Coming from all directions. Over her shoulder, she said, "Beatrix, you doing this, or is he?"

Greenson smiled. "Me."

"Can you do anything about the ghouls he's controlling?" she asked Beatrix.

"Yes," Beatrix said, her tone deep and emotionless. She sounded almost as monotone as the ghouls now.

Greenson laughed. "You can't stop me, Beatrix. You aren't strong enough."

"I have skills you don't," Beatrix said. "The dead are mine."

"Not anymore," he said. "Your amulet gives me the ghouls. *He* gives me the rest."

From the darkness a swarm of dead bodies moved forward into the light. Cary swallowed hard. She couldn't tell if they were all ghouls or not, but there were a lot of them now. That many walking dead bodies was just so so icky.

She braced herself against her own kneejerk reaction. So far, no actual ghosts. Just walking dead. No problem. She could handle this.

The ghouls shuffled forward until they lined up behind Greenson, an army of ragged beings that couldn't be killed—except by Beatrix—waiting in a silence full of anticipation. Behind Cary, Beatrix breathed out a few words. Cary had to force herself not to flinch as the ghouls behind her stepped forward, bracketing her on both sides.

"You sure sending them forward is a good idea?" she asked Beatrix. She was worried for the poor ghouls, since they weren't exactly here of their own free will.

From her peripheral vision, she realized there were a lot more bodies than there had been just a few minutes ago.

"How many did you call?" Cary hissed.

"Enough," Beatrix said. "The dead answer me. All of them."

Cary closed her eyes, briefly because she was afraid to take her eyes off the scene too long, but obviously there were more than ghouls flanking her. And every part of that idea made her want to run screaming down the tunnel.

For some reason, walking dead bodies was so much worse than vampires, even though they were essentially the same thing. Maybe because vampires were still in control of themselves and aware. Whatever the difference was, Cary was definitely not a zombie person. And this felt like being surrounded by zombies.

What she wouldn't give for a vampire about now. Not that that would help. It would just be nice to face something she was used to. Even an ordinary, familiar demon seemed preferable.

Behind Greenson's dead army, a faint reddish glow rose, illuminating the tunnels further.

Cary groaned. She should have known better than to ask for the familiar. She really should have known better.

"Oh hell," Cary muttered as at least five scary looking monsters of the demon variety stalked into the midst of the ghouls and other assorted dead people.

While Beatrix might be able to handle all the dead things—and Cary sincerely hoped she could—the demons were another disaster all together. That tingling of residual magic crawled over her skin again, so strong this time, her stomach rebelled. She leaned forward and braced a hand on her thigh as the roll of nausea passed.

"You okay?" Deacon asked from just behind her shoulder.

He rested a hand on her back, but she shivered to dislodge his touch. Her nerves had gone from normal to oversensitive in a blink.

"Fine," she said so he wouldn't misinterpret her actions. "Lot of stuff being thrown at me right now. Can't see where it's coming from. Demon magic? Do demons do magic?"

She was too busy trying not throwing up to remember. That seemed to be something she should know already, but her brain wasn't offering up the information. They did throw power around. Holland had done that. But she wasn't seeing any of the light shows that came with those types of attacks.

"Anyway," she said, "whatever is happening is making my nerves hum. I'll be okay. Just… Wow. A lot." She straightened and shook hard to dislodge the creepy-crawly sensation.

What the hell was causing this reaction? Still no vampires in the mix—the last Master she'd faced *had* made her want to throw up when he'd attempted to use his power on her—and no obvious magical attacks. Not being able to see what was causing these sensations left her edgy.

It meant there was still another shoe waiting to drop.

She hated that. "Okay, so whatever that is, it's not going to work. You can stop. Even if I throw up, you won't get through me. In fact, you're not getting through me period." The intensity of sensation eased. She hid her relief. "So everyone just go back to where you came from, and Greenson if you would just turn yourself into the police, that'd be great. Okay? We're done here, right?"

The silence that followed her ridiculous statement was deafening, but it gave Cary some room to evaluate the dangers around her. Five demons in front of her, an army of dead people, a serial killer, and their own army of dead things ready to launch against Greenson's group. But something seemed odd.

The demons.

Had Greenson raised and freed some just for this? Just to get to Beatrix? That seemed overkill. And how hadn't he been killed when the demons got free? And where were the demon hunters when he was freeing random demons?

And what the hell was she missing?

She knew something about this wasn't right, something important. Her spine tingled with awareness of danger that seemed to encompass everywhere at once. What was she missing? What was she missing?

The sudden lunge of the first row of Greenson's dead disrupted her focus, and she had to brace against her instinctive squeal of disgust. The wave of dead hit up against her shield, some bouncing backward, some hanging against it like an invisible hand kept them upright, some lost body parts to the effort.

Gross.

She stood her ground, grateful the line of attack had stopped far enough back that nothing could touch her. Another wave lunged, faster than she would have thought dead things could move. And then one of the demons threw itself at her, a flaming lava-like body of sulfur smelling menace. It slammed against her shields just in front of her, its claw-like hands reaching toward her. She was absolutely certain she wouldn't like those claws getting anywhere near her throat.

Lucas cursed. Deacon mutter something to him. Then to her, "Cary?"

"I'm good," she said, grunting when the demon threw itself so hard at her, she actually felt a vague sense of its impact. "We're good. Just, you know, don't run out into that right now."

"How are you doing this?" Lucas asked, his voice gravely, his leopard obviously near the surface.

"It's what I do," she said as a second demon flew on ragged bat wings toward them.

It flew up to the ceiling and attempted to dive bomb them. Flames spread out from its mouth as it hit her shield, the entire overhead section of the tunnel alight with the demon's fire and hissing screams.

"That hurting your ears?" she asked Deacon.

"Little bit," he said. "The echo."

"Yeah." She winced again as the demon screamed so loud dirt filtered from the ceiling. "I really hope they don't bring this whole place down on top of us."

Or catch anything on fire! Did the Mor-Gin come with some sort of magic fire extinguishing feature? It would be a good addition to an underground magic realm. But given the age of the place...

Next to her ear, Deacon said, "Can you survive a tunnel collapse?"

"Yeah." She hoped. "It'll just be messy and hard to explain. There are buildings above us. Other people could get hurt." She didn't have any idea what part of Portland they were under at the moment, but if the Mor-Gin collapsed, she was terrified it would take some of the downtown with it.

She gave the ceiling a leery glance just as more flames from the bat-winged demon flared above them. The heat from all the fire made her sweat, which reminded her she was still wearing her jacket, which reminded her she had a sacrificial dagger in her pocket. None of which was any good to her at the moment, but it did mean she didn't want to discard her jacket. Just in case someone managed to get through the magic pocket and remove the dagger.

"I can do this all night," Greenson said as another wave of dead people threw themselves at Cary's shield.

"So can I," she called back over the shrieks of another flying demon.

She braced her legs, steadying herself as more bodies scrambled at her and more flames circled them. Plops of what looked like lava rolled her direction, pooling a few feet away at the base of her protective shield. She frowned at it. That might not reach them, but if it burned through the ground, that could cause a lot of trouble. Yet, she didn't have any direct way to cool or stop the lava.

Sometimes, being a Kevlar vest without any actual magic of her own could be frustrating.

The lava piled up against her shield in a small, fiercely hot hill. And the sounds of melting rock were like the tinkling of bells amidst the screams and screeches of the attacking demons and dead people.

"He won't need to stop until sunrise," Beatrix said quietly.

"Then we'll stand here until then," Cary said. She knew they probably needed a better plan, but right then, all she wanted was to keep the people with her alive. And the best way for her to do that was to just stand here with them behind her while her Protector magic did its thing.

She hoped the other leopards in the tunnels didn't try to come help from the rear. She wouldn't be able to help them from here.

"I'm keeping the leopards away from the fight," Deacon said as if reading her thoughts.

"How are you doing that?" she asked.

"They won't help until I call," he said, not answering her question.

She faced a ghoul as it scrambled at her face with blood covered, decaying fingers. "I think we have some things to talk about," she said to Deacon.

"Later," he said.

"We can't just stay here forever," Justin said, sounding young, scared, and frustrated at once.

"They'll wear themselves out," Cary said. "Or the sun will come up and all the ghouls and dead things will have to go to sleep." She risked a glance at Beatrix. "That's how it works right? Nothing up while the sun's up?"

Beatrix nodded. "But that's a long ways away." Her eyes were narrowed as she stared at the dead thing still scrambling toward Cary.

Cary faced the animated corpse again, and watched as it seemed to deflate, settling onto the ground, a pained moan hissing between its clenched teeth. By the time the sound ended, the things eyes had closed and all hint of animation had left the body. It was just a fully dead carcass taking up space.

Cary raised her brows, and to Beatrix said, "What did you just do?"

"I can put them to rest one at a time," Beatrix said, "but without sacrificial blood, I can't lay them all down."

"And unless you're willing to sacrifice one of your friends," Greenson called. "I can call as many dead as you quiet." He hadn't moved from his position several feet away. He watched and occasional made a hand gesture that sent another wave of monsters their way.

"No sacrificing needed," Cary said sharply.

She grunted as another of the demons threw a series of lava daggers at her. The lava crystalized as it hit her shield, becoming little black blades scattered around in a half circle in front of her. Several of them dropped onto, and into, the body Beatrix had quieted. Since no blood came out, Cary assumed whoever that poor sap was, he'd been dead for a while and wouldn't mind the extra holes.

"No one needs to sacrifice anything," she repeated. "If you haven't noticed, we're just fine. I'm sorry you're all bored waiting for them to wear out, but that's what you're going to do so I can keep you safe. Do not argue with me. It'll just piss me off."

She took a step forward, despite Deacon reaching out and grabbing her arm. The line of attack was forced back the foot she'd gained. The small but growing hill of lava hissed steam as if it had come into contact with water. Then it too turned to chinking, snapping stone.

Hey, a newly formed stalactite, Cary thought. Or stalagmite? She couldn't remember which was which. Anyway, that solved the lava hill problem. Cool.

She tried another step forward, but a wave of real ghouls, not just dead bodies, flowed toward her and she stopped instinctively, not wanting to get too close to them. She heard a hiss, and glanced over her shoulder. Deacon was holding one of Beatrix's hands, which held a wickedly sharp blade.

"She was going to use her own blood," Justin said, tugging at Deacon's hold. The young man might as well have been tugging at a steel post.

"No spilling blood while there are demons running around," Cary barked. Though the fact that there were five freed demons thrashing at her shields once again raised her concerns that she'd missed something important in all this.

Like where was the demon god? And the demon hunters? And how had Greenson survived releasing five demons?

And why had the demon god given Greenson the ability to raise the dead now, when it had sent him to find Beatrix before. If Lud could raise the dead itself, why would it even need Beatrix, or Justin's amulet?

None of that made sense. And when things didn't make sense, Cary worried. She took another step forward, pushing the attack farther back.

Greenson roared. He gestured at his army and they charged forward, demons, dead, and ghouls alike, all in one thick writhing wave of bodies, blood, and fire.

Cary stopped, braced and leaning into the attack to keep her balance. Behind her, she knew Deacon was moving the others closer to her, keeping them near enough for her to protect. She'd have given him a thankful smile if she'd been able to spare the attention, but the row upon row of attacks, forced her to focus on simply holding her ground.

And despite her efforts, she felt that crawl over her spine that said danger was near. Since they were under attack, the new sensation caught her full attention. What the hell?

Suddenly the dead that had been flanking her, the ones Beatrix had called and controlled, surged forward, throwing themselves at Greenson's army.

Cary shouted a denial but the sound was lost in the chaos of noise, bodies slamming into bodies, the wet squishy sounds of decaying flesh being impacted, the crunch and snap of bones, the tearing and screaming. She had to remind herself these were all dead things, already dead. But the abomination of what was happening to their corpses disgusted her.

And, she realized with a throat closing punch of disgust, the ghouls were in a feeding frenzy amidst all the dead. They were gorging on the fallen, whether the bodies were animated or not, feasting on the dead even while the dead tried to fight for Greenson or Beatrix.

"Stop this," Cary shouted to Beatrix. "It's not necessary."

"They are mine to control," Beatrix said, her toneless, deep voice a rumble of thunder over the noise.

"Then stop them from—"

She cut herself off when blood splattered across Greenson's face. Where the hell had the blood come from?

Despite the carnage, the fight hadn't resulted in any blood because everything fighting had been dead too long or was a demon which would hardly be injured by anything in the fight.

Greenson rubbed the blood on his face, glancing at it as if he couldn't quite make sense of what it was. He was still staring at his hand when the ghouls circled him. He looked up in time to realize his danger. He gripped the amulet, shouting something. Even from a distance, Cary felt the wave of what must have been his will. The ghouls' movements slowed so much it was like watching a stop action film in reverse. And for a few seconds, Greenson smiled in triumph.

Then the pointed end of a glowing white sword of fire erupted from his chest in a spray of blood.

His eyes widened, shock and surprise. He opened his mouth but nothing came out. Slowly he slid forward on the flaming sword until he dropped to the ground. The ghouls swarmed onto him. And finally, Greenson screamed.

But it was too late.

Cary, eyes wide, looked up at the wielder of the fire sword.

The demon god that was Oliver Holland's father smiled at her. And she realized what she'd been missing.

"Oh shit," she said. "We're all inside a containment circle."

38

"What are you talking about?" Deacon said, his hands on her shoulders as he eased her backward a few steps.

She was so shocked she didn't think to argue with him. "The demons…" She nodded to the five random demons now lined up behind the god, as well as the god himself. "They aren't freed. It was a trap. We're *inside* a containment circle."

"Which means?" Deacon said, though his tone implied he already had a hint.

"The demon has his full power here."

No wonder she'd been feeling and sensing danger since entering this section of the tunnels! No wonder her Protector magic couldn't pinpoint the threat. They'd quite literally been encircled by threat the minute they crossed the line of Greenson's circle.

She stared up at the monster that took up most of the cavern, both horrified and confused. "Why?" she shouted up to it. "Why kill him and let the ghouls have him, after everything he's done to help you break into our realm?"

She'd been so certain the demon would use Greenson's body and his amulet to control the body so it wouldn't die immediately…

"Ghouls are cursed," Lud said in its deep, bone-jarring voice.

242

The demons in the tunnel had stopped attempting to get at Cary and the others and were now bowing to the god, murmuring something quietly in a pitch that just sounded like buzzing insects to her. The circling dead had stilled as well, but for the ghouls currently eating Greenson. She worked very hard not to look at or listen to that feeding.

"For me to control his body," Lud said, "to keep his body functioning, he'd have to be cursed to rise as a ghoul after death." It glanced behind Cary. "The amulet doesn't control the dead. Greenson failed to get the correct tool."

Cary backed closer to Beatrix and Justin. "Yeah, he wasn't the brightest bulb I guess," she said, attempting to keep the demon focused on her. "Maybe should have picked a better patsy."

Lud's chuckle made Cary's skin crawl.

"His sacrifice was the last I needed," it said.

She narrowed her eyes. It was implying it could leave the containment circle now that it had killed the human who'd called it. That was how this tended to work if the human was stupid enough to go *inside* the circle with the demon.

Where they were currently, stupidly, trapped.

But... "If you leave the circle now," she said, "in that form, you sacrifice a huge chunk of your power." Given the thing was a literal god, having it enter her realm even with a fraction of its power could be world ending.

But it had to move from the Mor-Gin out into her realm as well. Would that cost it more if it wasn't in a human body? Or would it gain power from moving through another magical realm before entering hers? Was being inside the Mor-Gin worse or better? Was this all part of Lud's plan? She had no way of knowing without asking Lud. Except revealing her ignorance seemed like a bad idea. Well, revealing any more than she already had.

"You won't be able to reclaim your son," she added, hoping she was right about that.

Really, it was just a guess. But Holland had been a pretty badass demon, a long lived, crafty, powerful sonofabitch. And he'd escaped his father and remained free for centuries. Cary was betting it would be no small feat to return the reluctant Holland to the demon lands.

The demon tilted its head to one side to contemplate her. Cary braced herself to take an attack. When it didn't immediately happen, she also had to brace herself against fidgeting under the demon's glowing red cat's eye stare. It was very good at being intimidating.

Where the hell were the demon hunters?

A fireball formed on the center of the demon's hand and he tossed it at her casually, as if throwing a ball. She watched the ball spin and explode harmlessly a foot in front of her. The heat from the blast still washed across her skin and reminded her of getting too close to an active kiln. It was a surprisingly dry heat, like desert heat, and it sucked the moisture from the air, making breathing more difficult.

"My son is both in this realm and not now," the demon said, his tone almost pleasant. A casual conversation between friends. "I sense him. After you, he was no longer here fully. You could not have returned him to another realm."

But the demon didn't sound so sure about that. She wondered just what it had learned from Holland about her. Besides her name.

"You are not a hunter," Lud said. "You are not able to banish demons on your own."

"Speaking of hunters, they'll be here soon." Cary gestured at the other demons bowing their heads. "Too much activity for them to ignore."

The god chuckled again. "They are busy. Your world will burn."

"Oh, I really wish you wouldn't do that. I haven't finished my laundry yet."

Lud frowned. "What is 'laundry'? Some sort of spell?"

She shrugged. "I have to wash my clothes." She gestured to her leather jacket and t-shirt beneath. "They're dirty now. And I have piles of the stuff at home. Been busy. You know. It builds up. My mother would be very disappointed in me if the world ended and I still had piles of laundry lying around."

"Cary?" Deacon said under his breath.

She ignored him. She might sound like she was cracking up under the pressure—and she wasn't entirely convinced she wasn't—but she did have a reason for talking nonsense. Stalling tactic combined with confusing her enemy.

Sometimes it even worked.

"You are very strange," Lud said.

"So I've been told."

"Your world will die. I will reclaim my son."

"Sure, sure. But would you mind telling me why you want him?" she said. "I mean, you two don't seem particularly close. He did go to a lot of trouble to avoid you. So…why bother?"

"It is beyond the scope of your understanding, human."

She shrugged. "Probably. Just thought I'd ask." She met its intimidating gaze for a long silent moment. Waiting it out.

Somewhat to her surprise, the silence got to the god before she broke and started babbling.

"He must fulfill his duty to me," Lud said. "His purpose."

"Which is…?" She circled her hand in a please-continue gesture.

Though it was hard to do, she made an attempt to relax her stance, hoping it looked like she was no longer terrified or on the verge of peeing herself.

Lud watched her closely, like a child might watch an ant. Just before stepping on it. "He must fulfill his destiny."

"Yeah, that doesn't really explain much, but okay." She shrugged. Behind her, Deacon continued to hold her shoulders, his presence and the strength in his hands pretty damned comforting.

Lud tossed another casually thrown fire ball at her, which exploded in a bright white shower of sparks.

She blinked to clear the spots from her vision. "Well, that was rude."

"He's testing you?" Deacon murmured.

"Yup," she said. "What do you want from Beatrix and Justin?" she asked Lud. If it wasn't in the mood to explain more about the situation with Holland, maybe she could ferret out other bits of information.

So much for not showing her ignorance. Oh well.

Mostly though, she just needed the thing to keep talking so the hunters had time to get here. If she let the god walk out of the circle now, she was pretty sure her world was fucked.

"The necromancer will control the dead body I need," Lud said matter-of-factly. "Or her brother dies. If they cooperate, they will continue in my realm."

"That doesn't sound like a reward," Justin murmured.

Cary had to agree. While she'd never personally been inside a demon realm, given what came out of them, she was pretty sure she didn't want to live in one.

"If they resist," Lud continued, "they will bath in never ending flames for all eternity."

"That sounds really awful," Cary said. "So I won't be allowing that."

"You cannot stop me, Cary Redmond," Lud said.

With so much condescension it set her teeth on edge. She scowled. "I can stop you from hurting Justin and Beatrix."

Another flashing ball of white hot flames hit off her Protector magic, this time so hard she was forced back a step into Deacon. He took her weight and helped her keep her balance, but his low growl made her nervous. The last thing she needed was him getting mad enough to attack a demon god.

"You stay behind me," she warned him. "No matter what this thing tries. Promise me."

Deacon grunted, but didn't promise. She opened her mouth to force the issue, but the demon was watching too closely and she didn't want to hint at the real nature of her powers, just in case it was smart enough to guess or had heard of Protectors. She didn't want to help the demon god gain information it might not have.

"I can't read your thoughts," Lud said. "Why not?"

That surprised her. She had no idea. Probably her magic, but she'd never had cause for it to work that way before. "Got me," she said truthfully. "Probably for the best though. I'm not thinking very nice things about you."

It chuckled. "You will be soon."

That didn't sound good. "I doubt that very much, but what makes you think so?"

"You will be mine. I will be in you."

Ew. "No," she said firmly.

"My son will be surprised to see you. It will be amusing to watch him realize I've come for him in your body."

Cary blinked. For a heartbeat, two, she couldn't comprehend what Lud had just said. It didn't compute at all, like the words hadn't been words in any kind of human language that she might hope to understand.

"Huh?" she said because she couldn't form any other coherent response. What?

Deacon's hands tightened on her shoulders, enough pressure to snap her out of her dazed confusion and focus on making sure no one—like her angry leopard boyfriend—risked their lives trying to attack the demon god.

"The witch," Lud said. "She was much easier to influence. I could read her thoughts. I could control her thoughts."

"Which witch," Cary said, then winced at the phrasing. That sounded weird out loud.

"Greenson chose her well. She was a lure, not a sacrifice." The demon's mouth stretched into what it probably thought was a smile, the gesture revealing rows of sharp pointy teeth. "And you took the bait."

"Yeah, I'm still not getting this," she said. But she realized now that the woman she'd saved last night had been a witch of some kind.

"She didn't remember my slave," Lud continued. "She thought you were to blame for her loss."

"Loss?"

"Her great love. You ensured she couldn't join her. She cursed you to be a ghoul after death for interfering."

Cary felt her eyes bulging as her heart thumped so hard in her chest it hurt. "I'm cursed to be a ghoul now?"

Ah, that was so not good! She didn't want to be a ghoul. First, she didn't want to die. But she really really didn't want to be a ghoul after she died.

"You manipulated that poor woman into thinking *I* was the bad guy last night? That was really mean of you."

The ridiculousness of accusing a blood thirsty demon of being "mean" was not lost on her.

"Well, whatever," she said, "you're not getting my body, ghoul or not."

"What makes you think you can resist?" Lud asked. And suddenly that same sexy, handsome human man it had become last night appeared in front of them.

Cary rolled her eyes. "I'm not falling for that handsome man thing," she said. "I've had to deal with handsomer men than you who wanted to kill me. I'm immune."

"Your leopard is not," the man said, smiling at Deacon.

"Stop that. Don't torment him." She glanced at Deacon, whose eyes were so yellow now there wasn't much of his human self left in them. His jaw worked and a ripple of movement through his face hinted that he was on the verge of shifting. Damn it.

"Hey," she said, snapping her fingers in front of his face. "If you're seeing that man from last night, ignore it. Look at me."

She forced his face around, roughly to get his attention. He actually snarled at her. She gave him a look and for a flickering moment his rage dimmed.

"The demon is fucking with you," she said, "and if you buy it and get yourself killed, I will never forgive you."

He turned his face away from her, pulling in several deep breaths.

"My prince," Lucas said, coming up closer to Deacon. "What can I do?"

"Prince?" Cary said. "Well that's something we have to talk about later, isn't it?"

The very human chagrin and annoyance that filled Deacon's expression filled her with relief. She might even forgive him for hiding something from her as important as the fact that he might be a prince.

Maybe.

"You are not like normal humans," Lud said, still in the sexy man form, but its voice was no longer laced with seduction.

"That's rude, too," Cary said. "Lot of humans are just like me. Now, stop with the trying to seduce me. We both know that won't work. And if you keep torturing my boyfriend, I'm gonna get really pissed."

"This is what it took for you to admit to being my girlfriend?" Deacon asked under his breath.

She noted his voice was a little more his own now, his control seeming to return. Which made her embarrassment worthwhile.

"We'll discuss that later too," she said primly. "Prince." She took a moment of pleasure in his wince, then returned her attention fully to the watching demon. "Learn everything you wanted to with that little stunt?" she asked.

"Yes," it said. "The night is waning. You will join me now."

She felt the tug of its powers, its will, that same sensation she'd felt coursing through her when she and Aidan had combined to send the god away. Only this time the will, combined with whatever magic demons had, was directed at her. The tug of its power hit her so strongly, she took a step toward it before stopping herself. She set her feet, legs wide, and settled into her stubborn Protector stance.

When the tugging turned into a jerking pull, she leaned back a little to offset the power and said, "No."

"How can you resist?" it asked, reaching for her physically now, its hands stretched toward her as if it could reach through the space between them and force her close.

She might have given her usual flippant response, but the power of the demon's compulsion got so strong she had to put her full concentration on resisting. How could the damned thing affect her like this when it was still a threat to the others? It had threatened Beatrix and Justin both with very bad things. Right now, Cary was the only thing standing between them and a future of burning in never ending flame, or worse. No matter how much the damned demon god wanted to take over her body, it needed Beatrix which made it a threat to Beatrix, which meant Cary should be immune to this stupid pull.

Irritated, she doubled down on staying right where she was. "No," she said again, using the same tone she used to scold Fred when he did something wrong.

The demon leaned closer, its human face starting to contort with strain. She narrowed her eyes, glaring at it as she held her ground.

"I will not be your ghoul," she said. "I already have a boyfriend." She was amused enough by her own bad joke she smiled. The smile showed teeth.

"You will be mine," Lud hissed, losing any hint of humanness from its voice again.

"No," she repeated. And she pushed back with her resistance. She blinked in surprise when the demon actually took a step backward.

The demon blinked in surprise too.

"How?" it demanded.

She had no idea. But it seemed a bad idea to admit that out loud. "Leave my realm and never come back," she said. There wasn't the power in her words that had been there in their last fight, when Aidan's will had backed hers up. So she pulled in a deep breath, let it out slowly, and said again, "Leave my realm and never come back."

Her voice had gone deep enough she almost didn't recognize it. That was cool. She repeated the phrase and *pushed* again.

Fiery lava spread over Lud's human form as it exploded back into its true form. It roared and the tunnel lit with burning heat and flames. Cary covered her eyes with one hand against the blinding flash of light.

When the light faded, Lud was gone. Cary slowly lowered her hand, looking around. The other five demons were gone too. The dead army stood motionless and staring at nothing. The ghouls, still feasting on Greenson's corpse, never even looked up.

She winced at that. In the hoopla, she'd forgotten about the ghouls eating Greenson. She glanced back at Deacon and the others. Lucas and Deacon exchanged a frown.

"Is he gone?" Deacon asked.

"Just like that?" Lucas asked.

A scream from farther up the tunnel pierced the air. Cary's heart lurched. "Shit. It left the circle. It's free."

3 9

ary tore up the tunnel, racing after Deacon and Lucas. Those screams were their people under attack, and both shifters had rushed off to help before Cary could stop them. She'd taken just enough time to order Beatrix to quiet the dead then get out of the tunnels with Justin, before she followed Deacon.

She skidded to a stop at a curve in the tunnels, horrified by the slight of all six demons attacking the leopards. Most were in their animal forms, dodging and fighting against the invaders. They were fast, and strong, but a shapeshifter, even a group of them, couldn't hold out indefinitely against *six* demons. Especially when one of them was a god.

Small fires were popping up around the area, lava pooled here and there, and smoke pillowed in a thick gray mass at the roof of the tunnel.

Shit. Fire inside a tunnel was so not good. They'd be suffocated if not burned out. She could probably keep them breathing and safe from flames but only if everyone was together. Again, she wondered if the sorcerers who'd created the Mor-Gin had put any spells in place to prevent fire. And if they had, would it stop demon flames?

She spotted Deacon still in his human form rushing at a shifter who was in the way of the bat-winged demon. Deacon wrapped his arms around the leopard and rolled them both beyond the demon's attacking claws. Cary's heart stopped as she watched that near escape. Then she raced into the den.

How did she get everyone in one place? She needed them all to clump up so she could protect them. She lurched between a fanged-toothed demon as it lunged at Lucas, getting between him and the demon in time to send the demon flying backward. She scowled at the rip in her leather coat sleeve. Marianne was going to kill her for getting this nice leather torn. Especially since it was spelled not to do that very easily.

Damned demons.

Over her shoulder, she screamed, "We have to get everyone together so I can block the attack."

Lucas nodded and started calling to the other shifters. Together they moved through the fight, Cary wincing as fire, rocks, and lava bounced off her shield. The smell of blood and sulfur made her gage. To her immense relief, though, the flames and everything burning snuffed out when it came into contact with her shield. At least she could prevent them from being overwhelmed by a raging fire.

She caught Deacon's eye as he ducked under a line of flames, shielding one of his people.

"Get your ass over here," she shouted. "Get your people over here."

Deacon glanced around the room and suddenly shifters were racing toward her, as if Deacon had somehow silently told them to move. She and Lucas gathered them in a group, Cary standing between them and the demons as the attack intensified. She flinched at the sparks and heat, watching as Deacon dodged toward her, pushing his people in front of him.

She screamed his name as one of the five minion demons dove at him. He ducked and rolled away, but the demon still caught him, racking a long slice down his shoulder. He continued the roll until he was on his feet again, and in the next blink he was in leopard form.

To her relief, the wound healed with the shift. She'd never been so grateful for his shifter nature and his ability to shift so fast before. In leopard form, he barreled through the tunnel, lifting one of his fallen people in his mouth and dragging the wounded shifter with him as he worked to reach Cary.

Lud rose to an impressively scary height in the tunnel, making the ceiling tremble and dirt rain down onto them. She coughed, panic clogging her throat as the god looked first at her, then swung its gaze to Deacon still too far away for her to protect.

"No!" she screamed as a line of yellow-white lava shot from the demon's open palm. She reached toward it as if she could stop the lava from reaching Deacon by desperation alone.

To her surprise, the column of glowing liquid death slowed, not much, but enough, just enough for Deacon to lurch out of the way. Then it sped again, slamming into the dirt floor where he'd just been and hardening into a line of crackling black rock.

Okay. That was a new trick.

Lud glared at her, its eyes glowing white now, like mini suns burning into her. "You cannot resist me for long, human. You are mine."

"You've already sacrificed a lot of your power leaving the circle," she said, stepping forward enough to keep the god's attention on her while Deacon dragged the other shifter toward the safety of her magic. "Entering my ghoulish body won't give you that back." She still wasn't sure how the Mor-Gin affected all this, but she'd have to worry about that later. "You've already lost. And we'll send you to your realm a fallen god." She lowered her voice. "The others will eat you alive when you return."

She wasn't sure if she was making all of this up or if it was true. And she didn't care. From the corner of her eye, she could see Deacon and the wounded shifter were almost to her. She just needed to distract Lud for a few more minutes. There were other shifters in the area that hadn't reached her yet either. She had to stall long enough for them to get close.

The five minion demons charged her magics, testing, working around the edges, trying to get in. She was good with that. Let them focus all their attention on her. Every attack on her meant a few more seconds for the remaining leopards to reach her or get out of the tunnels all together.

The demon let loose a screech, so piercing Cary had to cover her ears. The shifters covered their heads and ears, their sensitive hearing taking the brunt of the god's scream. Those inside her protection looked uncomfortable. Deacon threw his head back, his mouth wide open. She couldn't hear him over the noise, but she was horrified to see blood drip from his nose and ears.

Panic swelled fast and hard. She didn't know what to do and she couldn't think over the ear-shattering demon scream and the fear pummeling her senses.

"Shut up," she yelled into the noise.

She couldn't even hear her own voice, but she yelled the command again and tried once more to use the hunter's trick of willing something to happen. It didn't seem to work this time, though, because the demon continued to screech. Deacon collapsed against the floor, the wounded shifter he'd been carrying curled into a tight ball, its muzzle lifted as it soundlessly howled in pain.

Another wave of panic exploded through her. "Shut up," she commanded. The fuzzing bubble of her own power rose through her blood, a sensation she'd only experienced once before.

In the fight against Holland.

She grasped that sensation and used it, throwing her arms wide to encompass more of the tunnel, willing her protection to spread out over a bigger space. She used that sense of her own power, her own shields and pushed, expanding the bubble of safety, the shock of it forcing the lesser demons back.

The god's howl became muted, like there was cotton in her ears now. She could almost think beyond the noise. She focused on keeping her shield spread wide, gently rolling it over the other shifters in the room. She walked closer to Lud, her movements pushing her protections out farther, wider, encompassing more and more space even as she closed the distance between her and the god. The five minions tumbled around her, their continued attacks frantic and fierce.

She ignored them, her full focus on Lud. Aloud, she said, "You aren't a god here. You gave that up. And I will not let you hurt them." She felt the truth and power in her tone, now that the panic had eased, she felt the strength of her will in her bones. Sheer, stubborn will.

She held up a hand to cover her eyes from another blinding flash of lava shot at her, but even the heat from the attacks were muted now.

Lud stopped howling and snarled at her. "You are mine," it said, crouching. "I will have you."

"I'm no good to you now," she said. "And I will not let you free in my realm."

It lifted its lip. "You can't stop me. You can only stand between me and others."

She had a moment's hesitance at that. It was right. She couldn't do much but stand between it and its potential victims. But right now, that was enough because she couldn't bear the thought of anyone being killed when she might be able to prevent it.

As if sensing its hit on her confidence, Lud laughed. "You are nothing but a barrier. A wall." It leaned close, and despite the distance that had just been between them, it was suddenly right in her face, close enough its hot sulfur-laced breath washed over her face. "I break walls all the time," it hissed.

"You're going to have to break me to win," she said, steeling herself for his attack.

"Broken, you will be mine to control." It smiled. "And I will regain my strength as soon as I have my son."

"You're no god anymore," she said quietly.

"And you're no longer useful to me alive," it said back.

Deacon's howl sounded behind her, but she kept her gaze on the demon. Deacon and his people were safe now, and would remain safe for as long as she stood her ground. She could give them time to get out, to leave the tunnels, get out of the Mor-Gin, and reach safety. Maybe they could even find a way to close the Mor-Gin down, cutting Lud off from their realm. She could stay here all night if that's what it took.

She smirked when Lud reached for her and its hand crumbled into an odd, distorted shape when it couldn't force its way through her magic. "You will go back," she told it. "You will not stay here. Not on my watch."

"Nor mine," a new voice said, deep and echoing and hollow.

Cary blinked when she realized it was Beatrix.

She straightened from the demon as dead bodies marched past her, swarming over Lud. He tossed them aside, casually, carelessly. But still they came, body after body, lurching into the demon's sharp, lava rock touch, filling the space between the demon and Cary until she had to move backward or risk getting overrun herself.

Lud frowned at the swarm of bodies, swatting at them. The other demons were covered in the dead, their struggles leaving a growing pile of corpses around them. Cary might have felt bad about those bodies except that they were already dead.

Amidst the marching horde, the ghouls moved in shuffling circles, feasting on the fallen, making room for more dead to reach their targets.

She had the ridiculous, and maybe a little hysterical, thought that the ghouls were going to get fat eating so much tonight. She had to swallow a laugh that would no doubt be just a touch insane.

She fell back a few more feet as yet more bodies crammed into the tunnel, crawling over the top of each other to reach the six demons now buried under the sheer numbers.

From wherever she'd been, Beatrix was suddenly at Cary's side. Cary glanced at her, wondering where all the bodies were coming from, but a little afraid to ask. She was also wondering where Beatrix had gotten the blood sacrifice to call so many dead.

"I told you to get out of here," Cary said.

"You aren't the boss of me," Beatrix said with a slight tilt to her lips.

The necromancer's almost smile surprised a laugh from Cary.

"Do I want to know where they're coming from or where you got the blood?" Cary asked as even more bodies filled the tunnel. It was so crowded now she was afraid the air would get thin soon. Then she remembered dead people didn't breathe.

"Greenson spilled enough blood for me to work," she said. "And… there are two dead leopards. Their blood gives me more to work with."

Cary closed her eyes. Damn it, she hadn't realized, hadn't had time to realize some of the shifters had been killed.

"They were dead before we got here," Deacon said.

She spun to face him. He was in human form, and naked, but the blood from his nose and ears seemed to be gone. "You can hear? Your brain didn't explode?"

"I'm fine." He nodded at the piles and piles of bodies. "How long will that stall them?" he asked Beatrix.

"Another few minutes," she said.

Shit. Cary had been hoping this was over. But even as she looked back she saw demon limbs breaking through the thick blanket of dead. Deacon was right. This was a distraction, but the corpses weren't enough to stop the demons permanently.

"We need to get them out of here and to safety," she said, nodding back at the shifters. Those who weren't seriously hurt were tending the wounded. They would all heal fast if their injuries weren't life threatening, but they were some distance from an exit.

She spotted Justin helping one woman who'd shifted back to her human form to her feet, then gesturing toward the tunnel out. To Beatrix, Cary said, "Can you keep them swarming from a distance, or do you have to stay here?"

"I can work from a short distance," Beatrix said. She gestured toward the bodies. "The ghouls are under their own power right now, so they'll keep eating and clean this up after we leave."

Cary tried not to flinch at the ickiness of that.

"But I can only keep the dead swarming for a little while longer," Beatrix continued. "The sacrifices will only feed the magic for so long."

Cary cursed. "Let's move. Deacon? You're okay?"

He jerked her close, surprised her with a hard kiss, then moved back to his people, ordering them to their feet, sending them back up the tunnels. Cary shook her head to clear the surprise, ignored Beatrix's smirk, and gestured the necromancer to follow the shifters.

She took up the rear, watching over her shoulder as the pile of dead reached toward the tunnel ceiling. The small fires that had sprung up during the attack, the ones she hadn't been able to snuff out with her shields, were smothered by all the corpses—one less thing to worry about.

And at the edges of the pile of dead, the ghouls ate.

From the midst of the mess, she heard Lud hiss. The sound of his voice rolled through the dense wall of bodies.

"We aren't finished, Cary Redmond."

Oh boy. This wasn't over yet.

40

They reached the breech in the magic barrier out of the Mor-Gin fast, thanks to the shifters moving at top speed and a couple of them carrying Beatrix and Justin. Once Deacon had his people on the move, he picked up Cary and ran with her, keeping to the rear of the group so her magic would guard their backs.

She might have argued with him about being carried, but she was starting to feel the exhaustion of the night, and she needed to conserve her strength, knowing she wasn't done with Lud yet.

Also she couldn't run this fast under her own speed, even in Protector mode.

But mostly, she just wanted to wrap her arms around Deacon, ensuring herself he was still strong and alive. Watching him almost killed several times had definitely taken a few years off her life.

Deacon hurried his people through the realm breech, an invisible barrier this time that Cary barely sensed when they stepped through it, and to the wooden ladder twenty yards beyond. They'd entered the Mor-Gin from this ladder earlier in the night, so Cary knew a private, unused basement was above, a place they could sneak out of without drawing too much attention to the wounded. They'd even left back-packs with spare clothes there, just in case. Given the number of naked people heading up the ladder, Cary was grateful for both the private basement and the spare clothes. The shifters didn't pay attention to nudity. But everyone on the downtown streets at this time of night would. And the less attention they attracted the less questions they'd have to answer.

Right now, any breaks they could get were good.

She stayed at the rear of the group, watching their backs, counting seconds, trying not to rush anyone. A couple of the shifters were seriously injured and needed help up the ladder. The fact that so many of them had been hurt helping her, that two of them had died, left a knot of guilt in her throat she knew would come back to haunt her later. But for now, she just needed them away and safe.

She had no idea how to deal with Lud and keep him from erupting into her realm after that, but she'd worry about the demon god once everyone else was out of the tunnels.

She was so focused on ensuring all the shifters made it up the ladder that, at first, she mistook the tingling along her spine as something to do with the magic barrier all those yards behind her. When she realized danger was coming, she patted Deacon's arm and nodded back into the Mor-Gin.

"They're coming?" he asked.

She nodded. "Get everyone out. I'll keep them occupied until you're all safe."

"You know I'm not going anywhere, right?" he said.

She wanted to argue, but the truth was, she needed someone to protect or the demons would slaughter her the minute everyone else was safely out of their reach. She didn't want Deacon in danger, though. Not after watching him almost die.

"We'll stay too," Justin said. Beatrix nodded.

"You guys are who they're after," Cary said. "You have to leave."

"The god wants your body," Beatrix said. "You're the cursed one."

Cary scowled over her shoulder. That was inconveniently true. "Fine, but what can you do? Aren't all the dead bodies…well, not dead exactly. But probably in the middle of being eaten now."

Justin exchanged a look with Beatrix. She sighed and nodded.

From under his shirt, he removed two necklaces. One had a charm of clear crystal encased in gold hanging from a silver chain, the second an obsidian stone without any circling metal encasing it hanging from a gold chain. The obsidian was smooth and shaped like a tiny pyramid. The clear crystal was rough and jagged. Both stones seemed to have a slight luminescence.

"Okay, what are those?" Cary said. "And if they're helpful, why haven't you used them before now?" From farther up the tunnel, she heard the Lud's scream.

Most of the shifters had made it up the stairs. But Lucas and Sherri hung back. "Go on, you two," Cary ordered. "I want you safe."

Lucas shook his head. "We owe you."

"You most certainly do not," she snapped. "Get out of here. You have kids to raise."

"You should leave," Deacon said, settling a hand on Lucas's shoulder. "I'll watch her back."

Both remaining shifters hesitated, their gazes jumping back down the tunnel, then up the ladder. One of the leopards already at the top called down to them to hurry, they were going to block off the exit with the heavy shelving and boxes filling the basement.

"Excellent idea," Cary said.

Not that she thought it would help much against a demon god, even a weakened one, but anything that slowed it down was a great plan.

Cary waved at the two shifters to hurry. "Don't worry," she said. "I've got this." There was a lot of false confidence in that statement, she thought as both Lucas and Sherri hurried up the ladder.

She faced the tunnel and the distant but quickly growing glow from the demons. "Back into the Mor-Gin or wait here?" she asked Deacon.

"Here. Maybe the barrier will…slow it down. Or drain its power more."

He didn't sound any more sure of that than she was, but it was worth a try. If the barrier didn't slow the monsters, Cary being inside it or outside it wouldn't make any difference.

To Justin she said, "Okay, explain those amulets of yours. Make it quick. We've got about twenty seconds."

She was only exaggerating a little.

"One funnels magic, the other absorbs it," Justin said.

Cary appreciated his efficiency, but… "Meaning?"

"The obsidian will absorb any magic thrown at it by the demons. The crystal can take that magic and throw it back."

"That is really really cool," Cary said. "Why the hell haven't you been using those already?"

"They'll only work for a short period of time before they burn out," Justin said. "I'm not sure they can take the magic of a demon god for long."

"Great, okay," Cary said. "Why did you bring them?"

"Just in case," Justin said.

She titled her head in a slight shrug of acknowledgement.

The scent of sulfur proceeded the demons up the tunnel, coating her throat. She considered the twenty yards of space separating her from the breech in the Mor-Gin's barrier, wondering if she should get just in front of it or stay back near the ladder where she was. She had no idea how that extra magic was going to affect the coming fight or how it would affect Justin's amulets. Or if the demons could even get through it. Not knowing made her gut tight. Waiting made things worse.

She was not good at waiting.

Sweat trickled down her temples and she really wanted to take off her coat, but still didn't dare. She fingered the pocket with the dagger in it, wondering again if it would work as a weapon against the demons or if it might help them given it was covered in sacrificial magic and blood designed to call the god.

"So," she said, bracing her legs wide in anticipation of the approaching attack, ensuring she was in front of the others and the ladder leading above ground. "We've got something more offensive to work with in Justin's amulets, but they won't help for very long. We've got a demon god on the loose who is freed from human confinement, along with five henchmen. The dead Beatrix used to slow them down are mostly ghoul food now. The ghouls are probably so busy gorging they won't be much help. There are no demon hunters in sight. The magical realm and its wonky barrier may or may not complicate things. And I haven't the foggiest idea how to send freed demons back to their realms."

She nodded. "Okay. None of that bodes well for our chances, does it?"

She didn't miss how no one argued that point with her.

As the demons finally came into view, Lud at the front, Cary's heart pounded so hard her chest hurt.

"I will destroy you now," it said. "I will take what my son wanted and rend it to ash!"

She swallowed hard. Unless it had given up completely on going after...well the entire rest of the world, she should be able to stand between it and the exit from the tunnels and be safe. Except, it could probably just melt through the ceiling and leave. Or bring the entire roof of the tunnel down on them. Or...

She sucked in steadying breath. A demon god, weaker though it might be now, was still a god that could basically do whatever the hell it wanted. Which was a very bad thing for the rest of the world. So Cary had to stand, for as long as she could, and hope they found a way to send the thing back *before* it got out and caused more disaster.

Sure. No problem.

She sighed.

When the demons reached the invisible line between the Mor-Gin and her realm, Lud hesitated. Cary dared to hope the barrier would confine them. In fact, the demons held their place inside the barrier so long, she started to feel a rush of relief.

Then Lud smiled and stepped through.

The remaining demons followed, letting out loud roars, hisses, and screeching screams. A crackling boom echoed through the tunnels, like something in the distance had imploded. Behind the demons, where there had been an open tunnel, there was now a solid wall of stone and dirt.

Cary's mouth fell open. "Did it...did it just destroy the Mor-Gin?" she asked.

"Looks like it might have," Deacon said.

She glanced up at the ceiling. "The city?" she whispered. Had parts of the city just dropped into the void?

"I'm not hearing any screams, not feeling the vibration of collapsing buildings," he murmured. "I'd hear something if the destruction affected our realm."

Cary let out a very slow breath. Boy, she hoped like hell Deacon's hearing was accurate.

Before she could fully grasp the implications of what Lud had just done, though, a stream of fire rolled toward them in a battering ram of heat and pressure that slammed against her shield. The flames flared out in a blinding wall that completely blocked her view of the demons beyond.

Wincing as the heat washed over her, even though the fire itself didn't get close enough to burn, she tried listening for hints and warnings from beyond the wall of flame. All she heard was the crackling hiss of leaping fire. The wall hung there without snuffing out, going on and on, not showing any signs of dying down. But her protective magics were holding.

She leaned into them, letting her determination fuel the shield, not even sure that would work since she couldn't feel the bubbling presence of her power at the moment. One way or the other, she'd hold here until the demon was banished back to its hell.

Or she died.

She really didn't like the sound of that second option though.

From behind her, she heard Beatrix's hard breathing and Deacon's low growl. Justin was eerily silent. She risked a brief look back. He was staring at the fire, the obsidian charm in his palm.

To Beatrix, so she didn't disrupt Justin's concentration, Cary said, "Is he pulling in the magic from that fire?"

Beatrix nodded. Her eyes were wide as she stared at the flames. For the first time tonight, Cary saw fear in the young woman. This wasn't the dead she was used to handling, and she didn't have any more of her own help to call on. The dead hadn't stopped the demons. They'd barely slowed them down.

Cary wanted to reach back and comfort Beatrix, but she was a little afraid to move, in case her movements shifted the shield somehow and drew the firewall closer. That didn't normally happen. But then again, she didn't normally face off against a demon god.

And she'd thought Lud's son had been scary.

The fire surrounding them flowed like a never-ending curtain of heat, and the fact that it wasn't burning anything above them down was a damned miracle. Or maybe her magic was preventing that. Maybe Justin's amulet was pulling in enough of the magic to stop a full-blown disaster. Or maybe Lud just had that much control over the flames.

Whatever it was, she was just glad they weren't setting the building above them on fire—at least not yet.

She concentrated on her shield, letting Justin do what he could. She felt Deacon's hand on her shoulder, a reassuring bit of support. She'd thought having him here distracting her would weaken her focus. At that moment, without any way to end this and not knowing how to stop a *god*, she'd never been so grateful for someone else's presence.

Unfortunately, his loyalty might just get him killed. But they'd gotten his people—most of his people—out of the tunnels before the Mor-Gin had been destroyed. That counted as something.

She wanted to say more to Deacon, but breathing against the press of the fire was getting harder. She could feel the roar of it in her bones now, the power of it tingling across her skin in harsher bites. Prickles of pain were starting to nudge at her, just a little, but enough to make her nervous. The wall of flames wasn't getting any closer, her power was holding, but she was feeling it now, despite the distance.

More flame seemed to join the original wall, making it *feel* thicker and stronger. She still couldn't see the demons. She had no idea what they were doing back there. For all she knew, this was the power of a minion and Lud had already left. She groaned at the possibility even as she had to brace her legs to keep steady under the increasing attack.

Damn it, she should have thought about that before.

To Deacon, "Can you see beyond the flames? Can you tell if Lud is still even there?"

"It's still there," Justin answered, surprising Cary.

"How do you know?" she asked.

"Its power is being absorbed by my amulet," Justin said. His voice was quiet and strained. "And it's too strong to be the minor demons."

Cary wasn't sure whether to be relieved or not. Maybe Lud was so angry with her, it hadn't occurred to it to just leave.

That was good?

The thought of the demon leaving sparked another level of worry, though. She had no idea what stepping through the Mor-Gin, what collapsing the Mor-Gin, had done to Lud's powers—strengthened or weakened them—but that didn't seem to matter. Even weakened, Lud was beyond dangerous. If the god finally decided to leave her to the minor demons, there wasn't much she could do to prevent it from causing absolute chaos above ground. Even without its full god strength.

But since the demon hunters seemed to be no-shows, she had to come up with some way to keep the god here until Justin's amulet was ready to use.

Usually, she just taunted the bad guys, which was a great, although scary, way to keep their attention on her. Somehow taunting a god— any more than she already had—seemed a super bad idea, though. Especially since Lud was mad enough at her already.

She leaned in as another wave of strength poured into the flame wall. Overhead, sprinklers she hadn't noticed before rained water down on them. The water did nothing to penetrate the flames, but it couldn't hurt. Maybe it would even keep the fire from spreading. Though, getting wet wasn't a very pleasant sensation just then. Steaming in her clothes was even less pleasant.

She really wanted to take off her jacket but was afraid of leaving the dagger in her pocket unattended.

The dagger...

Something Aidan had said, or maybe something she'd read, started to surface.

Could she bind the demon again? Was that possible with a freed demon? Aidan had mentioned sending the demons back using the "stuff" used to call them. Angie had told her about magic circles and how she set them. A lot of witches used stuff. People who summoned demons used stuff too. Salt to make the circle. Chalk drawings. Runes. Magic words or incantations.

Daggers and blood.

Cary strained to remember what Greenson had done to call Lud. She couldn't remember everything, but she remembered a chalk circle, a lot of incantations, and a bit of Latin. What was that phrase? Damn, her memory wasn't this good, especially when she was scared. She did remember Greenson using the dagger to cut himself and then call the demon. Oh wait, the one phrase was, *Vocationem ore exíbit gládius acútus*.

She'd looked that up. As best she could tell, it meant something like, "heed my call." But another way it was translated included the phrase "with a sharp edge."

She touched her pocket, opening the seal she'd put on it. Angie had told her that while things like salt and chalk were great visual aids for setting a circle, a witch could form one with just a really good mental image and a pointing finger. Since Greenson had used chalk, the mental image part of circle forming might not work in this case. But Aidan had said all of that stuff was just for show anyway.

That it just took a stronger will.

Cary didn't have a lot of faith in her own willpower, but her Protector magic gave her what she needed when she needed it to keep her charges safe. And right now, what she needed was the will of a demon hunter.

And maybe a little of her own blood.

Deacon was going to hate this.

$\mathcal{C}$ary pulled out the dagger, then to Deacon said, "I'm going to try binding these things in a circle again. That way we can keep them here and contained."

"If *you* bind it," Deacon said, "doesn't that mean it needs to kill you to get free again? And aren't you currently cursed to be a ghoul, which will give it a body it can animate with Beatrix's help, and allow it its full powers if it escapes your hold?"

"Yeah, that's the down side of the plan." The part she'd almost forgotten about. Oops. "But I'm protecting you all so I won't die. And a containment circle will keep the things from getting out. And maybe with Justin's amulet we can send it back."

Only…

They were all going to have to be inside the containment circle. Outside of it, they wouldn't be able to use Justin's amulet. Outside it, she wasn't sure she could bind the demons. Greenson had been inside the circle with Lud, when he'd used his own blood and when he'd used sacrifices. If she had to do what Greenson did to make this work, she'd have to be inside the containment circle when she spilled her own blood.

And to ensure her own magic kept working, she'd have to have the others inside with her so she had someone to protect.

"This is a bad plan," Deacon said.

"I knew you'd say that." She also agreed with him, but she wasn't going to admit that out loud.

"Let me do it," Beatrix said. "I'm used to dealing in blood and death. I'll make a good blood offering."

Cary considered that. She'd still be the one forming the circle and doing the calling. Technically, without killing her, Beatrix would be the "sacrifice." That was closer to what Greenson had done, and it wouldn't bind Cary by blood to the demon.

But it went against her instincts to let Beatrix take the risk. The move would essentially feed her blood to the god, even if only a bit of it. She couldn't let the woman take that chance.

Beatrix moved up a little so Cary could see her without having to turn away from the demon's wall of flame. "Let me," Beatrix said. "I need to help."

"Justin," Cary said, "how are you doing? We're probably going to need that magic to send the demon back once the circle is set."

"Almost...there," he said, quiet and breathless. "When I release this... It will break... The amulets. Maybe... One shot."

"One shot." Cary nodded. She glanced at Beatrix, who looked firm and determined. Then she exchanged a look with Deacon who looked worried but ready.

"This will work," Cary said. "This will work."

Oh boy, she hoped this worked.

"Deacon, keep me upright as I don't know how much this will take out of me. Beatrix, stay nearby. I'll have to cut you just as I set the circle. Sorry in advance about the pain."

Beatrix didn't comment. She just held out her arm, her sleeve rolled back, her bare skin wet from the sprinklers. Thin white lines crisscrossed her forearm, proof this wasn't the first time Beatrix had been cut.

That didn't make Cary feel any better.

She raised the dagger, hovering it over Beatrix's arm. She hoped she could do this. Cutting someone with a sacrificial dagger wasn't exactly in her comfort zone. Forming magic circles wasn't either.

She pulled in a deep, bracing breath, then started drawing the mental circle just as Angie had described. A line of blue flame, moving clockwise, hitting the four cardinal points…

She let her eyes drift almost closed as she concentrated on making the circle strong, solid, impenetrable once set. Just as the line reached its starting point, just as the circle was about to close, Cary dragged the dagger over Beatrix's arm, wincing at the woman's hiss of pain. Blood dripped from the cut, plopping to the dirt and water at her feet, creating a puddle of red. Cary repeated the Latin phrase Greenson had used, pouring her will and intention into the circle, locking it into place with a final push.

Aloud, she said in English, "Heed my call, Ho'Lud."

A scream from the other side of the flames pierced all other sound, so loud Cary felt like her ears were going to burst. Beside her, Beatrix dropped to her knees, covering her ears. Deacon cried out at the sound, and suddenly his hands weren't on her anymore. She risked a quick look. He'd shifted to his leopard form. But she couldn't tell if he'd done that on purpose.

She wanted to check on Justin, but just then the wall of flame vanished. Steam enveloped the area, thick as fog. And from the fog, Lud stepped forward like a harbinger of death, its rock skin making the crinkling sounds of cooling lava.

"What have you done, human?" it intoned, the power in its voice now like nothing Cary had heard before.

Oh boy. What had she done?

She wanted to open her mouth and say something, but a movement behind the demon distracted her. A flash of pale blond fur.

What the…?

She felt her mouth drop open as she realized… Buck?

What the hell was her dog doing here? And *inside* the circle. With all these demons. And not close enough for her to protect.

Shit shit shit shit.

She faced the god's glowering, glowing anger. She had to keep its attention on her until Buck reached her and the safety of her protective magic.

"You wanted me," Cary said to Lud. "Well, here we are bound together again."

"How?" it hissed. "I was free."

"I'm just that talented." But also, she didn't know for sure. She'd guessed this would work. Hoped it would. But she didn't understand how or why it had. If she survived, she'd ask…well, someone for an explanation.

She leaned in closer to Lud because from the corner of her eye she saw Buck inching toward her. "And it's time for you to go back to where you came from."

The demon got its face as close to Cary's as her magic allowed, which was terrifyingly close as far as Cary was concerned. Its sulfur-scented breath washed heat and death over her.

"You will die now, Cary Redmond. I will have your body. But you will suffer first."

"Yeah, no." She feigned more confidence than she felt.

Buck was within leaping distance. The other five demons seemed completely focused on her and her small group, awaiting the directions of their god, but one, the bat-winged bastard, did flicker a glance toward Buck. Damn it.

"Justin?" Cary asked without looking away from Lud.

The god leaned back and glanced at Justin.

"Now!" Cary shouted.

She covered Beatrix with her own body as a line of power shot over their heads, hitting Lud in the chest. The shot was so strong and solid, the demon actually flew backward, slamming into the edge of the containment circle. Because she was bound to the circle, Cary felt the hit, so hard it momentarily stole her breath. She blinked back the shock of that and stared at Lud, on its knees, its head bent forward…

A gaping hole at the center of its chest.

Cary gasped. Wow.

Yay?

The power from Justin's amulet cut off abruptly. She heard the tinkling sound of shattering glass and when she looked back, Justin was on his knees, the remains of the clear crystal lay in tiny glittering shards around his knees. The obsidian stone was also broken into several pieces. And Justin looked about to pass out.

But they'd managed to seriously wound the god!

She faced Lud again, ready to will it back to its realm, hoping her own magic would feed her will.

Only to see Lud's wound starting to close.

Fuck. It was healing. She stood away from Beatrix, stepping a foot closer to the god, as close as she dared without leave her charges vulnerable. From the corner of her eyes she searched for Buck but could no longer see him. She hoped he was somewhere behind her now.

She narrowed her eyes at the five minor demons. If she got rid of the god, would they go with it? Or would she have to send them back as well?

She glanced at Lud, the wound in its chest was still huge, but closing fast, the lava just under its skin flowing inward in a spiral, the top layer cooling back into black rock. Its attention seemed to be on healing from a shot of its own power. She looked back at the bat-winged demon who'd spotted Buck and attacked Deacon.

She pushed her anger and will forward, and hissed, "Go back. Be gone. Leave this realm." The deep cadence of her voice surprised her, and she blinked at the sound, breaking her concentration.

The bat-winged demon screeched and launched toward her.

She swallowed her surprised squeak and refocused her will and anger. That thing had wounded Deacon. It was going home. She let her command out again, ignoring the sound of her own voice now as she will the demon gone.

It dropped its head back and screamed, then seemed to fold in on itself, spinning and writhing as it shrank into a pinpoint. And blinked out.

Whoa.

That was kind of cool. She focused on another minor demon and tried again. This one went without protest, stepping backward through a hole in the worlds she couldn't see. Huh? Was it scared or just being pragmatic?

She checked on Lud again. It was heaving in large gasps like breaths, its whole body growing and shrinking as the wound continued to close.

Shit. She focused on another minor demon. This one didn't particularly want to leave and raced toward her in a flash that left a light trail behind it. It's scaly red skin and sharp black horns were almost comic in their stereotypical demon look. She braced for it to bounce off her shields, heard Deacon in his leopard form hiss a warning.

And to her utter shock, a huge three headed beast leapt from behind the demon, landing on top of it, sending it sprawling to the ground. The demon's cry cut off mid-bellow as the beast's middle head snapped the creature in half.

When the animal turned all three heads to look at her, Cary's mouth dropped open.

She recognized Buck in the eyes of that creature. Though nothing else about him was the same. He was the size of a small bus, taking up a huge chunk of the tunnel, even when compared to Lud and the other demons. His heads were sort of dog like, but with red eyes and seriously huge sharp teeth. There was a lot more slobber, too. And in place of Buck's usual blond fur was a thick, slightly scaly black hide that glistened with a hint of green. His tail was thick and had spikes on the end. And his four paws were now tipped with wicked looking black razor claws.

Holy hell. This was his demon dog form? No wonder they were called hellhounds.

"Buck?" she murmured.

The beast woofed in a surprisingly familiar answer. Then he spun and without ceremony ripped one of the remaining two minor demons into multiple pieces.

Cary squeezed her eyes shut as guts and demon body parts sprayed around the circle.

The fifth demon vanished without any effort on Cary or Buck's part—which seemed a prudent move on its part—leaving only the god.

A fully healed god now, Cary realized as it stood. A black mass of crackling rock skin over a moving layer of lava, its cat's eyes glowing white instead of red again, all heat and anger. So much anger.

All focused on her.

4 2

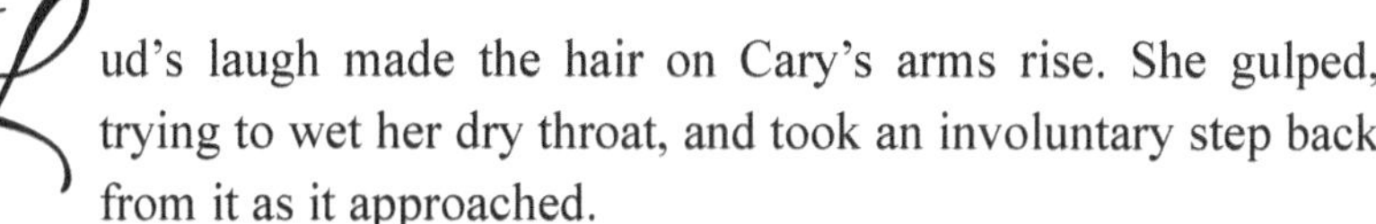

*L*ud's laugh made the hair on Cary's arms rise. She gulped, trying to wet her dry throat, and took an involuntary step back from it as it approached.

She was still protecting the people behind her, she reminded herself. So even if it really really wanted to kill her and her alone, it would still hurt the others if she died. Bad guys couldn't get around her Protector magic that way. So she and the others were all okay.

She hoped.

Its laugh didn't bode well for her, though.

Deacon leapt forward, landing between her and the demon, his hissing growl low and deadly. But against a god, even a shapeshifter wasn't strong enough. And they were out of magic to slow Lud down. Especially since she didn't believe she had the will to hold the circle indefinitely. Even with her magic helping to strengthen her will, she felt it wobbling in the face of the danger Buck was in because he still wasn't behind her and within her protection.

Buck snarled at Lud, as if he'd sensed her thoughts, but the god flicked its hand and Buck whined a little, backing off.

Oh, poor Buck. He'd had enough trouble with demon abuse in his life. He didn't need some god pushing him around. The god's gesture sparked her anger, which helped tamp down her fear. She put a hand on Deacon, keeping him within her protection and made sure she was between the god and the twins.

"You've failed," the god said, the power in its voice making her bones hurt. "You will all bow down to me now."

"I got rid of your other pets," she said, though she didn't sound as cocky as she'd have liked.

A thrust of the demon's power, this time pure unadulterated energy, slammed into her shield. She groaned as the strength of it washed over her. Her skin tingled so much in the wake of all that magic it was painful, like her nerves were on fire.

"You cannot stand forever," the demon said. "My powers are stronger than yours. Protector."

Cary closed her eyes as the terror washed over her again. It knew what she was. "How did you figure it out?" she asked. There was no point in prevaricating now.

"It was in my son's head. It has taken me time to unravel the meaning. He killed your kind."

"So he said," she sighed.

Tears pricked at her eyes. She forced them back. If she had to die, she'd die trying to protect the world from a demon god. She could accept that. But she really couldn't stomach the deaths of the others, especially Deacon and Buck, because she'd failed. There was still more she wanted to say, to do.

And, damn it, she was cursed to be a ghoul. What a crappy way to end.

Her gut hurt. "You know how he did it?" she asked, out of morbid curiosity. "You know he failed to kill me?" she also felt the need to point out.

"He is weaker here," the god said. "And thanks to your circle, linking me back to my realm, I am at full strength again."

"Yup. I did that, didn't I?" Well, that one researcher would be pleased to know they were right while everyone else was wrong about the loss of power being permanent.

She narrowed her eyes. Lud hadn't mentioned whether or not it knew how to kill her. If it just kept throwing power at her, she might fall eventually. But with the others still in danger, she had at least a chance.

Unless the demon released all claim on hurting everyone in her world indefinitely going forward.

Not likely. It was a grave threat to her realm. And she stood between it and the world. For as long as she could hold out, she would.

She glanced down at Deacon as another shot of pure power slammed against her shield. She winced, her fingers clenching in the leopard's fur. "Sorry," she murmured.

In a blink, Deacon shifted. "Don't apologize," he said. "Ever."

She forced a smile that got wiped away as pain ripped through her body in a breath-stealing shock. This was worse than facing an army of bad guys. A god's power really hurt, despite her magic. She was relieved to see neither Deacon nor the twins seemed to feel anything yet, though. So far, she was keeping them safe. She could hold out a bit longer.

Another hit of Lud's power nearly brought her to her knees, but Deacon supported her, keeping her upright and just a little in front of him so her powers would keep working. She knew that cost him, that he wanted to protect her. But by letting her keep him safe, he *was* protecting her. The fact that he did that much made her chest ache with feelings she wouldn't ever be able to say aloud.

She glanced at Buck, too far away. The poor thing was cowering at the edge of the circle, a faint whine from the left and right heads making a sort of white noise under another rush of god power washing over Cary's shield.

Buck's middle head lifted his lips in a snarl. A low growl vibrated through the circle, almost outside her hearing range. Deacon frowned, glancing at the demon dog. Another hit of power made Cary see spots and for a few seconds she couldn't breathe.

A rippling of almost unheard sound, the kind that made her hair stand on edge but she couldn't really hear, came from all three heads now, and as she watched from the corner of her eye, Buck's crouch took on an expectant sort of energy.

The kind of crouch an animal took before it leapt.

She opened her eyes wide, tried to cry out in warning, but another powerful blast of energy from Lud shocked through her. She screamed as her shields flared with bright light in protest of the hit, her nerves lit up with pain that matched. She only remained standing now because Deacon had his arms around her waist, but every part of her hurt as the god sent another round of power at her.

She couldn't focus enough to find will or anger or even breathe. She couldn't feel much of anything now either. Not the bubbling of her powers in her veins. Not the tingling of the god's magic along her skin. Even the pain was so white hot, she could barely feel it.

A small part of her brain struggled to remember how she'd held off an army. If she could just recreate that space, that bubble, maybe she could fend off the demon for a little bit longer. But the power was a lot stronger from a single god than even an army of supernatural beings. She couldn't think behind the continued rain of hits. Her mind went numb.

Even as she felt her shield move closer.

She forced her eyes open, not even realizing she'd closed them, and stared at Lud. Fine. It would kill her. But she was going to make it rip her into so many pieces it wouldn't be able to use her body—there wouldn't be enough left to raise as a ghoul.

Another hit wracked her. She screamed. And her shield edged closer. When the pain faded enough for half a breath, she met the demon's gaze again, silently daring it to do its worst.

It smiled back, the gaping black hole of its mouth seeming to suck her in, dragging her those final steps toward death.

From the edges of her consciousness, she heard Deacon cry out her name. And the sounds of three demon dog heads roaring.

The flash of black scaly skin barreling into Lud forced Cary back to awareness, breaking her out of the downward spiral. She watched in horror, still trying to regain her senses, as Buck clamped three huge jaws down on Lud's torso. The god actually screamed in pain, a sound Cary hadn't heard from it before, even when it had been wounded by its own power.

Buck tightened his jaws, his teeth digging past the rocky exterior of Lud's body and into the rolling lava beneath. And with a sound like tearing fabric, a hole opened in the air, a rip into another realm. Beyond, Cary could see red steaming rocks, a blood red sky, and heat like hell itself poured out.

Without loosening his hold on the now struggling god, Buck glanced at her. All three sets of eyes meeting hers with that soulful sweetness that she recognized in her friend and pet.

"Buck?" she tried to say aloud. But she couldn't make any sound.

The middle head winked one eye at her, or so she thought. And then with another sound of rending, like the earth opening up, Buck leapt through the hole between realms.

Taking the god with him.

Cary blinked, panic filled her. She tried to take a step toward the hole in space and time but her knees buckled. And then the tear knitted back together, like a strange sort of zipper. Closing off the demon realm.

Trapping Buck inside.

"No!" She dropped to the ground, not even Deacon's strength enough to hold her up anymore. Tears she only barely felt poured down her cheeks.

Buck.

She covered her face with her hands, crying so hard she shook. Deacon's arms encircled her and she leaned into him even though she could barely feel his touch. Her body hurt so much, her soul ached so deeply, she was barely aware of anything beyond that pain.

Oh Buck, what have you done?

The failure of losing the very being who'd started her on her journey as a Protector was like no pain she'd ever felt before. And for a few moments, even the knowledge that he'd saved the world by sacrificing himself wasn't enough to quell her grief.

"Cary," Deacon murmured against her ear.

From the quiet firmness, she had the sense he'd said her name a few times trying to get her attention. When she could bring herself to raise her head, she tried to look at him. But her tears were still too thick, blurring her vision.

She sniffled and rubbed her fists across her eyes, trying to clear her sight. A thick, warm puff of breath against her cheek, the feel of a rough tongue over her skin. She frowned. Deacon wasn't in his leopard shape. That wasn't him.

She rubbed her eyes harder and glanced to one side.

Buck, in his mundane dog form, let out a deep woof, and licked her face again.

"Break the circle now," Deacon said.

Cary blinked a few times in realization and mentally broke the circle, cutting a line through the blue light she could only see in her mind. Her ears popped as if depressurizing. Buck let loose another woof and licked her face again before settling on his haunches, looking for all the world like nothing had just happened.

She took her beloved demon dog's furry face between her hands. "What did you do?"

Buck snuffled at her cheek in answer.

"He just jumped back out," Deacon said, answering her question for Buck. "I'm not sure how."

"I think I need to learn more about demon dogs," Cary murmured. But from the recesses of her memory, of that first meeting with Buck and Jaxer, she remembered something Jaxer had said about…adult demon dogs opening passages between realms? Oh, she definitely had to look that up when she got home.

Buck barked and licked her face again. She laughed, and hugged him close, burying her face in his warm fur.

"I'm so glad you're safe," she whispered. And held on to her friend for a very long time.

4 3

Cary, Deacon, Buck, and the twins made their way above ground just as the sun was rising. Lucas and Sherri had remained by the exit, removing the barriers blocking it and opening the trapdoor for them as if they knew it was safe now. Cary glanced between them and Deacon, her eyes narrowed in speculation, as the shifters helped Beatrix and Justin up the ladder.

Deacon followed the twins, carrying Buck as if the dog weighed nothing. Given the size Buck had been earlier, Cary wondered at the look of him now, all snuggly golden Labrador in Deacon's arms. Buck's tongue hung out of his mouth, and he seemed to be smiling as Deacon set him down. No one would ever guess that sweet dog could rip holes between this realm and the demon world.

Lucas handed Deacon a stack of clothes, and Cary remember Deacon had shifted several times and had been naked for a lot of the night. Wow, she'd really been distracted that she'd forgotten that. She kept a hand in Buck's fur, mostly not watching while Deacon got dressed. Then followed Lucas out of the bar that had hidden this particular trap door into the tunnels, stepping outside into the sharply cold predawn air.

She let out a long breath, fogging the space in front of her, weariness and relief leaving her pleasantly numb. The city was still standing. Nothing had fallen apart or collapsed or caught fire. Everything was as it should be.

Beatrix and Justin leaned on each other, Beatrix with her arm pressed to her stomach. The blood wasn't flowing anymore, but she might have a new scar.

"You should have that checked out at the hospital," Cary said, without much hope they'd follow through.

Beatrix smiled a little. "We can take care of it."

"What will you do now?" Cary asked. While keeping one hand on Buck's head, she leaned into Deacon, who had his arms around her.

The twins exchanged a look. Beatrix answered. "I need to make sure the ghouls didn't escape the collapse of the Mor-Gin. I'll do that tonight."

That reminded Cary they'd left the bodies of the two dead leopards behind in the Mor-Gin. She had no idea what had happened to them with the bubble realm's destruction. She absently rubbed at her chest. Another heartache. Another regret to add to her list.

But the world was still here and no one else had died. That had to count.

"Then we'll be moving on," Justin continued. "New town. New home. Somewhere no one knows us."

"Somewhere no one can find us," Beatrix said.

Cary was about to ask if they'd continue selling their powers when a familiar person turned the corner and crossed the mostly empty street to them.

"Hey, you all survived," Aidan said. "I was hoping that would happen."

"Where the hell have you and the other hunters been?" Cary asked.

"Taking care of all the demons popping up around the city all night so you could concentrate on Lud," Aidan said matter-of-factly.

"Oh," Cary said.

Aidan smiled. "I knew you could handle it."

Cary snorted. "I had some help." She rubbed Buck's head affectionately. Buck thumped his thick tail in pleased response.

Aidan stared at Buck a moment, her head titled to one side. "Huh," she said.

Cary narrowed her eyes, waiting for the demon hunter to say more about Buck.

Instead, she said, "Well, glad to know everyone survived and the god is back where it belongs. Call me if you need me again."

Cary blinked a few times as the hunter continued down the road, strolling along as if nothing had happened last night and hell hadn't nearly broken loose all over Portland. Aidan was halfway up the road before she turned back.

In a voice surprisingly easy to hear for the distance, even though Aidan wasn't shouting, she said, "Cary, let me know if this Protector thing doesn't work out. You'd make a hell of a demon hunter."

"No," Deacon and Cary said at the same time.

Aidan chuckled, titled her head in a slight shrug, and ambled off.

Cary was almost home before she realized Aidan had called her a Protector.

LIGHT SNUCK IN PAST HER CLOSED EYELIDS. CARY BLINKED A FEW times and opened her eyes. To see Deacon leaning over her, his brow furrowed.

"You're awake," he said.

Cary groaned. "Oh no, did I pass out again?"

He nodded, smiling slightly.

She pressed a hand to her forehead. "How long this time?"

"Four days. Only a little less worrying now that I know what to expect."

She shook her head and dropped her hand back to the bed.

"How do you feel?" he asked.

She assessed, not really surprised this time to realize, "I feel great.

These healing sleeps really get me through the aches-and-pains portion of my job."

"I hate your job," he said.

"I know." Sometimes she did, too.

"I talked to Angie a couple days ago," he said, "to assure your friends you were okay."

She smiled. "That was very considerate of you."

He shrugged. "I had an ulterior motive."

"Being?"

"I asked Angie to talk to the witch who'd cursed you to be a ghoul after death."

"Oh yeah." That. Cary made a face. "What'd Ang say?"

"She called back this morning to let me know everything was settled. The witch removed the curse after Angie explained what had happened, how the demon had tricked her. Apparently, the woman was pretty pissed at Greenson, though. Probably good he died before she could curse him, or he'd be the ghoul now."

"Not that he didn't deserve it," Cary said. But boy was she glad that wasn't her post-death fate anymore. "Thanks for taking care of that."

"You would have made a terrible ghoul anyway," he said. "You'd only want to eat donuts and pizza."

She snorted. "Don't forget coffee. And nachos." She sat up and stretched, then dragged her fingers through her hair, taking in her surroundings. In her own bed, in her own bedroom, in her own pajamas, only Deacon there this time around.

"Did you change me into my PJs?" she asked.

He smiled, the worry in his expression when she'd first opened her eyes gone now. "I only peaked a little. I promise."

"Ha! How are the dogs? Buck?"

"Fine. Like nothing happened."

Pickles and Fred had rolled him over in enthusiastic doggy greetings when she and Deacon and Buck had walked through the door. Then all three dogs had fallen back into their usual rhythms, heading to the kitchen for a well-earned breakfast.

Cary didn't remember much after that, so she assumed she'd passed out sometime after feeding them but before she'd stumbled into bed herself.

"Have you been here this whole time?" she asked.

"No family emergencies to drag me away this time," he said. He cupped her cheek and kissed her, deep and lingering.

Cary's heart thumped pleasantly as a tingling of awareness started low in her stomach. By the time he eased back, her hormones were urging her to return to the kissing. And maybe more.

"This is a nice way to wake up," she murmured. His expression made her tingles intensify. "We should probably just scrap the idea of a normal date, huh? Maybe it's just not going to be our thing."

"No," he said firmly. "Tomorrow night. Dinner and a movie. A real date. Even if we have to leave halfway through so you can protect someone. We're going to have that date."

"We've already had sex," she reminded him even as her body reminded her she'd like a little more of that sex please.

"Which means I can seduce you after the date without hesitance," he said.

She chuckled. "You could always seduce me now." She wrapped her arms around his neck, beyond grateful just to be alive, to know she hadn't lost him or anyone else she loved four nights ago.

She'd have to think about that "love" part of all this at some point. But right now, she pushed it aside to enjoy the erotic charge of watching Deacon's eyes spark with lust.

"Food first," he said. "You're going to need your energy."

"Pizza?" she asked hopefully.

"I'll go make the call."

He rose from the side of her bed and she admired the view of him walking away.

A memory from the crazy fight with the god had her narrowing her eyes. She called after Deacon just as he disappeared out the bedroom door, "Maybe over food, you can explain to me why Lucas called you a prince."

From farther down the hall, Deacon called back, "Sure. After you explain all about this wizard trying to kill you."

Cary winced. She'd almost forgotten about that. She groaned and flopped back down onto her bed, not anticipating that conversation.

Maybe she could seduce Deacon before they got to that part. That would definitely distract him. She grinned.

Oh boy.

THANK YOU

Thank you for reading book 2 in the Cary Redmond series! I hope you're enjoying Cary's adventures.

For those of you familiar with the Portland area, and specifically, the "Shanghai" tunnels, I hope you'll forgive me for taking some literary license with them. The myths about Portland's underground are as fun as the true history. But given Cary is living in a magical world, I felt the need to add…well, a bit more magic.

If you'd like to read more about Cary's history and how she got "tricked" into becoming a Protector, the short story *When Cary Met Jaxer* is the place to start—that's also where she met Buck! There are more short stories in the series—some out now, some on the way—which you can learn more about at my website (http://www.katsimons.com) or through my newsletter (http://eepurl.com/OxQQL).

For a sneak peek at book 3 in the series, The Trouble with Leopard Queens and Shifter Wars, keep reading.

And if you're curious about Aidan the Demon Hunter, I've included a bonus flash fiction short story after the excerpt. (Pay attention to the title.)

Thanks again for continuing on this journey with Cary!

~ Kat

THE TROUBLE WITH LEOPARD QUEENS AND SHIFTER WARS

A CARY REDMOND NOVEL, BOOK 3
EXCERPT

1

"You think we can get through this one without anything going wrong?" Deacon asked, his golden gaze sparking with the same combination of frustration and heat that Cary felt.

This was their fourth attempt at a real date.

Attempt being the operative word.

The first had gone… Well, it had started well. But then she'd been forced out of the movie theater to deal with a pissed off werewolf caught in mid-shift. That had taken the rest of the night. And while she'd enjoyed meeting Deacon's sister for the first time, she didn't think that evening qualified as a successful first day. Shame because she'd really wanted to see that movie.

The second date, they'd only gotten as far as the parking lot downtown before Cary got called away by her bosses to protect a young wizard from an irate vampire. That had been interesting. Two powerful adversaries facing off and Cary standing there in her pretty black date night dress trying to stop a fight.

Fun!

Heavy on the sarcasm.

And then to add insult to injury—literally—there'd been the

mugger afterward. Poor guy would likely never recover from the shock of having Cary jump between him and his intended target so fast he grabbed Cary's arm instead of the woman's purse. The fact that his hand got an electric shock after touching her had been interesting. She'd never had that happen before with a mundane human. But she'd stopped questioning the ways of her Protector powers a long time ago.

On their third attempt at a date, they'd made it into the restaurant and started their first course before disaster struck. She was still having nightmares about that night.

She sighed and nibbled at a breadstick. "So long as we get through dinner this time, I'll be good."

Because while she really wanted to see this latest superhero movie —research!—she mostly just wanted to eat. She'd spent the day with Lucy, one of her best friends and her personal martial arts trainer, working on her self-defense skills. And Lucy was a brutal teacher. Cary needed the training, now more than ever. She'd entered her seventh year as a Protector and that meant she was cut off from all the support she'd had during her first six years of on-the-job training.

Fortunately, that "support" didn't count her friends or Deacon.

And Lucy was taking her responsibilities for making sure Cary could defend herself even without her powers very seriously.

Deacon grinned. "Soreness gone away yet?"

"Nearly." Cary made a face. She healed fast—which was good since, like any good Kevlar vest, she took the occasional hit while jumping between bad guys and good guys. But Lucy had worked her so hard at the dojo that Cary's muscles were *still* recovering. That had been one hell of a workout.

"I think I could officially throw someone over my head now, though," she said brightly.

Being a perfectly ordinary human woman who'd gotten tricked into this particular job as a Protector left her short a few skills. She was a purely defensive superhero. She could jump between bad guys and good guys and keep the good guys safe from pretty much anything— guns, demon fire, magic and mayhem, walking dead (that had been a gross assignment), rushing cars, knives, vampires, shapeshifters...

Anything or anyone that wanted to hurt, maim, or kill another, would run up against Cary's shields and stop right there, no passing Go, no collecting two hundred dollars.

But that was all she could do. She had *no* offensive skills.

Well, there was that one time she'd managed to level a supernatural army with her powers, but she still didn't even know how she'd done that, so it didn't really count.

She'd gone to college with the intentions of becoming a veterinary technician, maybe eventually a vet. She'd never learned how to fight, taken martial arts, or so much as tried to shoot a gun. She was wholly unprepared for the job she'd ended up in. In fact, she hadn't even known the magical world existed before becoming a Protector. The only really good thing she had going for her was the ability to put herself in the middle of danger and then just stubbornly stand there.

That stubbornness had annoyed more than one bad guy in the past.

"I'm glad Lucy's increased your training," Deacon said.

"I've survived six years without being able to do all this," she pointed out. Much to Lucy's chagrin since she'd been trying to train Cary in self-defense skills for more than five years. "My powers help when I need them."

"I wasn't thinking of your normal job," he said darkly, his gaze narrowed.

"Oh, yeah, that."

Turned out there was a wizard out to get her for reasons that were still unclear. But whoever he was, he wanted her dead and knew how to get around her powers to kill her. He just had to be aiming for her with no interest in hurting anyone else around her. And the bastard had gotten close twice now. It was a little nerve-wracking if she were to be honest. But she wasn't about to admit that to Deacon.

"I still think you should consider—"

"No," she said firmly. "I have to stay here and work. I can't run away and hide." Especially not to Deacon's mother.

Especially given who Deacon's mother was!

"It wouldn't be running away," he insisted. "We have this charity event every January. It would just be two weeks away. Long enough for Jaxer to track down the wizard."

Jaxer was Cary's former mentor and someone who wasn't supposed to be helping her this year. But he'd been sneaking around trying to uncover more information about this wizard threat for her, under the excuse that it had to do with something that happened right before she was cut loose.

"The Nags won't let me go into hiding," she pointed out. "Or on a holiday or however you want to spin this."

The Nagumwasuck were her bosses, the North American Fae who made Protectors. They infused them with magic and through a series of premonitions and old-fashioned research, sent Protectors out to save the day. They couldn't stop all the bad things in the world from happening. No one could. But they did their best to stop some of it, and Cary respected that.

She wasn't thrilled with how they'd tricked her into becoming a Protector, but still, what they did try to do for this world deserved some consideration. Although she would never admit that out loud to them, ever ever. And they were kind of a pain in her ass. Which was why she called them Nags—mostly to annoy them but also because they were.

"They've had no compunction about interrupting our dates," she said, "what makes you think taking me off to Eugene will stop them?"

She sighed as their food arrived. Pizza. A large pizza she felt perfectly justified in eating half of because of all the work she'd done with Lucy today. Deacon would eat his half of the pizza plus his calzone and pasta dishes because he had a shapeshifter metabolism. She really really envied him that metabolism.

She was halfway through her first slice—authentic New York style cheese and pepperoni, *yum*—before she finished her reasoning. "The Nags will still demand I do something while I'm away. I'll either have to protect someone there, or I'll be called back to Portland. And I don't dare try to avoid my job."

If she did, the Nags would cut off all their support. They paid her, which was useful, but more importantly, they had a protective glamour on her house that kept anyone she didn't want to find her home from finding it. Her house was one of the few places she could be certain she was safe. And with a wizard out to kill her, she needed that safety more than ever. But it wasn't just the wizard that wanted her dead. She'd built up a lot of enemies in six years of stopping bad guys from doing exactly what they wanted. If they ever discovered where she lived, she'd never be safe again.

Deacon didn't know about the glamour. No one beyond the Nags and Jaxer knew. Not even her best friends. She was still deciding whether to tell Deacon or not.

They'd only known each other for two and a half months. They hadn't even exchanged presents at the holidays because the thought of it had wigged her out. She was still adjusting to the idea of this mate-boyfriend thing.

He'd claimed they were mates on the first night they'd met. At this stage she believed him. But the permanence of it was intimidating.

Though it turned out that, technically, because she was a human, she could break the bond at any time. Deacon couldn't walk away that easily, not now that they'd slept together. For him, the permanence of the thing was a lot more real and it would cost him to break their bond —if he even could anymore.

She had the freedom to walk away from their relationship, even now, if she wanted to.

Thing was, she really didn't want to.

"They can leave you alone for a week," Deacon insisted. "You still get to have a life outside of protecting people."

"Right," she said with no little sarcasm. The Nags had never taken her life into consideration when it came to doing her job.

She finished off her first slice and moved on to a second. The one truly lovely thing about eating with Deacon was she never felt self-conscious about how much pizza she could eat—especially when he could always eat so much more than she could. He was used to shapeshifters and all shapeshifters with their super high metabolisms ate a lot. There was something relaxing in knowing she wouldn't be judged if she decided to eat this entire pizza by herself.

"Let's change subjects," she said, because she didn't want to think about her job anymore. "Your control…" A delicate topic. "How are you doing?"

"Better."

She narrowed her eyes. "You nearly ripped that werewolves arm off," she pointed out. All the wolf had done was make a snide comment to her—which was pretty typical bad guy behavior when she was thwarting their attempts to hurt people.

"I only broke it a little," he said, almost defensively. "And it healed."

"It was over the top and unnecessary. He was already restrained."

"He threatened you."

"Deacon, they *all* threaten me. You know that. You've been there. Why isn't your control coming back?"

That was the million dollar question. Leopard shifters lost their minds a little right after finding their mates, and it apparently took a lot of sex to make them feel settled and secure in the bond. At which point, their control supposedly returned. At least that was according to Deacon's mother.

Cary was still traumatized that this information came from his *mother*.

Deacon shrugged. "We haven't been together long enough I suppose."

"We have been having sex all the time."

"Are you complaining?"

"Ha! You should know better than that."

"Guess my leopard needs more of you still."

She scowled, not sure whether to take that as a compliment or not. She lowered her voice. "How much more? I mean, every spare moment hasn't been enough?"

"That's how it is with mates," he said, in that terrifyingly matter-of-fact way that left her a little breathless.

"Really? All the time? They don't have other things to do? Like jobs and laundry and walking the dogs and stuff. How do other mates do it?"

He smiled a little. "Eventually the frequency slows. But never the intensity."

Her heart thumped harder at that thought. Because so far the intensity had been…intense. One thing still bothered her though. "Our current frequency is about as much as we can work in around everything else in life, and yet you're still not yourself. What happens if—" She cut herself off, afraid to say more aloud.

Since she was human, their bond was different. And since Deacon's control hadn't returned yet, despite them following his mother's advice (ah!) and having sex a lot—and it had really been a lot over the last three weeks—Cary was starting to worry. More than she'd wanted to let on.

He reached across the table and squeezed her hand. "I'll be fine. We'll be fine. It just takes time." He dropped his gaze to the table. "Unless you're rethinking us being together."

"Stop." She tightened her grip on his hand. "That's not what I was talking about."

He met her gaze again and nodded. But the uncertainty was there, in his eyes and her gut. She wanted him in her life. She was pretty sure she'd fallen in love with him somewhere in the last few months. But there was a lot still that scared her about this relationship. A lot of things that apparently still scared him too.

Which was weirdly reassuring.

"I just want your control back so you can stop feeling so edgy," she said. "And maybe go back to work."

"Getting tired of my company?" he said, only half joking.

"Yeah, you're tough to take." She rolled her eyes. "No. You just do good work, and I don't like that you haven't been able to do your job." He and his family ran animal shelters around the country, taking in both ordinary animals as well as the more exotic species. They were no-kill shelters and the family ensured those animals who couldn't be adopted were sent to appropriate sanctuaries. Cary loved that his work involved rescuing animals, and she'd felt a little guilty that their mate situation, and his slipping control over his leopard side, meant he'd had to take a hiatus from that work.

"Caitlin is handling things fine in my absence. And there's email. I haven't been cut off entirely."

She let out a long breath. "Okay."

"You don't sound sure?"

"I'm worried. I'm worried you might not every get your control back and that will suck a lot."

"We could talk to my mother about it," he offered. "Another good reason to go stay with my parents for a week."

She suppressed a shudder. "You want me to ask your mother why all the sex I'm having with her son isn't working?"

"Not working?" He contrived to look offended, though she saw his lip twitch with amusement.

"You know what I mean," she said, her cheeks warming. "It's been working just fine for orgasms."

"I'm glad to hear that."

"But not for your control," she finished.

"She's really the best person to talk to for answers."

Cary sighed. She'd only just recently found out his mother was basically the queen of the leopards—at least the west coast leopards. A little fact he'd failed to mention when they'd first met. His mother being the leader of his people was intimidating enough. The thought of discussing their mate issues with her, their *sex* life, was almost more than she could contemplate.

"I'm not sure I need answers enough to face that conversation," she admitted. She ignored Deacon's suppressed smile. "And I did a piss poor job of subject change here. Let's try another topic. Something innocuous."

They went on to debate the various merits of New York style pizza versus Chicago style—she only threatened to leave him once when he defended Chicago style—and that led into other food related topics which were safe and easy date conversation.

The complications of her job and their relationship could wait. At least until after the movie.

Or so she'd thought. But when they stepped out of the restaurant, a tingle crawled down her spine. A too-familiar sensation. One she'd been learning to interpret for the last six years.

Danger.

Someone was in need of her particular brand of help.

~

Don't miss The Trouble with Leopard Queens and Shifter Wars
Book 3 in the Cary Redmond series
Coming Soon!

BONUS FLASH FICTION

DEMON SAYS, A DEMON HUNTER SHORT STORY

DEMON SAYS

Aidan put her hands on her hips and stared at the demon through eyes that were just brown enough most people could pretend they weren't really red. The demon stared back with its claws on the foggy black mass that passed for its hips. Aidan pursed her lips. The demon scrunched its mouth up in a passable imitation despite not having lips. Aidan clicked her teeth. So did the demon.

This had to be the weirdest hunt she'd ever gone through.

"Do you know what you're doing?" the ratty little man next to her asked. "What's happening?"

"Do you want to take over?"

"No! No."

"Then shut up."

The demon put its hands behind its back and smiled. Aidan smiled too as she put her hands behind her back.

Hunts were never the same. A lot of different things had to be taken into consideration. The type and age of the demon called, the religious background used in the calling, the beliefs of the demon, the beliefs of the one who called the demon, the original deal, the forfeit, the price. Sometimes even the weather and the phase of the moon had to be considered. But really the paraphernalia used in a fight with a demon came down to window dressing.

All a hunter really needed was will. A will stronger than a demons.

The demon moved to the edge of the containment circle. It waited.

Aidan looked right into its big red eyes as she stepped to the edge of her side of the circle.

"Wait! What are you doing? He'll kill you." The ratty man whose life she was saving pulled at her hand where it still rested behind her back.

"Afraid if he kills me, you'll be next?"

"You know what he'll do to me," the man whined. "He promised me all kinds of horrors if I didn't fulfill our second bargain."

"They always do." She had little sympathy for this particular case. The man—Fred—had bargained away his soul for a pittance.

The demon started to move its hands forward, but Aidan shook her head. "Ah, ah. That was three. The smile counted."

A deep growl rose from what was roughly the center of the oil black ooze that made up the demon's body. Aidan met the growl passively. After a minute, the demon bobbed its head.

The fight continued.

Aidan took one step away from the edge of the ring. The demon, after letting loose another growl, took one step backward. Aidan dropped her hands to her sides. Her gaze locked with the demon's as he followed suit. She raised one eyebrow in an expression that would have been amusement on anyone else.

The demon's brows rose over the glowing pits of his eyes.

It smiled.

Aidan smiled. "You lose. I only raised one."

Its brows snapped back down. A keening sound started from the center of the circle. And with a howl of outrage, the demon vanished, leaving behind the scent of sulfur.

BOOKS BY KAT SIMONS

THE CARY REDMOND SERIES

1 - The Trouble Black Cats and Demons

2 - The Trouble with Ghouls and Serial Killers

3 - The Trouble with Leopard Queens and Shifter Wars

CARY REDMOND SHORT STORIES

When Cary Met Jaxer

When Cary Met Pickles

When Cary Met Marianne

TIGER SHIFTERS SERIES

1 - Once Upon a Tiger

2 - Along Came a Tiger

3 - Here There Be Tigers

4 - Her Tiger To Take

5 - To Tempt a Tiger

6 - Down Will Come Tiger

7 - To Catch a Tiger

8 - What a Tiger Wants

9 - Taming Her Tiger

Tiger Shifters Series Vol 1 (Books 1 - 3)

Tiger Shifters Series Vol 2 (Books 4 - 6)

ABOUT THE AUTHOR

Kat Simons earned her Ph.D. in animal behavior, working with animals as diverse as dolphins and deer. She brought her experience and knowledge of biology to her paranormal romance and urban fantasy fiction, where she delights in taking nature and turning it on its ear. Her Tiger Shifter series combines romance and the otherworldly with heart-pounding action adventure. Her latest urban fantasy romance series follows the adventures of Protector Cary Redmond as she tries to manage her personal life while saving the world. A lot.

After traveling the world, Kat now lives in New York City with her family. She is a stay-at-home mom and a full time writer.

For more on Kat and her future books:

Website: http://www.katsimons.com
Newsletter: http://eepurl.com/OxQQL